KU-632-430

THE BINDING

Emmett Farmer is working in the fields when a letter arrives summoning him to begin an apprenticeship. He will work for a book binder, a vocation that arouses fear, superstition and prejudice — but one neither he nor his parents can afford to refuse. He will learn to hand-craft beautiful volumes, and within each he will capture something unique and extraordinary: a memory. If there's something you want to forget, he can help. Your past will be stored safely in a book and you will never remember your secret, however terrible. In a vault under his mentor's workshop, row upon row of books — and memories — are meticulously stored and recorded. Then one day Emmett makes an astonishing discovery: one of them has his name on it . . .

SPECIAL MESSAGE TO READERS

THE ULVERSCROFT FOUNDATION
(registered UK charity number 264873)
was established in 1972 to provide funds for
research, diagnosis and treatment of eye diseases.
Examples of major projects funded by
the Ulverscroft Foundation are:-

- The Children's Eye Unit at Moorfields Eye Hospital, London
- The Ulverscroft Children's Eye Unit at Great Ormond Street Hospital for Sick Children
- Funding research into eye diseases and treatment at the Department of Ophthalmology, University of Leicester
- The Ulverscroft Vision Research Group, Institute of Child Health
- Twin operating theatres at the Western Ophthalmic Hospital, London
- The Chair of Ophthalmology at the Royal Australian College of Ophthalmologists

You can help further the work of the Foundation
by making a donation or leaving a legacy.
Every contribution is gratefully received. If you
would like to help support the Foundation or
require further information, please contact:

THE ULVERSCROFT FOUNDATION
The Green, Bradgate Road, Anstey
Leicester LE7 7FU, England
Tel: (0116) 236 4325

website: www.foundation.ulverscroft.com

THE BINDING

BRIDGET COLLINS

LARGE
PRINT

First published in Great Britain 2019
by
The Borough Press
An imprint of HarperCollins*Publishers*

First Isis Edition
published 2019
by arrangement with
HarperCollins*Publishers*

The moral right of the author has been asserted

Copyright © 2019 by Bridget Collins
All rights reserved

A catalogue record for this book is available
from the British Library.

ISBN 978–1–78541–762–7 (hb)
ISBN 978–1–78541–768–9 (pb)

Published by
F. A. Thorpe (Publishing)
Anstey, Leicestershire

Set by Words & Graphics Ltd.
Anstey, Leicestershire
Printed and bound in Great Britain by
T. J. International Ltd., Padstow, Cornwall

This book is printed on acid-free paper

CAVAN COUNTY LIBRARY
ACC No. S/17526
CLASS NO. F LP
INVOICE NO. 11399 Ulvers
PRICE €23.79

For Nick

PART ONE

PART ONE

CHAPTER
ONE

When the letter came I was out in the fields, binding up my last sheaf of wheat with hands that were shaking so much I could hardly tie the knot. It was my fault we'd had to do it the old-fashioned way, and I'd be damned if I was going to give up now; I had battled through the heat of the afternoon, blinking away the patches of darkness that flickered at the sides of my vision, and now it was nightfall and I was almost finished. The others had left when the sun set, calling goodbyes over their shoulders, and I was glad. At least now I was alone I didn't have to pretend I could work at the same pace as them. I kept going, trying not to think about how easy it would have been with the reaping machine. I'd been too ill to check the machinery — not that I remembered much, between the flashes of lucidity, the summer was nothing but echoes and ghosts and dark aching gaps — and no one else had thought to do it, either. Every day I stumbled on some chore that hadn't been done; Pa had done his best, but he couldn't do everything. Because of me, we'd be behind all year.

I pulled the stems tight round the waist of the sheaf and stacked it against the others. Done. I could go home now ... But there were shadows pulsing and

3

spinning around me, deeper than the blue-violet dusk, and my knees were trembling. I dropped into a crouch, catching my breath at the pain in my bones. Better than it had been — better than the splintery, sickening spasms that had come unpredictably for months — but still I felt as brittle as an old man. I clenched my jaw. I was so weak I wanted to cry; but I wasn't going to, I'd die first, even if the only eye on me was the full, fat harvest moon.

"Emmett? Emmett!"

It was only Alta, winding her way through the stooks towards me, but I pushed myself to my feet and tried to blink the giddiness away. Above me the sparse stars slid one way and then the other. I cleared my throat. "Here."

"Why didn't you get one of the others to finish? Ma was worried when they came back down the lane and you weren't with —"

"She didn't need to be worried. I'm not a child." My thumb was bleeding where a sharp stalk had pierced the skin. The blood tasted of dust and fever.

Alta hesitated. A year ago I'd been as strong as any of them. Now she was looking at me with her head on one side, as if I was younger than she was. "No, but —"

"I wanted to watch the moon rise."

"'Course you did." The twilight softened her features, but I could still see the shrewdness in her gaze. "We can't make you rest. If you don't care about getting well —"

"You sound like her. Like Ma."

"Because she's right! You can't expect to snap back as if nothing's happened, not when you were as ill as you were."

Ill. As if I'd been languishing in bed with a cough, or vomiting, or covered with pustules. Even through the haze of nightmares I could remember more than they realised; I knew about the screaming and the hallucinations, the days when I couldn't stop crying or didn't know who anyone was, the night when I broke the window with my bare hands. I wished I *had* spent days shitting my guts helplessly into a pot; it would have been better than still having marks on my wrists where they'd had to tie me down. I turned away from her and concentrated on sucking the cut at the base of my thumb, worrying at it with my tongue until I couldn't taste blood any more.

"Please, Emmett," Alta said, and brushed the collar of my shirt with her fingers. "You've done as good a day's work as anyone. Now will you come home?"

"All right." A breeze lifted the hairs on the back of my neck. Alta saw me shiver and dropped her eyes. "What's for dinner, then?"

She flashed her gappy teeth in a grin. "Nothing, if you don't hurry up."

"Fine. I'll race you back."

"Challenge me again when I'm not wearing stays." She turned away, her dusty skirts flaring about her ankles. When she laughed she still looked like a child, but the farmhands had already started sniffing round her; in some lights now she looked like a woman.

I trudged beside her, so exhausted I felt drunk. The darkness thickened, pooling under trees and in hedges, while the moonlight bleached the stars out of the sky. I thought of cold well-water, clear as glass, with tiny green flecks gathering at the bottom — or, no, beer, grassy and bitter, the colour of amber, flavoured with Pa's special blend of herbs. It would send me straight to sleep, but that was good: all I wanted was to go out like a candle, into dreamless unconsciousness. No nightmares, no night terrors, and to wake in the morning to clean new sunlight.

The clock in the village struck nine as we went through the gate in the yard. "I'm famished," Alta said, "they sent me out to find you before I could —"

My mother's voice cut her off. She was shouting.

Alta paused, while the gate swung closed behind us. Our eyes met. A few fragments of words drifted across the yard: *How can you say . . . we can't, we simply can't . . .*

The muscles in my legs were shaking from standing still. I reached out and steadied myself against the wall, wishing my heart would slow down. A wedge of lamplight was shining through a gap in the kitchen curtains; as I watched, a shadow crossed and crossed again. My father, pacing.

"We can't stay out here all night," Alta said, the words almost a whisper.

"It's probably nothing." They'd quarrelled all week about the reaping machine, and why no one had checked it earlier. Neither of them mentioned that it should have been my job.

A thud: fists on the kitchen table. Pa raised his voice. "What do you expect me to do? Say no? That bloody witch will put a curse on us quick as —"

"She already has! Look at him, Robert — what if he never gets better? It's her fault —"

"His own fault, you mean — if he —" For a second a high note rang in my ears, drowning out Pa's voice. The world slipped and righted itself, as if it had juddered on its axis. I swallowed a bubble of nausea. When I could concentrate again, there was silence.

"We don't know that," Pa said at last, just loud enough for us to hear. "She might help him. All those weeks she wrote to ask how he was doing."

"Because she wanted him! No, Robert, *no*, I won't let it happen, his place is here with us, whatever he's done, he's still our son — and *her*, she gives me the creeps —"

"You've never met her. It wasn't you that had to go out there and —"

"I don't care! She's done enough. She can't have him."

Alta glanced at me. Something changed in her face, and she took hold of my wrist and pulled me forwards. "We're going inside," she said, in the high, self-conscious voice she used to call to the chickens. "It's been a long day, you must be ravenous, I know I am. There better be some pie left, or I will kill someone. With a fork through the heart. And *eat* them." She paused in front of the door and added, "With *mustard*." Then she flung it open.

7

My parents were standing at either end of the kitchen: Pa by the window, his back turned to us, Ma at the fireplace with red blotches on her face like rouge. Between them, on the table, was a sheet of thick, creamy paper and an open envelope. Ma looked swiftly from Alta to me and took a half step towards it.

"Dinner," Alta said. "Emmett, sit down, you look like you're about to faint. Heavens, no one's even laid the table. I hope the pie's in the oven." She put a pile of plates down beside me. "Bread? Beer? Honestly, I might as well be a scullery maid . . ." She disappeared into the pantry.

"Emmett," Pa said, without turning round. "There's a letter on the table. You'd better read it."

I slid it towards me. The writing blurred into a shapeless stain on the paper. "My eyes are too dusty. Tell me what it says."

Pa bowed his head, the muscles bunching in his neck as if he was dragging something heavy. "The binder wants an apprentice."

Ma made a sound like a bitten-off word.

I said, "An apprentice?"

There was silence. A slice of moon shone through the gap in the curtains, covering everything in its path with silver. It made Pa's hair look greasy and grey. "You," he said.

Alta was standing in the pantry doorway, cradling a jar of pickles. For a second I thought she was going to drop it, but she set it down carefully on the dresser. The knock of glass on wood was louder than the smash would have been.

"I'm too old to be an apprentice."

"Not according to her."

"I thought . . ." My hand flattened on the table: a thin white hand that I hardly recognised. A hand that couldn't do an honest day's work. "I'm getting better. Soon . . ." I stopped, because my voice was as unfamiliar as my fingers.

"It's not that, son."

"I know I'm no use now —"

"Oh, sweetheart," Ma said. "It's not your fault — it's not because you've been ill. Soon you'll be back to your old self again. If that was all . . . You know we always thought you'd run the farm with your father. And you could have done, you still could — but . . ." Her eyes went to Pa's. "We're not sending you away. She's asking for you."

"I don't know who she is."

"Binding's . . . a good craft. An honest craft. It's nothing to be afraid of." Alta knocked against the dresser, and Ma glanced over her shoulder as she swung her arm out swiftly to stop a plate from slipping to the floor. "Alta, be careful."

My heart skipped and drummed. "But . . . you hate books. They're wrong. You've always told me — when I brought that book home from Wakening Fair —"

A look passed between them, too quick to interpret. Pa said, "Never mind about that now."

"But . . ." I turned back to Ma. I couldn't put it into words: the swift change of subject if someone even mentioned a book, the shiver of distaste at the word, the look on their faces . . . The way she'd dragged me

9

grimly past a sordid shopfront — A. *Fogatini, Pawnbroker and Licens'd Bookseller* — one day when I was small and we got lost in Castleford. "What do you mean, it's a *good craft?*"

"It's not . . ." Ma drew in her breath. "Maybe it's not what I would have wanted, before —"

"Hilda." Pa dug his fingers into the side of his neck, kneading the muscle as though it ached. "You don't have a choice, lad. It'll be a steady life. It's a long way from anywhere, but that's not a bad thing. Quiet. No hard labour, no one to tempt you off the straight and narrow . . ." He cleared his throat. "And they're not all like her. You settle down and learn the trade, and then . . . Well. There're binders in town who have their own carriages."

A tiny silence. Alta tapped the top of a jar with her fingernail and glanced at me.

"But I don't — I've never — what makes her think that I —?" Now none of them would meet my eyes. "What do you mean, I've got no choice?"

No one answered. Finally Alta strode across the room and picked up the letter. "'As soon as he is able to travel'," she read out. "'The bindery can be very cold in winter. Please make sure he has warm clothes.' Why did she write to you and not Emmett? Doesn't she know he can read?"

"It's the way they all do it," Pa said. "You ask the parents for an apprentice, that's how it works."

It didn't matter. My hands on the table were all tendons and bones. A year ago they'd been brown and muscled, almost a man's hands; now they were no one's. Fit for nothing but a craft my parents despised. But why would she have chosen me, unless they'd asked her to? I spread my fingers and pressed, as if I could absorb the strength of the wood through the skin of my palms.

"What if I say no?"

Pa clumped across to the cupboard, bent down and pulled out a bottle of blackberry gin. It was fierce, sweet stuff that Ma doled out for festivals or medicinal purposes, but he poured himself half a mug of it and she didn't say a word. "There's no place for you here. Maybe you should be grateful. This'll be something you can do." He tossed half the gin down his throat and coughed.

I drew in my breath, determined not to let my voice crack. "When I'm better, I'll be just as strong as —"

"Make the best of it," he said.

"But I don't —"

"Emmett," Ma said, "please . . . It's the right thing. She'll know what to do with you."

"What to *do* with me?"

"I only mean — if you get ill again, she'll —"

"Like in a lunatic asylum? Is that it? You're packing me off to somewhere miles from anywhere because I might lose my wits again at any moment?"

"She *wants* you," Ma said, clutching her skirts as if she was trying to squeeze water out of them. "I wish you didn't have to go."

"Then I won't go!"

"You'll go, boy," Pa said. "Heaven knows you've brought enough trouble on this house."

"Robert, don't —"

"You'll go. If I have to truss you up and leave you on her doorstep, you'll go. Be ready tomorrow."

"Tomorrow?" Alta spun round so fast her plait swung out like a rope. "He can't go tomorrow, he'll need time to pack — and there's the harvest, the harvest supper . . . Please, Pa."

"Shut *up!*"

Silence.

"Tomorrow?" The blotches on Ma's cheeks had spread into a flush of scarlet. "We never said . . ." Her voice trailed off. My father finished his gin, swallowing with a grimace as if his mouth was full of stones.

I opened my mouth to tell her it was all right, I'd go, they wouldn't have to worry about me any more; but my throat was too dry from the reaping.

"A few more days. Robert, the other apprentices don't go until after the harvest — and he's still not well, a couple of days . . ."

"They're younger than he is. And he's well enough to travel, if he did a day in the fields."

"Yes, but . . ." She moved towards him and caught his arm so that he couldn't turn away. "A little more time."

"For pity's sake, Hilda!" He made a choking sound and tried to wrench himself away. "Don't make this any harder. You think I want to let him go? You think that after we tried so hard — fought to keep a pure house — you think I'm proud of it, when my own father lost an eye marching in the Crusade?"

Ma glanced at Alta and me. "Not in front of —"

12

"What does it matter now?" He wiped his forearm across his face; then with a helpless gesture he flung the mug to the floor. It didn't break. Alta watched it roll towards her and stop. Pa turned his back on us and bent over the dresser as if he was trying to catch his breath. There was a silence.

"I'll go," I said, "I'll go tomorrow." I couldn't look at any of them. I got up, hitting my knee against the corner of the table as I pushed back my chair. I struggled to the door. The latch seemed smaller and stiffer than it usually was, and the clunk as it opened echoed off the walls.

Outside, the moon divided the world into deep blue and silver. The air was warm and as soft as cream, scented with hay and summer dust. An owl chuckled in the near field.

I reeled across to the far side of the yard and leant against the wall. It was hard to breathe. Ma's voice hung in my ears: *That bloody witch will put a curse on us.* And Pa, answering: *She already has.*

They were right; I was good for nothing. Misery rose inside me, as strong as the stabbing pains in my legs. Before this, I'd never been ill in my life. I never knew that my body could betray me, that my mind could go out like a lamp and leave nothing but darkness. I couldn't remember getting sick; if I tried, all I saw was a mess of nightmare-scorched fragments. Even my memories of my life before that — last spring, last winter — were tinged with the same gangrenous shadow, as if nothing was healthy any more. I knew that I'd collapsed after midsummer, because Ma had told me so, and that I'd been on the way home from Castleford; but no one had explained where I'd been, or what had happened. I must have been driving the cart — without a hat, under a hot sun, probably — but when I tried to think back there was nothing but a rippling mirage, a last vertiginous glimpse of sunlight before the blackness swallowed me. For weeks afterwards, I'd only surfaced to scream and struggle and beg them to untie me. No wonder they wanted to get rid of me.

I closed my eyes. I could still see the three of them, their arms round one another. Something whispered behind me, scratching in the wall like dry claws. It wasn't real, but it drowned out the owl and the rustle of trees. I rested my head on my arms and pretended I couldn't hear it.

I must have drawn back instinctively into the deepest corner of darkness, because when I opened my eyes Alta was in the middle of the yard, calling my name without looking in my direction. The moon had moved; now it was over the gable of the farmhouse and all the shadows were short and squat.

"Emmett?"

"Yes," I said. Alta jumped and took a step forward to peer at me.

"What are you doing there? Were you asleep?"

"No."

She hesitated. Behind her the light from a lamp crossed the upper window as someone went to bed. I started to pull myself to my feet and paused, wincing, as pain stabbed into my joints.

She watched me get up, without offering to help. "Did you mean it? That you'd go? Tomorrow?"

"Pa meant it when he said I didn't have any choice."

I waited for her to disagree. Alta was clever like that, finding new paths or different ways of doing things, picking locks. But she only tilted her face upward as if she wanted the moonlight to bleach her skin. I swallowed. The stupid dizziness had come back — suddenly, dragging me one way and then another — and I swayed against the wall and tried to catch my breath.

"Emmett? Are you all right?" She bit her lip. "No, of course not. Sit down."

I didn't want to obey her but my knees folded of their own accord. I closed my eyes and inhaled the night smells of hay and cooling earth, the overripe sweetness of crushed weeds and a rank hint of manure. Alta's skirts billowed and rustled as she sank down beside me.

"I wish you didn't have to go."

I raised one shoulder without looking at her and let it drop again.

"But . . . maybe it's the best thing . . ."

"How can it be?" I swallowed, trying to fill the crack in my voice. "All right, I understand. I'm no use here. You'll all be better off when I'm — wherever she is, this binder."

"Out on the marshes, on the Castleford road."

"Right." What would the marshes smell of? Stagnant water, rotting reeds. Mud. Mud that swallowed you alive if you went too far from the road, and never spat you back . . . "How do you know so much about it?".

"Ma and Pa are only thinking about you. After everything that's happened . . . You'll be safe there."

"That's what Ma said."

A pause. She began to gnaw at her thumbnail. In the orchard below the stables a nightingale gurgled and then gave up.

"You don't know what it's been like for them, Emmett. Always afraid. You owe them some peace."

"It's not my fault I was ill!"

"It's your fault you —" She huffed out her breath. "No, I know, I didn't mean . . . just that we all need . . . please don't be angry. It's a good thing. You'll learn a trade."

"Yes. Making books."

She flinched. "She chose you. That must mean —"

"What does it mean? How can she have chosen me, when she's never even seen me?" I thought Alta started to speak, but when I turned my head she was staring up at the moon, her face expressionless. Her cheeks were thinner than they had been before I got ill, and the skin under her eyes looked as if it had been smudged with ash. She was a stranger, out of reach.

She said, as if it was an answer, "I'll come and see you whenever I can . . ."

I let my head roll back until I felt the stone wall against my skull. "They talked you round, didn't they?"

16

"I've never seen Pa like that," she said. "So angry."

"I have," I said. "He hit me, once."

"Yes," she said, "well, I suppose you —" She stopped.

"When I was small," I said. "You weren't old enough to remember. It was the day of Wakening Fair."

"Oh." When I glanced up, her eyes flickered away. "No. I don't remember that."

"I bought . . . there was a man, selling books." I could recall the clink of my errand-money in my pocket that day — sixpence in farthings, so bulky they bulged through my trousers — and the heady, carefree feeling of going to Wakening Fair and slipping away from the others, wondering what I'd buy. I'd wandered past the meat and chickens, the fish from Coldwater and the patterned cottons from Castleford, paused at the sweetmeat stall and then turned towards another a little further away, where I'd caught a glimpse of gold and rich colours. It was hardly a stall at all, only a trestle table guarded by a man with restless eyes, but it was piled high with books. "It was the first time I'd seen them. I didn't know what they were."

That curious, wary expression was on Alta's face again. "You mean . . . ?"

"Forget it." I didn't know why I was telling her; I didn't want to remember. But now I couldn't stop the memory unfolding. I'd thought they were boxes, small gilt-and-leather chests to hold things like Ma's best silver or Pa's chessmen. I'd sauntered over, jingling my money, and the man had glanced over both shoulders before he grinned at me. "Ah, what a golden-haired

17

little prince! Come for a story, young sir? A tale of murder or incest, shame or glory, a love so piercing it was best forgotten, or a deed of darkness? You've come to the right man, young sir, these are the crème de la crème, these will tell you true and harrowing tales, violent and passionate and exciting — or if it's comedy you're after, I have some of those too, rarest of all, the things people get rid of! Have a look, young sir, cast your eyes over this one . . . Bound by a master in Castleford, years ago."

I hated the way he called me *young sir*, but the book fell open as he passed it to me and I couldn't give it back. As soon as I saw the writing on the pages I understood: this was lots of pages all squashed together — like letters, lots of letters, only in a better box — and a story that went on and on. "How much is it?"

"Ah, that one, young sir. You have wonderful taste for a young 'un, that's a special one, a real adventure story, sweeps you off your feet like a cavalry charge. Ninepence for it. Or two for a shilling."

I wanted it. I didn't know why, except that my fingertips were prickling. "I only have sixpence."

"I'll take that," he said, clicking his fingers at me. The wide smile had gone; when I followed his darting gaze I saw a knot of men gathering a little way off, muttering.

"Here." I emptied my pocketful of farthings into his palm. He let one drop, but he was still staring at the men and didn't stoop to pick it up. "Thank you."

I took the book and hurried away, triumphant and uneasy. When I reached the bustle of the main market I stopped and turned to look: the group of men was advancing on the man's stall, as he threw the books frantically into the battered little cart behind him.

Something warned me not to stare. I ran home, holding the book through my shirt-cuff so that I didn't stain the cover with my sweaty fingers. I sat on the barn steps in the sun — no one would see me, they were still at the fair — and examined it. It wasn't like anything I'd ever seen. It was a deep, heavy red, patterned with gold, and it was as soft to the touch as skin. When I opened the cover, the scent of must and wood rose up as though it hadn't been touched for years.

It sucked me in.

It was set in an army camp in a foreign country, and at first it was confusing: full of captains and majors and colonels, arguments about military tactics and a threat of court martial. But something made me go on reading: I could see it, every detail, I could hear the horses and the snap of wind against the canvas, feel my own heart quicken at the smell of gunpowder ... I stumbled on, absorbed in spite of myself, and slowly I understood that they were on the eve of a battle, that the man in the book was a hero. When the sun rose, he was going to lead them to a glorious victory — and I could feel his excitement, his anticipation, I felt it myself —

"What in hell's name are you doing?"

It broke the spell. I clambered instinctively to my feet, blinking through the haze. Pa — and the others behind him, Ma with Alta on her hip, everyone back from the fair already. Already . . . but it was getting dark.

"Emmett, I asked what you were doing!" But he didn't wait for an answer before he plucked the book away from me. When he saw what it was his face hardened. "Where did you get this?"

A man, I wanted to say, just a man at the fair, he had dozens and they looked like boxes of jewels, in leather and gold . . . But when I saw Pa's expression something shrivelled in my voice box and I couldn't speak.

"Robert? What . . .?" Ma reached for it and then pulled away as if it had bitten her.

"I'll burn it."

"No!" Ma let Alta slip staggering to the ground, and stumbled forward to catch Pa's arm. "No, how could you? Bury it!"

"It's old, Hilda. They'd all be dead, years ago."

"You mustn't. Just in case. Get rid of it. Throw it away."

"For someone else to find?"

"You know you can't burn it." For a moment they stared at each other, their faces strained. "Bury it. Somewhere safe."

At last Pa gave a brief, curt nod. Alta gave a hiccup and started to whimper. Pa shoved the book at one of the farmhands. "Here. Package this up. I'll give it to the gravedigger." Then he turned back to me. "Emmett," he said, "don't ever let me see you with a book again. You understand?"

I didn't. What had happened? I'd bought it, I hadn't stolen it, but somehow I had done something

20

unforgivable. I nodded, still reeling from the visions I'd seen. I'd been somewhere else, in another world.

"Good. You remember that," Pa said.

Then he hit me.

Don't ever let me see you with a book again.

But now they were sending me to the binder; as though whatever danger Pa had warned me against had been replaced by something worse. As though now I *was* the danger.

I looked sideways. Alta was staring down at her feet. No, she didn't remember that day. No one had ever spoken about it again. No one had ever explained why books were shameful. Once, at school, someone had muttered something about old Lord Kent having a library; but when everyone snickered and rolled their eyes I didn't ask why that was so bad. *I'd* read a book: whatever was wrong with him, I was the same. Under everything, deep inside me, the shame was still there.

And I was afraid. It was a creeping, formless fear, like the mist that came off the river. It slid chilly tendrils round me and into my lungs. I didn't want to go anywhere near the binder; but I had to.

"Alta —"

"I have to go in," she said, leaping to her feet. "You'd better go up too, Em, you have to pack and it's a long way to go tomorrow, isn't it? Good night." She scampered away across the yard, fiddling with her plait all the way so I couldn't glimpse her face. By the door she called again, "See you tomorrow," without looking round. Maybe it was the echo off the stable wall that made it sound so false.

Tomorrow.

I watched the moon until the fear grew too big for me. Then I went to my room and packed my things.

CHAPTER
TWO

From the road, the bindery looked as if it was burning. The sun was setting behind us, and the red-gold blaze of the last sunlight was reflected in the windows. Under the dark thatch every pane was like a rectangle of flame, too steady to be fire but so bright I thought I could feel my palms prickle with the heat. It set off a shiver in my bones, as if I'd seen it in a dream.

I clutched the shabby sack in my lap and looked away. On the other side of us, under the setting sun, the marshes lay flat and endless: green speckled with bronze and brown, glinting with water. I could smell sodden grass and the day's warmth evaporating. There was a rank mouldering note under the scent of moisture, and the vast dying sky above us was paler than it should have been. My eyes ached, and my body was a map of stinging scratches from yesterday's work in the fields. I should have been there now, helping with the harvest, but instead Pa and I were bouncing along this rough, sticky road, in silence. We hadn't spoken since we set off before dawn, and there was still nothing to say. Words rose in my throat but they burst like marsh-bubbles, leaving nothing on my tongue but a faint taste of rot.

As we jolted along the final stretch of track to where it petered out in the long grass in front of the house I sneaked a look at Pa's face. The stubble on his chin was salted with white, and his eyes were sunken deeper than they'd been last spring. Everyone had grown older while I was ill; as if I'd woken up and found I'd slept for years.

We drew to a halt. "We're here."

A shudder went through me: I was either going to vomit or plead with Pa to take me home. I snatched the sack from my lap and jumped down, my knees nearly buckling when my feet hit the ground. There was a well-trodden path through the tufts of the grass to the front door of the house. I'd never been here before, but the off-key jangle of the bell was as familiar as a dream. I waited, so determined not to look back at Pa that the door shimmered and swayed.

"Emmett." It was open, suddenly. For a moment all I took in was a pair of pale brown eyes, so pale the pupils were startlingly black. "Welcome."

I swallowed. She was old — painfully, skeletally old — and white-haired, her face as creased as paper and her lips almost the same colour as her cheeks; but she was as tall as me, and her eyes were as clear as Alta's. She wore a leather apron, and a shirt and trousers, like a man. The hand that beckoned me inside was thin but muscular, the veins looped across the tendons in blue strings.

"Seredith," she said. "Come in."

I hesitated. It took me two heartbeats to understand that she'd told me her name.

"Come in." She added, looking past me, "Thank you, Robert."

I hadn't heard Pa get down, but when I turned he was there at my shoulder. He coughed and muttered, "We'll see you soon, Emmett, all right?"

"Pa —"

He didn't even glance in my direction. He gave the binder a long helpless look; then he touched his forelock as if he didn't know what else to do, and strode back to the cart. I started to call out but a gust of wind snatched the words away, and he didn't turn. I watched him clamber up to his seat and click to the mare.

"Emmett." Her voice dragged me back to her. "Come in." I could see that she wasn't used to saying anything three times.

"Yes." I was holding my sack of belongings so tightly my fingers ached. She'd called Pa *Robert* as if she knew him. I took one step and then another. Now I was over the threshold and in a dark-panelled hall, with a staircase rising in front of me. A tall clock ticked. On the left, there was a half-open door and a glimpse of the kitchen beyond; on the right, another door led to —

My knees went weak, like my hamstrings had been cut. The nausea widened and expanded, chewing on my insides. I was feverish and freezing, struggling to keep my balance as the world spun. I'd been here before — only I hadn't —

"Oh, damn it," the binder said, and reached out to take hold of me. "All right, boy, breathe."

"I'm fine," I said, and was proud of how distinctly I'd shaped the consonants. Then it all went black.

When I woke, there was sunlight dancing on the ceiling in a billowing net, water-wrinkles that overlapped the narrow rectangle of brightness that spilt between the curtains. The whitewashed walls looked faintly green, like the flesh of an apple, marred here and there with the solid froth of damp. Outside a bird whistled over and over again as if it was calling a name.

The binder's house. I sat up, my heart suddenly thumping. But there was nothing to be afraid of, not yet; nothing here but myself and the room and the reflected sunshine. I found myself listening for the sounds of animals, the constant restlessness of a farmyard, but all I heard was the bird and the soft rattle of wind in the thatch. The faded curtains billowed and a wider band of light flared across the ceiling. The pillows smelt of lavender.

Last night . . .

I let my eyes rest on the opposite wall, following the bump and curve of a crack in the plaster. After I'd fainted, all I could remember was shadows and fear. Nightmares. In this clean daylight they seemed a long time ago; but they'd been bad, dragging me over and under the surface of sleep. I'd almost fought clear of them, once or twice, but then the weight of my own limbs had pulled me under again, into a choking black blindness like tar. A faint taste like burnt oil still lingered in the back of my mouth. They hadn't been as bad as that for days. The draught raised goose-pimples on my skin. Fainting like that, into Seredith's arms . . . It must have been the fatigue of the journey, the headache, the sun in my eyes, and the sight of Pa driving away without a backwards glance.

My trousers and shirt were hanging on the back of a single chair. I got up and dragged them on with clumsy fingers, trying not to imagine Seredith undressing me. At least I was still wearing drawers. Apart from the chair and the bed, the room was mostly bare: a chest at the foot of the bed, a table next to the window, and the pale, flapping curtains. There were no pictures, and no looking-glass. I didn't mind that. At home I'd looked away when I walked past my reflection in the hall. Here I was invisible; here I could be part of the emptiness.

The whole house was quiet. When I walked out on to the landing I could hear the birds calling across the marsh, and the tick of the clock in the hall below, and a dull banging from somewhere else; but underneath it all was a silence so deep the sounds skittered over it like pebbles on ice. The breeze stroked the back of my neck and I caught myself glancing over my shoulder, as if there was someone there. The bare room dipped into gloom for a second as a cloud crossed the sun; then it shone brighter than ever, and the corner of one curtain snapped in the breeze like a flag.

I almost turned and climbed back into bed, like a child. But this house was where I lived, now. I couldn't stay in my room for the rest of my life.

The stairs creaked under my feet. The banister was polished by years of use, but the dust spun thickly in the sunlight and the whitewashed plaster was bubbling off the wall. Older than our farmhouse, older than our village. How many binders had lived here? And when this binder — Seredith — died . . . One day, would this house be mine? I walked down the stairs slowly, as if I was afraid they'd give way.

The banging stopped, and I heard footsteps. Seredith opened one of the doors into the hall. "Ah, Emmett." She didn't ask me if I'd slept well. "Come into the workshop."

I followed her. Something about the way she'd said my name made me clench my jaw, but she was my master now — no, my mistress, *no*, my master — and I had to obey her.

At the door of the workshop she paused. For an instant I thought she'd step back to let me go first; but then she strode across the room and bundled something swiftly into a cloth before I could see what it was. "Come in, boy."

I stepped over the doorsill. It was a long, low room, full of morning light from the row of tall windows. Workbenches ran along both sides of the room and between them were other things that I didn't have names for yet. I took in the battered shine of old wood, the sharp glint of a blade, metal handles dark with grease . . . but there was too much to look at, and my eyes couldn't stay on one thing for long. There was a stove at the far end of the room, surrounded by tiles in russet and ochre and green. Above my head papers hung over a wire, rich plain colours interspersed with pages patterned like stone or feathers or leaves. I caught myself reaching up to touch the nearest one: there was something about those vivid kingfisher-blue wings hanging above my head . . .

The binder put her bundle down and came towards me, pointing at things. "Lay press. Nipping press. Finishing press. Plan chest — behind you, boy — tools in that cupboard and the next one along, leather and cloth next to that. Waste paper in that basket, ready for use. Brushes on that shelf, glue in there."

I couldn't take it all in. After the first effort to remember I gave up and waited for her to finish. At last she narrowed her eyes at me and said, "Sit."

I felt strange. But not sick, exactly, and not afraid. It was as if something inside me was waking up and moving. The looping grain of the bench in front of me was like a map of somewhere I used to know.

"It's a funny feeling, isn't it, boy?"

"What?"

She squinted at me, one of her milky-tea eyes bleached almost white by the sun on the side of her face. "It gets you, all this. When you're a binder born — which you are, boy."

I didn't know what she meant. At least . . . There was something *right* about this room, something that — unexpectedly — made my heart lift. As if, after a heatwave, I could smell rain coming — or like glimpsing my old self, from before I got ill. I hadn't belonged anywhere for so long, and now this room, with its smell of leather and glue, welcomed me.

"You don't know much about books, do you?" Seredith said.

"No."

"Think I'm a witch?"

I stammered, "What? Of course n —" but she waved me to silence, while a smile tugged at the corner of her mouth.

"It's all right. Think I've got this old without knowing what people say about me? About us." I looked away, but she went on as if she hadn't noticed. "Your parents kept books away from you, didn't they? And now you don't know what you're doing here."

"You asked for me. Didn't you?"

She seemed not to hear. "Don't worry, lad. It's a craft like any other. And a good one. Binding's as old as the alphabet — older. People don't understand it, but why should they?" She grimaced. "At least the Crusade's over. You're too young to remember that. Your good fortune."

There was a silence. I didn't understand how binding could be older than books, but she was staring into the middle distance as if I wasn't there. A breeze set the wire swinging, and the coloured papers flapped. She blinked and scratched her chin, and her eyes came back to mine. "Tomorrow I'll start you on some chores. Tidying, cleaning the brushes, that sort of thing. Maybe get you paring leather."

I nodded. I wanted to be alone here. I wanted to have time to look properly at the colours, to go through the cupboards and heft the weight of the tools. The whole room was singing to me, inviting me in.

"You have a look round if you want." But when I started to get to my feet she gestured at me as if I'd disobeyed her. "Not now. Later." She picked up her bundle and turned to a little door in the corner that I hadn't noticed. It took three keys in three locks to open it. I glimpsed stairs going down into the dark before she put the bundle on a shelf just inside the doorway, turned back into the room and pulled the door shut behind her. She locked it without looking at me, shielding the keys with her body. "You won't go down there for a long while, boy." I didn't know if she was warning or reassuring me. "Don't go near anything that's locked, and you'll be all right."

I took a deep breath. The room was still singing to me, but the sweetness had a shrill note now. Under this tidy, sunlit workshop, those steep steps led down into darkness. I could feel that hollowness under my feet, as if the floor was starting to give. A second ago I'd felt safe. No. I'd felt . . . *enticed*. It had turned sour with that glimpse of the dark; like the moment a dream turns into a nightmare.

"Don't fight it, boy."

She knew, then. It was real, I wasn't imagining it. I looked up, half scared to meet her gaze; but she was staring across the marsh, her eyes slitted against the glare. She looked older than anyone I'd ever seen.

I stood up. The sun was still shining but the light in the room seemed tarnished. I didn't want to look in the cupboards any more, or pull the rolls of cloth out into the light. But I made myself stroll past the cupboards, noting the labels, the dull brass knobs, and the corner of leather that poked a green tongue round the edge of a door. I turned and walked down the aisle of space, where the floor was trodden smooth by years of footsteps, of people coming and going.

I came to another door. It was the twin of the first one, set into the wall on the other side of the tiled stove. It had three locks, too. But people went in and out — I could tell that from the floorboards, the well-trodden path where even the dust lay more lightly. What did they come for? What did she do, the binder, beyond that door?

Blackness glittered in the corners of my eyes. Someone was whispering without words.

"All right," she said. Somehow she was beside me now, pulling me down on to a stool, putting weight on the back of my neck. "Put your head between your knees."

"I — can't —"

"Hush, boy. It's the illness. It'll pass."

It was real. I was sure. A fierce, insatiable, *wrongness* ready to suck me dry, make me into something else. But she'd forced my head down between my knees and held me steady, and the certainty drained away. I was ill. This was the same fear that had made me attack Ma and Pa . . . I clenched my jaw. I couldn't give in to it. If I let myself slip . . .

"That's good. Good lad."

Meaningless words, as though I was an animal. At last I straightened up, grimacing as the blood spun in my head.

"Better?"

I nodded, fighting the acid creep of nausea. My hands were twitching as though I had the palsy. I curled them into fists and imagined trying to use a knife with fingers I couldn't trust. Stupid. I'd lose a thumb. I was too ill to be here — and yet . . . "Why?" I said, and the word came out like a yelp. "Why did you choose me? Why *me*?"

The binder turned her face to the window again and stared into the sunlight.

"Was it because you were sorry for me? Poor broken-minded Emmett who can't work in the fields any more? At least here he'll be safe and solitary and won't upset his family —"

"Is that what you think?"

"What else could it be? You don't know me. Why else would you choose someone who's ill?"

"Why else, indeed?" There was an edge to her voice, but then she sighed and looked at me. "Do you remember when it began? The fever?"

"I think I was . . ." I took a breath, trying to steady my mind. "I'd been to Castleford, and I was on my way back — when I woke up I was at home —" I stopped. I didn't want to think about the gaps and nightmares, daytime terrors, sudden appalled flashes of lucidity when I knew where I was . . . The whole summer was ragged, fever-eaten, more hole than memory.

"You were here, lad. You fell ill here. Your father came to get you. Do you remember that?"

"What? No. What was I doing here?"

"It's on the road to Castleford," she said, with a faint smile. "But with the fever . . . you remember it, and you don't. That's partly what's making you ill."

"I can't stay here. This place — those locked doors. It'll make me worse."

"It will pass. Trust me. And it will pass more quickly and more cleanly here than anywhere else you could go."

There was a strange note in her voice, as though she was almost ashamed.

A new kind of fear tugged at me. I was going to have to stay here and be afraid, until I got better; I didn't want that, I wanted to run away . . .

She glanced at the locked door. "In a way," she said, "I suppose I did choose you because you're ill. But not in the way you think. Not out of pity, Emmett."

Abruptly she swung round and pushed past me, and I was left staring at the dust that swirled in the empty doorway.

She was lying. I'd heard it in her voice.

She *did* pity me.

But perhaps, after all, she was right. There was something in the silence of the old house, the low rooms filled with steady autumn sunlight and the still order of the workshop, that loosened the dark knots inside me. Day after day went by, until the place wasn't new or strange to me any more; then week after week . . . I learnt things by heart: the crinkling reflections on my ceiling, the gappy seams in the patchwork quilt on my bed, the different creak of each tread under my foot when I came downstairs. Then there was the workshop, the gleam of the tiles around the stove, the saffron-and-earth scent of tea, the opalescent gloop of well-mixed paste in a glass jar . . . The hours passed slowly, full of small, solid details; at home, in the busyness of farm life, I'd never had the time to sit and stare, or pay attention to the way a tool looked, or how well it was made, before I used it. Here the clock in the hall dredged up seconds like stones and dropped them again into the pool of the day, letting each ripple widen before the next one fell.

The tasks Seredith gave me in the workshop were simple and small. She was a good teacher, clear and patient. I learnt to make endpapers, to pare leather, to finish with blind or gold tooling. She must have been disappointed at the way I fumbled — how I'd paste a page to my own fingers, or gouge a square of pristine calfskin with a sharp centre-tool — but she said nothing, except, occasionally, "Throw it away and start again." While I practised she'd go for a walk, or write letters or lists of supplies to be ordered by the next post, sitting at the bench behind me; or she'd cook, and the house would fill with the smell of meat and pastry. We shared the rest of the chores, but after a morning bent over painstaking work I was glad to chop wood or fill the copper for laundry. When I felt weak I reminded myself that Seredith had done it all on her own, before I came.

But everything I did — everything I saw her do — was preparing materials or practising finishing; I never saw a block of pages, or a complete book. One evening when we were eating dinner in the kitchen I said, "Seredith, where are the books?"

"In the vault," she said. "Once they're finished, they have to be kept out of harm's way."

"But —" I stopped, thinking of the farm, and how hard we all worked, and how it had never been enough; I'd argued continually with Pa, asking for every new invention to make it as productive as possible. "Why don't we make more? Surely, the more we make, the more you can sell?"

She lifted her head as if she was about to say something sharp; then she shook her head. "We don't make books to sell, boy. *Selling* books is wrong. Your parents were right about that, at least."

"Then — I don't understand —"

"It's the binding that matters. The craft of it, the dignity. Say a woman comes to me for a book. I make a book for her. For *her*, you understand? Not to be gawped at by strangers." She slurped soup from her spoon. "There are binders who only think to turn a profit, who care about nothing but their bank balance, who, yes, sell books — but you will never be one of them."

"But — no one's come to you . . ." I stared at her, thoroughly confused. "When am I going to start using what you're teaching me? I'm learning all these things, but I haven't even —"

"You'll learn more soon," she said, and stood up to get more bread. "Let's take things slowly, Emmett. You've been ill. All in good time."

All in good time. If my mother had said it, I would have snorted; but I stayed silent, because somehow it *was* a good time. Gradually the nightmares grew fewer, and the lurking daytime shadows receded. Sometimes I could stand for a long time without feeling dizzy; sometimes my eyes were as clear as they used to be. And after a few weeks I didn't even look twice at the locked doors at the end of the workshop. The benches and tools and presses murmured comfort to me: everything was useful, everything was in its place. It didn't matter what it was all for, except that a glue brush was for glue, and a paring knife for paring. Sometimes, when I paused to gauge the thickness of a scrap of leather — in places it had to be thinner than a fingernail or it would fold badly — I would look up from the dark scurf of leather shavings and feel that I was in the right place. I knew what I was meant to be doing, and I was doing it — even if I was only practising. I *could* do it. That hadn't happened since before I was ill.

I missed home, of course. I wrote letters, and was half glad and half miserable to read their replies. I would have liked to be at the harvest supper, and the dance; or rather, I *would* have liked it, before . . . I read that letter over and over again, before I crumpled it up and sat looking out past my lamp-flame into the blue dusk, trying to ignore the ache in my throat. But the part of me that yearned for music and noise was the old, healthy part; I knew that silence, work and rest were what I needed now. Even if, sometimes, it felt so lonely I could hardly bear it.

The quiet days wore on, as if we were waiting for something.

When was it? Perhaps I'd been there a fortnight or a month, the first day I remember clearly. It was a bright, cold morning, and I'd been practising gold tooling on a few odd scraps of leather, concentrating hard. It was difficult, and when I peeled away the foil to see an uneven, indistinct print of my name I cursed and rolled my neck to ease the ache out of it. Something moved outside, and I looked up. The sun dazzled me, and for a moment all I saw was a shape outlined against the light. I narrowed my eyes and the glare softened. A boy — no, a young man, my age or maybe older — with dark hair and eyes and a pale, gaunt face, watching me.

I jumped so much I nearly burnt myself on the tool I was using. How long had he been there, watching me with those black stony eyes? I put the tool carefully back on to the brazier, cursing the sudden tremor that made me as clumsy as an old man. Who did he think he was, lurking there, spying?

He knocked on the glass. I turned my back on him, but when I looked over my shoulder he was still there. He gestured sideways to the little back door that opened on to the marshes. He wanted me to let him in.

I imagined him sinking gently into the mud, up to his knees, then his waist. I couldn't bear the thought of speaking to him. I hadn't seen anyone except Seredith for days; but it wasn't just that, it was his stare, so steady it felt like a finger pressing between my eyes. I kept my face averted from the window as I swept the parings of leather to the ground, tidied the scraps of gold foil into their box, and loosened the screw of the hot type-holder so that I could tap the letters out on to the bench. In a minute they'd be cool enough to put back into their tray. A spacer, like a tiny brass splinter, fell to the floor and I bent to pick it up.

When I straightened to flick it on to the bench, his shadow still hadn't moved. I sucked the sting out of my burnt finger and conceded defeat.

The back door had swollen — when was the last time it had been used? — and stuck in the frame. When I managed to get it open my heart was drumming with exertion. We stared at each other. At last I said, "What do you want?" It was a stupid question; he clearly wasn't a tradesman with a delivery, or a friend of Seredith's here for a visit.

"I . . ." He looked away. Behind him the marsh shone like an old mirror, tarnished and mottled but still bright. When he turned back to me his face was set. "I've come to see the binder."

I wanted to shut the door in his face. But he was a customer — the first one since I'd arrived — and I was only an apprentice. I stepped back, opening the door wider.

"Thanks." But he said it with a sort of effort, and stood very still on the step, as if walking past me would soil his clothes. I turned and went back into the workshop: now he was inside he was no longer my problem. He could ring the bell or call for Seredith. I certainly wasn't going to stop work for his sake. He hadn't apologised for disturbing me, or watching me.

I heard him hesitate, and follow.

I made my way back to the bench and bent over the piece of tooling I'd been working on. I rubbed at one of the words to see if I could make the letters a bit clearer.

The tool had been too hot on the second try — or I'd let it linger too long — and the gold had blurred; the third was a little better but I hadn't pressed evenly. There was a chilly draught from the open workshop door, and quiet footsteps. He was behind me. I'd only looked at him for a second, but I could still see his face as clearly as if it was reflected in the window: white, smudged with shadows, with red-rimmed eyes. A deathbed face, a face no one would want to look at.

"Emmett?"

My heart skipped a beat, because he shouldn't have known my name.

Then I realised: the tooling. *EMMETT FARMER*. It must have been just large enough for him to read from a few feet away. I picked up the leather and slammed it over, face down. Too late, of course. He gave me a crooked, empty smile, as if he was proud of noticing, as if he was pleased that I'd blenched. He started to say something else.

I said, "I don't know if the binder is taking commissions at the moment." But he went on looking at me with that odd, thirsty half-smile. "If that's what you've come for. And she doesn't sell books."

"How long have you been here?"

"Since harvest-time." He had no right to ask; I didn't know why I answered, except that I wanted him to leave me alone.

"You're her apprentice?"

"Yes."

He looked round at the workshop, and back at me. There was something too slow, too deliberate in his look to be mere curiosity. "Is it a — good life?" A twist of contempt in his voice. "Here, alone with her?"

The sweet scorched smell of the tools on the stove was making my head ache. I reached for the smallest, an intricate centre-tool that never came out properly in gold. I wondered how it would feel to bring it down on the back of my other hand. Or his.

"Emmett —" He made it sound like a curse.

I put the tool down and reached for a new piece of leather. "I have to get on with this."

"I'm sorry."

Silence. I cut the leather into a square and fixed it to a piece of board. He was watching me. I fumbled and nearly caught my thumb with the scalpel. It felt as if there were invisible threads tangled between my fingers. I turned to him. "Do you want me to go and find Sere — the binder?"

"I — not yet. Not just yet."

He was afraid. The realisation took me by surprise. For an instant I saw past my own resentment. He was as frightened and miserable as anyone I'd ever met. He was desperate. He stank of it, like fever. But I couldn't pity him, because there was something else, too, in the way he looked at me. Hatred. He seemed to hate me.

"They didn't want me to come," he said. "My father, I mean. He thinks binding is for other people, not us. If he knew I was here . . ." He grimaced. "But it'll be too late when I get home. He won't punish me. How could he?"

I didn't answer. I didn't want to wonder what he meant.

"I wasn't sure. I didn't think . . ." He cleared his throat. "I heard she'd chosen you and I thought I'd come and — but I didn't think I wanted — until I saw you there . . ."

"Me?"

He took a breath and reached out to brush a speck of dust off the nipping press. His forefinger trembled, and I could see the pulse beating at the base of his neck. He laughed, but not as if anything was funny. "You don't care, do you? Why should you? You've got no idea who I am."

"No, I haven't."

"Emmett," he burst out, stumbling on the syllables, "please — look at me, just for a second, please. I don't understand —"

I had the sensation that I was moving, the world racing past me too quickly to see, the speed drowning out his words. I blinked and tried to hold on, but a sickening current lifted me up and whirled me downstream. He was still talking but the words sang past me and away.

"What's going on?" Seredith's voice cut him off.

He spun round. Red crept over his cheeks and forehead. "I'm here for a binding."

"What are you doing in the workshop? Emmett, you should have called me at once."

I tried to master the nausea. "I thought —"

"It wasn't Emmett's fault, it was mine," he said. "My name is Lucian Darnay. I did write."

"Lucian Darnay." Seredith frowned. A strange, wary expression swept over her face. "And how long have you been talking to Em — to my apprentice? Never mind." Her eyes went to me before he could answer. "Emmett?" she said, more softly. "Are you — well?"

The shadows swirled round me, blacking out the corners of my vision; but I nodded.

"Good. Mr Darnay, come with me."

"Yes," he said, but he didn't move. I could feel his desperation pulsing out in dark waves.

"*Come*," Seredith repeated, and at last he turned and moved towards her. She reached for her keys and started to unlock the door at the far end of the workshop; but she didn't look at what she was doing, she looked at me.

The door swung open. I caught my breath. I didn't know what I had expected, but there was a glimpse of a scrubbed wooden table, two chairs, a hazy square of sun on the floor. It should have been a relief, but a tight claw closed round my chest. It looked so tidy, so austere — and yet . . .

"Go in, Mr Darnay. Sit down. Wait for me."

He drew in a long, slow breath. He glanced at me once, the fierceness in his eyes as unreadable as a riddle. Then he walked to the door and through it. When he sat down he kept his back very straight, as if he was trying not to shake.

"Emmett, are you all right? He should never have . . ." Her eyes searched my face for a reaction they didn't find. "Go and lie down."

"I'm fine."

"Then go and mix up a jar of paste in the kitchen." She watched me walk past her. I had to make an effort to take smooth steps and not stagger. Black wings were beating around me and it was hard to see where I was going. That room, that quiet little room . . .

I sat down on the stairs. The light lay on the floorboards in a silvery lattice. The shape of it made me think of something — half-remembered nightmares, a flash of Lucian Darnay's face, his hungry black eyes. The darkness hung in front of me for a long time, like a fog; only there was something new in it, a flash like teeth, sharper than I could bear. Not hatred — but something that would have torn me apart if it could.

Then it closed round me, and I was gone.

CHAPTER
THREE

I surfaced gradually into a grey soft day and the muffled sound of rain. There was another noise too, one I couldn't identify right away: I stared at the ceiling and wondered idly what it was. A swish, a pause, a human breath, swish . . . After a long time I turned my head, and saw Seredith sitting at the table beside the window, her head bent. There was a kind of wooden frame set up in front of her, and piles of folded paper. She was sewing the folded pages together, along one way and then the other, and the thread whispered as it pulled taut. I watched her for a long time, lulled by the rhythm of it: in, pull, out, over, in . . . She tightened a stitch, cut the thread, reached for the spool, cut a new length, and tied it on. The room was so quiet I heard the little click as the knot bit. She looked round, and smiled. "How do you feel?"

"I . . ." I swallowed, and the sharp dryness in my mouth brought reality back. I ached all over. My wrist stung, like a Chinese burn. I glanced sideways, confused for a second. I was tied to the bed with a strip of whitish cloth. The fabric was rucked up into a narrow fold that cut into my flesh, as though I'd fought to get away.

"You were having terrors," Seredith said. "Do you remember?"

"No." Or did I? An echo of screams, a flash of dark eyes watching me . . .

"Never mind. Now you're awake I'll untie you."

She stood up, putting her needle down carefully on the half-sewn pile of paper, and bent over me to pick with gnarled fingers at the knot. I lay still, not looking at her. What had I done? Had I gone mad, again? Last time, when it got really bad, I'd hit out at Ma and Pa. Alta had been afraid to come near me. Had I attacked Seredith?

"There." She dragged the chair to my bedside and settled into it with a sharp breath. "Are you hungry?"

"No."

"You will be. Five days you've been out."

"Out?"

"Two more days of rest. At least. Then you can try getting up."

"I'm fine. I can get up now." I wrenched myself into a more upright position, and grabbed the side of the bed to steady myself against the sudden drag of dizziness. Slowly the spinning stopped, but it had taken all my strength and I let my head drop back on to the pillow. I squeezed my eyes shut, forbidding myself to cry. "I thought I was getting better."

"You are."

"But —" I didn't want to think about how it must have been, one frail old woman against her crazed, hallucinating apprentice. I might have hurt her, or worse . . .

She shifted. "Open your eyes."

"What?"

"Look at me. That's better." She leant towards me. I smelt soap and glue and the leather of her apron. "It was a relapse. But the worst is over."

I turned my face away. I'd heard Ma say that before, and every time it'd had slightly less conviction.

"You can trust me, boy. I know a little about binder's fever. Normally it isn't so bad, but . . . you will recover. Slowly, of course."

"What?" I raised my head so suddenly it sent a flash of pain across my temple. There was a *name* for what was wrong with me? "I thought it was just — madness."

She snorted. "You're not insane, boy. Who told you that? No, it's an illness like any other. It's a sort of temporary frenzy."

An illness, like influenza or scurvy or the flux. How I wanted to believe it. I looked down at the red creases in my wrist. Further up my arm there were two bluish smudges like fingerprints. I swallowed. "Binder's fever? What's it got to do with binders?"

She hesitated. "Only binders get it. That is . . . not binders, but people who could be binders. When you have the calling . . . sometimes it goes wrong, in your head. It's how I knew you'd be a binder, boy — and a good one. It's nothing to be ashamed of. And now that you're here, it will pass."

"Do all binders get it?"

"Not all, no." A spatter of rain rattled the window. She glanced up, and I followed her gaze; but there was nothing out there, only the grey emptiness of the marshes, and wet veils of fog. "One of the greatest binders of all nearly died of it," she said. "Margaret Pevensie. She was a widow in the Middle Ages, and she bound over twenty books — that was a lot, in those days. A few of them survived. I travelled to Haltby, once, to see them." Her eyes came back to me. "My old master used to say that the binderbound fever was what made someone an artist, not a mere artisan. I always thought he was teasing me, but if he was right . . . well, you'll make a good apprentice."

I laid my hand over the bruises on my arm, fitting my fingers into the marks. The wind murmured in the thatch and drove another gust of rain against the window-pane, but the house was thick-walled, solid, as old as rock. Binder's fever, not madness or weakness.

"I'll get you some soup." She got up, put the reel of thread and the loose folded pages into the pocket of her apron, and lifted the sewing frame.

I craned forwards. "Is that . . .?"

"Lucian Darnay's book. Yes. It will be."

His name was like a hook that snagged my insides and jerked tight. Lucian Darnay, the boy who hated me. The hook sank deeper, tugged harder. "What are you making for him?" Seredith glanced at me, but she didn't answer. "Can I see?"

"No." She strode past me to the door.

I tried to get to my feet, but the room spun. "Was it —"

"Get back into bed."

"— him, Seredith, was it — did I get ill again because of him, or — who was he, why did he . . .?"

"He won't come back. He's gone."

"How do you know?"

Her eyes slid away. A timber creaked above, and suddenly the house felt fragile, as if the thick walls were nothing but a dream.

"I'll fetch you that soup," she said, and closed the door behind her.

For a while after that, Seredith locked herself in the workshop in the afternoons. She didn't tell me what she was doing, and I didn't ask: but I knew she was working on Darnay's book. Sometimes, when I'd finished my chores, I leant against the door, half listening and half dreaming, trying to make sense of what I heard. Most of the time it was silent — a peculiar heavy silence, as if the whole house listened with me, every fibre of wood and plaster tuned to the absence of sound — but now and then there would be banging, or scraping, and once there was the clunk of an overturned pot. As it got colder my joints tingled and ached from standing still for so long, but I couldn't wrench myself away. I hated the compulsion that held me there, waiting for something I didn't understand; but it was irresistible, a mixture of curiosity and dread, driven by the nightmares that still haunted me, even now I was getting better.

They were rarer now, and they'd changed — the formless black terrors had sharpened into clear dreams, full of sunlight — but they were just as bad. Ever since that day, the fear had a face: Lucian Darnay's. I saw him again and again, his fierce eyes, his last look at me before he walked to the half-open door at the end of the workshop. I saw him sit down, straight-backed, in that quiet, bright, terrible room, and a surge of panic went through me — because in my dream it wasn't him sitting there, it was me.

They were trying to tell me something. I didn't know what I was frightened of: but whatever it was, it lived in Seredith's locked room. When I woke and couldn't get back to sleep I sat by my window, letting the sharp night air dry the clamminess of my skin, and tried to understand; but no matter how much I turned it over in my head, no matter how much I tried to see past the fear, there was nothing except Lucian Darnay, and that half-glimpsed room. Whatever happened in there, it seeped out, setting my teeth on edge, bleeding into my dreams.

I asked Seredith about him one evening when I was scouring a pan and she was making stew. She didn't look up, but her fingers stumbled and knocked half an onion on to the floor. She bent slowly to pick it up. "Try not to think about Lucian Darnay," she said.

"Why won't you show me his book? All I'm learning is this endless finishing work, I thought I was supposed to . . .?" She rinsed the onion and went on chopping it. "Seredith! When are you going to —"

"I'll teach you more soon," she said, pushing past me into the pantry. "When you're well again."

But day after day passed, until I was nearly as strong as I'd ever been, and she still didn't tell me.

★ ★ ★

Autumn changed into winter. In our day-by-day life — the monotonous, meditative routine of work and food and sleep — I lost track of time. The days rolled round like wheels, full of the same chores and the same hours of finishing work, marbling paper, paring leather or gilding the edge of a dummy block. Mostly, my practice-pieces ended up in the old barrel Seredith used as a waste-bin; but even when Seredith stared down at one of the papers and said, without smiling, "Keep that one," it went into the plan chest and stayed there, out of sight. Nothing ever seemed to get used. I almost stopped wondering when they'd be good enough, or when I'd see a real book; and maybe that was what Seredith wanted. In the still silence of the workshop I concentrated on small things: the weight of the burnisher, the squeak of beeswax under my thumb. One morning I looked out and saw, with a shock, that the reeds were poking through a thin layer of snow. I'd noticed the cold, of course, but in a distant practical way that made me move my work closer to the stove and dig out a pair of fingerless gloves. Now it hit me: I'd passed months here, nearly a quarter of a year. Soon it would be the Turning. I took a deep, chilly breath, wondering how — if — we would celebrate it, alone in the middle of nowhere. It hurt to imagine my family surrounded by evergreens and mistletoe, toasting absent friends in mulled ale . . . But Seredith hadn't said anything about letting me go home, and if deep snow fell the roads would be impassable. Not that anyone had come, since Lucian Darnay, except the weekly post. The post-cart still stopped at our door, and the driver scuttled inside to bolt a mug of hot tea before he went on; until one day, a few weeks later, the clouds were so low and the air so ominously stagnant that he shook his head when I invited him inside. He threw a packet of letters and a bag of supplies onto the ground at my feet as quickly as he could before huddling into his nest of blankets. "Going to snow again, boy," he said. "Not sure when I'll be back. See you in the spring, maybe."

"The spring?"

A sharp blue eye glinted at me from the space between his hat and scarf. "Your first time out here, isn't it? Don't worry. She always makes it through."

With that he clicked to the shivering horse, and jolted off down our path towards the road. I stood there watching until he was out of sight, in spite of the cold.

If I'd known . . . I racked my brain to remember what I'd said in my letter to my family — the last one this year . . . But what would I have added? Wished them a happy Turning, that was all. In a way I was glad that home felt so far away, that I could stand there and feel nothing, as if the freezing air had numbed my mind as well as my fingers.

A fit of trembling seized me, and I went inside.

He was right. It snowed that night, sieving it down in a silent blizzard, and when we woke the road was hardly a ripple in the whiteness. I was meant to light the stove first thing, but that morning when I walked into the workshop Seredith was already awake and at her bench. She was watching a bird hop and flutter outside, leaving neat tracks like letters. A drift of flour from the paste she'd been mixing made it look as if the snow had come through the window.

She'd lit the stove, but I shivered. She looked round. "There's tea ready. Oh, and is there anything you need? I'm writing a list for the next order from Castleford."

"The postman said he wouldn't be back till spring." I was so stiff with cold that I nearly spilt the tea when I tried to pour it.

"Oh, Toller's a fool. It's too early for winter. This will thaw in a few days." She smiled as I glanced involuntarily at the bank of snow that rose halfway up the far window. "Trust me. The real snows won't be here until after the Turning. There's enough time to prepare."

I nodded. That meant I could write another letter home, after all; but what would I say?

"Go out to the storehouse and take stock." I looked at the glittering snowdrifts and a thin chill ran up my back. She added, "It'll be cold," with a glint in her eye that was half mockery, half sympathy. "Wrap up well."

It wasn't too bad when I got down to it. I had to move boxes and sacks and huge jars to see what was there, and after a little while I was panting with exertion and too warm to keep my hat on. I dumped the sack I'd been moving and leant against the side of the doorway to catch my breath. I let my eyes linger on the woodpile, wondering if it would be enough to get us through winter. If it wasn't, somehow I'd have to find more; but in this wide bare landscape there was no wood to gather or trees to cut down. A cloud had come up to cover the sun, and a breeze whined in my ears like someone sharpening a knife a long way away. It was going to snow again. Surely Seredith was wrong about the thaw.

I should have got back to work. But something caught my eye — something too far away to see clearly, struggling along the faint line of road like an insect stuck in white paint. At last the dark blot grew into the shape of a horse, hock-high in the snow, with a fat hunchbacked speck of a rider. No — two riders, looking as small as children until I realised that the horse was a huge shaggy Shire horse. Two women, the one behind straight-backed, the other sagging in front and slipping sideways at every step. Long before I could see their faces clearly, their voices carried across the snow: a desperate mutter of encouragement, and above that the thin desolate keening I'd thought was the wind.

When they stopped in front of the house, and one woman dismounted awkwardly into the snowdrift, I should have gone to help her. Instead I watched as she struggled, coaxing and tugging and finally heaving the other woman off the horse as if she was a doll. The shrill wailing went on, high, inhuman, only hiccupping and starting again when the women stumbled on their way to the front door. I caught a glimpse of wide glazed eyes and loose tangled hair and lips bitten bloody; then they were huddled in the porch, and the bell jangled off-key.

I turned back to the ordered familiarity of the storeroom; but now there were shadows lurking behind every pile and looking out at me from every jar. Who would drag themselves through this snow, unless they were desperate? Desperate for a binding ... Like Lucian Darnay. But what could a book do? What could Seredith do?

In a moment she would open the door to the women. Then she'd take them through the workshop to the locked room ...

Before I had time to think I had crossed the little yard and skirted the side of the house so I could slip inside by the back door. I paused in the passageway and listened.

"Bring her in." Seredith's voice.

"I'm trying!" Breathless, a village accent, stronger than mine. "I can't get her to — come on, Milly, please —"

"Didn't she want to come? If she doesn't agree, I can't —"

"Oh!" A brief laugh, sharp with bitterness and fatigue. "Oh, she wanted to come, all right. Begged and begged, even in this snow. And then half a mile down the road she went like a rag doll — and she won't stop this bloody *noise* —"

"Very well." Seredith said it without heat, but it was enough to cut her off. The wailing went on, sobbing and quavering like a trickle of water. "Milly? Come here. Come inside. I can help you. That's good, now your other foot. Good girl."

Something about her tone reminded me of when I'd first come here. I turned my head and focused on the wall in front of my face. A thin crust of windblown snow clung to the rough plaster, as intricate and granular as salt crystals.

"That's better. That's good." It was like Pa, murmuring to an edgy mare.

"Thank goodness." The woman's voice cracked. "She's gone mad. You'll make her better. Please."

"If she asks me to. There we go, Milly. I've got you now."

"She can't ask — her mind's gone —"

"Let go of her." A pause, and the keening faded a little. The other woman sniffed. Seredith added, more gently, "You've done all you can. Let me look after her now." I heard the workshop door open, and the three sets of footsteps: Seredith's familiar tread, the lighter step of the other woman and a dragging, halting shuffle that made my scalp crawl.

The door closed again. I shut my eyes. I could count the time it took them to walk along the worn boards to the locked door, the moment Seredith unhooked her keys and put them to the locks . . . I thought perhaps I heard it open and shut again, unless it was the knock of my heartbeat in my ears.

Whatever happened behind that door, it was happening now, to the woman who looked like a wounded animal.

I didn't want to know. I forced myself to go back to the storeroom. I still had work to do. But when I'd hauled the last sack back into place and chalked up the last numbers on the wall, it was as if no time at all had passed. It was nearly sunset, and I'd had nothing to eat or drink all day. I stretched, but even the ache in my shoulders was distant and unimportant.

When I walked into the workshop the room was dim and grey. A fine flurry of snow crackled against the windows.

"Oh!"

I spun round, catching my breath. The other woman, not the mad one but the tall, straight-backed one who'd brought her . . . Stupid. Somehow I knew that everyone went in there on their own, alone with the binder. Of course Seredith would have told this woman to wait outside. I was an idiot to have jumped like that.

"Who are you?" she said. She was dressed in shapeless blue homespun, and her face was weather-beaten and freckled, but she spoke like I was a servant.

"The binder's apprentice."

She gave me a wary, hostile look, as if she belonged here and I didn't. Then she sank slowly back on to her seat next to the stove. She'd been drinking from my mug; a thin ribbon of steam rose from it and dispersed in the air.

"Your . . . friend," I said. "Is she still — in there?"

She looked away.

"Why did you bring her here?"

"That's her business."

No, I wanted to say, no, I don't mean that, I mean what's happening to her, why bring her *here*, what can Seredith do? But I hated the way the woman had turned away, dismissing the question. I sat down, deliberately, and reached for the jar of flour-paste, rummaged in a drawer for a clean brush. I had some endpapers cut and ready to be glued out; I could do that without concentrating, while the room filled with a silent hum from the locked room . . .

But it wasn't locked now. If I went and turned the handle the door would open. And I'd see . . . what?

A gobbet of paste dropped from my brush onto the workbench, as if someone had spat over my shoulder. The woman was pacing, her heels clicking on the floor at every turn. I kept my eyes on my work, on the dirty rag I was using to wipe the paste away.

"Will she die?"

"What?"

"Milly. My friend. I don't want her to die." I could hear how hard she'd tried not to say the words aloud. "She doesn't deserve to die."

I didn't look up until I felt her come close to me. The scent of wet wool and old saddles rose from her clothes. If I looked down I could see the hem of her skirt, the old blue linsey stained along the bottom edge with splashes of mud. "Please. I heard that sometimes they die."

"No." But my heart turned over. For all I knew . . .

"You liar." She swung away, her breath rasping in her throat. "I didn't want to bring her. She was desperate. I said to her, an old witch, why go to the old witch? You know it's wrong, it's evil, stay strong, don't give in. I should never . . ." She caught herself, as if she'd realised how loudly she'd spoken, but after a moment she started again. "But today she was crazy, I couldn't hold out any longer. So I brought her to this awful place, and now she's been in there for . . ." Her voice trembled and died.

"But you said — you asked Seredith to help her . . ." I bit my tongue.

But she didn't seem to hear me, let alone realise that I'd been eavesdropping earlier. "I just want her back, my lovely Milly, I just want her to be happy again. Even if she has to sell her soul for it. I don't care if it's the devil's bargain, whatever the old bitch has to do, all right, she can do it! Bring Milly back, that's all. But if she dies in there . . ."

The devil's bargain. Was that what Seredith did? The bitch, the old witch . . . I tried to lay the coloured paper on top of the white, but I missed. Clumsy hands, stupid trembling hands. *Even if she has to sell her soul.* But what did that have to do with books, with paper and leather and glue?

The sun came out between two slabs of cloud. I looked up into a pinkish mist of sunlight. It stung my eyes; for a split second I thought I saw an outline, a dark silhouette against the dazzle. Then the sun was gone, and the young man was too. I blinked away reflexive tears, and looked past the after-image to my work. I'd let the paper cockle, and I'd let it dry; when I tried to peel it away it ripped. I ran my thumb over the sticky white scar that ran across the feathered patterning. I had to start again.

"I'm sorry, I didn't . . ." She strode to the window. When she glanced at me her eyes were in shadow but her voice had a pleading edge. "I don't know what I'm saying. I didn't mean that. Please don't be angry. Please don't tell her — the binder — will you? Please."

She was afraid. I screwed up my botched endpaper and threw it away. Not just afraid of Seredith, afraid of me too . . .

I took a deep breath. Cut more papers. Mix more paste. Glue out the pages, lay them down, nip in the press, hang them up to dry . . . I didn't know what I was doing, but somehow I carried on. When I came back to myself the room was so dim it was hard to see, and a pile of glued papers were waiting to be put between pressing boards. It was like waking from a dream. There'd been a sound, the door opening.

Seredith's voice, dry as stone. "There's tea on the stove. Bring it here."

I froze, but she wasn't talking to me. She wasn't looking in my direction, she hadn't seen me. She was rubbing her eyes; she looked drained, infinitely weary. "Hurry," she said, and the woman scurried towards her with a spilling teapot and chinking cups.

"Is she — all right?"

"Don't ask foolish questions." A moment later she added, "In a minute she will be ready to see you. Then you should hurry home, before more snow falls."

The door closed. A pause. A spray of snowflakes brushed the window like a wing. So much for the thaw. In a while the door would open again. I willed myself not to turn round when it did.

"Come on, my dear." Seredith led the keening girl out into the workshop — only now she was docile, quiet.

And then they were embracing, the other woman laughing with relief, sobbing, "Milly," over and over again while Seredith slowly, deliberately locked the door behind them.

Alive, then. Sane, then. Nothing terrible had happened. Had it?

"Thank goodness — oh, look at you, you're well again — thank you —"

"Take her home and let her rest. Try not to speak to her of what's happened."

"Of course not — yes — Milly, sweetheart, we're going home now."

"Gytha. Home . . ." She pushed the tangled hair away from her forehead. She was still gaunt and grimy but not long ago she'd been beautiful. "Yes, I should like to go home." There was something empty and fragile in the words, like a cracked glass.

The woman — Gytha — led her into the hallway. "Thank you," she called again to Seredith, pausing at the door. Without anyone pushing her Milly was inert, her face so calm it looked like a statue's. I swallowed. That uncanny serenity . . . It made the hairs on the back of my neck rise. My heart said, *wrong, wrong, wrong.*

I must have made a noise, because she looked at me. I met her eyes for an instant. It was like looking into a mirror and seeing no one there.

Then they were gone, and the door closed. A second later I heard the front door open and shut. The house sank back into the muffled snow-silence.

"Emmett?" Seredith said. "What are you doing in here?"

I turned to the bench. In this light my tools looked like pewter, and a silver smear of glue glinted on the wood like a snail's trail. The pile of finished endpapers was all shades of grey: ashes-of-roses, ashes-of-peacock, ashes-of-sky.

"I thought I asked you to sort out the stores."

A draught flicked a fine sand of ice against the window and set a wire swinging above my head. There were more papers hanging there; more dim wings, more pages than we could ever use.

"I finished. I made more endpapers."

"What? Why? We don't need —"

"I don't know. Because it's something I know how to do, I suppose." I looked round. There were rolls and rolls of book-cloth, piled like logs on the shelf, all sombre and shadowy in this silvery half-dusk. The cupboard below held goatskins, a box of leather scraps, bottles of dye . . . And next to it — the door was swinging open, the catch needed seeing to — the boxes of tools glinted dully, their tiny elaborate feet poking up into the light. Reels of gold foil gleamed. In front there were presses, another long bench, the board-cutter, the plough . . . "I don't understand," I said. "All this — to decorate books that you don't even sell."

"Books should be beautiful," Seredith said. "No one sees, that's not the point. It's a way to honour people — like grave-goods, in olden times."

"But whatever happens in your locked room . . . that's the real binding, isn't it? You make books for people, in there. How?"

She made a sudden movement, but when I looked at her she was still again. "Emmett . . ."

"I've never even seen —"

"Soon."

"You keep *saying* —"

"Not now!" She staggered, caught herself and dropped into the chair by the stove. "Please, not now, Emmett. I'm tired. I'm so tired."

I walked past her, to the locked door. I ran my hand down over the three locks. It took an effort. My shoulder prickled with the impulse to pull away. Behind me Seredith's chair scraped on the floor as she turned to look at me.

I stayed where I was. If I waited long enough, this fear would pass: and then I would be ready. But it didn't. And underneath it, like a sickness I hadn't known I had, was a black misery, a sense of loss so strong I could have wept.

"Emmett."

I turned on my heel and left.

In the next few days we didn't speak of it again; we only talked about the chores and the weather, treading carefully, like people edging across new ice.

CHAPTER
FOUR

I woke out of a dream of fire. I opened my eyes and blinked away the flickering red light. I'd been in a palace, a maze made of flames, so high and hot they sucked the air out of my lungs, and for a moment I thought I caught the bitter scratch of smoke in my throat; but the room was dark and when I breathed all I could smell was the subtle metallic scent of snow. I sat up, rubbing my eyes.

Knocking. That was what had woken me: a hard pounding at the front door that hardly paused. And someone shouting. There was a bell jangling too, a continuous clanging like an alarum.

I dragged myself out of bed and pulled on my trousers. The boards were cold under my bare feet, but I didn't bother about shoes. I stumbled out into the passageway and stood there for a second, listening. A man's voice, breathless. "I know you're there!" The door juddered in its frame. "Come out or I'll smash your fucking windows. *Out!*"

I clenched my fists. At home Pa would have reached for his rifle, and when he swung the door open whoever was there would have stammered and fallen silent. But this wasn't my house, and I didn't have a rifle. I crossed the passageway to knock at Seredith's door. "Seredith?" I didn't have time to wait for an answer. I pushed it open and peered round, trying to make out where her bed was. I'd never been in this room. "Seredith, there's someone outside. Are you awake?"

Nothing. I could just see the pale crumple of her pillows and rucked sheets, next to the window. She wasn't there. "Seredith?"

Something muttered in the darkness. I whirled round. She was curled in a chair in the corner of the room, shielding her head as if the sky was about to fall. Her eyes were open, gleaming at me. Her face was so pale it seemed to hover in the air. "Seredith. There's someone knocking at the door. Should I answer? What's going on?"

"Come for us," she muttered, "they've come, I knew they would, the Crusade, the Crusade . . ."

"I don't understand." My voice wavered and I clenched my fists. "Should I open the door? Do you want to talk to him?"

"The Crusaders, come to burn us all, come to kill us — nowhere to run now, hide, hide in the cellar, don't give up the books, die with the books if you must —"

"Seredith, please!" I dropped to my haunches in front of her, so that my eyes were at the same level as hers. I pulled gently at one of her wrists, trying to uncover her ear. "I don't know what you're talking about. Do you want me to —"

She recoiled. "Who — get away from me — who who who —"

I rocked backwards, off balance. "It's me! Seredith, it's Emmett."

Silence. The pounding stopped. We stared at each other through the dense grainy dark. I could hear her hoarse breathing, and my own. There was the smash of glass from downstairs. "Hey!" the man yelled. "Come out here, you old bitch!"

Seredith shuddered. I tried to take her hand but she scrabbled backwards into the corner of the room, scraping frantically at the plaster. Her face was gleaming with moisture and her mouth was half-open. For a second she'd known who I was, but now she was staring past me, her lips trembling, and I didn't dare touch her again.

I stood up. She caught at my shirt and tugged. I nearly fell. "Seredith." I peeled her fingers away one by one. They were brittle and clammy, and I was afraid that I'd break the bones. "Let go of me. I have to —"

I pulled too hard, and she cried out. But as she shook the pain from her wrist, her eyes seemed to clear. "Emmett," she said.

"Yes."

"I was dreaming. Help me back to —"

"It's all right. I'll go. You stay here." I walked into the passage on shaking legs.

The man's voice rose, clearer now that the window had gone. "I'll smoke you out! You come out here and talk to me, witch!"

I don't know how I got to the bottom of the stairs, or slid the bolts on the front door, but suddenly I was in the open doorway. The man in front of me startled and stepped back. He was smaller than I'd expected, and his face had a pointed, ratty look. Behind him more dark figures turned their heads. One of them had a torch. So I *had* smelt smoke.

He squared up to me as if he thought he was as tall as I was, though he had to tilt his head back to look me in the eye. "Who the hell are you?"

"I'm the witch's apprentice. Who the hell are *you?*"

"Get her down here."

"What do you want?"

"I want my daughter back."

"Your daughter? She's not here. No one's here but —" I stopped.

"Don't try to be smart. You know what I'm talking about. You bring her book out here, right now, and give it to me. Or —"

"Or what?"

"Or we burn this house to the ground. And everything in it."

"Look around you. It's been snowing. These walls are three feet thick. You really believe you can just set light to the house? With one torch? Why don't you and your makeshift army —"

"You think we're that stupid?" The man gestured to his friend, who hefted a covered bucket and grinned. A slosh of liquid dribbled over the side and I smelt oil. "You think we'd come all this way to make empty threats? You want to take me seriously, son. I mean it. Now *bring me that book.*"

I swallowed. The house had thick walls, and there was snow on the thatch; but I'd seen the barn at Greats

Farm on fire one winter, and I knew that if the flames took hold . . . "I don't know where it is," I said. "I —"

Seredith's voice said, from behind me, "Go home."

"That's her," one of the dark figures said. "The old woman. *That's* her."

The man glared over my shoulder. "Don't you order me, you old hag. You heard what I said to your — whatever he is . . . I want my daughter's book. She had no right coming here to you."

"She had every right."

"You mad old bitch! She sneaked out without my permission, and then she comes home half-empty — looks at me like she doesn't even know who I am —"

"It was her choice. All of it was her choice. If you hadn't —"

"Shut up!" He jerked forwards; if I hadn't been there maybe he would have hit her. I caught a whiff of sour beer on his breath, mixed with something stronger. "I know your lot. I'm not having you sell my daughter's book to some —"

"I don't sell books. I keep them safe. Now *leave*."

There was a silence. The torchlight danced on the man's face. He glanced backwards, licking his lips, and his friends stared at him. His hands opened and closed like claws.

A breeze ruffled the grass and set the torch-flame fluttering. For a moment I felt a damp breath on my cheek, blowing away the scent of smoke; then it died, and the flames leapt upwards again.

"All right," he said. "All right, we'll do it your way." He grabbed the bucket of oil from the other man, and lumbered heavily back to the door. "I want that book burnt. If you won't bring it to me, I'll burn the house down with the book in it."

I tried to laugh. "Don't be a fool."

"I'm warning you. You'd better come out here."

"Look at us — an old woman and an apprentice, you can't really —"

"Watch me."

My grip tightened on the door frame. The blood was thrumming in my fingers so hard that it felt like the wood might leap out of my grasp. I looked at Seredith. She was staring at the man, white-faced, her hair straggling over her shoulders. If I'd never seen her before I could have believed she was a witch. She said something too low to catch.

"Please," I said, "she's old, she hasn't done anything wrong, whatever happened to your daughter —"

"*Whatever happened*? She was bound, that's what happened! Now, you move out of the way, or I swear I'll burn you along with everything else —" He lunged at me and dragged me forwards. I stumbled away from the door, surprised by the strength of his grip; then I flung my arm up to break his hold. I staggered to the side but by the time I got my balance someone had grabbed me from behind. The other man swung his torch in front of me as if I was an animal. The heat prickled on my cheeks and I blinked away stinging tears. "And you," he shouted, through the doorway, "you come out too. You come out and we won't hurt you."

I tried to pull away from whoever was holding me. "You mean you'll just leave us out here in the snow? Miles from anywhere? She's an old woman."

"Shut up!" He turned on me. "I'm being kind, warning you at all."

I wanted to throttle him. I forced myself to take a deep breath. "Look — you can't do this. You could be deported — you don't want to risk that."

"For burning a binder's house to the ground? I've got ten friends'll swear I was in the tavern the whole night. Now, get the old bitch out here or she'll get smoked into a kipper with the rest."

The front door slammed. A bolt shot home.

Melted snow ran off the roof in a sudden dribble, as if a pool had formed and overflowed. The breeze lifted and died again. I thought I heard it whine in the broken window. I swallowed. "Seredith?"

She didn't answer. I pulled away from the man who'd been holding me. He let me go without a struggle.

"Seredith. Open the door. Please." I leant sideways to peer through the jagged space where the window had been. She was sitting on the stairs like a child, her legs crossed neatly at the ankles. She didn't look up. "What are you doing? Seredith?"

She murmured something.

"What? Please, let me in —"

"That's it. The bitch wants to burn." There was a strident note in his voice, like bravado; but when I looked back at him he gave me a wide rotten-toothed grin. "She's made her choice. Now get out of the way."

He lurched forwards and sloshed oil on the wall by my feet. The smell rose like a fog, thick and real.

"Don't — you can't — please!" He went on grinning at me, unblinking. I turned and hammered at the last shards of glass in the window, smashing them away with the side of my fist; but the window was too narrow to get through. "Seredith, come out! They're going to set the house on fire, *please*."

She didn't move. I would have thought she couldn't hear me, except that her shoulders rose a little when I said *please*.

"You can't set fire to the house while she's in it. That's murder." My voice was high and hoarse.

"Get out of the way." But he didn't wait for me to move. Oil splashed on to my trousers as he went past. He poured the last dregs against the side wall and stood back. The man with the torch was watching, his expression open and interested, like a schoolboy's.

Maybe it wouldn't be enough. Maybe the snow on the roof would quench it, or the walls would be too thick and too damp. But Seredith was old, and the smoke would be enough to kill her, if she was inside.

"Hey, Baldwin. Get the other bucket. Round the side." He pointed.

"Please. Please don't do this." But I knew it was no good. I spun round and threw myself against the door. I pounded on the wood with my fists. "Seredith! Open the door. Damn you, *open the door*."

Someone caught my collar and pulled me back. I choked and nearly fell.

"Good. Keep him back. Now."

The man with the torch grunted and stepped forwards. I scrabbled desperately to break free. The seam of my shirt ripped and I almost fell into the space between the torch-flames and the door. The smell of oil was so strong I could taste it. It was on me, on my trousers and hands; the smallest leap of a spark and I'd be on fire. The burning torch hovered in front of my eyes, a spitting mass of talons and tongues.

Something thudded into my back. I'd walked backwards into the door. I leant against it. Nowhere to go now.

The man raised the torch like a staff and tilted it until it was right in front of my face. Then he lowered it. I watched it flicker, almost touching the base of the wall, almost close enough to catch.

"No."

My own voice; but not my own. My blood rose and sang in my ears like a flood, so loud I couldn't hear myself think.

"Do this and you will be cursed," I said, and in the sudden quiet it was as though another voice spoke underneath mine. "Kill with fire and you will perish in fire. Burn in hatred and *you* will burn."

No one answered. No one moved.

"If you do this, your souls will be stained with blood and ash. Everything you touch will go grey and wither. Everyone you touch will fall ill or run mad or die."

A sound: faint, faraway, like something drawing closer. But the voice coming from inside me wouldn't let me pause to listen. "You will end hated and alone," it said. "There will be no forgiveness, ever."

Quietness spread out around me like a ripple in a pond, deadening the hiss of the wind and the scratch of the flames. But inside that quiet there was something new, ticking, like drying wood or leaves falling.

The men stared at me. I looked round, meeting their eyes, letting the other voice look through me. My hand rose to point at the man who had threatened me, steady as a prophet's. "Go."

He hesitated. The ticking broadened into a crackle, then a hiss, then a roar.

Rain.

It fell in ropes, as sudden as an ambush, blinding me, driving through hair and clothes in seconds. Icy water ran down the back of my neck and sprayed off my nose when I gasped with the shock of it. The man swung his torch sideways to catch the shelter of the overhanging roof, but the wind blew a curtain of rain over it, and then there was no light at all. There was shouting, a few stifled, panicked cries, and the sounds of a man stumbling in the dark. "He called down the rain — fuck this, let's go — the magic —"

I blinked, but there were only blurred shadows, running and disappearing like wraiths. Someone called, someone answered, someone grunted and swore as he tripped and struggled to his feet; and then the noise retreated, I heard a far-off mutter of voices and horses, and they were gone.

I shut my eyes. I was soaked to the skin. The marsh hissed and rumbled under the rain, answering, echoing. The thatch whispered its own note as the wind hummed through the broken window. There was the smell of mud and reeds and melted snow.

I was cold. A spasm of shivering took hold of me and I leant forward, bracing myself as if it came from outside. When it was over I blinked the water off my eyelashes and blew the strings of rain away from my mouth. The dark had lessened, and now I could make out trembling, silvery edges to things: the barn, the road, the horizon.

I turned round and stared through the window. Even now it made my neck tingle, to turn my back on the vast emptiness where the road was. But I'd heard them go. I called softly, "Seredith? They've gone. Let me in."

I wasn't sure if I could really see her, or whether my brain was inventing the ghostly blur in the darkness. I wiped the water out of my eyes and tried to make her out. She was there, sitting on the stairs. I leant as close to the edge of the broken glass as I could. "Seredith. It's all right. Open the door."

She didn't move. I don't know how long I stood there. I murmured to her as if I was trying to tame an animal: the same words, over and over again. I started to forget what was my voice and what was the rain. I was so cold I went into a sort of dream, where I was the marsh and the house as well as myself, where I was slippery wet wood and claggy mud . . . When at last the bolt was shot back, I was so stiff and shrammed that I didn't react straight away.

Seredith said, "Come in, then."

I limped inside and stood dripping on the floor. Seredith rummaged in the sideboard; I heard the scratching of match after match as she tried to light the lamp. At last I crossed to her and gently took the box. We both jumped at my touch. I didn't look at her until the lamp was burning and I'd put the glass chimney over the flame.

She was trembling, and her hair was sticking out in a clump; but when she met my eyes, she gave me a wry almost-smile that told me she knew who I was. She reached for the lamp.

"Seredith . . ."

"I know. I shall go to bed, or I'll catch my death."

That wasn't what I'd been going to say. I nodded.

"You'd better go too." She added, too quickly, "You're sure they've gone?"

"Yes."

"Good."

Silence. She stared at the lamp, and in the soft light her face could have been young. At last she said, "Thank you, Emmett."

I didn't answer.

"Without you, they would have burnt the house down before the rain came."

"Why didn't you —"

"I was so afraid when I heard them knocking." She stopped. She took a pace towards the staircase, and turned back. "When they came, I dreamt . . . I thought they were the Crusade. There hasn't been a Crusade here for sixty years, but . . . I remember them coming for us. I must have been your age. And my master . . ."

"The Crusade?"

"Never mind. Those days are over. Now it's only a few peasants, here and there, that hate us enough to murder us . . ." She laughed a little. I'd never heard her say *peasants* like that, with contempt.

Something inside me tipped. I said, slowly, "But they didn't want to murder us. Not really. They wanted to burn the house." A pause. The flame bobbed, so I couldn't tell if her expression had changed. "Why did you lock yourself in, Seredith?"

She reached for the banister and began to climb the stairs.

"*Seredith.*" My arms ached with the effort to stop myself reaching for her. "You could have died. *I* could have died, trying to get you out. Why the hell did you lock yourself in?"

"Because of the books," she said, turning so suddenly I was scared she'd fall. "Why do you think, boy? Because the books have to be kept safe."

"But —"

"And if the books burn, I will burn with them. Do you understand?"

I shook my head.

She looked at me for a long time. She seemed about to say something else. But then she shivered so violently she had to steady herself, and when the spasm had passed she seemed exhausted. "Not now," she said. Her voice was hoarse, as if she'd come to the last of her breath. "Good night."

I listened to her footsteps climb to the landing and cross to the room where she slept. The rain swirled through the broken window and rattled on the floor, but I couldn't bring myself to care.

I was aching all over with cold, and my head was spinning with tiredness; but when I shut my eyes I saw flames spitting and clawing at me. The noise of the rain separated into different notes: the percussive hiss of water on the roof, the whisper of the wind, human voices . . . I knew they weren't real, but I could hear distinct words, as if everyone I had ever known had surrounded the house and was calling to me. It was fatigue, only fatigue, but I didn't want to fall asleep. I wanted . . . Most of all I wanted not to be alone; but that was the one thing I couldn't have.

I had to get warm. My mother would have parcelled me up in a blanket and wrapped her arms round me until I stopped shivering; then she would have made me hot tea and brandy, sent me to bed and sat beside me while I drank it. The familiar ache of homesickness threatened to overwhelm me. I went into the workshop and lit the stove. Outside there was a hint of light, a crack between the clouds and the horizon; it was later than I'd realised.

It occurred to me, vaguely, that I had saved Seredith's life.

I brewed tea, and drank it. The flames dancing in my head began to subside. The voices grew fainter as the rain slackened. The stove creaked and clicketed and smelt of warm metal. I sat on the floor, leaning against the plan chest, with my legs spread out in front of me. From this angle, and in this light, the workshop looked like a cave: mysterious, looming, the knobs and screws

of the presses transformed into strange rock forma-
tions. The shadow of the board cutter on the wall
looked like a man's face. I rolled my head round, taking
it all in, and for a second I was filled with a fierce
pleasure to have saved it all: my workshop, my things,
my place.

The door at the end of the room was ajar.

I blinked. At first I thought it was a trick of the light.
I put down my cold mug of tea and leant forward, and
saw the gap between the door and the jamb. It was the
door on the left of the stove: not the room where
Seredith took people, but the other door, the one that
led down into the dark.

I almost kicked it shut. I could have done that, left it
unlocked but closed, and gone to bed. I almost did. I
reached out gently with my foot, but instead of pushing
it shut I edged it open.

Blackness. An empty shelf just inside, and beyond
that a flight of stairs going down. Nothing more than
I'd seen before. Nothing like the bare light-filled room
behind the other door, except for the cold that breathed
from it.

I stood up and reached for the lamp. I wasn't sleepy
any more. Tension pricked in my fingertips and itched
between my shoulder blades. I pushed the door wide
open and went down into the dark.

It smelt of damp. That was the first thing I noticed: a
thick, muddy scent like rotting reeds. I paused on the
stair, my heart speeding up. Damp was almost as bad as
fire; it brought mould and wrinkled paper and softened
glue. And it smelt of age and dead things, smelt

wrong . . . But as I turned the corner of the staircase and lifted the lamp, what I saw was nothing out of the ordinary: a little room with a table and cupboards, a broom and a bucket, chests that were marked with a stationer's label. I almost laughed. Just a storeroom. At the far end — although it wasn't far, only a few steps across — there was a round bronze plate in the wall, like a solid wheel, intricate and decorative. The other walls were piled high with chests and boxes. The air felt as dry as it had upstairs; perhaps I'd imagined the smell.

I turned my head, half thinking I'd heard something. But everything was perfectly still, insulated from the noise of the rain by the dense earth beyond.

I put down the lamp and looked about me. There was a drawer balanced on a pile of boxes, full of broken tools waiting to be repaired or thrown away, and a row of glass bottles filled with dark liquid that looked like dyes or ox gall for marbling paper. I nearly tripped over three fire-buckets of sand. On the table there was a humped parcel wrapped in sackcloth, and some tools. I didn't recognise them; they were thin, delicate things with edges like fish's teeth. I brought the lamp closer. Next to the bundle there was another cloth, spread out to cover something. This was where Seredith worked, when I was upstairs in the workshop.

I reached out and unwrapped the bundle, as gently as if it was alive. It was a book-block, neatly sewn, with thick dark endpapers threaded with white, like tiny roots reaching through soil. The blood sang in my fingertips. A book. The first book I had seen, since I'd been here; the first since I was a child, and learned that they were forbidden. But holding it now I felt nothing but a kind of peace.

I brought it to my face and inhaled the smell of paper. I almost opened it to look at the title page; but I was too curious about what was under the other bit of sacking. I put the block down and drew back the cloth. Here was the cover Seredith had been making. For a moment, before I understood what I was seeing, it was beautiful.

The background was black velvet, so fine it absorbed every glint of light and lay on the bench like a piece of solid darkness. The inlay stood out against it like ivory, shining softly, pale gold in the lamplight.

Bones. A skeleton, the spine curled like a row of pearls round pale twigs of legs and arms, and the tiny splinters of toes and fingers. The skull bulged like a mushroom. They were smaller than my outstretched hand, those bones. They were as small and fragile as a bird's.

But it wasn't . . . it hadn't been a bird. It was a baby.

CHAPTER
FIVE

"Don't touch it."

I hadn't heard Seredith come into the room, but some distant, watchful part of me wasn't surprised to hear her voice. I didn't know how long I had been standing there. It was only when I stepped back — carefully, as though there was something here I was afraid to wake — that I felt the stiff chill in my joints, the pins-and-needles in my feet, and knew it had been a long time. In spite of my care I knocked my ankle against a box, but the hollow sound was muffled by the earth beyond the walls.

I said, "I wasn't going to touch it."

"Emmett . . ."

I didn't answer. The wick of the lamp needed trimming, and the shadows jumped and ducked. The bones gleamed against their bed of black. As the light danced back and forth I could have made myself believe that they were moving; but when at last the flame steadied they lay quiet.

"It's only a binding," she said. She shifted in the doorway, but I didn't look at her. "It's mother-of-pearl."

"Not real bones." It came out like mockery. I hadn't meant it to, but I was glad, fiercely glad, at the way it cut through the silence.

"No," she said softly, "not real bones."

I stared at the shining intricate shapes on the velvet until my eyes blurred. At last I reached out and pulled the cloth down over them; then I stood looking down at the coarse brown hessian. Here and there, where the weave was loose, I could still see the smooth edge of a femur, the nacreous curve of the skull, a miniature, perfect finger-bone. I imagined her working on them, crafting tiny shapes out of mother-of-pearl. I shut my eyes and listened to my blood pounding, and beyond that the dead quiet of walls and earth.

"Tell me," I said. "Tell me what you do."

The lamp murmured and guttered. Nothing else moved.

"You know already."

"No."

"You know, if you think about it."

I opened my mouth to say *no*, again; but something caught in my throat. The lamp-flame flared, licked upwards and then sank to a tiny blue bubble. The dark took a step towards me.

"You bind — people," I said. My throat was so dry it hurt to speak; but the silence hurt more. "You make people into books."

"Yes. But not in the way you mean."

"What other way is there?"

She walked towards me. I didn't turn, but the light from her candle grew stronger, pushing back the shadows. "Sit down, Emmett."

82

She touched my shoulder. I flinched and spun round, stumbling back into the table. Tools clattered to the floor and skittered away. We stared at each other. She had stepped back too; now she put her candle down on one of the chests, and the flame magnified the trembling of her hand. Wax had spattered the floor; it congealed in a split second, like water turning to milk.

"Sit down." She lifted an open drawer of jars off a box. "Here."

I didn't want to sit, while she was standing. I held her gaze, and she was the first to look away. She dumped the drawer down again. Then, wearily, she bent to pick up the little tools I'd knocked off the table.

"You trap them," I said. "You take people and put them inside books. They leave here . . . empty."

"I suppose, in a way —"

"You steal their souls." My voice cracked. "No wonder they're afraid of you. You lure them here and suck them dry, you take what you want and send them away with nothing. That's what a book is, isn't it? A life. A person. And if they burn, they die."

"No." She straightened up, one hand clutching a tiny wood-handled knife.

I picked up the book on the table and held it out. "Look," I said, my voice rising and rising, "this is a person. Inside there's a *person* — out there somewhere they're walking round *dead* — it's evil, what you do, they should have fucking burnt you."

She slapped me.

Silence. There was a thin high ringing in the air that wasn't real. Automatic tears rose in my eyes and spilt down my cheeks. I wiped them away with the inside of my wrist. The pain faded to a hot tingling, like salt water drying on my skin. I put the book down and smoothed the endpaper with my palm where I'd rumpled it. The crease would never come out entirely; it stood out like a scar, branching across the corner. I said, "I'm sorry."

Seredith turned away and dropped the knife into the open drawer by my side. "Memories," she said, at last. "Not people, Emmett. We take memories and bind them. Whatever people can't bear to remember. Whatever they can't live with. We take those memories and put them where they can't do any more harm. That's all books are."

Finally I met her eyes. Her expression was open, candid, a little weary, like her voice. She made it sound so right — so necessary; like a doctor describing an amputation. "Not souls, Emmett," she said. "Not people. Just memories."

"It's wrong," I said, trying to match my tone to hers. Steady, reasonable ... but my voice shook and betrayed me. "You can't say it's right to do that. Who are you to say what they can live with?"

"We don't. We help people who come to us and ask for it." A flicker of sympathy went over her face as if she knew she'd won. "No one has to come, Emmett. They decide. All we do is help them forget."

It wasn't that simple. Somehow I knew it wasn't. But I had no argument to make, no defence against the softness of her voice and her level eyes. "What about that?" I pointed to the child-shape under the sacking. "Why would you make a book like *that*?"

"Milly's book? Do you really want to know?"

A shiver went over me, fierce and sudden. I clenched my teeth and didn't answer.

She walked past me, stared down at the sacking for a moment, and then slid it gently to one side. In her shadow the little skeleton shone bluish.

"She buried it alive," Seredith said. There was no weight to the words, only a quiet precision that left all the feeling to me. "She couldn't go on, she thought she couldn't go on. And so she wrapped it up, one day when it wouldn't stop crying, and she laid it on the dung heap and pulled rubbish and manure over it until she couldn't hear it any more."

"Her baby?"

A nod.

I wanted to shut my eyes, but I couldn't look away. The baby would have lain like that, curled and helpless, trying to cry, trying to breathe. How long would it have taken, before it was just part of the dungheap, rotting with everything else? It was like a horrible fairy tale: bones turned to pearl, earth turned to velvet. But it was true. It was true, and the story was locked in a book, shut away, written on dead pages. My hand tingled where I had smoothed out the endpaper: that thick, veined paper, black as soil.

"That's murder," I said. "Why didn't the parish constable arrest her?"

"She kept the child a secret. No one knew about it."

"But . . ." I stopped. "How could you help her? A woman — a girl who killed her own child — like *that* — you should have . . ."

"What should I have done?"

"Let her suffer! Make her live with it! Remembering is part of the punishment. If you do something evil —"

"It was her father's, too. The man who came to burn this book. He was her father, and the child's."

For a moment I didn't understand what she meant. Then I looked away, feeling sick.

There was the rustle of sackcloth as Seredith drew it back over the bones, and the creak of the box as she perched on the edge of it, holding on to the table to steady herself.

At last she said, "I'm not being fair to you, Emmett. Sometimes I *do* turn people away. Very, very rarely. And not because they've done something so terrible I can't help; only because I know they'll go on doing terrible things. Then, if I'm sure, I will refuse to help them. But it has only happened three times, in more than sixty years. The others, I helped."

"Isn't burying a baby terrible?"

"Of course," she said, and bowed her head. "Of course it is, Emmett."

A breath. "You said, *what books are* . . . So every book," I said, "every book that's ever been bound, is someone's memories. Something they've chosen to forget."

"Yes."

"And . . ." I cleared my throat. Suddenly I could feel the imprint of my father's hand on my cheek, the stinging blow he'd given me years ago, as if the pain had never really faded. *Never let me see you with a book again.* This was what he had wanted to protect me from. And now I was an apprentice; I was going to be a binder.

"You think," I said slowly, "you think I'm going to do what you do."

She didn't even glance at me. "It will be easier," she said, from a long way away, "if you don't despise it. Despise books — despise the people who need help — and you despise yourself. Your work."

"I can't," I said. "I won't. It's not . . ."

She laughed. It was so close to her usual amused snort that my stomach twisted. "Yes, you can. Binders are born, not made. And you're a binder born, boy. You may not like the idea of it much now. But you'll grow to understand. And it won't let you rest. It's a great force, inside you. It's what made you ill, when . . . You're stronger in it than most binders I've known. You'll see."

"How do you know? You might be wrong —"

"I know, Emmett."

"How?"

"The binder's fever gave you away. You will be a good binder. In every sense."

I shook my head. I went on shaking it, even though I didn't know why.

"Sometimes," she said, "what we do is very difficult. Sometimes it makes me angry or sad. Sometimes I regret — if I'd known what the memories were, I wouldn't have —" She stopped and glanced away. "Much of the time it doesn't even touch me. But sometimes I am so glad to see the pain go away that if that were the only person I had ever helped it would still be worth it."

"I'm not doing it. It's wrong. It's — unnatural."

She lowered her head, inhaling so deeply I saw her shoulders move. The skin under her eyes looked as fragile as the bloom on a moth's wing: one touch and it would brush away and leave bare bone. She said, without looking at me, "It's a sacred calling, Emmett. To have another person's memory entrusted to you . . . To take the deepest, darkest part away from them and keep it safe, forever. To honour it, to make it beautiful, even though no one will ever see it. To guard it with your own life . . ."

"I don't want to be a glorified gaoler."

She jolted upright. For a long moment I thought she would hit me again. "This is why I didn't tell you before," she said, finally. "Because you're not ready yet, you're still struggling . . . But now you know. And you're lucky to be here. If you had gone to a bindery in Castleford you'd have had your scruples beaten out of you long ago."

I held out my finger and slid it through the candle flame, once, twice, slowing down until I could hardly bear it. There were too many questions; I concentrated on the pain and let my mouth decide. "So why *am* I here?"

She blinked. "Because I was the nearest. And —" She stopped.

Her eyes slid away from mine. She kneaded her forehead, and for the first time I noticed how flushed her cheeks were. "I'm exhausted, Emmett. I think that's enough for today. Don't you?"

She was right. I was so tired that I could feel the world spinning. I nodded, and she stood up. I reached out to help her but she ignored me. She picked her way through the narrow space back to the door.

"Seredith?"

She paused, but didn't turn. Her sleeve had fallen back as she leant against the wall, and her wrist was like a child's.

"Yes?"

"Where are the books? If you keep them safe . . ."

She held her arm out to point at the circular plaque on the wall. "On the other side of that," she said, "there's a vault."

"Can I see?"

"Yes." She turned, reaching for a key that hung round her neck; then her hand tightened on it. "No. Not now. Another time."

I'd only asked out of curiosity. But there was something in her face — or something *not* in her face, something that should have been there . . . I pushed my tongue into the sharp space between two of my teeth and stared at her. Strands of her hair clung to her forehead, sticky with sweat. She reeled. I stepped towards her, but she stumbled back as if she couldn't bear me to get too close. "Good night, Emmett."

I watched her turn, bracing herself in the doorway as though she was fighting to stay on her feet. I should have let her go, but I couldn't stop myself. "Seredith

. . . What happens if the books burn? Do the people die?"

She didn't look at me. She shuffled to the stairs and began to climb them. "No," she said. "They remember."

I was so tired I couldn't think. Seredith had gone to bed; I should go too. If only I'd gone to bed an hour ago, instead of sitting down next to the stove in the workshop . . . Sleep. I wanted to step right off the edge of consciousness. I wanted that darkness more than anything. I wanted not to be here.

I sat down. Or rather, I found that I was already sitting, cramped on the floor with my legs folded, my back against a box. I didn't have the energy to find a better position. Instead I wrapped my arms round my knees, put my head down, and slept.

When I woke, the first thing I felt was a kind of peace. It was almost pitch-black — the candle had gone out — and I felt as though I were drifting, disintegrating painlessly in the subtle currents of the dark. Then some of what had happened came back — but small, too far away to hurt me, like reflections in a silver cup. I got up and groped my way up the stairs, yawning. I'd thought it was the middle of the night, and the greyish light streaming through the workshop windows made me blink and rub my eyes. It was still raining, although now it was a thin quiet mizzle, and the snow only clung to the ground in a few places, grimy and pockmarked. Seredith had been right about the thaw; the post would get to us at least once more before winter really set in.

The stove had gone out. I hesitated, wanting to leave it and go upstairs to bed; but it was morning, and there was work to do . . . Work. I didn't want to think about work. I crouched down and remade the fire. By the time it was going properly I was a little warmer, but the deep, cold quiet of the house needed more than the stove to thaw it. I hadn't boarded up the broken window; but it wasn't that, it was something else. I shook my head, wondering if my ears were playing tricks on me. It was like the way the snow had muffled every sound — or a feeling of distance, as if everything I heard was an echo . . .

Tea. The caddy was almost empty. I put water on to boil and went to get a new packet from the pantry. As I crossed the hall I turned my face away from the moist draught that blew in through the jagged-edged window. As soon as I'd had something hot to drink I'd find a bit of millboard —

Seredith was curled on the stairs, her head resting against the banister.

"Seredith? Seredith!"

It was only when she moved that I knew I'd been afraid. I pulled her gently to her feet, appalled at how light she was, and the heat that was seeping from her skin. She was clammy, and her face was flushed. She muttered something, and I bent close to hear her. "I'm all right," she said. Her breath was foul, as if something was rotting inside her. "I was just . . . sitting down."

"Yes," I said. "Let's get you to bed."

"I'm perfectly all right. I don't need . . ."

"I know," I said. "Come on." I half pushed and half lifted her upwards, step after step, and then along the passage to her room. She clambered into bed and pulled the blankets over herself as if she was freezing. I hurried downstairs to get her a jug of water, and herb tea to bring the fever down, and more blankets; but when I came back into the bedroom she was already asleep. She'd undressed, and her clothes were crumpled in a pile on the floor.

I stood very still, listening to the silence. I could hear Seredith's breathing — faster, louder than it should have been — and the faint crackle of rain against the window; but behind that, and my own blood in my ears, there was nothing but the solid emptiness of the house and the marshes beyond. I was more alone here than I'd ever been.

I sat down. In this light, sleeping, Seredith looked even older; the flesh on her cheeks and below her jaw sagged, so that the skin was stretched thin over the bones of her nose and eyes. A scab of spittle clung to the corner of her mouth. She murmured something and turned over, and her hands twitched and clutched the quilt. Her skin was a chalky, yellowish colour against the faded indigo-and-white of the patchwork, while here and there the shadow of a raindrop crawled across the cotton.

I looked around. I had never been in here in daylight. There was a little fireplace and a padded window seat, and a mossy-looking armchair, but it was almost as bare as my room. There were no pictures, or ornaments above the hearth. The only decoration on the walls was the light from the window, the faint lattice, the sliding silver of the rain-shadows. Even my parents had more than this. And yet Seredith wasn't poor; I knew that, from the lists of supplies we sent to Castleford every week, and the sacks that Toller brought back for us. I had never thought about where her money came from. If she died —

I looked down at her face on the pillow, and a kind of panic seized me. It was an effort to stop myself from waking her up and pouring the tea forcibly down her throat; it was best to let her sleep. I could light a fire, bring damp cloths, have some honey dissolved in water for when she woke of her own accord . . . But I sat still, unable to leave her. It had been the other way round, so many times — that she'd watched at my bedside while I slept, as patient as stone — but she'd never made me feel as though I should be grateful. For the first time I wondered whether her brusqueness had been deliberate. My throat ached.

An hour later, through the rain, I caught the distant creak and rumble of a cart, and at last the off-key jangle of the bell. The post. I lifted my head, and a perverse part of me wanted him to go away again, to leave me in this strange, bereft peace; but I got to my feet and went down to open the door.

"Seredith's sick. I don't know who to . . . Can you send someone?"

He squinted at me above the collar of his coat. "Send someone? Who?"

"A doctor. Or her family." I shook my head. "I don't know. She writes letters, doesn't she? Tell the people she writes to."

"I —" He stopped, and shrugged. "All right," he said. "But don't count on them coming."

He drove off. I watched until the cart was a tiny blot in the mottled expanse of brown grass and half-melted snow.

CHAPTER
SIX

The house was so quiet it was as if the walls were holding their breath. Every few hours, during that day and the days that followed, I had to go outside and listen to the dry wind in the reeds, just to be sure that I hadn't gone deaf. I went and got a spare pane of glass from the storeroom to fix the broken window, but as I was fitting it I found myself putting down my tools with unnecessary vehemence, tapping on the glass harder than I needed to. I was lucky not to break it. And when I sat at Seredith's bedside I coughed and fidgeted and picked at the paring callus on my forefinger. But no sound I could make was enough to break the silence.

At first I was afraid. But nothing changed: Seredith didn't get better, she didn't get worse. She slept for hours, at first, but one morning when I tapped on her door she was awake. I'd brought her an apple and a cup of honeyed tea, and she thanked me and bent over the cup to breathe in the steam. She'd slept with the curtains open — or rather, I hadn't closed them for her the night before — and the sky was full of grey-bellied clouds being torn apart by the wind. Here and there the sun flashed through. I heard her sigh. "Go away, Emmett."

I turned. Her face was damp, but the bright flush had left her cheeks and she looked better. "I mean it. Go and do something useful."

I hesitated. Now that she was awake, part of me wanted to ask her questions — all the questions that had been brewing since the first time I walked through the bindery door; now that she had no reason not to tell me . . . But something inside me baulked at the idea of so many answers. I didn't want to know; knowing would make it all real. All I said was, "Are you sure?"

She lay back down without answering. After a long time she dredged up another heavy breath and said, "Don't you have better things to do? I can't bear being *watched*."

It might have stung, but somehow it didn't. I nodded, although her eyes were closed, and went out into the passage with a sense of relief.

I was determined not to think, so I set myself to work. When I collapsed on the lowest stair in the hall and looked at the clock, I saw that I'd been at it for hours: cleaning and filling the lamps, scrubbing the floor and wiping out the kitchen cupboards with vinegar, sweeping the hall and sprinkling the floor with lavender water, polishing the banister with beeswax . . . They were jobs that my mother would have done, at home, or Alta; I'd have rolled my eyes and trod unconcerned footprints across their clean floors. Now my shirt clung to my back and I smelt rank and peppery with sweat, but I looked round and was glad to see the difference I'd made. I'd thought that I was doing it for Seredith, but suddenly I knew I'd been

96

doing it for myself. With Seredith ill, this was no one's house but mine.

I got to my feet. I hadn't had anything to eat since the morning, but I wasn't hungry. I stood for a long time with one foot on the stair above, as if there was a decision to be made: but something made me turn again and go into the passage that led to the workshop. The door was closed and when I opened it there was a blaze of daylight.

I stoked the stove extravagantly because I'd chopped the wood myself, and no one could see me wasting it. Then I tidied methodically from one side of the room to the other, straightening shelves, sharpening tools, oiling the nipping press and sweeping up. I tidied cupboards and discovered old supplies of leather and cloth I hadn't known we had, and a stash of marbled paper at the bottom of the plan chest. I found a bone folder carved with faint scrimshaw flowers, a book of silver leaf, a burnisher with a thick, umber-streaked agate . . . Seredith was tidy, but it was as if she'd never thrown anything away. In one cupboard I found a wooden box full of trinkets, wrapped in old silk as if they were important: a child's bonnet, a lock of hair, a daguerreotype mounted in a watch case, a heavy silver ring that I tilted back and forth in my palm for a long time, watching the colours slide from blue to purple and green. I put that box back carefully, pushing it behind a pile of weights, and once it was out of sight I forgot it almost at once. There was a box of type that needed sorting, and jars of dye so old they needed to be poured away, and little dry nubs of sponge that needed washing. It all gave me pleasure — an unfamiliar sensuous pleasure, where everything — the neatness of a blade, the wind in the chimney, the yeasty smell of stale paste, the logs collapsing into ash in the stove — was distinct and magnified.

But this time, when I'd finished, what I felt wasn't satisfaction but fear, as if I had been preparing for an ordeal.

When I'd taken Seredith's dirty clothes away, her keys had been in the pocket of her trousers. Now they were in mine. Not the key that she wore round her neck, but the keys to the other doors, the front and back of the house, and the triple-locked doors at the end of the workshop . . . Their weight in my pocket felt like part of my body. The sense of possession I'd had blurred into something else.

I looked out at the expanse of marsh. The wind had died and now the clouds were massed in a thick grey bank, while the glints of water lay still as a mirror. Nothing stirred; it could have been a picture painted on the window-pane. Dead weather. What would they be doing at home? It was slaughtering time, unless Pa had started early; and there were repairs to be made, tools and tack and a back wall of the barn that needed seeing to . . . If we were going to run a hawthorn fence across the top of the high field, as I'd suggested last year, we would need to plant it soon. My nerves tingled at the memory of sharp thorns jabbing into cold fingers. For an instant I thought I could smell turpentine and camphor, the balm Ma made to ward off chilblains; but when I lifted my hand to my nose my palm smelt of dust and beeswax. I'd sloughed that life off like a skin.

I raised my head and listened. There was no sound from anywhere. The whole house was waiting. I took the bundle of keys out of my pocket, and walked round the lay press and along the worn floorboards to the far door. My heart thudded but the three keys went into the three locks and turned cleanly, one by one.

Seredith had kept the hinges well oiled. The door swung back as easily as if someone had opened it from the other side. I don't know why I had expected it to be stiff. My pulse sped into a sudden crescendo that sent black specks whirling across my eyes; but after a few seconds my vision cleared and I could see a pale, bare room, with high uncurtained windows like the workshop. A table of scrubbed wood, with two chairs facing each other across it. The floor and walls were bare. I put the keys down on the table and the sound of it startled me.

I had no right to be here. But I had to be. I stood still, resisting the crawling sensation at the base of my spine.

Against the mottled grey of the windows the binder's chair stood out in silhouette. It was straight-backed and simple — less comfortable than the one nearest to the door — but somehow I knew it was Seredith's chair. I drew the other one out from the table, hearing the legs bump as I dragged it over the uneven floor, and sat down. How many people had waited here to have their memories taken away? Enough to wear a path into the floorboards, coming and going . . .

How did it feel? I could imagine the sick fear in the pit of your stomach, the terror that flickered when you tried to see past the point of no return, to the person you would be . . . But the moment itself? To have something wrenched out of the deepest part of you — how did *that* feel? And afterwards, when you had a hole inside you . . . I saw again the blankness in Milly's eyes as she left, and clenched my jaw. Which was worse? To feel nothing, or to grieve for something you no longer remembered? Surely when you forgot, you'd forget to be sad, or what was the point? And yet that numbness would take part of your *self* away, it would be like having pins-and-needles in your soul . . .

I took a deep breath. It was too easy to imagine sitting here, in this seat; I ought to put myself in Seredith's chair. What would it be like to be her? To look into someone's eyes and then do — *that* — to them? The thought of it made me feel sick, too. Whichever way you looked at it . . . Seredith had called it *helping*. But how could that be right?

I stood up, caught my ankle on the side of the table, and steadied myself on the back of the chair. The carving cut into my palm, not hard enough to hurt but enough to take me by surprise. I looked down at the shape of it, the gleam of bluish light on the wooden scroll.

So many times it had been the light catching on something that brought on the illness. The latticed sun falling on the hall floor, the slant of daylight seen through a half-open door . . . I knew how it began, the bright shape — not quite a memory — that fitted like a key into a hole in my mind, and the sickness that spilt out. And now I felt the same shock of recognition and fear. I cringed instinctively, waiting for the blackness to swallow me. It would be the end, the abyss. Now that I was here, in the place I was most afraid of . . . the source, the heart.

My knees gave way. I dropped into the chair, bracing myself as if for a crash. But my mind stayed steady. A beam creaked, a mouse scratched in the thatch above the window. The darkness rolled and sucked like a tide, at arm's length; and then, instead of drowning me, it receded.

I held my breath. Nothing happened. The darkness drew back and back, until I felt exposed, drenched in grey daylight until my eyes watered.

Time passed. I looked down at my hands on the scrubbed table. When I'd left home, they'd been dead white and spidery. Now there was a callous on my left forefinger from paring leather with a knife that was too blunt, and my left thumbnail was long so that I could position a finishing tool without burning myself. But it was the shape of them — thin but not bony, strong but not bulky — that made me see them for the first time. They weren't a farmer's hands — not like Pa's — but they weren't an invalid's hands, either. I would have known that they were a bookbinder's hands; and not just because they were mine.

I turned them over and looked at the lines on my palms that were supposed to tell me who I was. Someone — was it Alta? — had once told me that your left hand showed the fate you were born with, and your right showed the fate you made for yourself. My right hand had a deep, long line down the centre, cutting my whole palm in half. I imagined another Emmett, the Emmett who might have taken over the farm, the way my parents always planned: an Emmett who hadn't got ill, and hadn't ended up here, alone. I saw him look back at me with a grin, pushing his chilblained hands into his pockets, and then turn towards home, whistling.

I bowed my head and waited for the sudden sadness to pass; but it didn't. Something gave way inside me, and I started to cry.

At first it was as involuntary as being sick: great paroxysms like retching, each spasm driven by an unpitying reflex that made me gasp and sob for air. But slowly the urgency eased, and I had the time to catch a lungful of air between sobs; and then at last I wiped the wetness and snot off my face, and opened my eyes. The sense of loss was still sharp enough to make the tears rise again, but I blinked them away and this time I managed to master my breath.

When I raised my head the world was empty, clear, like a cut field. I could see for miles, I could see where I was. There'd been shadows at the corners of my vision for so long I'd grown used to them, but now they had gone. This quiet room wasn't terrible, it was only a room; the chairs where two people could sit opposite each other were only chairs.

I paused for a moment, testing the place where the fear had been, as though I was checking a rotten tooth with my tongue. Nothing — or no, maybe a sharp faint echo of pain: not the dull ache of decay but something cleaner, like a gap that was already healing. There was a scent in the air like earth after rainfall, as if everything had been freshly remade.

I picked up the keys and left without locking the door behind me.

I was ravenous. I found myself in the pantry, gorging on pickles out of a jar — and then, sated, I was so exhausted I couldn't see straight. I'd meant to take a bowl of soup up to Seredith, but I fell asleep at the kitchen table with my head on my arms. When I woke up the range had gone out and it was nearly dark. I lit it again — covering myself and the clean floor with ash — and then hurriedly warmed the soup and carried it up to Seredith's room. The bowl was only slightly hotter than tepid, but no doubt she'd be asleep anyway. I pushed the door open with my foot and peered round.

She was awake, and sitting up. The lamp was lit, and a glass bowl of water was perched in front of it to focus the light on a shirt she was patching. She looked up at me and smiled. "You look better, Emmett."

"Me?"

"Yes." She peered at me and her face changed. Her fingers grew still, and after a moment she put the shirt down. "Sit."

I put the tray on the table next to her bed and drew the chair up beside her. She reached out and pushed my jaw with one finger, tilting my face towards the lamplight. It wasn't the first time she'd touched me — she'd often corrected my grip, or leant close to me to

103

show me how something should be done — but this time I felt it tingling on my skin.

She said, "You've made your peace with it."

I looked up, into her eyes. She nodded to herself. Then, with a long sigh, she sat back against her pillows. "Good lad," she said. "I knew you would, sooner or later. How does it feel?"

I didn't answer. It was too fragile; if I talked about it, even to her, it might break.

She smiled at the ceiling, and then slid her eyes sideways to include me. "I'm glad. You suffered worse than most, with the fever. No more of that for you. Oh" — she shrugged, as if I'd spoken — "yes, other things, it won't ever be easy, there'll always be a part of you missing, but no more nightmares, no more terrors." She stopped. Her breath was shallow. Her pulse fluttered in the skin above her temple.

"I don't know anything," I said. It took an effort to say it. "How can I be a binder when I don't even know how it works —"

"Not now. Not now, or it'll turn into a deathbed binding." She laughed, with a noise like a gulp. "But when I'm well again I'll teach you, lad. The binding itself will come naturally, but you'll need to learn the rest . . ." Her voice tailed off into a cough. I poured a glass of water and offered it to her, but she waved it away without looking. "Once the snows have gone we'll visit a friend in Littlewater. She was my . . ." She hesitated, although it might only have been to catch her breath. "My master's last apprentice, after I left him . . . She lives in the village with her family, now. She's a good binder. A midwife, too," she added. "Binding and doctoring always used to go together. Easing the pain, easing people into life and out of it."

I swallowed; but I'd seen animals being born and dying too many times to be a coward about it now.

"You'll be good at it, boy. Just remember why we do it, and you'll be all right." She gave me a glinting sideways look. "Binding — our kind of binding — has to be done, sometimes. No matter what people say."

"Seredith, the night the men came to burn the bindery . . ." The words came with an effort. "They were afraid of you. Of us."

She didn't answer.

"Seredith, they thought — the storm . . . that I'd summoned it. They called you a witch, and —"

She laughed again. It set her off coughing until she had to grasp the side of the bed. "If we could do everything they say we can do," she said, "I'd be sleeping in silk and cloth-of-gold."

"But — it almost felt like —"

"Don't be absurd." She inhaled, hoarsely. "We've been called witches since the beginning of time. Word-cunning, they used to call it — of a piece with invoking demons . . . We were burned for it, too. The Crusade wasn't new, we've always been scapegoats. Well, knowledge is always a kind of magic, I suppose. But — no. You're a binder, nothing more nor less. You're certainly not responsible for the weather." The last few words were thin and breathless. "No more, now."

I nodded, biting back another question. When she was well I could ask whatever I wanted. She smiled at me and closed her eyes, and I thought she'd fallen asleep. But when I started to rise she gestured at me, pointing at the chair. I settled myself again, and after a while I felt my body loosen, as if the silence was undoing knots I hadn't known were there. The fire had nearly gone out; ash had grown over the embers like moss. I ought to tend to it, but I couldn't bring myself to get up. I moved my fingers through the focused ellipse of lamplight, letting it sit above my knuckle like a ring. When I sat back it shone on the patchwork quilt, picking out the curl of a printed fern. I imagined Seredith sewing the quilt, building it block by block through a long winter. I could see her, sitting near the fire, frowning as she bit off the end of a thread; but in my mind she dissolved into someone else, Ma or Alta or all of them, a woman who was young and old all at once . . .

The bell jangled. I struggled to my feet, my head spinning. I'd been drowsing. For a while, on the edge of wakefulness, I'd heard the noise of wheels and a horse, trundling down the road towards the house; but it was only now that I made sense of it. It was dark outside, and my reflection stared back at me from the window, ghostly and bewildered. The bell jangled again, and from the porch below I heard an irritable voice muttering. There was a glimmer of light from a lantern.

I glanced at Seredith, but she was asleep. The bell rang, for longer this time, a ragged angry peal as if they'd tugged too hard at the rope. Seredith's face twitched and the rhythm of her breathing changed.

I hurried out of the room and down the stairs. The bell clanged its impatient, discordant note and I shouted, "Yes, all right, I'm coming!" It didn't occur to me to be afraid, until I had shot the bolts and swung the door open; then just too late I hesitated, wondering if it was the men with the torches, come back to burn us to the ground. But it wasn't.

The man in front of me had been in the middle of saying something; he broke off and looked me up and down. He was wearing a tall hat and a cloak; in the darkness only his shape was visible, and the sharp flash of his eyes. Behind him there was a trap, with a lantern hanging from the seat-rail. The light caught the steam rising from the horse, and its plumes of breath. Another man stood a few feet away, shifting from foot to foot and making an impatient noise between his teeth.

"What do you want?"

The first man sniffed and wiped his nose on the back of his glove. He took his hat off, handed it to me and stepped forward, forcing me to let him cross the threshold. He pulled his gloves off finger by finger and laid them across the brim of the hat. He had straggling ringlets that hung almost to his shoulders. "A hot drink and a good dinner, to start with. Come in, Ferguson, it's perishing out there."

"Who the hell are you?"

He glanced at me. The other man — Ferguson — strode inside and stamped his feet to warm them, calling over his shoulder to the trap-driver, "Wait there, won't you?" He put his bag down on the floor with a heavy chinking thud.

The man sighed. "You must be the apprentice. I am Mr de Havilland and I have brought Dr Ferguson to see Seredith. How is she?" He walked to the little mirror on the wall and peered into it, stroking his moustache. "Why is it so dark in here? For goodness' sake light a few lamps."

"I'm Emmett."

He waved me away as if my name was incidental. "Is she awake? The sooner the doctor sees her, the sooner he can get back."

"No, I don't think she —"

"In that case we will have to wake her. Bring us up a pot of tea, and some brandy. And whatever you have to eat." He strode past me and up the stairs. "This way, Ferguson."

Ferguson followed him in a waft of cold air and damp wool, reaching back in an afterthought to shove his hat at me. I turned to hang it on the hook next to the other one, deliberately digging a fingernail into the smooth felt. I didn't want to take orders from de Havilland, but now that the door was shut it was so dark I could hardly see. I lit a lamp. They'd left footprints across the hall floor, and thin prisms of compacted mud from the heels of their boots were scattered on the stairs.

I hesitated. Resentment and uncertainty tugged me in different directions. At last I went into the kitchen and made a pot of tea — for Seredith, I told myself — and took it upstairs. But when I knocked, it was de

Havilland's voice that said, "Not now." He had a Castleford accent, but his voice reminded me of someone.

I raised my voice to call through the door panel. "You said —"

"Not now!"

"Emmett?" Seredith said. "Come in." She coughed, and I pushed open the door to see her clutching at the bedcovers as she tried to catch her breath. She raised her head and her eyes were red and moist. She beckoned me in. De Havilland was at the window, with his arms crossed; Ferguson was standing at the hearth, looking from one to the other. The room seemed very small. "This is Emmett," Seredith managed to say. "My apprentice."

I said, "We've met."

"Since you're here," de Havilland said, "maybe you would ask Seredith to be reasonable. We've come all the way from Castleford and now she is refusing to allow the doctor to examine her."

She said, "I didn't ask you to come."

"Your apprentice did."

She shot me a look that made my cheeks burn. "Well, I'm sorry that he wasted your time."

"This is absurd. I'm a busy man, you know that. I have pressing work —"

"I said I didn't ask you to come!" She turned her head to one side, like a child, and de Havilland rolled his eyes at the doctor. "I'm perfectly all right," she said. "I caught a chill the other night, that's all."

"That's a nasty cough you have." It was the first time I'd heard the doctor speak to her, and his voice was so tactful it was positively unctuous. "Perhaps you could tell me a little more about how you're feeling."

She worked her mouth childishly, and I was sure she was going to refuse; but her eyes flicked to de Havilland and at last she said, "Tired. Feverish. My chest hurts. That's all."

"And if I might . . ." He moved to her and picked up her wrist so swiftly she didn't have time to pull away. "Yes, I see. Thank you." He looked at de Havilland with something in his eyes that I couldn't interpret, and said, "I don't think we need intrude any longer."

"Very well." De Havilland walked past the bed, paused as if he was about to speak, and then shrugged. He took a step towards me, the way he'd done before, with an absent-minded determination that meant I had to move out of his way. Ferguson followed him, and I was alone with Seredith.

"I'm sorry. I was worried."

She didn't seem to hear me. She had her eyes closed, and the broken veins in her cheeks stood out like red ink. But she knew I was there, because after a minute she flapped at me, dismissing me without a word.

I went out into the passage. The lamplight spilt up the stairs and through the banisters, edging everything in faint gold. I could hear them talking in the hall. I walked to the top of the stairs and paused, listening. Their voices were very distinct.

". . . stubborn old woman," de Havilland said. "Really, I apologise. From what the postman said, I was under the impression that she had asked —"

110

"Not at all, not at all. In any case, I think I saw enough. She's frail, of course, but not in any real danger unless her condition gets worse suddenly." He crossed the hall and I guessed that he was picking up his hat. "Have you decided what you'll do?"

"I shall stay here and keep an eye on her. Until she gets better, or —"

"A pity she's all the way out here. Otherwise I would be very happy to attend her."

"Indeed," de Havilland said, and snorted. "She's a living anachronism. One would think we were in the Dark Ages. If she must carry on with binding, she could perfectly well work from my own bindery, in comfort. The number of times I've tried to persuade her . . . But she insists on staying here. And now she's taken on that damned apprentice . . ."

"She does seem somewhat . . . obstinate."

"She's infuriating." He hissed a sigh through his teeth. "Well, I suppose I must endure this for a while and try to make her see sense."

"Good luck. Oh —" There was the sound of a clasp being undone, and a clink. "If she's in pain, or sleepless, a few drops of this should help. Not more."

"Ah. Yes. Good night, then." The door opened and shut, and outside there was the creak and rumble of the trap drawing away. At the same time there were footsteps as de Havilland climbed the stairs. When he saw me he raised the lamp and peered at me. "Eavesdropping, were you?" But he didn't give me time to answer. He brushed past me and added, over his shoulder, "Bring me some clean bedding."

I followed him. He opened the door of my bedroom and paused, quirking his head at me. "Yes?"

I said, "That's my room — where'm I supposed to —"

"I have no idea." Then he shut the door in my face and left me in darkness.

CHAPTER
SEVEN

I slept in the parlour, huddled in a spare blanket. The settee was shiny horsehair and so slippery that in the end I had to brace myself with one foot on the floor to stop myself sliding off. When I woke up it was freezing and still dark, and I ached all over. I was disorientated; for a moment I thought I was outside somewhere, surrounded by the dim hulks of winter ruins.

It was so cold I didn't even try to go back to sleep. I stood up with the blanket still wrapped round my shoulders and staggered stiffly into the kitchen. I stoked the range and boiled a kettle for tea, while the last stars faded over the horizon. There was a clear sky, and by the time I'd drunk my tea and made a pot to take upstairs the kitchen was full of sunlight.

As I crossed the landing I heard my bedroom door open. It struck me for the first time how familiar the sound had become: I knew, without thinking, that it was my door and not Seredith's.

"Ah. I was hoping for shaving water. Never mind, tea will do. In here, please."

I blinked away the after-image of the kitchen window that was still hovering in my vision. De Havilland was standing in my doorway in his shirtsleeves. Now it was light I could take in his appearance better — the ringlets of lightish, greyish hair, the pale eyes, the embroidered waistcoat — and the disdainful expression on his face. It was difficult to tell how old he was: his hair and eyes were so washed out that he could have been forty or sixty. "Hurry up, boy."

"This is for Seredith."

For a second I thought he was going to object. He sighed. "Very well. Bring another cup. The hot water can come later." He pushed ahead of me and went into Seredith's bedroom without knocking. The door swung closed and I caught it with my elbow and backed into the room after him.

"Go away," Seredith said. "No, not you, Emmett."

She was sitting up, her face haloed by wisps of white hair, her fingers clasping the quilt under her chin. She was thin, but there was a good colour in her cheeks, and her eyes were as sharp as ever. De Havilland gave her a thin smile. "You're awake, I see. How are you feeling?"

"Invaded. Why are you here?"

He sighed. He brushed a few nonexistent specks of dust off the moss-coloured armchair and sank into it, hitching his trousers up delicately at the knee. He turned his head to take in the room, pausing here and there to note the cracks in the plaster, and the scarred foot of the bed, and the darker diamond of blue where the quilt had been patched. When I put the tray down beside the bed he leant past me to pour tea into the solitary cup, and sipped from it with a flicker of a

114

grimace. "This is tiresome. Suppose we stop wasting time and behave as if I was concerned for you," he said.

"Rubbish. When have you ever been concerned for me? Emmett, will you get two more cups, please?"

I said, "It's all right, Seredith, I'm not thirsty," just as de Havilland said, "One will suffice, I think." I clenched my jaw and left without looking at him. I went to the kitchen and back as quickly as I could, but when I glanced at the cup as I reached the top of the stairs I saw a feather of dust curled round the inside. If it had been meant for de Havilland I would have left it, but it wasn't. By the time I opened Seredith's bedroom door, swinging the cup from my finger, Seredith was sitting bolt upright with her arms crossed over her chest, while de Havilland lolled back in his chair. "Certainly not," he said. "You're an excellent binder. Old-fashioned, of course, but . . . Well. You would be useful to me."

"Work in your bindery?"

"You know my offer still stands."

"I'd rather die."

De Havilland turned to me, very deliberately. "So glad to see you finally managed to find your way back to us," he said. "Perhaps you would be kind enough to pour Seredith a cup of tea before she expires of thirst."

I didn't trust myself to reply. I poured dark tea into the clean cup and gave it to Seredith, cradling her hands in mine to make sure that she held it securely. She glanced up at me and some of the ferocity went out of her face. "Thank you, Emmett."

De Havilland pinched the bridge of his nose with his finger and thumb. He was smiling, but without

115

warmth. "Times have changed, Seredith. Even apart from the question of your health, I wish you would reconsider. This lonely existence, miles from anywhere, binding ignorant, superstitious peasants . . . We have worked very hard, you know, to better our reputation, so that people begin to understand that we are doctors of the soul and not witches. You do the craft no credit at all —"

"Don't lecture me."

He smoothed a strand of hair away from his forehead with splayed fingers. "I am merely making the point that we learnt from the Crusade —"

"You weren't even alive during the Crusade! How dare you —"

"All right, all right!" After a moment he leant over and poured himself another cup of tea. By now it was like dye, but he didn't seem to notice until he took a sip and his lips wrinkled. "Be reasonable, Seredith. How many people have you bound, this year? Four? Five? You can't have enough work to keep yourself busy, let alone an apprentice. And all peasants with no understanding of the craft at all. They think you're a witch . . ." He leant forward, his voice softening. "Wouldn't it be pleasant to come to Castleford, where binders command some respect? Where *books* command respect? I am quite influential, you know. I attend some of the best families."

"*Attend* them?" Seredith echoed. "A binding should be once a lifetime."

"Oh, please . . . When pain can be alleviated, who are we to withhold our art? You are too set in your ways."

116

"That's enough!" She thrust her tea aside, slopping it over the patchwork. "I am not coming to Castleford."

"This inverse snobbery is hardly in your best interests. Why you prefer to rot away in this godforsaken place —"

"You don't understand, do you?" I had never heard Seredith struggle to control her anger, and it made my own gorge rise. "Apart from anything else, I can't leave the books."

He put his cup down on its saucer with a clink. The signet ring on his little finger glinted. "Don't be absurd. I understand your scruples, but it's quite simple. We can take the books with us. I have space in my own vault."

"Give you my books?" She laughed. It sounded like a twig cracking.

"My vault is perfectly safe. Safer than having them in the bindery with you."

"That's it, is it?" She shook her head and sat back against her pillows, gasping a little. "I should have known. Why else would you bother to come? You're after my books. Of course."

He sat up straight, and for the first time a hint of pink seeped into his cheeks. "There's no need to be —"

"How many of your own books actually end up in your vault? You think I don't know how you pay for your new bindery and your — your *waistcoats*?"

"There's nothing illegal about trade binding. It's merely prejudice."

"I'm not talking about trade binding," she said, her mouth twisting on the words as if they tasted bitter.

"I'm talking about selling true bindings, without consent. And that *is* illegal."

They stared at each other for a moment. Seredith's hand was a white knot of tendons at her throat; she was clutching the key she wore round her neck as if it was in danger of being wrenched away from her.

"Oh, for goodness' sake," de Havilland said, getting to his feet. "I don't know why I bother."

"Neither do I. Why don't you go home?"

He gave a theatrical sigh, raising his eyes to the cracked plaster on the ceiling. "I'll go home when you're better."

"Or when I'm dead. That's really what you're waiting for, isn't it?"

He made a little mocking bow in her direction and strode towards the door. I leant back against the wall to let him pass, and he caught my eye and started, as if he'd forgotten I was there. "Hot water," he said. "In my bedroom. Immediately." He slammed the door behind him with a bang that made the walls tremble.

Seredith looked at me sidelong and then ducked her head, plucking at the quilt as if she was checking that the pattern was complete. When she didn't say anything, I cleared my throat. "Seredith . . . If you want me to make him leave . . ."

"And how would you do that?" She shook her head. "No, Emmett. He'll go of his own accord, when he sees that I'm recovered. It won't be long." There was something sour in the way she said it. "In the meantime . . ."

"Yes?"

She met my eyes. "Try not to lose your temper with him. You may need him, yet."

But that flicker of complicity wasn't much consolation, as the days went on and de Havilland showed no sign of leaving. I couldn't understand why Seredith put up with him, but I knew that without her permission I couldn't tell him to go. And knowing that it was my own fault that he was there didn't make it easier to bite my tongue when he poked quizzically at the lumps in a salt-pork stew, or threw me a couple of shirts and told me to wash them. Between my chores, looking after Seredith and the extra work he made, there was no time for anything else; the hours passed in a blur of drudgery and resentment, and I didn't even set foot in the workshop. It was hard to remember that a few days ago, before de Havilland came, I'd felt as if the house belonged to me: now I was reduced to a slave. But the worst thing wasn't the work — I'd worked harder than this, at home, before I got ill — it was the way de Havilland's presence filled the house. I'd never known anyone who moved so quietly; more than once, when I was stoking the range or scrubbing a pan, I felt the chill touch of his gaze on the back of my neck. I turned round, expecting him to blink or smile, but he went on watching me as if I was a kind of animal he'd never seen before. I stared back, determined not to be the first to look away, and at last he let his eyes travel past me to what I was doing, before he drifted silently out of the room.

One morning he passed me at the foot of the stairs as I carried a basket of logs in for the range. "Seredith is asleep. I'll have a fire in the parlour."

I clenched my jaw and dumped the wood in the kitchen without answering. I wanted to tell him to build his own fire — or something more obscene — but the thought of Seredith helpless upstairs made me swallow the words. De Havilland was a guest, whether I liked it or not; so I piled a couple of logs against my chest and carried them across the hall to the parlour. The door was open. De Havilland had turned the writing desk around and was sitting with his back to the window. He didn't look up when I came in, only pointed to the hearth as if I wouldn't know where it was.

I crouched and began to brush the remnants of the last fire out of the grate. The fine wood ash rose like the ghost of smoke. As I started to lay kindling I felt that creeping sensation at the base of my skull; it felt like a defeat to glance round to see if he was looking, but I couldn't stop myself. De Havilland leant back in his chair and tapped his pen against his teeth. He regarded me for what felt like a long time, while the blood began to hum in my temples. Then he smiled faintly and turned his attention back to the letter he was writing.

I forced myself to finish the fire. I lit it and waited until the flames had taken hold. Once it was burning well I stood up and tried to brush the grey smears off my shirt.

De Havilland was reading a book. He was still holding his pen, but it lay slackly between his knuckles while he turned the pages. His face was very calm; he might have been looking out of a window. After a moment he paused, turned back a page, and made a note. When he'd finished he caught sight of me. He put down his pen and smoothed his moustache, his eyes fixed on mine above the stroking hand that covered his mouth. Abruptly his vague, interested expression gave way to a gleam of something else, and he held out the book.

"*Master Edward Albion*," he said. "Bound by an anonymous binder from Albion's own bindery. Black morocco, gold tooling, false raised bands. Headbands sewn in black and gold, endpapers marbled in red nonpareil. Would you care to have a look?"

"I —"

"Take it. Carefully," he added, with a sudden sharp edge in his voice. "It's worth . . . oh, fifty guineas? Certainly more than you could ever repay."

I started to reach out, but something jarred in my head and I pulled back. It was the image of his face, utterly serene, as he read: words he had no right to, someone else's memories . . .

"No? Very well." He put it on the table. Then he looked back at me, as if something had occurred to him, and he shook his head. "I see you share Seredith's prejudices. It's a school binding, you know. Trade, but perfectly legitimate. Nothing to offend anyone's sensibilities."

"You mean —" I stopped. I didn't want to give him the satisfaction of asking what he meant, but he narrowed his eyes as if I had.

121

"It's unfortunate that you've been learning from Seredith," he said. "You must be under the impression that binding is stuck in the Dark Ages. It's not all occult muttering and the Hwicce Book, you know — oh." He rolled his eyes. "You've never heard of the Hwicce Book. Or the library at Pompeii? Or the great deathbed bindings of the Renaissance, or the Fangorn bindery, or Madame Sourly . . . No? The North Berwick Trials? The Crusades, presumably even you know about the Crusades?"

"I've been ill. She couldn't start to teach me properly."

"The Society of Fine Binders?" he said, raising an eyebrow. "The Sale of Memories Act of 1750? The rules that govern the issuing of licences to booksellers? Heavens, what *has* she taught you? No, you needn't tell me," he added, with a flick of disdain. "Knowing Seredith, you've probably spent three months on *endpapers*."

I turned away and picked up the full pan of ashes. My face was hot.

As I left, trailing a cloud of ash-dust, he called after me, "Oh, and my sheets smell musty. Change them, will you? And this time make sure they are properly aired."

When I went to collect Seredith's tray, later that afternoon, she was out of bed: huddled at the window in her quilt, her cheeks flushed. She smiled when I came into the room, but there was an odd blankness in her eyes. "There you are," she said, "you were quick. How did it go?"

"What?" I'd been changing de Havilland's sheets.

"The binding, of course," she said. "I hope you were careful when you sent her home. If you tell them they've been bound, sometimes they can hear you, even though . . . Only in the first year or so, while the mind adjusts, but it's a dangerous time, you have to take care . . . Your father could never explain why, why that one thing gets through, somehow . . . But I wonder . . . I think, deep down, they know something's missing. You must be *careful*." She fretted, chewing on nothing as if she had a tooth loose. "Sometimes I think you started too young. I let you bind them before you were ready."

I set the tray down again; I tried to be gentle but the china jumped and rattled. "Seredith? It's me. Emmett."

"Emmett?" She blinked. "Emmett. Yes. I'm sorry. I thought, for a moment . . ."

"Can I . . ." My voice cracked. "Can I get you anything? Do you want some more tea?"

"No." She shivered and pulled the quilt closer round her shoulders, grunting a little, but when she looked up her eyes were bright and sharp. "Forgive me. When you're as old as I am, things sometimes . . . blur."

"It doesn't matter," I said, stupidly polite, as if she'd spilt something. "Shall I . . .?"

"No. Sit down." But for a long time she didn't say anything else. Cloud-shadows swept past, over the marsh and the road, as swift as ships.

I cleared my throat. "Seredith . . . a moment ago, who did you think I was?"

"He thinks I've kept you in ignorance, deliberately," she said. From the new acid in her voice I knew she meant de Havilland. "He thinks I'm a crotchet-monger.

123

A stubborn, backward old stick-in-the-mud. Because I think the craft is sacred. He laughs at that. It's all about power, for him. Money. He has no . . . reverence. I *know*," she said, although I hadn't said anything. "I know too many people still think we're witches. People spit over their shoulders when they talk about binders — if they talk about them at all, that is. People like your parents — well, your grandfather was a Crusader, wasn't he? Your father at least had the decency to be ashamed of that . . . But that's only ignorance. The way *he* does things —"

"De Havilland?"

She snorted. "That absurd name . . . No, it's all wrong. Binderies full of men who don't understand what they're doing — books for *trade* . . . We make books — we make beautiful books — out of love." She twisted round, and her face was as hard as I'd ever seen it. "Love. Do you understand?"

I didn't, exactly. But I had to nod.

"There's a moment when you start a binding, when the binder and the bound become one. You sit and wait for it. You let the room go silent. They're afraid, they're always afraid . . . It's up to you, to listen, to wait. Then something mysterious happens. Your mind opens to theirs, and they let go. That's when the memories come. We call that moment the *kiss*."

I looked away. I'd never kissed anyone except my family.

"You become each person you bind, Emmett . . . Just for a little while, you take them on. How can you do that if you want to sell them at a profit?"

124

My legs started to cramp suddenly. I shuffled my feet to ease the ache and then stood up to pace to the mantel and back to my chair. Seredith followed me with her eyes. A cloud blew across the sun, blurring her wrinkles and softening the shape of her face. "I don't want you to become the sort of binder he is, Emmett."

"I'd rather slit my own throat than be like —"

Her laugh had a dry painful rattle in it. "So you say now. I hope it's true." She huddled deeper into the quilt until it bunched over her shoulders like a deformity.

There was a silence. I curled my toes in my boots; I was cold, all of a sudden. "Why are you telling me this?"

"I think I will have that tea, now, please," she said. "I'm feeling a little better."

"Yes." I crossed the room and opened the door so clumsily it almost hit the wall.

De Havilland stepped back; he'd been standing just outside. "I need to speak to Seredith," he said. "Get out of my way."

I stood aside. Something in the tilt of his head told me he'd been listening. I hoped he had been; I wanted him to have heard what I'd said.

"And wipe that insolent smile off your face," he added. "If you were my apprentice I'd have you whipped."

"I'm not your apprentice."

He pushed past me. "You may be, soon," he said, and slammed the door.

That night I found myself walking downstairs in moonlight so bright I hadn't needed to light a candle. There was something strange about the way it clung to me, whispering at every step like cobwebs breaking. But I was searching for something. That was the only thing that mattered.

I was cold. My feet were bare. I looked down at them and the moonlight shimmered, billowing, moving as I moved. I was dreaming; but the knowledge didn't wake me. Instead it seemed to lift me up and carry me. Now I was in the workshop. Everything here was covered with a bloom of light. My shirt brushed the bench and left a dark smear, and the glimmering dust clung to the fabric. What was I looking for?

I went towards the door in front of me, the one that led down to the storeroom. But when I went through it — it didn't open, it dissolved under my touch — I was in the other room, the one with chairs and a table. It wasn't night any more. There was a young man sitting with his back to me. It was Lucian Darnay.

He turned as if he was going to look at me, but the world slowed down and before I caught sight of his face the dream gave way under my feet. For a second I was falling, dropping blindly through empty space; then I jolted awake, my heart pounding, my limbs still humming with tension. It took me a long time to master the muscles in my arms, but at last, when they would obey me, I sat up and wiped the sweat off my face. Another nightmare. Only it hadn't exactly been a nightmare; in spite of the fear, the strongest feeling was a kind of desperation, as if another split second would have shown me what I'd been looking for.

I'd thought it was the middle of the night, but I heard the clock strike seven and realised I'd overslept; it was time to stoke the range, and make Seredith's tea. I slid off the settee and went into the hall, with the blanket wrapped round my shoulders like a cloak. I stood in front of the stove for a long time, as close to it as I could get, until it warmed me through.

"I would like some tea, please."

I whirled round. De Havilland lowered himself into a chair and rubbed his brow with two fingers as if he was trying to get rid of a smudge. He was wearing a pale blue dressing gown embroidered with silver, but underneath he was fully dressed and his waistcoat and cravat were the ones he'd been wearing the day before. There were purplish shadows under his eyes.

At least he'd said "please". I didn't answer him, but I put the kettle on to boil and measured a spoonful of tea into the pot. The tea caddy was so old that the green-and-gold pattern was speckled with rust, and flakes of paint came off on my fingers when I opened it.

He yawned. "How often does the post come? Is it once a week?"

"Yes."

"Today, then."

"Probably." When the water boiled I poured it into the teapot. Steam rose into my face, stinging my cheeks with heat.

"Good." He got out his watch and started to wind it. The cog made a metallic scratching sound that made my back teeth tingle. The tea hadn't brewed for long enough but I poured it anyway; in the thin porcelain of de Havilland's cup it looked hardly darker than piss. He frowned at it, but he raised the cup to his mouth and sipped without commenting. Then he set it down with a precise clink, exactly in the centre of the saucer.

I got out the tray and laid it, not with the blue-and-white china, but with one of the pottery cups that Seredith and I used. There was no point taking her bread and butter — when Toller came I'd ask him to bring us some rennet, and then I could make her some junket — but for now I picked a few bits of dried apple out of the jar and added a spoonful of honey to the cup. I was so eager to get away from de Havilland that I slopped tea on to the tray as I picked it up.

He looked up as I walked past. "Where are you going?"

"I'm taking Seredith her breakfast."

"Oh." His eyes flickered as if something behind me had caught his attention. But when his gaze came back to me it was steady. His irises were the same pale brown as the weak tea. One of the points of his moustache was fraying; I had a prickling, hateful urge to reach out and rip it off his face.

"No need for that," he said. "I'm afraid she died in the night."

CHAPTER
EIGHT

It was so quiet in Seredith's room that it was like walking into a picture. Everything apart from the window was dim and shadowy. Beyond the glass the first morning light made a band of pale blue on the horizon. A cobweb was strung across the corner of the window pane like a sail. Flecks of dirt or dead grass had speckled the window sill, even though the latch was closed; but whatever wind had driven it through the gaps had died, and there was no sound, from anywhere.

He had put coins on Seredith's eyes to keep them closed. One was a sixpence, the other a half-guinea; the effect was grotesque, like a wink. It didn't matter, though, because the thing on the bed wasn't really Seredith any more. I stood at the foot of the bed and tried to remember that gaunt, shrunken face with its blind lopsided stare speaking to me, teaching me . . . But the room felt empty. Even her hair, her nightdress, had turned into inhuman, organic things, like mould or fungi. I tried to examine myself for some glimmer of grief or shock, but my brain disobeyed. The only things that seemed worthy of notice were the details: the faint metallic smell like melting snow, the dry stain in the

129

glass beside the bed, the fraying lace just below Seredith's chin.

What was supposed to happen now?

I reached out and touched the quilt. It was so cold it felt damp. Suddenly, absurdly, I wanted to bring her more blankets and build another fire in the hearth; it seemed lazy — unkind, even — to let her lie here in this icy stillness. I wanted her to have the dancing light and the whisper of the flames to keep her company . . . But what fool would heat a room with a corpse in it? And I could imagine de Havilland's face when he saw me climbing the stairs with a basket of logs. I turned away. There was no point in speaking, or straightening her collar where the ruffle was half folded inwards, or brushing her sleeve as I passed; she was gone, completely and finally gone, and to pretend otherwise was sentimental.

I shut the door behind me and went down the stairs. It was strange how the floorboards and banisters stayed solid, how they gleamed and dulled as my shadow passed over them, and how the creak of my footsteps was just a little too distinct: as though they were working hard to remind me that I was here and alive, while Seredith had slid into thin air.

"In here." De Havilland's voice, from the parlour. He had never once used my name.

More than anything I wanted to open the front door and walk out. If I went now and kept on walking I could be home by tomorrow morning. I'd stride into the farmyard, tired but triumphant. Alta would pause at the door of the dairy, blinking at me, until she dropped her bucket with a clang and threw herself into my arms. I'd tell Ma and Pa I was better, and we'd go back to how it was before. What would they be doing today? There was a drainage ditch that needed digging in the Low Field, and this clear cold weather was good for drawing turnips. Maybe Ma would have set up the smoker in the farmyard; for a moment I could smell thick woodsmoke and the hint of blood. It was like trying to imagine being a child again.

"In here, *now*. I know you're there."

I turned away, my insides aching. I couldn't go home. Even if my family were pleased to see me, I didn't belong there any more; I was a binder now, whether I liked it or not. And what if the binder's fever was still in my blood, like an ague? Perhaps I had to be a binder to keep it at bay. If I went home now, I'd always be afraid. I crossed the hall to the parlour, and made sure my voice was steady. "Yes, I'm here."

"At last." He was sitting on the settee, with an empty teacup and plate on the table him. He was glaring at the hearth. He'd made a fire, but it was too tightly packed; I knew that in a minute it would subside into nothing. "It's perishing in here. This chimney doesn't draw properly."

As if on cue, the flames sighed and flickered out. I didn't answer.

He clicked his tongue and glanced furiously at me, as if it was my fault. "On the writing table are two letters. When Toller comes, give them to him. Do you understand?"

I went to the table and picked them up. *Dr Ferguson, 45 The Mount, Castleford* and *Elijah Oaks, Undertaker, 131 High Street, Castleford*. "Is that all?"

He stood up and took a few steps towards the window. Outside a bird skimmed across the water, throwing a bright trail of droplets, and the rushes dipped, silvery, in the breeze; but when he turned back to me it was as if he'd been looking at a dungheap. "Sit down."

"I'd prefer to stand."

He pointed to a chair and smiled at me. I tried to stare him out, and failed. "Good," he said, when I lowered myself into the chair. He paused, nudged the remains of the fire with the poker and sighed before he resumed. "Seredith's death," he said, still stirring the ashes, "was . . . regrettable."

I didn't answer. Absurdly I found myself listening for movement upstairs.

"Although she was old. It is natural, after all. One generation fades as another matures. The old order gives way to the new. And so on."

"Can I go?"

He raised his eyes to me. Could I see a sort of distant surprise in his face, or was it a trick of the light? "No," he said. "I believe we have much to discuss. Please sit still. I find your fidgeting distracting."

I bit my lip.

"I am your master now. I am therefore responsible for you." He said it as if he were reading aloud. "Apparently you have some promise," he paused fractionally as if to suggest scepticism, "and it is clear that there is no question of you staying here."

"I can't stay here?" As soon as I said it, I realised how impossible it was. The thought of leaving was like a sudden rush of cold air into a wound.

"Certainly not. With whom? I have no intention of remaining in this house longer than I am obliged to. Seredith was an eccentric. Worse than a Luddite, resisting progress. I am afraid you have not been given the best opportunity to develop our art. Living like this, like a peasant . . ." He gestured with the poker as if to indicate me, and the room around me. "Her insistence on the — manual — part of the work, those incidental skills which any man with a modicum of dexterity can demonstrate . . . Accepting all the clients who came to her . . . Taking no pride in her work . . ."

"She did take pride in her work."

"None of those things," he went on, as though he hadn't heard me, "prepares you adequately for the great dignity of being a binder. A true binder has no need to sew or cut or . . ." He drew a limp loop in the air with the poker as if to suggest tasks he didn't even know the name for. "A true binder, boy, has *clean hands*."

I looked automatically at his hands. They were as white as a peeled willow switch.

"But you have to make the books," I said. "Someone has to make the books."

"Naturally. In my workshop in Castleford I have several good workers. They produce some very fine . . ." Again, that gesture with the poker. "Covers, and so on. But they are replaceable, that is the point. What I do —

133

what we do, that is the true art. To cheapen it with glue and dust and grime under one's fingernails is sacrilege." He smiled thinly. "I had encouraged Seredith for a number of years to employ an artisan so that she could concentrate on her true calling. When I heard she had apprenticed you I thought that for once she had heeded my advice. But then she told me that you would be a binder yourself, and that moreover you'd had the binderbound fever so badly she didn't dare let you set eyes on a book." His smile contracted, as though a stitch had pulled tight somewhere. "Don't worry, boy, I have no intention of asking you questions about that."

The blood roared in my ears. "I'm all right now."

"I should hope so." He put the poker back in the stand and turned to look at a picture on the wall. I hadn't realised how relentless his regard had been, but now I felt a surge of relief. "As it happens," he said, tapping the frame to adjust the angle, "it is useful for me that you are in fact a binder. Next week I have been requested by Lord Latworthy, and one of my usual clients in Castleford is also in need of my services. You will do for him, I think."

"What? Me? I can't —"

"I agree that you are not the deputy I would choose, given a free hand and all the time in the world. But the subject is a servant, I believe, so the binding itself will require very little finesse. To my client himself you will be polite, tactful and discreet — I trust you can perform that role creditably enough, Seredith never liked a fool . . ." He paused and flicked a glance over his shoulder. "Then, when I return, I will be better able to assess your talent and deal with you accordingly. If you are indeed a binder, I will take over your training. If not, you can earn your living in my workshop, with the craftsmen."

"I don't understand."

"I don't understand what you don't understand," he said, with a sort of bemused softness. "It is quite simple."

"No. You see . . ." I took a deep breath. "I've never bound anything. Anyone. I didn't know what it was until . . . Seredith told me, the night before she got ill. I can do some of the finishing work, but the — the other bit, the —" I didn't have words for it. That room, that clean, bare, terrible room . . . "I don't know what to do. I don't know how it works. I can't do it."

"How it *works* is a mystery, boy." He sighed. "I suppose you mean . . . the procedure. My goodness, she really didn't teach you anything, did she? Luckily it's easy enough, you merely have to lay hands on the subject and listen. As long as you take paper and a pen and ink, and make sure you're both sitting down, and that she's consented, you can hardly go wrong. There is the small matter of managing the memories — making sure you don't go too deep, and so on — but I'm sure your — er — apparently *exceptional* talent will see you through. A maidservant is not very important, after all."

"But —"

"It is unfortunate that you have no experience, but you will do your best. Bearing in mind, it goes without saying, that your future depends on it."

135

"But —"

"You had better pack a bag. If Toller delivers those letters today we will be leaving here tomorrow. From then on you will be living under my roof, and I don't know when you will be able to return."

I opened my mouth to speak, and he swung swiftly round. For a split second he simply looked at me — where had I seen that look before? — and my stomach tightened. Then he reached out for Seredith's teacup, held it up as though to propose a toast, and dropped it. It smashed. I looked down at the talons of blue-painted china.

"And," he said, very calmly, "you will *stop arguing*."

I didn't have much to pack. I had the few clothes I'd brought with me, and a few useful bits and pieces — a box of needles and thread, my folding knife, a razor and comb, and a nearly empty purse. It seemed a sparse collection when I spread it out on my bed, even when I added the things Seredith had given me: a couple of bone folders, curved and smooth with years of use, a magnifying glass, a pair of scissors, a paring knife and a cobbler's knife. I thought suddenly of the silver ring I'd found in the workshop, and wondered if I should take it to sell, just in case; now Seredith was dead, no one would know who had left it here, or why. Whoever they were, they were long gone. But it was still stealing.

I bundled everything into my sack and dumped it downstairs in the parlour — de Havilland was in my room, of course — and then stood for a long time at the window, watching the light change in the clear sky.

When Toller had come I'd given him the letters and tried not to think about how convenient it was that Seredith had died that night, and not the night after, when de Havilland would've had to let another week pass before he could send for the undertaker. Now there was nothing to do but wait. It was like a vigil, except that Seredith was alone behind a closed door. More than once I thought about lighting candles and sitting beside her, but my skin crawled at the thought of the deep chill in that room, and those mismatched coins staring blindly at the ceiling.

Once I'd packed, de Havilland retired to my room and shut the door. Maybe he was sleeping, but in any case I didn't hear anything. When the sun went down I went up and knocked, because even his voice would have been better than the silent shadows. He didn't answer. Both bedrooms were equally quiet, as if he was dead too.

I shuddered and laughed at the same time. I was getting fey; the best thing was to go downstairs and warm up. I wasn't hungry, but I made myself tea and gulped it down, thirsty for the heat. Then, without thinking about it, I went into the workshop.

The shapes of the presses and the clutter on the workbench were just visible against the last veil of light in the windows. It had been a long time since I'd been in here. Dust lay like a reproach on the bench; there was a damp odour in the air that explained why Seredith had always kept the stove going. I held my lamp up to the coloured tiles, but the glass mantle was so stained with soot that I struggled to make out the shades of russet and jade and earth.

Seredith's apron was on the floor, under the hook where it was supposed to hang — although she'd hardly ever taken it off. I picked it up, and the leather was cold and stiff. How long had it been here, forgotten, on the floor? She'd worn it so long that the bib and waist kept the shape of her body, and it smelt of her, of glue and whetstone and soap.

It hit me then, that she was dead.

I hadn't realised I'd loved her till that moment. At first I tried to stay quiet, in case de Havilland heard; but after a while I didn't care, and no one came. I crawled into a corner of the workshop like a child, and buried my face in the old stained leather, blotting out the space and the darkness. Seredith wasn't in that desiccated body upstairs; she was here, I was holding her. I could almost hear her sigh of amusement mixed with sympathy, and her voice: "Come on, now, lad, you'll make yourself ill again. All right, lad, it'll be all right . . ."

In the end it soothed me. Somehow a sob turned into a yawn. I folded the apron into a pillow and wedged it between my head and shoulder. Slow tears rolled into my collar and dampened my chest. When I blinked my eyelids grew heavier and heavier. For a moment I danced on the edge of darkness; and then, out of a gentle maelstrom of fragments, I found myself walking downstairs. There was something strange about the moonlight, the dusty glimmer of it, the silky sound it made as I moved through it. I knew I was dreaming

— the same familiar dream — and the realisation set the fragments whirling again, threatening to settle in a different pattern. I glimpsed the corner of the bindery, the shapes of lay press and board-cutter; then in a fog of moonlight I was on the stairs again, and the only thing that mattered was that I was searching for something. This time I knew that I had to go through the door at the far end of the workshop; and when I got there it would be the other room, and Lucian Darnay would be sitting at the table, about to look up at me.

The world shivered and melted in an instant. I jerked upright and a pain shot through my neck and shoulder. I was on the floor, chilled to the bone. A fold of Seredith's apron was digging into my cheek. There was the sound of a door shutting very near to me, and footsteps going down the steps on the other side.

I crawled out from under the bench, wincing at the crick in my neck — Ma would say it served me right for falling asleep on a cold floor — and got unsteadily to my feet. The desperate urging of the dream hadn't quite left me, and my heart was beating faster than it should have been; but the footsteps and the closing door had been real, and a line of lamplight spilt along the sill. It was so faint I could only just see it, but it was there. Someone — de Havilland — was down there. And now I could make out muffled sounds: thumps, a clatter of something falling, a thin voice humming snatches of melodies.

I opened the door. For an instant I was back in my dream, and I expected to be in the other room, looking at Lucian Darnay's back — I was close, so close, he'd

139

turn and when he met my eyes I'd *know*. I reached out and held on to the doorframe. In front of me the steps led down to the storeroom as I'd known they would. It took me a moment to shake off the clinging sense of desperation; then I was standing in the lower room, dazzled by the sudden blaze of light. There were three lamps, perched on the table and an upturned bucket at the side of the room, as if he'd wanted to eradicate the dark entirely. He'd pushed the clutter and boxes back against the wall, pell-mell, and a huge chest sat in the centre of the floor, its lid flung back. From where I was I couldn't see what was in it.

De Havilland stepped back, his arms full of books. The whole wall behind him was yawning open, swinging on hidden hinges, the bronze boss throwing a snub-nosed shadow on the plaster; the darkness beyond was deep, not a cupboard but a room. The walls of the vault were lined with shelves, but they were mostly empty. Only a few ranks of spines remained, where the books were too high to reach easily. The gold tooling caught the light, glinting in lines or leaves or names: *Albert Smith, Emmeline Rivers née Rosier*. De Havilland hummed a bar of a tuneless melody, paused, and then reached out for one more volume, leaning back and contorting himself so that he didn't drop the rest.

"What are you doing?"

He looked round, and the high jaunty humming stopped. "Apprentice," he said, his voice sibilant and slushy. "What are *you* doing? Out of bed at this hour? I don't believe Seredith would have stood for it."

140

"I was in the workshop. I heard you."

"I am doing some very important work," he said. He took a few staggering steps to the chest and collapsed forward to let the books drop into it. His movements were looser than before, and he reeled as he raised his head. There was a brandy glass on the shelf inside the vault door, with nothing but an amber glint at the bottom. "Since you're here, pass me one of those boxes, will you? I think any more and this will be too heavy to lift."

I took a deep breath. Seredith was upstairs, and he was here, ripping books off the shelves, drinking, *singing*.

I didn't move. He pushed past me and upended a box on to the floor, kicking the debris aside so that he could thump the box down next to the chest. I caught a whiff of alcohol on his breath as he swung back to the vault and selected another armful of books. I bent and picked up a scorched centre-tool that had slipped out of its handle, but there was nowhere to put it. In the end I laid it carefully on the same bucket where the lamps were perched.

De Havilland turned round again, holding four or five books this time. I could see from their spines that they were good, expensive bindings — one was thick with gold, and the top one was bound in a kind of leather cutwork that must have taken hours — but he didn't even read the names before he put them in the box. I drew closer and saw that the chest was nearly full. More books. Lovely things: one like an inlaid box, another like a lace handkerchief, one half-concealed that looked as though embers had sprayed out across scrubbed pale wood.

"What are you doing with —"

He'd ducked into the vault again. "No," he said, tried to push a book back on to the shelf it had come from and missed. It opened in a splash of paper and thumped to the floor. "No, no" — more books, and now he wasn't even trying to put them back, they all flapped and fell like dead birds — "yes, lovely . . ." That one he put into the box, with a gesture that might have been careful if he'd been sober. "Yes, yes — oh wait . . ." He'd added the last of them to the *yes* box, but now he blinked and took it out again, squinting at the spine as if it had bitten him. It was bound in grey-green silk, blind-tooled with patterns of overlapping leaves, with here and there the glimmer of silver, like reflections on a river. I wanted to reach out and pluck it out of his grasp. "Whoops," he said, and giggled. "Lucian Darnay. Might be a bit tactless to send that one."

"What?"

"Can't have you take *that* one when you visit the Darnays," he said, as if I was in on the joke. He peered into the chest, nodding to himself as though he'd brought in the last of the harvest, and then wove his way back to the vault. He threw the book inside and shut the door with a thud. "Should do it," he added. "If he isn't happy with that lot . . ."

"The Darnays?" I said. "You're sending me to —"

"Don't mention it!" he said, swinging round. "Don't you dare mention it. Sometimes they can hear that, you know, even if everything else is gone, and then you wouldn't believe the trouble you can get into, with hysterical customers wanting their books back, or rebindings, or . . . Don't tell me — no, of course Seredith didn't teach you, damn the woman . . ." He sighed. "When you see him, you behave as if the name means nothing. Got it?"

That gaunt black-and-white face. A flash of dark eyes, fierce as a hawk's.

"What's the matter?" He narrowed his eyes. I thought dimly that I must be in a bad way, if he noticed through the haze of drunkenness . . . "What is it? Pull yourself together."

"I can't go to see Lucian Darnay."

"Don't be ridiculous. It wasn't even you who bound him, was it? In any case, you probably won't see him. It's Darnay senior who matters. Just look at them all with respect and deference and you'll be fine." He muttered, as if to himself, "Respect, deference, with that face . . . Heaven help us."

I didn't answer. The dragging, desperate dream-sense that I was missing something important had come back, stronger than it had ever been. What was it trying to tell me? What had I been searching for? Lucian Darnay had been about to turn, to tell me . . .

De Havilland yawned. He fumbled for his keys and locked the vault door.

"You've got the key," I said. "Seredith wore it all the time. How did —"

"Seredith gave it to me." He turned to stare at me. His expression was level; his eyes were red-rimmed, but now you wouldn't have known he was drunk. "A binder's books are a sacred trust. As her confidant and colleague —"

"But you said they were going to the Darnays."

He tilted his head, as if he would forgive me one mistake but no more. "Don't meddle in things you don't understand."

"I understand enough." I swallowed. "I heard her say she didn't want you to have the books. She didn't give it to you, you must have —"

"Don't you *dare* accuse me, boy." He raised his hand, pointing one finger upwards; it was more of a threat than anything else he could have done. "Nothing that you have seen tonight is any of your business. Put it out of your mind. If you mention it to anyone . . . well, it will be the worse for you. That's all."

I heard myself say, "You took it from her body. You knew that was the only way you could get it. You watched her die, and then you took the key from round her neck, because that was the only thing you cared about. Why would she have given it to you? She would have given it to *me*."

The room was as still as stone. If I could have taken the words back, I would have done.

At last he said, very softly, "I think, after you have been to the Darnays', there will be work to be done. I do not like your spirit, boy. I think you will have to be entirely broken."

Somewhere out of sight a pile of books collapsed with a slithering thud; then everything was quiet again.

144

"Go to bed," he said. "We will pretend that you were there all night. *Go.*"

I turned and began to climb the stairs. I was shaking, and he could see it.

"To address your . . . concern," he said, so suddenly I almost tripped, "she did not trust you with a key, because the books in that vault were none of your business. Her secrets are not your secrets. Get that into your head, or you will go mad."

But I remembered the certainty I'd felt. He was wrong. There was something in there that did concern me — that was *mine*, as surely as my own bones. I understood, too late, what I'd been looking for: Lucian Darnay's book. An answer to a riddle that was deeper inside me than my heart —

"And she *did* trust me," he said, "no matter how it might have seemed to a stranger, because I am her son. And whatever love you think there was between her and you, you may put it out of your mind. She was as cold as ice, and if you think you were anything more than her slave, you are a fool."

CHAPTER
NINE

The undertaker and the doctor arrived the next morning, early. It was foggy, with a biting damp that seemed to crawl under my skin, and the mist had got inside my head, too. Details flickered out of the blankness and were swallowed again: Ferguson shaking the moisture off his coat on the hall floor, "What a journey to do by night, we were lucky the horses didn't break a leg," his voice too loud for the house; a man who looked more like a carpenter than an undertaker shaking my hand with a frigid grip, smelling of peppermint; the sound of their feet coming past, later, shuffling and awkward with the weight of a loaded bier. We were summoned to witness the death certificate in the parlour — "a mere formality," the doctor said, as if I might be too nervous to write my name in such august company — but for the rest of the time I waited in the workshop, beside the stove, packing it with wood as if I could keep it burning forever. De Havilland's words came and went in my ears. I was almost sure that Seredith had loved me, in her way: but if de Havilland was her son, maybe he knew her better than I did. *Cold as ice* . . . It was like vertigo: everything I thought I knew about her was wavering, slipping through my fingers. Now all I wanted was to leave as soon as possible; but when at last de Havilland called from the hall, as impatient as if he'd been shouting for hours, it took an effort to get to my feet.

The doctor had brought his own carriage, and he and de Havilland huddled inside it while the undertaker — what was his name? Oaks, was that it? — helped me load the boxes and trunks on to the roof. The coachman watched us with a baleful neutrality, as if his eyeballs had iced over. De Havilland had only brought a small bag when he arrived, but now the carriage creaked under the weight. I recognised the chest and the box he had filled with books, and there were more: one box clinked gently, and another seeped golden ink from the bottom. I hesitated, but there was no time to find the leaking bottle, and anyway it was de Havilland's now. I tied the boxes in place while de Havilland murmured irritably in the carriage below.

The undertaker set off before us. I stood for a moment watching the tarpaulin-covered cart trundle along the road: if you didn't know, you'd think he was a farmer or a craftsman, taking a load of wares to market. I wondered whether I should feel anything, as Seredith's body was carried further and further away; but I didn't. It was only when I was in the carriage, watching the bindery recede, that the sadness grabbed me by the throat. De Havilland studied my face with those pale eyes — a parody of Seredith's — and I tried to stare him out. If I could make him look away first . . . But I couldn't. Had I really been her slave? Maybe the Seredith I'd loved had never existed, and I'd been a fool all along . . . I dug my nails into my thighs, trying to distract myself with the pain. He turned back to Ferguson and went on with their conversation as if I wasn't there.

It was a long journey. After a while the swaying suspension of the carriage on the bumpy road made me feel sick. I was glad not to have to talk; but as the mist closed against the windows and the cold crept into my limbs, I began to feel less and less real. Even the clouds of their breath were more solid than mine. Once, we got out to piss — by that point we had skirted the marshes and the road was bordered by woods on both sides — but the fog amongst the dark bars of the trees made the world seem so distant and comfortless that I wanted to get back into the carriage. But every minute that we creaked along was an eternity; de Havilland and Ferguson's conversation might have been interesting if I had recognised the people they gossiped about, but as it was I tried to shut it out along with the rumbling of the wheels. What did I care about Lord Latworthy, or the Norwoods or the Hambledons, or whether Honour Ormonde was marrying for love or money? I thought I'd give my little finger for a few moments of silence; but then, at last, they stopped talking and it was worse. Now, if I wanted it, I had time to wonder about Seredith, or my family, or where I was going.

Castleford built itself up around us slowly: first as looming shapes and faint echoes, then as shadows behind a thicker fog, tinged with a miasma of sewage, coal fumes and brick-dust. We rattled past a building site where a clamp of firing bricks smouldered, pouring out acrid smoke that made de Havilland cough and spit neatly into a handkerchief; then through wider streets where the traffic rumbled beside us and the smoke had the choking, ammoniac note of old manure. He pulled up the shutters and we sat in a grey semi-dark, while I fought my nausea; but it didn't keep out the noise. Horses snorted and neighed, men shouted, women shrieked, dogs barked, and all the time there was a lower hum of wheels and machinery and more, an indistinguishable cacophony. I didn't remember Castleford being like this — but then, I was here after months of living out on the marshes, where there hadn't even been the noise of animals to break the silence. I shut my eyes and imagined Seredith's — my — workshop, abandoned but still solid and quiet, and held the thought of it like a talisman.

When at last we came to a halt I was stiff and numb, and my head was pounding. De Havilland clambered out of the carriage and clicked his fingers at me from the pavement. "Come on, boy. What are you dallying for?"

I'd been waiting for the doctor to get out ahead of me, but he settled himself more comfortably into the corner and I realised that he was going on without us. Awkwardly I climbed past him and found myself in the street. The coachman hissed through his teeth at the cold, crossing his arms across his chest. The carriage stayed where it was.

I looked about me, pulling my coat tighter against a gust of chilly, sooty wind. We were in a road of tall brick houses and wide, bare pavements, carpeted in patches with dirty snow. Railings ran along the front of every house, between uniform front doors with steps leading up to them. There was a bay tree in a glazed pot standing on the doorstep of the nearest house, and from ten feet away I could see the smuts clinging to the leaves, like black mould.

"For goodness' sake, stop dawdling." De Havilland mounted the steps and rang the bell, and I hurried after him. There was a brass plaque beside the door, with an elegant line of engraving: *De Havilland, S.F.B.* Whatever I had been expecting, it wasn't this.

A severe-looking woman with a bun and a pince-nez around her neck answered the door, and stepped aside with a smile to let de Havilland in. The smile congealed when she saw me, but she said nothing except, "I'm so glad you're back, Mr de Havilland. Mrs Sotherton-Smythe is most in need of your services. Mr Sotherton-Smythe even threatened to go to someone else, if you were away much longer."

"While his wife's books are in our vault? Hardly," he said, with a quick humourless laugh. "What is it? She's found out about the latest mistress, I suppose?"

She cleared her throat, glancing at me, but de Havilland fluttered a hand in the air. "Don't worry, this is my new apprentice. He'll learn it all eventually. Did you make an appointment for her?"

"Not yet, sir. But I will send him a note in the afternoon post."

"Good. I'll see her tomorrow. Check he's settled his last bill before you write, though." He strode ahead of me down a tiled hallway. On one side was a half-open

150

door, with another plaque: *Waiting Room*. Through the gap I saw a pale, fashionable parlour, the wallpaper patterned with reeds and birds, a spread of periodicals on a table, and sprays of unseasonable flowers in a porcelain vase. There was another door at the far end, but I didn't have time to see more before de Havilland paused and frowned over his shoulder. "Will you hurry up? Anyone would think you'd never been inside a house. This way."

The severe secretary had disappeared — into another room on the other side of the passage, I thought, hearing the latch click — and I sped up, so that I was nearly at de Havilland's heels as he pushed through a jib door and out into a cramped yard. Opposite us there was a lopsided, shabby building. Shadows crossed back and forth behind grimy windows. De Havilland picked his way across the puddles and yanked the door open. "This is the workshop," he said. "You'll sleep in the room upstairs. Well, come *in*, boy." He took a few steps into the dingy passage and slapped a door on his left so it swung open. There were four or five men in the room beyond, all bent over benches or presses. One of them drew himself up, a hammer in his hand, and started to say something; but when he saw it was de Havilland he touched his forehead and said, "Afternoon, sir."

"Good afternoon, Jones. Baines, Winthorn, there are some boxes that need to be brought in from the street. They're on the roof of the carriage outside the front door. Bring them round, will you? Oh — the chest can go to my office. Everything else in here." He didn't even glance at the men putting down their work. One of them was in the middle of covering a corner with leather, and I saw him grimace as he pulled it apart so it wouldn't dry half-finished. They shuffled past us, but de Havilland still didn't seem to see them. "Jones, this is my new apprentice. He'll be sleeping upstairs and working with you."

"Apprentice binder, sir?"

"Yes. But as it happens he knows how to do some of the . . ." de Havilland gestured vaguely at the lay press. "The . . . er . . . *physical* crafts, so while he is learning to bind he may as well be of use in here." He turned to me. "I shall summon you when I need you. The rest of the time, you may take your orders from Mr Jones."

I nodded.

"It goes without saying that you are not allowed in the house unless I call for you." He turned and left. A moment later I heard the swollen door drag across the lintel and thud shut.

The man next to the window raised his head and watched him pick his way across the yard, his mouth pursed in a silent contemptuous whistle. The three of them didn't swap a glance, but after a pause they all started work again at the same moment. I pushed my hands into my pockets, trying to warm my fingers, waiting for Jones to ask my name; but he bent over the lay press and went on banging the back of an unbound book with his hammer.

I cleared my throat. "Mr Jones —"

Someone snorted. When I looked at him — the man closest to the door, who was tilting a finished book this way and that, checking the definition of the tooling he

152

had done — he rolled his eyes at me. "It's not Jones, it's Johnson. Bastard doesn't bother getting our names right."

"Can't get his *own* name right," one of the others said, without looking up. "De Havilland, my Frenchified arse."

I said, "Mr Johnson, then."

But Johnson still didn't answer. The other man shrugged and laid the book down on the table at the side of the room. "Wrap this up, will you?"

It took a second before I realised he was talking to me. I picked my way awkwardly through the aisle between the benches. By the time I'd reached the table he'd gone back to his station next to the stove. He said, scrutinising the end of a tooling wheel, "Brown paper and sealing wax. Label it with the name and volume and mark it 'Vault'. Then fill in a card. I'll show you what to do with that in a minute."

Johnson asked casually, between hammer-blows, "Who was that you've just finished?"

"Runsham." They all laughed.

I picked up the book. It was a slim, small volume, half-bound in leather and marbled paper. I hesitated, but no one was watching me, so I opened it and glanced inside. The endpaper had a thread peeling away where it hadn't been cleanly cut, and there were no whites before the title page. *Sir Percival Runsham, Vol. 11.* On impulse I rolled the fly between my fingers: the grain direction was wrong. I flicked through and stopped, at random. The writing was elaborate and hard to read, full of thorny flourishes . . . *her figure and* decided plumpness, I congratulated her husband on her fecundity, so splendidly demonstrated, and asked him when the new addition was expected; imagine my horror and confusion when he responded with, at first, bewilderment and then offence . . .

"Pity it's not trade, that one," Johnson said. "Runsham'd give some collector a good laugh." He gave the book in the press a final bash, and then started to undo the wooden screws. "You ever seen him make a speech, Hicks? I heard him once at the Town Hall. On his hobby-horse, shouting about the rights of the lower classes . . . The man can't help embarrassing himself. No wonder he gets bound twice a year." He slid the book out of the press, discarded the wedges of wood, and peered at the rounded spine. "That'll do. Well, are you going to wrap that up? Or are you too much of a *proper* binder to bother with the hard work?"

I dragged a sheet of paper towards me and began to wrap the book up as quickly as I could. I fumbled and made a bad job of it; then I realised I hadn't made a note of the name, and had to undo the package to check it again. Finally it was done. I dripped wax on the knot and sealed it with a monogram, an elaborate "d" and "H". I should have guessed that de Havilland wasn't his real name. A tiny shiver of gladness went through me: whatever Seredith's surname was, he'd chosen to change it. He hadn't liked her, or trusted her, or understood her. What did he know, about whether she'd loved me? But the flicker of warmth only lasted an instant: I was here, and it didn't matter any more.

154

Once I'd labelled the parcel the younger man — Hicks? — took it from me and pointed at a stack of cards. "Write the name, the volume and the date on one of those. At the top right, put 'vault'. Now, follow me."

Outside, in the little passage, there was a sack hanging from the wall. He dropped the parcel in. "The books for the vault go in here. The bank only sends the armoured coach once a month, so we keep the door into the street locked and no smoking, all right? You lose a book, you lose your job. Books for trade are kept through there until de Havilland collects them." He pointed at the door opposite us. "See this box here? Cards go through that slot. Every evening they go to the old bat for filing. Got it?"

"I think so."

"Right." The two men who had gone to get the luggage were trudging, heavily laden, across the yard. Hicks pulled the door open for them. They puffed and grunted as they carried the boxes inside and into the workshop. "What's all that, then? Your indenture fee?"

"In a way."

He opened his mouth, squinted at me, and shut it again. After a second he said, "Well, you'd better come in and start making yourself useful."

They set me to wiping the benches — smuts from the stove stained the rag black as soon as I wiped it over the wood — and then to sweeping. The light was fading fast, and I thought they'd stop work when it was dark; but when it was too dim to make out the dust on the floor they lit lamps and went on with what they were

155

doing. It was cold everywhere except next to the stove, and the greasy, acrid smell of coal turned my stomach. I hadn't eaten since breakfast, but no one asked me if I was hungry.

"You can empty the pail into the dustbin at the back," Hicks said. "It's next to the coal shed — oh never mind, I'll show you. You can bring some coal in at the same time. Stoke the stove and then you can call it a day, how's that? Coming out for a pipe, Johnson?"

I followed them down the passage to the far end of the building. The street outside was a narrow, badly-lit lane. It was hard to believe that the row of tall elegant houses was only the other side of the bindery yard. A jumble of walls, jutting corrugated-iron roofs and sheds spilt out on to the unpaved road, and the frost-hardened mud had formed deep ruts, glinting with long streaks of ice. Hicks jabbed his thumb at a low lean-to. I emptied my bucket into the dustbin and began to load the coal scuttle. A dog was howling in one of the cottages opposite. Someone swore at it, and then at a baby that started wailing.

"Gentlemen," a shrill voice said, "gentlemen, please . . ." I looked up. An old woman was picking her way through the frozen channels of filth. Hicks swapped a glance with Johnson and flicked away the match he'd used to light his pipe. "Don't turn away from me, gents. I know what you're thinking but I'm not begging. You're binders, ain't you? Well, I've got something you'd like."

"We're not binders," Johnson said. "You want the binder, go knock at the door in Alderney Street."

156

"I tried. That bitch at the door won't let me in. Come on, gents . . . I'm desperate, all right? But I promise you I've got some lovely stuff. Men'll be queuing up for my memories. Honest."

Hicks drew in a lungful of smoke and the ember brightened in the bowl of his pipe. "It's Mags, isn't it? Listen . . . It's a nice offer. But that's not our job. Even if . . ." He stopped.

"Come on. I won't charge much. A couple of shillings, that's all, for years and years. All the best bits. Whatever you want. Sex. Men beating me. There was a murder in my street, I saw it happen —"

"I'm sorry. Why don't you try one of the backstreeters? Fogatini might be interested. On the corner of the Shambles and Library Row. He might be more —"

"Fogatini?" She spat, thickly. "He's got no taste. He said he didn't sell the one from last month, but that's just an excuse, he's as dry-fisted as a lizard."

Johnson said, suddenly, "Where's your kids, Mags?"

"Kids? Ain't got no kids. Never had a husband, either."

"Lived like this all your life, have you?" There was a bitter edge in his voice that wasn't quite mockery. "You sure of that?"

She blinked and wiped her forehead with the inside of her sleeve, in a strange, disjointed gesture; and suddenly I saw that it wasn't age that had ravaged her face and given that set blankness to her eyes. "It ain't kind to laugh at me."

"I'm not laughing. You've sold enough. Go home."

"I just need a couple of bob. Come on, gents. A genuine slice of life on the streets. Plenty of dukes and earls would pay guineas for that. It's a bargain."

"Mags . . ." Hicks tapped his pipe against the side of the lean-to, although he hadn't finished it. "You've asked before, remember? When Johnson here took you inside for a cup of tea? Or did that go along with everything else, last time?" There was a pause. Mags dragged her hand back and forth over her forehead. "Never mind. Go and find a better way to earn your living, or there'll be nothing left of you."

"Earn a living?" She gasped a laugh and flapped her ragged cloak at him like a dark bird. "You think this is a *living*? A *life*? I don't care any more, I want it all gone, I'd rather be one of them drooling lunatics you see outside Fogatini's when he's gone too deep, I *want* there to be nothing left of me —"

Johnson pushed in front of Hicks and took her by the elbow, swinging her round so hard that one of her legs buckled and she nearly fell. "That's enough. Get out of here. Or I'll call the police."

"All I want is a couple of shillings — one shilling, then. Sixpence!"

He dragged her a few yards down the road and then pushed her. She reeled, glared at him as if she might spit in his face, and then picked her way through the seascape of dirt. As she rounded the corner I heard her cough, a deep throaty sound as if that was her real voice at last.

Johnson strode back towards us. "It's a foul night. I'm going in."

158

Hicks nodded and pushed his pipe into his pocket. Neither of them waited for me; I loaded the last few handfuls of coal into the scuttle and followed. As they went through the door I heard Hicks say, "Does she have kids, then?" and Johnson answer, "Three, living. They'll be in the workhouse. While some lucky bastard reads all about motherly love." Then the door closed behind them.

When I'd stoked the stove I picked up my sack from the corner of the room, and one of the others said, "Upstairs. The room at the back." No one said good night to me. I climbed the stairs, my legs shaking with fatigue. When I came to the little window on the landing I could see my breath. Ferns of frost had already crept across the dingy glass.

The room was tiny, and dirty, and bitterly cold. In one corner there was a sagging bedstead, with a couple of blankets trailing across it; I tried not to think about how many bodies had slept there before me. I could just catch the gleam of a chamber-pot underneath, and I breathed shallowly, afraid of what I might smell. But after a minute the cold got too much and I sank down on the bed and wrapped myself in the blankets; they stank of damp and must, but it might have been worse. The mattress had clumped into hillocks and the ticking had worn so thin I could feel the feathers pricking me. I felt as if I'd never be warm again.

Someone shouted in the street outside. I wrapped the blankets round my shoulders and got up to look out, but the single street-lamp was too feeble and the window pane too encrusted with soot for me to see anything. Whoever it was fell silent. Now there was only the sporadic howling of a dog, and a baby crying. I could feel the greasiness of coal in the grain of my fingertips and crunching between my back teeth. The longer I stayed here the deeper it would get; until nothing would wash it away completely, until even my bones were black.

I shut my eyes. An image came to me, as sharp as a memory: Alta at the door of the dairy, dropping her bucket — her eyes wide with delight — and then running across the yard to hug me. I could almost smell the earthy, ammoniac tang of the pigsty, and the creamy sweetness of new milk draining away from the upturned bucket. At home no time would have passed since I left; it would still be late summer, everyone would be the same, the jobs that I hadn't finished would be waiting for me. Or — no — if only I could unravel further, to before I started to fall ill: right back to last winter, when I still knew who I was. Back to when I worried about the thorn hedge in the High Field, or whether Ma would notice I'd used her good knife to skin a rabbit. But it was stupid to wish something impossible. I opened my eyes and wiped them on my sleeve.

I couldn't go home. But if I was still here in a few days' time, de Havilland was going to send me to the Darnays, for my first binding.

I was afraid. The realisation should have made it easier; but as soon as I'd thought it, I knew I couldn't run away. After I had been to the Darnays, and it was all over . . . *then* I could choose. Maybe I'd think of

160

somewhere else to go — or find a way to return to the bindery, where I belonged. But until then, I had to stay. Or I would be frightened for the rest of my life, without even knowing what I was frightened of — except that it had to do with Lucian Darnay, and the nightmares.

I lay down on the bed. The pillow was waxy with old hair oil. I curled into myself as tightly as I could, ignoring the scratchy lumps of mattress, and stayed very still. At last I began to warm up a little, but the cold held me hovering on the edge of sleep. Through my dreams I heard the banging of doors and the shouts of a drunken scuffle, and the chiming of clocks all over the town; but I suppose I must have fallen asleep properly at last, because when Hicks banged on the door in the morning I woke disorientated and heavy-headed, struggling to remember my own name.

CHAPTER
TEN

Three days later, de Havilland sent me to the Darnays'. He'd summoned me the afternoon before, sending Miss Brettingham, his secretary, into the workshop with a note; when I went to see him — in a cluttered, over-furnished sitting room that was hung so thickly with pictures that the walls hardly showed — he was distracted, poring over a huge marbled ledger while his fingers riffled through a pile of flimsy bills. "Oh yes," he said, "you. Mr Darnay is expecting you tomorrow evening. I'm sending him a delivery at the same time, so don't forget to pick it up from Miss Brettingham. In her office, opposite the waiting room." He raised his eyes and looked me up and down, wincing. "I shall send some appropriate clothes over to your room tonight. Make sure you wash, will you?" He gestured with his pen, dismissing me, and tutted as it flicked specks of ink over his accounts.

"But I —"

"I don't have time. I'm leaving for Latworthy Place first thing in the morning, and I have a lot to do. If you have questions, please ask someone else."

"Who?"

"That one, for example. *Go.*"

When I went up to my room at the end of the day I found an unfamiliar suit on my bed: pale grey, with a blue waistcoat and a clean stiff-collared shirt. It was so out of place in that dirty little room that from the doorway it looked as if an aristocrat had crawled on to the bed to die. When I took a step closer and held up my candle I saw there were shiny shoes, too, and a brushed felt hat, and an ivory box that contained cufflinks and a collar-stud. There was no need to try any of it on; I already knew that everything would be uncomfortable and ill-fitting. I laid it on the cleanest bit of floor, and tried to ignore it; but all through the night I was conscious of its flattened limbs reaching out for me.

The next afternoon I did my best to wash off the day's grime and then shave in icy water, but I'd been right about the clothes and when I walked past the workshop Hicks whistled and called, "Hey, lads, look at His Nibs," and the others dissolved into gales of laughter. De Havilland had taken his carriage to Latworthy, and I had to take a cab; I'd never hailed one before and I stood for ages on the pavement of Alderney Street before a cabbie finally drew up and asked me pityingly if I was lost. For a moment I thought I'd forgotten the Darnays' address. Miss Brettingham had shown me the "delivery" — the chest that de Havilland had filled with books — and I manhandled it on to the seat before I hauled myself up, wishing he could have sent it by post.

I watched Castleford roll past us, but my heart was beating so fast that only fragments seemed to emerge from the blur: a row of new houses, a pillared portico on a corner, shop windows hung with bright swatches of fabric. I could almost believe that it was all an elaborate hoax, and if we'd taken another route I could have peered sideways and seen how flimsy the houses were, how they were only painted greyboard ... I didn't recognise myself, either. I was an impostor, in this silvery-grey suit and pale waistcoat, clenching my toes in shoes that were too tight. I tried not to imagine trying to bind someone, but I couldn't stop myself. I'd fail, and nothing would happen at all; or — worse — it would bring the binder's fever back, and I'd lose control of myself, drown in the black fever-visions, be taken off shrieking to a madhouse ... And what if Lucian Darnay was there, watching? I didn't want to think about him, either. The faint, bitter taste of dread spilt onto the back of my tongue.

The cab rattled on, over the bridge and past the castle — a great mass of ochre stone, half-ruined — and suddenly there was more traffic. Carriages materialised alongside us, close enough to touch. For a few minutes we seemed to be carried in the current; then, at last, the cab slowed and turned into a side street. It was quiet here, and there were rows of bare plane trees along the edge of the roadway.

"Here."

"What?" I craned forward to hear him.

The cabbie pointed with his whip. "Number three," he said. "See the 'D' on the gate? This is it."

I got out of the cab and managed to drop the chest on to the pavement at my feet with a thud. I'd been so preoccupied that I hadn't thought about how to pay the cabbie, and for an instant I panicked; but my hand had already gone into my pocket, and I felt the cool weight of a sovereign against my fingers. Perhaps de Havilland — or Miss Brettingham — had been unexpectedly thoughtful; or more likely the suit hadn't been washed since it was last worn.

The cab drove off. I took a deep breath. In front of me the gate was knotted like a vine, a wreath of iron tendrils surrounding that elaborate D. A gravel drive led across a wintry, cross-quartered lawn to a wide front door set with panels of stained glass. The house was double-fronted, built of old red brick, with tall curtained windows with light behind them. There were symmetrical urns and knobs along the top where the roof met the facade. A house this big would have two entrances, wouldn't it, like de Havilland's — one for gentlemen, and one for ordinary people. I tried to remember Miss Brettingham's instructions. *Be respectful, but not obsequious. Remember you are representing Mr de Havilland . . .* The tone of her voice had left me in no doubt that Mr de Havilland was a great man, and I could scarcely hope to live up to him.

That meant the front door. I crouched to pick up the chest, feeling the ache already creeping across my shoulders. A few months ago I couldn't have lifted it at all. I was supposed to give it to Mr Darnay — *before anything else, give it to him — only him, no one else, you understand?* — but it would be all I could do to get it into the house. Sweat was already starting out on my forehead. My shirt collar rubbed, and I imagined it beginning to wilt, stained grey by the smoke in the air.

Did I imagine the quiver of a curtain at one of the upper windows? I told myself I had; but I could feel a gaze following me down the path, and I was glad to get to the front door. I wedged the chest against the doorframe and managed to ring the bell; then I stood there, my arms trembling under the weight. In front of me the stained-glass panel — a lamp and its flame surrounded by a green ribbon — juddered and leapt. A tremor hummed in my knees, too strong to be the distant vibration of carriage-wheels on cobblestones. My breath was coming very fast.

"Good afternoon, sir," someone said.

But it didn't matter who she was — a quiet voice, a lace cap, a pimple on her forehead — because I could see past her into the hallway; and Lucian Darnay was there, halfway down the stairs, and the ground lifted off its anchor and rocked on a sea of darkness.

Somehow I stayed on my feet. Somehow, when Darnay — Lucian — no, *Darnay* took the chest out of my arms and led me through to another room, I managed to follow, fighting for my balance at every step. Somehow I even heard myself answer him, although I didn't know what he'd said, or what I replied; somehow I sat down and blinked until the world swam back into focus. I was sitting at a polished table, an oval of ebony that gleamed like a mirror. It was a dark room, and although there was grey daylight at the windows the lamps on the wall had been lit. There was a fire in the grate. The fireplace was the colour of raw meat, veined with fat; the wallpaper was a darker shade of the same colour, mottled with burgundy flowers. Against the wall on the far side of the room there was a tall glass-fronted case full of curios. I squinted at the shapes, trying to see past the glare of the gaslight to make out what they were: a plume of feathers, a flight of butterflies under a bell jar, the disembodied grin of a huge jawbone . . . My ears still rang, like someone running their finger round the rim of a glass, but it was almost faint enough to ignore.

"My father will be down in a minute. Will you take something? A glass of sherry? We've just finished lunch, I'm afraid. Dinner isn't till eight."

"Thank you." It was a relief when he turned and busied himself with a decanter. I exhaled a long breath and squeezed my legs together to stop my knees shaking. He didn't remember me. The first time we'd met, he'd stared at me as if he despised me. Now there was nothing, no recognition in his eyes, no trace of hatred or fury — only a trace of contempt that I guessed from the cast of his face was habitual, and nothing to do with me.

"There." He put the glass down in front of me, and I made myself meet his eyes.

"Thank you." My voice came out steadier than I'd expected. I took a sip of the sherry, and felt the warmth of it run down my throat.

"These are for my father, I take it?"

"Yes." I should have moved to stop him before he opened the chest, but he flicked open the clasps with such assurance that it was done before I could say

167

anything. He lifted four or five books and turned them over to look at their spines before dropping them back into the chest with deliberate disdain. He paused once, frowning at the book I had half-glimpsed when de Havilland was packing it, pale and flecked with red-gold like embers on a table; but in the end he flung that one back with more force than the others. As he examined them I had time to observe him. He had changed; the shadows under his eyes were gone, and his face had filled out. There was a flush on his cheeks that would be florid in a few years' time, and his eyes had a kind of dullness to them, like smeared glass; but all in all he was handsome. It was hard to believe that he was the same man I'd seen at Seredith's, the one whose gaunt, bleak face had given me nightmares.

I heard the door open. Another voice said, "You must be de Havilland's deputy."

I half rose to my feet; but the white-haired man in the doorway wagged his finger and gave me a twinkling benevolent smile. "Sit down, young man." He walked straight past his son, and took my hand in both of his. His skin was warm and dry. Now he was close I could see that he wasn't as old as I'd thought, in spite of his bony face and white hair; but he had a kind of ethereal quality, not quite fragile but unworldly. It was hard to imagine this man at the head of the Darnay factory empire. "How enchanting," he said. "You are almost a boy. And already binding for de Havilland! I see so few *useful* young men."

Lucian Darnay gestured towards the door. "Shall I . . .?"

168

"No, no, stay." Darnay senior stared at me as though he were trying to make out my soul. "What a shame he couldn't come himself — I understand Lord Latworthy poached him from under my very nose! Never mind, never mind, it is delightful to meet you instead."

"I'm sure he wished he could have come himself."

"Oh nonsense, nonsense," Mr Darnay said, but with an ease that softened the words. "Anyway, de Havilland has no doubt told you — sit *down*, Lucian! — of our poor Nell, and how she has suffered. No need" — he raised a finger — "to speak of her ordeals in front of my son, he is too *delicate*" — was I imagining that emphasis, or the clench of Lucian's jaw? — "to hear of other people's troubles. But I shall be glad when she is happy again."

"He told me you had a servant who needed . . ."

"Quite, quite." He nodded, excusing me for my awkwardness. "I think a plain binding would be in order. She is a plain girl, you know, not terribly bright, although naturally we are all very fond of her. Did you speak?"

"No," Lucian said. He poured himself a glass of brandy and drank half in one mouthful.

Something like sadness glinted in the older man's eyes, but when he turned back to me his face was perfectly composed. "It shouldn't take you very long. She's young, after all, and the miseries of the young are swiftly taken away. For the binding, I leave the details to your discretion. If you send it back to me bound within a week, that will be perfectly adequate."

"Send it back? I thought — the vault —"

169

"No, no. We have our own safekeeping here. And now I must leave you. I have business to attend to, and I'm afraid I shan't see you again. This time, at least. I do hope our paths will cross again soon."

He patted my shoulder, and swept out of the room.

"Oh, but Mr de Havilland sent these —" I gestured to the chest of books, but it was too late; the door had already closed.

Lucian watched him go. "Charming, isn't he?"

"I'm very glad to make his acquaintance." I realised that he hadn't asked me my name.

"Oh, of course, of course." He tilted his glass until the last drop ran down the bulb on to his tongue. "Why should you care what he's like? As long as he pays you well. Or pays de Havilland . . ."

"It's kind of him," I said, "to care about a servant's unhappiness. Not everyone would."

He laughed, poured himself another brandy, and drank it in one go.

"Like a doctor, aren't you," he said, without a question mark. "You come here and drain a boil. A huge throbbing carbuncle, the size of someone's whole life. Then you wash your hands and pretend you've never smelt anything but roses. And you walk away with heavier pockets, until the next time. So like a doctor. All for the benefit of mankind. Except that you're really doing it because men like my father like the taste of the pus . . ."

"That's disgusting."

"Isn't it?"

170

I looked away. A shadow moved across the glass of the curiosity cabinet, as if something inside had come to life: but it was only Darnay's reflection, as he crossed the room to the fireplace and held out his free hand towards the fire. The cufflink had fallen out of his shirt, and where it flapped open I could see the veins on his wrist, the ridges of his tendons. The skin there was so pale it was yellowish, like ivory.

When he spoke again he sounded tired, as if I wasn't worth the effort. "I'll send for her now, then. Do you need anything else?"

"No."

After a moment he shrugged. "As you wish. Here?"

"I suppose — yes." All I needed was a table and two chairs; maybe not even that. What had de Havilland told me, the day after Seredith died? *You merely have to lay hands on the subject and listen. As long as you take paper and a pen and ink, and make sure you're both sitting down, and that she's consented, you can hardly go wrong.* How could that be enough? A sense of unreality came over me, like when I used to dream I'd been chosen to be Midsummer King and I'd forgotten the steps of the dance. It was too late to explain to Mr Darnay that I was only an apprentice, and that I had no idea what to do. And the thought of how Lucian would look at me made sweat prickle on the back of my neck. I put my bag on the table, opened it, and took out a pile of paper, a pen, and a bottle of ink. I arranged them carefully on the table. Apart from that, the bag was empty. De Havilland's bill, already written out, was in the inner pocket.

Lucian rang the bell. As he waited for the maid he said, "How long do you need?"

"I don't know exactly."

"I understand de Havilland generally pauses for tea at four o'clock."

"I — no. Thank you."

"Fine. I'll get someone to bring your dinner when Nell comes out. Anything else you need, ring for Betty, all right?"

"All right."

For a moment he seemed about to add something else, but the maid came in and he turned away. "Please bring Nell here. And make sure they're not disturbed until Mr — excuse me . . .?"

"Farmer," I said. It made sense that his memories of visiting Seredith had gone, along with whatever else was in his book; but it still felt strange to have to tell him my name.

"Mr Farmer," he echoed, with a faint, mocking emphasis, as if it amused him. "Until Mr Farmer rings for his dinner." Finally he looked at me again, and a spark of malice leapt behind his eyes. "Good luck, Mr Farmer. I hope you find it . . . enjoyable."

I swung away, mastering the urge to hit him. *Enjoyable.* No wonder his father despised him. I was glad that he left the room, sliding out through the half-open door after the maid, or I might have betrayed myself. When he'd gone I sat down and ran my hands through my hair to wipe away the prickling sweat. The woody warmth of sherry lingered on the back of my tongue, tinged with bile. My heartbeat seemed to echo from every corner of the room, every surface reflecting a different timbre: glass, wood, marble, papered wall . . .

"This is Nell, sir."

I staggered to my feet, as if I'd been caught napping. The older maid bobbed and left, shutting the door with a tactful click that felt louder than a slam.

Nell. I hadn't known what I was expecting, until I was surprised.

She was . . . colourless. As though she'd been erased, like a pencil drawing; she was thin, the bones at the base of her neck knobbly and prominent, her face as vacant as a statue. And young — younger than me, younger than Alta. I pointed to the chair opposite me — something in the gesture made me think uneasily of de Havilland — and she obeyed; but her movements were oddly lifeless, devoid of either ease or effort. She wasn't *there*. I swallowed. Milly had been catatonic when she came to Seredith — but that had been a different, ferocious stillness, like the eye of a storm. This was just . . . negative.

"My name's Emmett. You're — Nell? Is that right?"

"Yes, sir."

"You don't have to call me sir."

It wasn't a question, and she didn't answer. I might have guessed she wouldn't, but it felt like a rebuff.

"Do you know why I'm here?"

"Yes, sir."

I waited. Nothing. She should have been pretty, in a mousy sort of way; she should have been shy, or coy, or infuriating, the way Alta was at her age. But she wasn't anything. I pressed one fingernail into the pad of my thumb, and said, as gently as I could, "Can you tell me, then? Why am I here?"

"You're here to wipe my memory."

"Well." But she was right; it was as good a way to put it as any. "Yes. If you want me to. Your employer — Mr Darnay." I despised myself for how pompous I sounded. "Mr Darnay said you were very distressed. Is that right?"

She looked at me. In anyone else it would have been a challenge; but on her face it was like the stare of an animal. She held it until I had to look away.

My collar was itching unbearably. I ran my finger around the back of it, and then stopped, self-conscious. *Make sure you're both sitting down, and that she's consented.*

"Look," I said, "all I need to know is that you want me to bind your memories. If you don't want that . . ."

She bit her lip. It was a tiny movement, but it was the first sign of life.

My heart leapt. I leant towards her, trying not to sound eager. "It would be all right, you know," I said. "It would be good, really, if you felt that you could go on as you are. Much better in the long run. Maybe you feel that you can be brave, and live with what's happened? Maybe you're stronger than you realised at first, when you asked —"

"I didn't ask. Mr Darnay did."

"Oh. Well, yes, I suppose." I hated the sound of my own voice, wheedling, desperately trying to find a way out of my problem. I clenched my jaw and thought of

174

Seredith. She'd want me to do my best, not for myself but for this grey child with her gaunt face and fixed stare. "All I mean," I said, trying to keep any feeling out of the words, "is that you can choose. No one can make you do anything you don't want to do."

"Can't they?"

I started to say, "Of course not," and then something in her face changed and I stopped. What was it, that flicker of expression? A narrowing of the eyes, as though I'd said something contemptible. She went on staring at me. The blankness seemed to come and go. For a few seconds I thought I saw hopelessness like a desert, featureless and impersonal, so vast that I couldn't grasp the scale of it. Then I wasn't sure. Maybe she was simple. Mr Darnay had said *not terribly bright*. I was being melodramatic; it was understandable, I was nervous, my stomach was churning.

She dropped her gaze. Her hands lay in her lap like gloves, the nails ragged down to the quick, dirt lying in lines across her knuckles. Her chest hardly moved when she breathed. "What do you want me to do?"

I sat back. The stiff edge of my collar dug into the back of my neck. *There is the small matter of managing the memories — making sure you don't go too deep . . .* I tried to push away the fear. Seredith had thought I could do this; she'd said I was a binder born. "Suppose you just . . . tell me about it. In your own words."

"About what?"

"Whatever you want — taken away."

She raised her shoulders an inch. Her mouth opened but no sound came out, and after a long time I glanced at the bell-pull. I could call the other maid and leave a message, slip out of the front door before the Darnays even had time to hear it . . . I stood up. Nell's eyes followed me, a second too late. It occurred to me — faintly, in the back of my brain — that perhaps she was drunk; but no, I'd have smelt it, or heard it in her speech . . . "Look, Nell," I said, curling my toes in the tight shoes until they ached, "I haven't been . . . I can't bind you, all right? I got sent here — well, by mistake. I'm an apprentice, and I haven't ever . . . I'll explain to Mr Darnay that it's not your fault, it's nothing to do with you. Mr de Havilland can come in a few days' time, I expect. But I can't do it now. Perhaps I shouldn't have said — I didn't mean to give you the impression — I thought maybe I could . . ." I stopped and added, more quietly, "Do you understand what I'm saying?"

She closed her eyes. "Yes," she said, and her voice sounded very far away.

"I apologise." It came out as stiff as my collar.

She didn't move. Something on her cheeks glinted, and I realised that she was crying — immovably, impersonally, like a statue in the rain. I turned away, and found myself in front of the display cabinet. An intricate Chinese box sat next to something small and shrivelled, like a prune. I leant closer and saw that it was a tiny head, with shells sewn into the eye-sockets. I turned back to Nell.

"Let's just sit here for a while. Then I'll ring the bell and explain to Mr Darnay." I couldn't ring the bell yet; it would look like I hadn't even tried.

"Sit here?"

"To — to rest, I mean."

She blinked, and more tears ran down her cheeks and dripped off her chin. Suddenly she scrubbed them away with her apron, and for an instant I saw the child she must have been — no, the child she *was*. "Rest? Here?"

Her voice was raw, as though some feeling had finally come to the surface; but I didn't know what it was. "Yes. If you'd like to."

"I —" She choked halfway through the word, as if there was something too dangerous to say. Then she nodded, and the mask of inertia dropped over her face again.

"Good." I breathed out, as slowly as I could, trying to ease the tension in my stomach. I pulled out the other chair so that I could look into the fire without craning my neck, and sat down next to her. The flames had sunk to bubbles of red-gold that grew on the logs like fungi, shrinking and spreading and multiplying, their roots tinged with blue. Slow warmth radiated from the hearth, easing the aches in my legs, the tightness that had been there since my journey to Castleford. If I raised my eyes the pattern on the wallpaper slid in and out of focus, from blotches to intricate curlicues and back again, the colour of flayed flesh. The gas lamps flared and whispered. Beside me, Nell's breathing slowed to the same pace as mine.

At last, after a long time, the clock chimed. I glanced at Nell. She was staring at the wall, so fixedly that I wondered if she was sleeping with her eyes open.

"I should call the maid," I said, softly. "Are you ready to go back to your work?"

She didn't respond. I got up, and bent towards her. "Nell?"

Nothing. She was awake, I was sure of it; maybe she'd gone into the same almost-trance that had come upon me, lulled by the silence and the warmth. I looked down at her, my heart aching for the prettiness she should have had. Then I said again, "Nell?" and put my hand gently on her shoulder.

The world lurched and swung. Then it turned inside out.

CHAPTER
ELEVEN

The misery was a grey river, dragging me over and under and through a life so quickly that I only caught glimpses of it. Days darted by. Nights blinked on and off like dark fireworks. I didn't exist, I was part of the icy current, an eye that could see but not speak. What was going on? I fumbled for myself — for my name, my body, anything — but there was no myself, and then no *I*.

A grey blur. The sense of speed almost unravelled me. And then, gradually, it slowed. I could see — I was seeing — I *was* someone else, looking at a world that was off-kilter, skewed by the otherness of alien eyes, the sheer otherness of *her*. Everything was the same but somehow so deeply different that I could have screamed — if I'd existed, if enough of me had been there to be afraid . . . It was steady now, full of details I would never have noticed, blurred where I would have looked more closely. Did I recognise — But I was too mixed up in her to know what I felt — only that she was looking at a front door with a stained-glass panel in the centre of it, a lighted lamp and a ribbon border. She was pleased, excited, warmth glowed in the pit of her belly. I felt her grip on the bell-pull, the strangeness of it, like an unfamiliar glove.

Things whirled past again. A voice, snatched away like a shout in high winds, ". . . not *this* door, the back!" and then it was lost, the scene swallowed by greyness and the rush of more. More flashes, more glimpses, vivid as fever-dreams, growing darker and darker with shadows that weren't exactly visible. A tiny bedroom, up under the eaves, greyish walls and peeling plaster. Cold. Nights that sucked her down with weariness. An old man — younger than he looked — who was kind to her. A black-and-white face that hardly knew she was there. A bosomy woman in an apron who slapped her cheek and pushed a spice bun at her with the same hand, in the same minute. Tidemarks of moisture on tiles, the damp that ate into her knees like lye. The old man squeezing her shoulder. The bedroom again. No key for the door. Staring at curling dingy paint while she squeezed one finger into the lock, trying to reach its innards with her fingernail. No luck. The winter, work that never stopped, the coal-bucket that wrenched her shoulder out of its joint, the old man sitting her down — "smudge on your face, dear . . . my handkerchief . . ." And the bedroom, frost on the black window, the old man, "Don't look so startled, I brought you . . ." Coal. Lying awake, sick with cold, nearly wishing he'd come again, praying he wouldn't. The door handle, clenching her fists as it turned, the old man. "Cold again?"

No. Greyness around her, muffling, smothering. Don't feel. No.

180

Cold morning. Shivering. "What's up with you? Psht, girl." Sick and sick again. No time to dry her uniform. The clammy touch of wet cloth on her skin. The floors, growing dirty as she watched. Dust deepening on the mantelpiece like snow. Crazy. The bedroom. The old man. The smell of the chamber-pot. Think about the smell, think about what you ate and what came out the other end, think about anything but this. No.

Spiders like black knots in corners. Bugs crawling on her arms, invisible. Dirt under her nails. Get it *out*. The sun, hot on her neck. Spring must have come while she wasn't looking. But everything grey, still grey. Choking on the smell of lilac.

A summer-house. The stink of musty cushions. Shaking too much to do up her buttons. The bedroom again, thick with heat, the slick of male sweat on her face. The bedroom, the study, dead summer silence and the suck of wet flesh on hers. The bedroom. Autumn. Blurring now. Grey flickers of her bedroom, over and over, the edges dulled. Winter.

The old man. The old man. The old man.

I gasped for breath. The air hit my lungs like acid. The study danced in front of my eyes, wavering and doubling as though I was drunk. But I was here, I was present again, and the nightmare was . . .

Real. It was still real. But now I was outside of it.

She was opposite me. Her eyes were closed. I shut my own to block her out, but in the darkness behind my eyelids I could see her memories — already fading, distant, unmistakably now someone else's, but still close enough to make me shiver. The old man. Darnay. In her mind she'd refused to give him a name, clinging to *the old man* as if it was the only bit of power she had over him. But it was Darnay. That benevolent glint in his eye, the warmth, the smooth unscrupulous enjoyment . . . My skin crawled. I'd liked him. *She'd* liked him. Before . . .

I tried to breathe deeply and coughed. It hurt to be back here, in my body. But the pain was good, the pain meant I existed, that she and I were separate.

"Sir?"

"What?" I looked up, blinking until my vision steadied.

She was half standing, half sitting, hovering between the chair and the table as if she didn't know where she was. "Did you want something? I'm sorry, I — must have dropped off — it's so warm in here."

"What? No. You didn't — I —"

"Are you unwell, sir? Shall I call someone?"

"No. *No.* Thank you. I just need — some time." I sounded hoarse, as if I hadn't spoken for days. "Nell . . ."

"Yes, sir?"

I looked down. My reflection in the ebony table was like a blurred moon against a dark sky. Shadows swirled in the depths, dancing away as soon as I looked at them directly. I jolted upright, suddenly afraid that I would be sucked under. Nell was twisting the hem of her pinafore, staring at me as if I was at death's door.

"Please go and rest," I said. "You're tired. Mr Darnay —" I stuttered on the name, but she didn't even blink. "Mr Darnay said you could. Someone else will make sure your work is done."

"Oh." She frowned. "Thank you, sir." She turned, paused for a moment mid-step, and then walked out, brushing her pinafore off as if she had only swept the hearth.

The door shut. The sound seemed to echo in my ears, growing into a hum and then a roar, drowning out everything else; then, at last, it faded, and I heard the murmur of the fire and the gaslights, and the faint thumps and voices of the people in the rooms beyond. The clock chimed a quarter, winding up scratchily to a peal that gathered momentum as it went. I took a long breath, testing my body for the old familiar sickness. The darkness bloomed for a second in the corners of my eyes, but as I exhaled I felt the illness pass, leaving nothing behind but exhaustion.

I got up to ring the bell for the maid, so she could call Lucian Darnay; but I paused with my hand outstretched, grimacing at the bitter taste in my mouth. The hearth, the reflection of the gaslights in the glass cabinet doors, the grandfather clock with its smug-faced rolling moon, the rich Persian rug on the floor ... I met the stare of the china spaniels on the mantelpiece, blank over their curled whiskers. I had dusted those, and ached to smash one against the wall, and I had been too frightened to do it. I had polished the grate, desperate to finish it before the old man came in and found me; I could feel the grit of the blacking under my fingernails, the smears I found on my thighs afterwards . . . Everything was tainted with Nell's memories.

I picked up my bag. Next to it on the table was a book-block: a neat pile of unsewn pages, covered with dense lines of writing. I caught my breath. I'd done that. I didn't remember, but I must have done, it was my own handwriting. I blinked, suddenly feeling the burn in my wrist. Of course it had been me; who else could it have been? It took me a long moment to master myself enough to reach out and pick up the pile of pages. I pushed them into the bag and slung it over my shoulder.

I didn't stop to think about what would happen when they found me gone, or what de Havilland would say when he heard I'd bolted. I slipped out into the hallway, my heart pounding as if I was a thief. Through the archway at the end of the passage was the hall, tiled with black and white, with a bank of ferns at one side and a figure behind them who stopped, appalled at the sight of me. I realised it was a mirror. The staircase curled above, hung with portraits, but I didn't pause to look up as I hurried to the front door. I bent to undo the first bolt, and fumbled with the next. My elbow caught a porcelain umbrella-stand and the base scraped loudly on the marble floor.

"Where are you off to?"

A cool, curious voice, one that made my hand slip on the handle of the latch. I spun round. It was Darnay; but the young Darnay, not the old. That was something.

"Going," I said.

"Going where? We're having dinner in an hour. De Havilland always stays."

"No."

"You can't go yet," he said. "Even if you're not hungry, my father will want to see you before you leave."

I shook my head.

"Are you *ill*?"

I opened my mouth to answer, but there was no point. Instead I turned to the door and wrenched the bolt as hard as I could. After a second's resistance it gave way. I reached for the third one.

"For goodness' sake, let the maid bring you some dinner. Then my father will come and pay you and *then* you can leave."

The bolt slid to the side with a sudden rattle. His shadow fell across me, and I felt his touch on my shoulder. I whirled round, swinging out blindly, and my fist thumped into his ribs. He staggered and grabbed at me.

"Just — calm down — I'm only —" His breath was sweet with alcohol fumes. For a second I fought him, breathless. His face in front of me blurred, flickering with Nell's overlaid memories: he had never paid attention to her, never offered her help . . .

He dragged at the strap of my bag, and it broke. I tripped and landed on my knees. The bag fell, throwing its contents across the floor. Nell's pages flew everywhere, a storm of white wings, and drifted slowly to the floor. In the silence, a door slammed somewhere in another part of the house.

He was the first to move. He glanced around, a quick furtive look, as though he was afraid someone had heard; then he pushed himself to his feet and started gathering the paper in handfuls, not quite carefully. "Come on," he said, "help me, will you?" But by the time I rose from my knees he was picking the last few off the side-table and pushing them into the bag with the rest. When he had finished I thought he was going to hand it to me: but he turned away.

"You can wait in the study. Come on." He went back the way I'd come without looking over his shoulder, and I walked helplessly behind him. He was sweating; the dampness made his hair clump together where it touched his neck, and his collar was greasy and translucent along the top edge.

I followed him into the study. He put my bag down on the table. A few white corners peeked out of the top, creased and dog-eared. He glanced at the clock and silently offered me another glass of sherry. I hesitated, but I took it. He watched me sip, and then poured himself more brandy.

"Did it — go well?"

I didn't answer.

He finished his brandy and stood watching me, idly stroking the neck of the decanter. "You binders," he said, in a new, almost friendly voice, as if he were a host and I were his guest. "You give me the chills. What's it like, when you're inside someone's mind? When they're naked, and helpless, and you're so close you can taste them? It must be rather like fucking to order. Is it?" But

186

he didn't expect me to answer. "And then you come grovelling to men like my father, for more."

Silence. The fire scratched and muttered in the hearth.

"There's a growing trade in fakes, you know. Does that concern you?" He paused, but he didn't seem surprised not to get an answer. "I've never seen one — well, as far as I know — but I'm curious. Could one really tell the difference? *Novels*, they call them. They must be much cheaper to produce. You can copy them, you see. Use the same story over and over, and as long as you're careful how you sell them you can get away with it. It makes one wonder who would write them. People who enjoy imagining misery, I suppose. People who have no scruples about dishonesty. People who can spend days writing a long sad lie without going insane." He flicked one fingernail against the decanter, punctuating what he'd said with a tiny clink. "My father, of course, is a connoisseur. He claims that he would know instantly if he saw a *novel*. He says that a real, authentic book breathes an unmistakable scent of . . . well, he calls it 'truth', or 'life'. I think maybe he means 'despair'."

On the wall next to the window there was a dark landscape in an elaborate frame: mountains, a foaming cataract, a half-ruined bridge overgrown with ivy. I focused on it. I wanted to be there, standing on the cracked stone parapet, where the noise of water would drown out Lucian's soft voice.

"Then again," he said, "it makes me wonder about you. The binders. What is it like to steal a soul? To take

187

misery and make it . . . innocuous? To heal a wound so that it can be inflicted again, for the first time?"

"That's not —"

"You tell people that you're helping. Taking away pain, making the bad things go away . . . So respectable. Visiting the grief-stricken widows, the neurotic spinsters, smoothing over excesses of emotion . . ." He shook his head. "You make it all bearable when nothing else can. Is that right?"

"I —"

He laughed, and then stopped so suddenly the silence hung like an echo. "No," he said, at last. "That's what you hide behind. If that was all you did . . ." He inhaled through his teeth. "De Havilland sees the same servants, over and over. My father has whole *shelves* of books." He pointed at the air with a sharp finger. "Mary, for five years. Marianne for three. Abigail, Abigail, Abigail . . . I can't remember how many times, because she was one of his favourites. Sarah, twice. Now Nell. And it'll be Nell over and over, until she's too old. And you'll come back for her, every year, and every year it'll be the same story, and you'll take it away for my father to gloat over — it's a double pleasure for him, to read the story from inside her head and then do it all again as if he's never touched her before."

"No."

"Yes, Farmer." His voice was like a scalpel: so sharp it took whole seconds before I felt the pain. "Why do you think he pays you so much? It's his vice, his clever evil little vice. And when they leave they're sucked dry, bound for the last time so they don't remember

188

anything, they'll deny he ever touched them, they'll tell everyone he's a lovely man, delightful, and if ever anyone tries to do something to stop him ... He laughs. You understand? He *laughs*, because he's safe. When I found out he sent me away and told me I was lucky it wasn't to the madhouse. And it's you — *you*, Farmer, and the rest of you, de Havilland and his friends — that let him do it. That's why he's safe. Because you come and do his dirty work."

"No," I said, "no, it isn't always, it isn't *meant* to be like that."

"You make me sick. I wish you were all dead. I wish I had the guts to kill you now."

I met his eyes. Now I recognised him: he had the same face that had looked at me in Seredith's workshop, hating and hating as if it was the only thing he could do. For a moment I saw the high windows behind him, the wide light of the marshes, and caught my breath.

I might have told him then. I wanted to. I wanted Seredith's ghost to haunt him. She had helped him, and now she was dead and he was glad; I wanted to see his expression change from disdain to fear, I wanted him to be ashamed. I opened my mouth. He deserved to know. But abruptly, unwillingly, I saw Seredith — just before she died, her hand clutching on the key that hung round her neck, refusing to give it up — and I couldn't say the words. No matter how much I wanted to throw it in his face, I couldn't. I turned away.

"I mean it," he said. "I'd kill you, if I wasn't too much of a coward."

An ember subsided in the grate with a soft rustle. One of the gas lamps flared, and for a moment the room was a different version of itself, full of uncanny light. When the jet steadied again nothing seemed real, not even Darnay standing there glaring at me. Suddenly I was very tired. "Yes, I expect you would," I said. There didn't seem to be anything else to say. I picked up my bag from the table where he'd left it.

"What are you doing?"

"I'm going."

"You can't. You have to see my father." He held out one arm as if he could bar my way. He was swaying, and his undone cuff flapped like a grimy wing.

I looked down at the glass he was holding, tilted now so that the last dregs gathered on the rim, and then into his face. Darkness shimmered over my vision. "Tell him I was taken ill, if you want."

"He'll be angry —" He cut himself off. "Look. You have to obey me. You're being paid to be here. You're a servant."

I was itching to hit him; and yet, at the same time, I wanted to fasten his cuff for him, as if he was a child. "Complain to de Havilland," I said. I stepped round him, towards the door.

"Wait. *Wait.* Come back right now."

I paused at the door. He reached for my shoulder, but now I was expecting it and I twisted sharply to break his grip. He stumbled and drops of brandy spattered the wallpaper.

"Please," he said. His eyes were bright and feverish, steadier than I would have expected.

190

"I'm going now. I'm sorry, Lucian."

He blinked. "What?"

"I just said — never mind. Goodbye." I started to open the door; but Lucian reached past me and slammed it shut with a bang. I hadn't realised he could move so quickly.

"I said *wait*," he snapped. His cheeks blazed red and he stank of brandy; but his voice was suddenly precise, and his eyes narrowed. "Did you just call me *Lucian*? Who do you think you are? My *friend*?"

"No, of course not."

"I should hope not. You need to remember your place. You're my father's pander, remember? You're *nothing*." He drew himself up to his full height. "How dare you speak to me like that? When I tell de Havilland —"

"Tell him. I don't care."

"You will be out on the streets. My father will make sure of that. You condescending — you *impertinent* —" He stopped, breathing hard. "A man — a boy like you . . ."

I said, as quietly as I could, "It's your name, isn't it? It's just a name."

"We are not equals, Farmer. Or should I call you . . ." He faltered, as if for a second he was surprised not to know my first name.

"You can call me Emmett if you want," I said. "I don't care a damn what you call me. And no, we're not equals. You think you're so much better than me, but if you knew —" I stopped. Something strange had happened to his expression.

"Emmett . . ." he said. "Emmett Farmer." He frowned, without taking his eyes off my face, as if he was trying to remember.

My heart stuttered.

He turned back to the chest of books on the table. He bent over it, picking up one, then another, putting them to one side. His movements were slow now, almost graceful, as though he had all the time in the world. At last he picked up the one he'd stared at before, a full leather binding, creamy white, with dark spatters of inlay edged with red-gold, as though falling ash had burnt its way through. It looked . . . damaged. I could almost feel Lucian's fingers on the calfskin.

"Emmett Farmer," he said, in a cool, wondering voice. "I knew I'd seen your name somewhere." He turned it over, sliding his hands over the pale skin. Then he turned the spine towards me.

I didn't move. His eyes stayed steady, daring me to react.

EMMETT FARMER.

Some part of me had known. The part of me that had ached with emptiness and misery, that had tried to find the book — *my* book — the night before de Havilland arrived. I hadn't been looking for Lucian. I'd been looking for myself.

Binder's fever. The nightmares, the sickness. De Havilland had called it the binderbound fever. In a flash the name made sense. I'd got ill because I was a binder myself. When Seredith bound me it hadn't worked, not completely, that was why I'd gone half-mad. And that was why I still felt like this, why

Lucian's fingers on the head of the book made me shudder.

"Give it to me." I still couldn't catch my breath.

"I think you'll find that it belongs to my father now. He has an arrangement with de Havilland."

"No!" I lunged for it. My fingers caught the edge, and my nerves sang as if I'd burnt myself. He'd jerked away just in time, and now he backed towards the hearth, laughing. He was holding the book behind his back, out of sight, but I could feel it there as clearly as if it was my own flesh.

"A game," he said. "How amusing."

I threw myself at him, again. This time he was prepared for it; but so was I. The study spun around us — a punch knocked the breath out of me — but I was winning, driving him back towards the fireplace, so furious I didn't care how hard he hit me. Then my arms were round him, my knee drove into his groin, and he bent over and retched, his arms suddenly loose. I dived for the hand that held the book and plucked it out of his grasp. I fumbled and it flapped open, but the pages were blurred, unreadable, as if I was seeing them through smoke. I squinted, trying to make them out — any word, anything — but my eyes wouldn't focus.

He gasped, "You bloody —" and reached for the bell-pull.

Old Darnay couldn't get it. Anything but that. I looked round, frantically — but there was nowhere to put it, no way to keep it out of their reach — they'd take it away from me —

I kicked aside the fire-guard and pushed it into the grate.

For a second it lay in the bed of flames, intact. My ears sang; I heard Lucian's voice, shrill and distorted, unintelligible. Time slowed until I could see the languid lick of the tallest flame, spreading into the air like oil into water.

Then the light leapt around it, and the pages caught fire.

PART TWO

CHAPTER
TWELVE

We shouldn't have been there, not that afternoon —
late in a silver-grey winter day with the sun dying redly
behind the trees — or any other time. We shouldn't
even have been in the woods on the other side of the
lake, where there were pits and man-traps to catch the
poachers. But the traps were ancient and rusted open,
so even if you stepped on them they sank deeper into
the leaf-mould without a quiver; and it was the easiest
way home, and I was freezing and in a hurry to get
back. For most of the day we'd been struggling to run a
thorn hedge across the top of the High Field, but we'd
got to it late, after the ploughing, and although the
earth wasn't frozen solid it was heavy and claggy with
frost. No matter how hard we worked, I was never
warm; the sweat left clammy edges round my collar and
neck where the wind blew through like a knife, and the
cold intensified every aching thud and jar of the spade.
The hawthorn saplings were awkward to handle and
caught my coat with their thorns; I was too clumsy to
disentangle them smoothly and I lost two buttons and
had to scrabble for them in the new-turned ditch.
Everything which would have been easy in better
weather took an effort. By the time we'd finished, a

thin, bitter snow had started to fall, and Pa hardly paused to assess the new line of dark hedge before he gathered the tools and threw them into the back of the cart. "Come on," he said. "I was hoping to dig some more turnips, but not in this weather. It won't last. Best get back to the house and wait it out. Tell you what, I'll look at that dibbling machine."

"I told you, it's the chain, it's got knocked out of shape somehow," I said, pitching my shovel into the back of the cart on top of the other. "I reckon you'll need a trip to the smith."

"Well, I'll check, see if you're right." He clambered up into the seat. "Come on."

I glanced at the sky. The clouds were ragged, and patches of lighter sky shone through; there were still a few hours of daylight left, and I didn't have to be back to feed the pigs for ages. It was cold, but the snow would stop in a little while and the wind had dropped. There would be time enough, over the winter, to huddle indoors by lamplight; now that the hedge was done I was restless, wanting to make the most of the day. "If we've finished here, Fred Cooper was going to go ferreting on Castle Down, and he said if I wanted to come . . ."

Pa was pulling his scarf more tightly round his face. He shrugged, but with an understanding gleam in his eye. "All right," he said. "I suppose there's not much else you could be doing. A couple of rabbits won't go amiss with your ma."

"Good." I hurried down the hill to the valley path, relishing my unexpected freedom. Behind me, Pa clicked to the horse and the cart rumbled away.

When I found him, Fred Cooper had already tried the lower warren without much luck, but we trudged up along the boundary of Lord Archimbolt's lands and the second lot of burrows yielded a good haul of rabbits. The sun was sinking and he was chivvying his ferrets back into their box when we saw a girl running towards us, silhouetted against the blazing streaks of cloud; for a second my heart jumped, hoping it was Perannon Cooper, but then I saw it was Alta. She waved and called to me, her voice blown away in a chill gust of wind. ". . . couldn't bear it," she panted, when she was within earshot, and gave Fred a friendly bob-curtsy. "So Ma said as long as I'd finished my chores I could come and help you carry the rabbits home."

"I don't need help with three rabbits, squirt."

She grinned and turned to Fred, pushing back the wisps of hair that blew across her face. "Hello, Fred. How are you? How's the scaly leg mite?"

"Oh, much better, thank you. Your ma's balm worked a treat." He caught my eye and explained, "Perannon's hens had it. Not me."

"Come on, Tally," I said, taking Alta's elbow and steering her down the hill. "We'd better get back. Thanks, Fred. See you again on Sunday, maybe?"

"I'll send your love to Perannon," he called, cupping his hands to his mouth, and went away laughing before I could answer.

We picked our way down the hill and into the trees. "Lazy-bones," I said. "You still haven't mended that shirt for me."

Alta shot me a sideways smile that was half admission, half defiance. But all she said was, "Trespasser," nodding back at the broken-down fence that I'd led her through.

I shrugged. Lord Archimbolt was as useless as his rusted man-traps — rumour had it that he was holed up in one room in the New House, groaning with rheumatism, all winter — and what was more, the land should have been ours. It *had* been ours, until seventy years ago. I wasn't going to let a rotten bit of fence keep me out, not if he couldn't even be bothered to keep it standing. As long as we kept to the path, out of sight, no one would notice; and if the rabbits were *technically* poached, because the boundary bulged out over the down to cover the warrens . . . well, there wasn't a gamekeeper, and no one else would care. I wanted to get home, now. The bite of evening was sharper in the air, and I pulled my coat tighter round my shoulders. "Come on, keep up. And don't wander off the path, there're man-traps around."

She nodded, sauntering along behind me with her skirts hoicked up. But as the path curved up through the woods towards home she broke away and scrambled down to the edge of the trees. I heard her crunch through the deep grass of the bank that lay between the woods and the old castle. Then there was the metallic scrape of hobnails on ice, and when I looked over my shoulder she was already halfway across the frozen moat, sliding a little at each step and giggling, her arms out to keep her balance. In front of her, the ruins of the tower stood out black and bare against a fiery sky.

"Alta! Come back!"

"In a minute!"

I cursed under my breath. It was freezing, and every inch of exposed skin already ached with cold. Soon it would be dark. When we were kids we used to dare each other to go into the ruins, in the spring and summer. I remembered the sunlit green of overgrown walls, the silty moat like jade-coloured satin, the deep soft silence until we exploded into giggles and shrieks of mock fear; but now, looking at the walls standing stark and rotten in the wintry landscape, I could almost believe that the place *was* haunted.

Alta skidded and lurched to the far side of the ice, and paused briefly to wave at me. Then she scrambled up and across the grass. She darted through a weather-eaten doorway.

"Damn it, Alta . . ." I took a deep breath. The frost in the air stung the back of my throat. I set off across the ice, steadier and more careful than Alta had been. This early in the year the ice was new — the moat froze over before anything else because it was so shallow, left undredged for centuries — and the millrace and the canals on the other side of the village hadn't even started to freeze; but it crackled instead of bending, and I got safely to the other side. By then, there was no sign of her — no movement or sound at all. The bare trees were like a pen-and-ink drawing against the sunset. "Alta!" Something stopped me raising my voice above a murmur. Slowly I clambered up the far bank and walked along it, hoping to catch a glimpse of her. At last I crossed through a narrow gap in a low hedge and found myself in the flat circle of grass that stood in front of the ruined tower. There was a massive wellhead in the centre, blocked up years ago; now it was a stone plinth with a prone, carved figure on it, like a tomb. To my left was a stone staircase that led to a door draped in threadbare ivy, and the empty windows in the tower above it were hung with bloody curtains of cloud.

Where was she? I cleared my throat and said, "Alta! For goodness' sake!" but my voice was small and husky.

Nothing. A long way away a single bird croaked and fell silent. I turned slowly, my neck tingling as if someone was staring at me; but the sensation stayed with me no matter which direction I faced. There was only the empty ice, empty windows, empty doors. Everything waited.

At last I turned back to the overgrown circle and the wellhead.

The effigy on the wellhead moved.

My heart jammed like a lock. I stumbled backwards, grabbing for a support that wasn't there. The last ray of the sun blazed out suddenly, dazzling me, throwing a crimson tinge across the moat and the sparse snow on the ground. I blinked. When my vision cleared the figure was sitting up, his face shadowed by a hood, his cloak and the stone plinth stained red by the sunset.

"You're trespassing," he said.

I took a step back, pushing my hands into my pockets. The blood tingled in my cheeks. A breeze sang a mocking note in the high windows.

"I'm just trying to find my sister." I swallowed. My voice had come out cracked and hoarse.

"Then she's trespassing too."

"So are you, if it comes to that."

"How do you know?" He jumped down from the stone and approached me. He was nearly my height, but not quite. He pushed his hood back, and I saw his face properly: thin, bony, dark-eyed. "Maybe I've got every right to be here. Unlike you."

I stared at him. The dusk was thickening around us, like ink spreading through water. In his dark cloak he looked like part of the landscape, as though the spirit of the place had come to life — or death: his white, gaunt face was like something you'd find in a grave. I took a deep breath; I had to make an effort to step around and past him, so that I could scan the far shadows for Alta. "I'm going in a minute," I said.

"What's your name?"

I didn't answer. Nothing moved, and now the distinct tracery of the trees was blurring into thicker shadows. I strained my eyes for a movement, or a flash of her dress.

"Let me guess. You look like . . . a Smith. No? Poacher? Farmer?" I couldn't help glancing at him, and he whistled through his teeth and grinned. "Farmer, really?"

I turned my back on him. The moat was dulling from silver to pewter as the light failed. Something rustled in the undergrowth, behind the gnarled rhododendron trees that sprawled across the far bank, but a moment later a fox slipped out on to the grass and ran away.

"Speaking of poaching, whose rabbits are those? You know the penalty for poaching is deportation?"

"Look —" I swung round, belatedly aware of the limp bodies that hung over my shoulder.

"Emmett!" Alta's voice rang off the walls, echoing so that for an instant I wasn't sure which direction it came from. Then I ran towards her, glad to turn my back on him. I came out through an arch on to a little stone jetty.

She was waving from across the moat. "I found apples," she called. "Old ones but they're still sweet. Who's that with you?"

He had followed me. I glanced at him once, and then said, "No one. Come back *now*."

She peered through the dim light. "Hello, no one," she said. "My name's Alta."

"Lucian Darnay," he said, and bowed to her. It was a low, sweeping bow, so exaggerated it seemed to take an hour; but she beamed and curtsied back as though she hadn't noticed the mockery.

"Come *on*, Alta. I'm freezing. We shouldn't be here anyway."

"All right, all right! I'm coming. I just want to —"

"I'm going." I turned and strode back towards the other side of the little island and the path that led to home.

"I said I'm *coming*." I kept on walking and Alta's voice petered out. I pushed my way through the reeds, testing the ice with one foot; in front of me there was a candled patch, but I edged out beyond it to where the ice was as smooth and white as plaster. I took a deep

204

breath and stopped to wait. When I turned I could just make her out, standing on the other side of the moat, almost lost in the dusk: a black figure among the trees. Darnay stood between us.

Did Alta say something? I wasn't sure. It might have been another sound, a bird or the mutter of wind in the undergrowth. But after a moment she sidled down to the edge of the ice — one arm twisted awkwardly, trying to hold the apples in the crook of her elbow — and out into the middle of the moat. But she didn't come the most direct way, straight across the water and past Darnay, to me; she wandered sideways, to the widest part of the water, where the ice would be —

It opened under her feet like a mouth. A second of disbelief — a cut-off yelp, not even long enough to be a scream — and she was gone.

I ran through air that held me back. My boots slid on dead grass, throwing me off balance; I couldn't breathe, as if it was my body and not Alta's that had gone through the ice.

"It's all right! Stay there!" He got to her first. She'd dragged herself to her feet, gasping, the dark water up to her waist. He threw off his cloak and used it like a rope to help her on to solid ground. Then he shook it out and wrapped it round her, pulling it tight so that she was a bundle of black cloth, with only her face showing. When I got to her he stood up and hoisted her to her feet after him. "Where do you live? How far is it?"

"Not far. Ten minutes' walk —"

"I'll take her. She'll catch her death."

"We'll be fine now. Thank you." But she was wheezing, with an awful hissing noise like a broken bellows. I raised my voice and reached out to her. "Alta, for pity's sake, what were you thinking? You could have —"

"It'll be quicker to ride. My horse is just across the bridge. Alta can direct me. Can't you, Alta?"

She coughed and nodded. "Please, Emmett — I'm so cold —"

I started to say, "Walking will warm you up," but she was shaking, and the icy water was soaking through Darnay's cloak. "Fine. Go on, then." I turned to Darnay. "You'd better get her back safe, or —"

But he was already running to the bridge, with Alta stumbling along after him. I watched the two of them disappear up the path and into the trees. In the dusk the rhododendron bushes seemed to inch closer once they'd passed, cutting off the path behind them, and soon I couldn't make out their backs; but the clear chilly air carried the sound of Darnay's voice, and the clink of hooves on the path as they rode away. Suddenly I was alone. The rabbits over my shoulder were heavy and their fur had the softness of mould. I shivered, in a compulsive spasm that left me feeling worse than before.

I turned and started to trudge back home.

When I got home no one noticed me. I stood at the bottom of the stairs in the kitchen, looking up: I could hear Ma fussing in the bedroom, her voice echoing in the grate as she laid a new fire, and Alta's hoarse replies. At the top of the stairs — where they would have seen me if they'd only looked down — Pa and Darnay were talking. Pa was hunching his shoulders the way he did when he spoke to the schoolmaster or the beadle from Castleford, who sometimes came here to visit his brother; Darnay said something and Pa laughed, with a quick obsequious gesture. Darnay smiled and swept his hair back from his forehead. He was wearing my best shirt. The cuffs were starting to fray, and it was yellowish round the collar with age.

I almost went into the kitchen to wait until he'd left; but instead I strode up the stairs and pushed past them, into Alta's bedroom. She was reclining on a bank of pillows like the heroine of a ballad, and the colour had come back into her cheeks. She looked so much better that when she spoke her hoarseness sounded like an act.

"Hello, Emmett."

I stood where I was, looking down at her. "You little idiot. I *told* you not to leave the path." Alta rolled her head to one side without answering, and stared into the fire. There was a smile playing round her mouth: a small, secret smile, as if she was alone. "Alta! Did you hear what I said?"

Ma looked up and frowned. "Why didn't you stop her, Emmett? You should know better. If it hadn't been so shallow —"

"It's all right, Ma," Alta said. "Lucian rescued me, didn't he?"

"Well, yes, thank goodness, but . . ." Alta started to cough. Ma leapt to her feet and bent over her. "Oh,

207

sweetheart. Shallow breaths, slow as you can. There, that's better."

"Can I have something to drink?"

"Of course." Ma hurried past me, with only a sideways glance to tell me I wasn't forgiven.

When she'd gone, Alta lay back on her pillows and closed her eyes. The coughing had brought a deeper flush to her cheeks.

"Thanks, Alta. Now they think it was all my fault." I drew in my breath. "Honestly. What on earth were you thinking?"

She opened her eyes. "I'm sorry, Em —"

"I should think so!"

"— but I couldn't help it."

"You should have looked where you were putting your feet. Anyway, you shouldn't have gone out on the ice in the first place. I *told* you . . ."

"Yes, I know." But she sounded preoccupied, as if she was listening to music no one else could hear. She bent her head, one finger following the pattern of the quilt.

"So . . ." But I didn't know what else to say. I leant forward, trying to see her face. "Alta?"

"I've said I'm sorry." She looked up, and sighed. "Please, will you leave me alone, Em? I'm ill. I've caught a chill, I think."

"And whose fault is that?"

"Why can't you just be kind to me, for once?" She went on before I could react. "All I want is to rest. I could have *died*, Emmett."

"Exactly! That's what I'm —"

"So just stop going on at me, will you? I want time to think." She shifted against her mountain of pillows, so that all I could see was the back of her head. Her plait was coming undone.

"Fine." I strode to the door. "Good. You just lie there and think about how stupid you were —"

"I wasn't stupid! I thought he'd save me, and he d —"

There was a silence.

I said, "Wait. *What?*" She didn't answer. I crossed the room to the bed in two steps. I grabbed her shoulder and rolled her over, not gently. "You did it on *purpose?* So he'd rescue you?"

She pulled away from me. "Emmett! Sssh — he's just downstairs —"

"I don't care! You threw yourself on to a patch of rotten ice so that some supercilious get you'd never met before would — *possibly*, you didn't even know he would — pull you out? How could you? What if you'd died? What if —"

"Sssssssh," she said, scrambling to her knees on the bed, her eyes wide. "Please, Em, please don't."

I took a deep breath. "I hope you have nightmares about drowning," I said. "I hope you wake up choking and screaming. Don't you *ever* take a risk like that again. You understand? Or I will kill you myself."

"You don't understand. You're just jealous, because Perannon Cooper wouldn't throw herself into a frozen river for *you!*"

I caught her eye. There was a pause; that smile began to creep into her face again, her attention turning to the mysterious music that I couldn't hear. I turned aside and pulled the curtain sideways to look out into the yard. It was dark, and there was nothing to be seen, but I could hear that the cows were restless in their stalls. Alta hadn't milked them, of course. A patch of stars blazed coldly over the gable of the threshing barn. When I was sure that I could speak calmly, I said, "Don't worry. I won't tell Ma and Pa."

I let the curtain drop and strode to the door.

"Emmett? Where are you going?"

I went out on to the landing and shut the door on her voice. The different strands of my anger tightened into one huge knot, until I had to press my hands against the wall to try and steady myself. In my mind's eye she stepped on to the ice and fell through, and Darnay swept past me, his dark cloak swirling. Even now, standing on the landing, with warm lamplight spilling up the stairs and Ma rummaging in the blanket chest at the end of the passage, I could feel the cold space around me, the stone walls, a red, tattered sky . . . I blinked. On the wall opposite me, Great-Aunt Freya's sampler advised me to *Behold the Daughter of Innocence, how beautiful is the Mildness of her Countenance.*

Ma called to me, over an armful of blankets, "What are you doing? Did you leave Alta on her own?"

"She's fine." I pounded down the stairs and into the kitchen; and then stopped dead. Darnay was there alone, standing next to the stove and looking idly at one of the prints on the wall. I swallowed, staring at him, taken aback by my own fury: but I couldn't stop myself thinking of Alta dropping through the ice, and the way

210

my feet had slipped under me as I tried to run. It was his fault. And then he'd swept her up without a second thought, as if he had a right to her. She might have *died*.

He looked round, but when he saw that it was me the expression on his face froze over so quickly I wasn't sure what it had been before. I said, trying to keep the anger out of my voice, "What are you still doing here?"

"Your father went to find me a cloak. My clothes are wet."

"That's my shirt."

"Your mother said I could borrow it. Your father's would've come to my knees." When I went on staring at him he shrugged and turned back to the stove. He was even thinner than I'd realised; the collar of my shirt hung loose on him, and I could see the top of his spine. He shifted, as if he could feel me looking.

"I see you've helped yourself to my trousers, too."

He turned round. There was a faint wash of red along his cheekbones, but his eyes were level and steady. "Your mother offered. She said you wouldn't mind. But perhaps you'd rather I took them off?"

"Of course not."

"If it's an imposition —" Abruptly he started to draw the shirt over his head. I caught a glimpse of his hip above his waistband, jutting under bone-white skin.

"Come off it!" I turned away instinctively. "Don't be grotesque."

"Thank you." A pause, then the rustle of fabric. "Don't worry, I'll return them at the earliest possible opportunity."

211

At last I thought it would be safe to look at him again. His hair was damp and rumpled and the red had spread across his cheeks. The shirt was even shabbier than I'd thought: it had worn so thin across the ribs that I could see the light through it, and I noticed for the first time that there was a puckered stretch of seam over his shoulder where Alta had cobbled it together. It gave him an air of being in fancy dress.

I took a long breath. "Thank you for rescuing my sister —"

"You're welcome."

"— but I think it's time for you to leave."

"Your father's just trying to find a cloak for me."

"Now."

He blinked at me, and frowned; then he looked down, tugging at one fraying cuff. I waited for him to move towards the door, but he stayed where he was, rolling the loose threads between his finger and thumb. "You don't seem very pleased that I brought your sister home."

I exhaled, slowly. "As I said. Thank you."

He shook his head. "I'm not asking you to thank me."

"Then what do you want, exactly?"

"Nothing! That's what I'm saying. All I did was bring her home." He added, "It's not as if Alta —"

"What about Alta?" I tried not to picture her face, a moment ago: flushed, her eyes sparkling, smiling to herself because this man had rescued her.

"Well . . ." He hesitated. Then he tilted his head, a glint in his eyes. "She didn't exactly . . . push me away."

He was laughing at her.

I flung myself at him. He staggered backwards and thumped into the wall, my forearm across his throat, his eyes wide. He tried to wrench himself away, gasping, but I leant all my weight on his larynx. He coughed out, "What the —"

"Don't talk about her like that!" I put my face a hand's-breadth from his, so close I could feel his breath on my mouth. "She's a child, all right? Just a stupid child."

"I never said —"

"I can see what you think of her."

"Let go of me!"

"Listen." I eased the pressure on his throat, but when he tried to pull away I grabbed his shoulder and shoved him back. His head thudded against the wall. "You're going to forget this ever happened, all right? If you come within a mile of Alta, or my parents, or me, I'll kill you. Or worse. You understand?"

"I think I've got the gist."

Slowly I let go of him. He straightened his collar — my collar — without breaking my stare; but his fingers were trembling, and I was pleased.

"Good. Then you'd better go," I said.

"You'll want your clothes back, I imagine."

"No." If Ma had heard me, she'd have been furious; but I didn't want them back, not now. "Keep them. Burn them." I looked him in the eye again, daring him to be surprised.

He tilted his head to one side, as if he was conceding a point; then he bowed low to me, with an over-elaborate courtesy that made me feel like a peasant.

Then he went out into the freezing dark without a backward glance.

CHAPTER
THIRTEEN

The next morning Alta fainted at the top of the stairs and was helped back to bed, delirious, insisting that the floor was about to give way; but there was no time for Pa and me to worry about her, because the snows had arrived in earnest and the sheep were in the Lower Field. All I remember of that day is a howling white blur as we laboured to get them to shelter, the sting of furious wind driving needles of ice into my face, the burn of freezing air in my throat and the thump of blood behind my eyes. The blizzard was so loud we had to shout to be heard: when we'd finally got the flock to safety, and we dragged ourselves back to the house and collapsed in the kitchen, I could still hear a high strain keening in my ears. The blood scalded my forehead and cheeks as it made its way back to the surface of my skin. Pa was cursing, too, but in a loose, relieved way that told me how worried he'd been. But we couldn't stay there for long — just a few minutes, to warm up and eat something; there was more work to be done, not to mention Alta's chores, now that she was ill.

The next night, just before dawn, the rotten corner of the woodshed roof gave way under the weight of snow, and after I'd fed the livestock, milked the cows and cleaned the dairy pans, I spent a freezing morning trying to repair it while meltwater ran down my sleeves and rolled down the back of my neck. Then it was the familiar drudgery of mucking out the pigsty and the stalls, chopping wood . . . all the little bits of work that had to be done, while the cold and the deep snow made every movement an effort. On top of it all we lost a shearling ewe, and when Pa refused to sell the carcass to Alfred Stephens for broxy I had to step between them before Alfred lost his temper. Everyone's nerves were on edge; even Ma snapped at me, and once, while she was waiting for the doctor to come to listen to Alta's chest, I found her in furious tears because she'd used salt instead of sugar in a seed cake.

In all of this, I had so little time to myself that it should have been easy not to think about Darnay. But somehow from time to time I'd look up from whatever I was doing and wonder about him: where he was, where he lived, whether he'd got home in his — my — shirtsleeves without catching a chill. He'd taken me at my word, and hadn't returned my shirt; I'd had to barter a spare one from Fred Cooper, and hope Ma didn't notice. It showed he wasn't as chivalrous as he'd pretended, and I was glad of it; and even more glad, fiercely glad, that I'd managed to warn him off Alta. But at the same time I was on edge, as if I was missing something, as if I was waiting.

It must have been a week or two before Alta recovered enough to ask about him. It was one evening after dinner, one of those days when the daylight seemed to have lasted an eternity but still not long

216

enough to get everything done. I was exhausted and aching all over, and the sun-bright snow had sown flickering stars in my field of vision. I would have gone to bed, but there was a fire in Alta's room, and mine was cold and dark and unwelcoming; so I tiptoed in and slumped in the chair beside her. It was warm, lit only by the fire and a single lamp, and the golden half-dark softened everything into a comforting blur: Alta's sleeping face, the intricate hearts and diamonds of the quilt, faded to a rusty pink, the worn curtains, the solid gleam of the iron bedstead . . . I stared into the fire, thinking of everything and nothing. I wondered when Springle would drop her litter, whether I could invite Perannon Cooper to Turning dinner, whether the Grove Field would be better for the sheep after all, and whether the tup Pa had insisted on would prove to be worth the money. But in the shadows behind all that, there was a figure — slim, dark-eyed, staring at me with a challenge in his face.

"Did Lucian come to see me?"

I started. "What?"

Alta rolled over, pushing damp strands of hair off her forehead, and said again, "Did Lucian come to see me? Ma said I'd been feverish for ages, and I can't remember."

"No."

"Not once?"

"No."

I could see her heartbeat fluttering in the notch above her collarbone. "He said he would."

"Well, he didn't."

"What about his clothes?"

I shrugged. Ma had said only that day, with an appalled in-breath, "Oh my goodness, he didn't come back for his shirt! And that expensive cloak . . . He'll think we're thieves."

I'd slipped out to the stables without a word, and worked myself into a sweat hauling more water for the horses than they needed.

"But that's awful," Alta said, "he'll think you've stolen them."

"He probably doesn't want them any more."

"He must do. And he said he'd come to see me. I don't understand why he hasn't."

"I expect he's forgotten that you exist."

She frowned, and huddled herself into a sitting position, the quilt wrapped round her shoulders. The movement made her cough. I reached out and took her hand, squeezing it with a steady, gentle pressure until she managed to breathe properly again. "You silly sausage," I said. "Look at you. You're like old Jenson's threshing machine, spluttering and choking all over the place."

She rolled her eyes. "I didn't mean to get ill."

"You did it to yourself," I said, keeping my voice as light as I could. "And all for nothing. All for some boy who hasn't even bothered to find out how you were doing. He's probably gone back to wherever he came from, anyway."

"He's Lord Archimbolt's nephew."

"What?"

Alta winced and pulled her hand out of mine; I must have gripped hers too hard suddenly. "Cissy Cooper told me. He's from Castleford, but he's staying with Lord Archimbolt to help run the estate or something. His family's awfully rich, Cissy says. Lord Archimbolt's bailiff told her grandpa's friend, and he told Cissy's father, and —"

I said, "So he lives in the New House? How long's he there for?"

"No one knows. Maybe forever. Maybe he'll inherit when Lord Archimbolt dies."

I got up, but it was a small room, and there was nowhere to go. I crouched down in front of the grate and jabbed the poker deep into the heart of the fire, trying to break the logs apart.

"He said he'd come and see how I was. He said he'd send for fruit from Castleford for me."

"Well, he clearly didn't mean it." The poker broke the spine of the largest piece of log, and it collapsed in a spurt of sparks.

"What's wrong with you, Emmett? Why do you hate him so much?"

I sat back on my heels. The draught lifted a fragment of bark and a fiery line crawled across its edge; then it flew upwards, whirling like a flake of grey snow. "You're better off without him," I said. "He won't — people like us don't — you couldn't . . . You know what I mean. Forget about him."

"No, I *don't* know what you mean." I glanced at her; she was leaning forward, her cheeks scarlet. "You don't know anything about him. Why shouldn't he care about me?"

"*Care* about you? Alta — you're a child he pulled out of a pond. That's all. Stop *thinking* about him, for pity's sake!" We glared at each other. "And in any case," I said, more slowly, "as you said, he promised to come back and see you, and he didn't. So draw your own conclusions."

Silence. The ashes flared and went pale. If I wasn't careful the fire would go out completely. I put the poker back and stood up.

"What did you say to him?"

"What?"

She narrowed her eyes. "You said something to him, didn't you?"

"Of course I didn't. I didn't need to. He was never going to come back and see you, Alta."

"You beast, Emmett!" She scrambled out of bed and flung herself at me. I fended her off, as gently as I could; but I was scared of hurting her, and she landed a thump on my shoulder, and then her palm cracked across my ear like a whip.

"Alta, stop it, for goodness' sake!"

"You're lying! *What — did — you — say?*" She punctuated each word with a blow. At last I caught her wrists and swung her on to the bed, not as softly as I should have done. For a few seconds we wrestled, as if we were children again, and then she went limp on the pillows, coughing. Her face was as red and damp as a little girl's, and her hair stuck darkly to her cheeks.

I sat down on the bed next to her, smoothing the nearest patch of quilt while she coughed herself to silence. "All right," I said. "Yes, I told him to stay away."

"Why?"

"Because I was afraid —"

"How could you?" She pulled herself upright and stared at me, her eyes fierce. Her voice scratched in her throat. "Emmett, how *could* you? I don't understand. He would have come to see me, he *would*. And then . . ."

"Yes, and *then*?"

She stared at me silently. Then she dragged the quilt up to cover her face.

"Alta."

She said, her voice muffled, "You've spoilt it! Everything. My whole life."

I rolled my eyes. "Don't be ridiculous."

"You don't understand!" Her face emerged from under the covers. "This was *it*, Em. I knew, the moment I saw him. I love him."

There was a silence. I waited for her to giggle and look away first; but she didn't. I'd never seen this expression on her face: certain, passionate, feverish. There was a tight, uncomfortable knot in my stomach. "Don't be absurd. You don't know him. How can you possibly say that?"

"I know," she said. "I knew the moment I saw him — it was love at first sight."

"That's just a fairytale, Alta. You have to know someone before you fall in love."

"I feel like I've known him my whole life! When I saw him — Listen, Cissy says . . ." She sat up, her eyes intense. "Cissy says that sometimes witches come in the night — no, *listen*, Em — and they leave you a pile of gold and when you wake up your memories are gone. So what if I already know him, only I've forgotten, and we've *actually* been in love before and that's why —"

"That's nonsense," I said. "For one thing, don't you think everyone else would notice if you suddenly lost your memory?"

"She says it happened to her second cousin, and that's why she's a bit funny in the head."

"You're not *that* funny in the head."

"Emmett, I'm serious!"

"Show me the gold, then," I said, sitting back and crossing my arms. "No? Exactly. Now stop being stupid."

"What would *you* know about love, anyway?" Suddenly she rolled over and buried her face in her pillow. She started to sob.

I stood up. Then I sat down again, reached out and touched her shoulder. She shrugged me off violently and went on crying. I gritted my teeth and tried to muster the strength of will to walk out; but I couldn't leave her like this, weeping as if her heart was broken. "All right, I'm sorry. Please don't cry. Come on, Tally . . . I'll make it up to you, I promise. He's only a boy. Lots more boys in the village." *But I want this one,* her voice retorted in my head. "Please stop it. Just stop it, Alta. Please. Please don't cry. Look," I tried to pull her over so that I could see her face, but she went stiff at my touch and I gave up. "I'm sorry. I was worried."

She said, her voice muffled, "You're sorry?"

"Yes. I didn't mean to upset you. I just —"

"Will you write to him? And apologise?"

I hesitated. She started crying again, more quietly. I told myself it was just a tantrum; but there was a desperate, despairing note in the sound that made me lean back and hiss through my teeth. "I suppose. If I must."

"And ask him to come and see me, like he said he would?"

"I — he won't come, Alta, I'm sure he won't."

She rolled over. Her face was flushed, her eyes bright and still brimming with tears. "Make him come."

I ran my hands through my hair. "All right," I said. "Just stop crying."

"Thank you." She wiped her cheeks with the insides of her wrists. She took a deep, shuddering breath. "I'm sorry I shouted, Em."

"You know I hate being called that."

"Sorry, *Emmett*." She gave me a watery grin and a joking punch on the arm. Out of nowhere a deep, nasty bit of me wanted to punch her back, harder. "You're the best."

"Thanks, squirt." I reached out and tugged her plait until she flicked it out of my reach. I stood up. "You'd better get some more sleep. I'll see you tomorrow."

"You'll go tomorrow morning, early?"

I nodded.

"Good night, then." She snuggled down into her blankets and pulled the quilt up to her chin. I was at the door when she said, sleepily, "Emmett?"

"Yes?"

"I'm going to marry him."

The driveway to the New House was deep in snow, clogged and white and silent. It was a grey day, heavy with the threat of another snowfall, and I was on horseback so I could get home as soon as I could. Every now and then a tree dropped a slithering load of snow on to the path, or a bird scuttled in a bush; but there was something about the quietness and the light that made me rein in my horse, anxious not to make too much noise.

At first glance, through the trees, the house looked dead: but when I came out on to the wide white space in front I saw that there was smoke coming from one of the chimneys, and the doorstep had been swept clear of snow. In summer the sandstone would have been the colour of honey, but in this light it was grey, like everything else. I scanned the windows for anything that moved, but the reflections clung so thickly to the glass that I couldn't see anything but pale sky. I jumped down, grabbed the string-and-brown-paper parcel of Darnay's clothes and crossed the open space to the massive front door. The battlemented tower loomed above me, and I felt a shiver of the same irrational foreboding I'd had in the ruins. But all I had to do was leave the package here, where someone would stumble over it. My letter — tucked behind the knot — was addressed to him, so they'd know who it was for. I hesitated; I wasn't sure of the right thing to do.

The longer I lingered here, the more chance there was of seeing him. Without giving myself time to think better of it, I pressed the bell-push as hard as I could; and then turned aside and leant against the cold wall of the porch. A bird landed on the roof above me with a scratch and a flurry of wings, and a few handfuls of snow drifted past. The door opened, sooner than I'd expected. It was him.

His eyes narrowed as if he was about to say something. But he didn't.

"I've got your clothes."

He dropped his gaze to the parcel I was holding, and then brought it back to my face.

"Here." I held the bundle out. He rocked back on his heels, and I realised he'd half expected me to hit him. Finally he took it from me.

"I've still got yours," he said. "I would have ridden over with them, only I gathered that I wasn't welcome."

"It doesn't matter."

"Thank you." He laced his fingers into the string, and looked up at me. "It must have gone against the grain, to come here."

He made it sound innocent; but the mockery was there, like a shard of glass in a bowl of water. "I wasn't expecting to see you," I said. "I thought there'd be a housekeeper."

"Oh, of course," he said. "As you see, this house is run like a well-oiled machine. In fact, I don't know why you didn't just leave it with the gatekeeper."

The gatekeeper's lodge was a ruin, with holes in the roof and half the windows gone. When I'd ridden past it I'd heard something scurry across the stone floor. I clenched my jaw and turned to leave.

"What's this?" As I looked over my shoulder he pulled the folded bit of paper out from behind the string.

"It's an apology. Alta told me to —" I stopped. With an effort I added, "I shouldn't have spoken to you like that."

"Spoken to me? You mean, attacked me?"

I turned round and looked straight into his eyes. "Don't test your luck," I said.

A silence. We stared at each other. It felt like being on a narrow bridge, high over a chasm: one tiny nudge and we'd both fall.

At last he lifted one shoulder and gave me a crooked almost-smile. "All right," he said. "What should I do now? Tip you sixpence?"

I didn't blink. It gave me a tiny flicker of satisfaction when he gave a quick huff of laughter and looked away. I said, "My sister would be delighted if you came to visit her."

"Visit her? Really?" He narrowed his eyes. "What happened? Did someone find out I was Piers Darnay's son and heir?"

I took a deep breath. "She wants to thank you properly."

"I rather got the impression that you didn't want me to see your family."

226

"Look, what I said . . . I'm sorry." It almost choked me. "She'd like to see you. You'd be welcome. That's all."

He nodded slowly, turning the envelope over in his fingers.

"You don't need to read that, now." I reached for it.

Quicker than thought, he whisked it away, out of my reach. "That's for me to decide."

I fought the impulse to wrestle it off him. I didn't trust myself to speak. I strode away through the snow, conscious of his eyes following me. It was a small victory when I mounted my horse in one smooth movement.

I wanted to ride away without looking back; but in spite of myself I paused where the drive began, and shot a glance over my shoulder. He was still standing in the doorway, although an icy wind was rattling the slates on the roof. He raised the hand that was holding my letter. "Give my regards to your parents," he called, his voice clear and flat in the snow-muffled quiet. "And tell your sister I'll see her soon."

Two days later I came into the yard to find his horse tethered beside the gatepost. I hadn't looked at her properly before — she was a chestnut mare, heavy and docile, the sort of horse that you'd ride if you were nervous about falling off — but I knew she was his from the quality of the saddle. No one from the village would ride with a saddle like that; if we could afford to own one, it would be too good to use.

I dumped my basket of kindling next to the woodpile. It was getting dark, and I almost tripped over a stray log that had fallen near my feet. I swore and caught myself on one of the new posts that held up the lean-to.

"Emmett?"

Alta's voice. The stable door opened and spilt lamplight across the cobbles. I blinked, shielding my eyes against the sudden glare. "You should be in bed," I said. "It's freezing."

"Springle's had her puppies. Come and look."

I jumped over the basket and hurried into the stable after her. It was warm with the fug of horses and hay, and Hefty whickered to me in greeting; but I brushed past him with only a quick pat on his nose. "How many?"

"Only two. But they're both alive."

I got to the furthest stall, which we'd kept empty, and hung over the end, peering into the straw. Springle was fussing, covering the pups with her body; but then she moved restlessly to the other corner, and I caught a glimpse of two small bodies, whip-tailed, one dark and the other whitish. I felt myself grinning.

"They've fed all right, and Pa checked them over, and they look healthy. And they're so *sweet*."

They were. I leant further over the end of the stall. Springle saw me and wagged her tail, but when I stretched my hand to her she ignored it and went back to the pups. They started to feed, their blind faces nuzzling into Springle's belly, and I would have sworn that I could hear the gulp of milk as it went down their throats.

"They're very small."

Darnay's cool, flat voice broke the spell, and I nearly lost my balance. He was behind me. "Yes," I said, steadying myself on a timber upright. "They are. Very small."

He took a step forward out of the shadows and stared down into the stall. He was wearing the same dark, expensive clothes that he'd had on before, and a thread of straw clinging to his lapel caught the light like a fine gold chain. He looked at the puppies as though he was wondering how to make a pair of gloves out of them. "Like little furry slugs," he said. "With tails."

"I know," Alta said. "Aren't they lovely? Budge up, Emmett." She hooked her feet into the crack between two planks and hoisted herself up next to me, squeezing me sideways so that Darnay could see too. "Oh look . . ."

"The black one'll be a ratter," I said. "Bet you."

"That's what Pa said!" Alta wrinkled her nose at me. The black pup gaped a blind, newborn yawn and settled into the straw. "How can you tell? I think you're both guessing."

"He just looks . . . determined." I caught Alta's eye and started to laugh. "He *does*! I'm not making it up."

"Anyway, that's the one Pa's keeping. He says we can't look after another bitch."

"So the white one's going to Alfred Carter?"

"No, he changed his mind, Mrs Carter said they've got too many already. We'll have to find somewhere else for her." A current of icy air slid down the back of my collar.

"Will you sell her?" Darnay said.

I glanced at him over Alta's head, and then away again. "She's a terrier," I said. "Not a carriage dog or a hunting hound."

"So . . .?"

"So if no one wants her, no one wants her."

"Don't, Em," Alta said. "I expect one of the Millers will take her. Or if the gypsies come back this year . . . They always want more dogs, don't they?" But the brightness in her voice was forced.

The little bodies were twitching now, in trusting puppy-sleep. "Yes," I said. "We'll find somewhere for her."

Darnay frowned. "What if you don't?"

I shot a quick look at Alta. She was staring down at the pups. She was pretending not to have heard, but the delight had gone out of her eyes. I said, "Don't worry about it, Darnay."

"What happens to her?"

I hesitated. Alta glanced up and down again. She picked up a strand of straw and started to play with it, pulling it through her fingers over and over. Darnay was watching her too.

I said, "If we don't, Pa will drown her." There was a silence, filled with the rustle of straw and the splash of one of the horses pissing.

"But surely —"

"You asked, Darnay. That's the answer."

"I see."

"Do you? We can't afford to be sentimental about animals, here."

Alta said, "Em, stop it, please don't —"

At the same moment, Darnay said, "Could I have her?"

Alta twisted sideways, hooking one arm over the edge of the stall. We both stared at him. At last I said, "What?"

"Could I . . .? I'd pay you for her. I'd take care of her. I've never — I may not be a farmer, but I'd try and make sure she was looked after."

"The puppy?"

"What? Yes. Who did you think I meant?"

"Why would you want a terrier?"

"I just . . ." He took a long breath. Something came and went behind his eyes. "Does it matter? I promise I'll look after her."

"Oh yes, that's perfect, thank you so much! And then she'll have a good home. Isn't that right, Em? Pa will be so pleased, thank you, Lucian!" As Alta jumped down Darnay reached past me, offering his arm to steady her. For a split second she hesitated, her hand not quite touching his, her face alight. Darnay smiled down at her, and she smiled back. She said, without looking at me, "Em, isn't he kind?"

"We can find someone else." I was glad when Darnay turned aside, his smile fading.

"Don't be silly! Of course you can have her, Lucian. After all, you saved my life. And now you've saved hers." She took a step towards him, her fingers curling into her palm as if she could still feel his almost-touch.

For a moment he looked into my eyes, with a level, unreadable expression. Whatever it was that had almost surfaced, it was hidden again now. Then he turned and said to Alta, "Thank you."

"I'll go and tell Pa." Alta walked away. Her eyes were shining. The stable door banged shut behind her, and I heard her start to cough in the cold air. Then it was quiet again.

Darnay peered into the stall, very still. I stared at him until he glanced back towards me. "You can't have her until she's three months old. At least."

He nodded. In the lamplight his face was tinged golden, like an ancient idol. A draught swirled a few stems of hay along the floor, and I felt a shiver start at the base of my spine. I clenched my teeth, determined not to let him see.

"I'd like to visit her, though. So that she gets to know me."

I had been about to walk away. I stumbled and caught myself; the hobnails on my soles scraped so loudly on the floor that Hefty shifted and blew through his mouth. Darnay's face was open and guileless; I let my eyes travel over his white collar, the stray strand of straw on his lapel, all the way down to his polished black boots. Somehow he had walked across the farmyard without getting them dirty.

I held out my hand. "Well played."

"What?"

"It's what you were after, isn't it? A standing invitation?"

He looked down at my outstretched hand. I pulled it back before he could shake it and use my own gesture to make me feel small.

"I've always wanted a dog, as it happens."

"Of course you have."

"And if your father would drown it, otherwise —"

I hissed air through my teeth. "Forget it. You've won."

"Look, I don't know what you think we're fighting about —"

"You don't have to try to charm *me*. You've already got the others kneeling at your feet."

He stared at me, a faint line between his brows. It made heat run through me like the beginning of a fever.

The door banged open. Alta said, "Pa's so pleased, Lucian. I knew he would be. Now let me get her out of the stall and you can hold her, only quickly 'cause Springle won't like it, but she can get a sniff of you at least, and — what's up with you two?" She looked from me to Lucian and back again. "Emmett, you look like you're constipated."

"Don't stay out long, Alta."

I walked away and left them together.

CHAPTER
FOURTEEN

I hoped Darnay would change his mind; but when he didn't come the next day I was filled with a perverse disappointment, as if someone I wanted to fight had apologised. The week after that was blank, white weather — not snowing, but with a sky that matched the drifts so closely that my eyes played tricks with distance. I tried not to think about Darnay, but it was easy to let my mind wander and my gaze slide over the unfamiliar softness of the contours, the smoothness of fields that should have been a different shape, and then . . . Once, slogging back through the deepest snow at the bottom of the High Field, I tripped over a hidden stone and went flying; and when I caught my breath again I didn't know where I was. It was only when I stumbled to my feet and steadied myself on the wall that I recognised the repair that I had been meaning to do for months, and shook my head incredulously that I had been — just for a second — lost, *here*. That night I slept badly, and all the day after that I felt itchy and irritable. Everything seemed to go wrong — I kicked over a bucket of milk, a pig got into the dairy when I was careless with the latch, the threshing barn roof threatened to give way and another of the ewes was killed by a fox. Pa was in as foul a mood as I was, and Ma didn't have time to worry about us, except when she set me to hauling water for laundry while she fed the chickens and did Alta's other chores. Finally I nearly took my finger off in the turnip-slicing machine; that brought me to my senses. I pilfered a slice of bread pudding while Ma's back was turned and took it into the stables to eat it while I watched Springle suckling her pups. But even the new pups were an irritant; for a long time I didn't know exactly why, until I realised they were a reminder of how he'd looked at me, and the way he could somehow make his disdain *stick*, even when he wasn't there . . .

"Lucian!"

I didn't know how long Alta had been calling. I shoved the last mouthful of pudding into my mouth and went out into the yard. She was at the window, waving; and there was the sound of hooves on the road beyond the yard, steadily getting nearer. But the snow muffled everything, so it took me off-guard when, hardly a moment later, he rode past the end of the wall and dismounted in front of me. We stared at each other. At last he nodded, with a sort of wary acknowledgement, and brushed himself down with exaggerated care. He'd been riding, and his coat smelt of horse and his high boots were flecked with mud; but I'd been working all day, and I knew that I stank of sweat and was covered with dirt and cobwebs and sheep muck. It should have made us even, but I turned away from him, feeling my cheeks flush. There was an axe lying next to the chopping block, and I reached for it stupidly, as if I'd been busy splitting logs; I grabbed the nearest chunk of wood and split it down the middle with a thunk.

Perhaps he would have said something in the pause that followed; but by that time Alta was in the doorway. "Come and see the puppies," she called, and I heard Lucian go to her. Had he hesitated, waiting for me to acknowledge him? I didn't care. I split another three logs before I went into the stable after them.

"She's going to have a big black patch, look," Alta was saying, cupping the puppy gently against her chest. "Here. Hold her."

"What if I drop her?"

"You won't," Alta said. "There. Isn't she sweet? What are you going to call her?"

"I hadn't thought about it." He lifted the puppy awkwardly. "You're right, she looks like someone's spilt something on her. An ink-stain. I suppose we could call her —"

"You're not going to call her Inkstain," I said.

He glanced round; he hadn't known I was there. "I wasn't suggesting we should. How about Spatter? Or Blot?"

"Splotch," Alta said. The puppy opened its mouth and yawned, as if it had heard, and Alta giggled. "There, you see? Splotch."

So Splotch it was. Darnay didn't seem to care; or at least, he only smiled when Alta smiled, as if all that mattered was that she'd suggested it. He treated the pup like a baby — tentatively, deferring to Alta on everything — and I despised him for it. It was so obvious what he was doing: every half-smile, every

236

tender tap on the puppy's nose was for Alta's benefit. And when he came to our farm — once every couple of days, after that — it was to see Alta, not the puppy. When her cough got worse again and she had to go back to bed for a week he spent hours at her bedside, playing games and teasing her while she gorged herself on the chocolates he'd ordered from Castleford.

I stayed away, at first. If he had to be here, I didn't want to see them together. But after a week or so, Ma pulled me into the pantry as I went past, and shut the door behind me with a click. "Emmett? I need to have a word with you."

"What? In here? It's freezing."

"It won't take long. It's about Alta. And — Mr Darnay."

Mr Darnay. My feelings must have shown on my face, because she cut me off before I could answer.

"Listen to me, Emmett. I know you don't like him — don't look like that, do you think we haven't noticed? — but you have to think of Alta."

"I *am* thinking of Alta, that's exactly why —"

"This might be a chance for her. If he falls in love with her —"

"That's mad! He won't."

"I know it's only a chance. But think of what it could do for her, Em. If he married her . . . It happens! Not often, I know, but she's very beautiful, and he just *might*. He's rich, and he's good-looking, and he's charming, and he's young. She won't get a better opportunity than this. Don't ruin it."

"You want to sell her at the highest possible price."

Ma tugged one earlobe, pinching it until her fingernail left a tiny red crescent. At last she said, "I don't expect you to understand. You're very naive, Emmett. Even more naive than Alta. But nevertheless I need your help."

"*Help?* What should I do, sing her praises to him? Tell him she'd be a fantastic f —"

"Don't you *dare*!"

There was a silence. I pushed my hands into my pockets and took a deep breath. "What do you want me to do?"

"Contrary to what you seem to believe," she said, with an edge to her voice, "we love Alta dearly and we don't want her to get hurt. I hope, I desperately hope that Mr Darnay might change her life. But if he doesn't, I don't want her reputation to suffer. We want to know that she's never — that no matter how she feels, she's never tempted to . . . fall."

"She thinks she loves him," I said. "Of course she's going to be tempted to *fall*."

"Well, then. All we want you to do is to . . . keep an eye on them. To make sure she doesn't."

"You want me to *chaperone* them? I have work to do, Ma, I don't sit around all day with my tatting!"

"Don't be silly, Emmett. I know you're busy. I don't mean all the time. Just now and then, when you have a spare moment, and they're alone together. We have to protect her."

I clenched my fists in my pockets and stared past her at a jar of preserved medlars. *Split-arses*, they'd called them at school. You had to let them rot before you could get your teeth into them.

"Ma . . . she'll get her heart broken."

"No one ever died of a broken heart."

"She's only a child."

"I was only a year older than her when I married your father. And this is a wonderful chance, Emmett. Can't you see that? What if someone offered *you* a better life?"

"If it was Darnay offering, I'd tell him where to . . ." Ma's eyes narrowed, and I caught myself in time. "I'd say no."

Ma sighed, picked up a couple of jars and pushed past me. In a brisk, brittle tone, she said, "Just make sure they know you might walk in unexpectedly, Emmett. Will you do that, please?"

"All right," I said. But she'd already gone.

I obeyed her. I didn't want to; I had to steel myself to it, at first, and every time I walked up the stairs to Alta's room I was already begrudging the time I was wasting on them. People thought winter was the quiet season on a farm, but if you didn't get the repairs and maintenance done before the spring came you'd be cursing — or rather, Pa would be cursing at me. And I resented Darnay's presence for other reasons, too — the way he looked at me, the way I was conscious of the stink of pig-muck or oil or sweat clinging to my shirt, the way he made my stomach churn. Somehow I always knew when he was under our roof, even when I hadn't seen him arrive. I used to hope that I'd catch him out, so I could tell him to leave and never come back; but he never looked guilty, or as though he had anything to hide. That was another thing I distrusted, that he never did anything more than tug Alta's plait or flick her cheek with his finger. He was *too* brotherly, as if she was nothing but a child.

But as the days went on I found myself spending more and more time with them. There were a few chores, after all, that I could bring inside. As the days grew shorter I was glad to sit in the lamplight, where I could see to mend tack or whittle trennels or pore over the seed catalogue, swotting for a long argument with Pa about the best proportions of fescue and timothy grass. It was bitterly cold — I'd brought Springle and the pups inside, so that their box could sit by the range — but because Alta was convalescing she always had a good fire in the grate. And sometimes it was almost pleasant: the warmth, Alta and Darnay talking in low voices or silently absorbed in a game, Darnay whistling a soft melody between his teeth while Alta made a mess of her embroidery. Sometimes, in spite of everything, I had to clench my jaw to stop myself laughing at something he'd said. Sometimes I had to dig my nails into my palms to remind myself not to let him charm me too.

It was one afternoon, nearly past sunset, and Alta had been in a bad mood all day. She'd tried not to show it in front of Darnay, but I knew the signs: she was curling a lock of hair jerkily round her finger, and now, suddenly, she was staring at me. "Don't you have something better to do, Emmett?"

240

"What?" I'd been watching the game of patience Darnay had laid out on her quilt, biting my tongue when he missed a jack of hearts that would have freed up a whole column.

"Why don't you go and do something useful? You don't have to stay here if you're bored."

"I'm fine, thanks."

"You're sitting there glowering."

I felt the blood come into my cheeks. Darnay had paused in his game; now he was looking from Alta to me, with a crease between his eyebrows. I'd tried so hard, these last few weeks, not to show how I felt about him. "Shut up, Alta."

"No one's making you sit here. Lucian is too well brought-up to say anything, but —"

"Alta." Darnay tapped his cards into a pile. "I'm fine."

"You're only being polite. Em, if you can't be civil, why don't you just *go away?*"

"I live here," I said. "I've got every right —"

"Don't you dare move, Lucian! I forbid you to go. Emmett, why don't you just —"

"Alta, you don't need to ask anyone to leave on my account," Darnay said. He met my eyes. "I'm sorry."

I stared back at him. "What for?"

"I only — all I meant was . . ." He blew out his breath through his teeth. There was a silence. He scraped the cards together into a pack without looking up. "Listen, Alta, it's getting late. I'll be back tomorrow."

"No!" She grabbed his sleeve and looked up at him, wide-eyed. "Please don't go yet."

He shot me a look and I shrugged. Then, abruptly, he shoved the pack of cards at me. "Shuffle those, will you?" He sat down and leant towards Alta, cupping her face gently so that she had to look straight at him. "It's not Emmett who's being rude, it's you," he said. "Stop it."

"Wh-what?"

"I'm fine. Emmett's fine. Either you behave, or we both go." She blinked at him, utterly bewildered; then, to my surprise, she laughed a little, fluttering her eyelashes. "You're right," she said. "I'm sorry, Lucian."

"It's all right." He laughed too and tapped her nose with his forefinger. "Now," he said. "Let me tell your fortune. Let's have a look." He took the cards and laid four in a line on the quilt. As he laid them out I saw her brush her own cheek as if she could still feel his touch. He raised his head. "Two of spades, two of hearts, knave of spades, ten of spades. Hmmm. Interesting."

"Is that bad?"

"No," he said, "not at all." He pointed at the two of hearts. "That's love. The two of spades before it means . . . I'm not sure. Maybe that you'll fight. Or you won't realise at first that's it's true love. And the knave of spades . . . A dark young man. You're going to fall in love with a dark young man. And he'll love you back. How's that?"

She looked at him, drawing in her breath. She wasn't smiling. For a moment I glimpsed the woman she would be. "Then what?" she said.

"Then . . ." He shuffled the cards back into the pack. "That's as far as it goes," he said lightly, and grinned at her. "I expect you'll live happily ever after. Now, you lie there and think about that, and I'll be back tomorrow. And I'll see if I can bring some of those candied fruits you like. All right?" He stood up.

She nodded. That odd, adult look was still on her face, like a white light shining on her. He reached down and ruffled her hair. "And no more tantrums," he said.

She watched him leave. If he'd turned back, he'd have seen the way she looked at him; but he didn't bother, he ran down the stairs like a schoolboy after the last lesson, grateful to have escaped.

He was in the kitchen when I caught up with him. I saw him through the half-open door, crouching on the floor, but when I came in he got to his feet with the puppy cradled against his chest. "I'll go in a minute," he said. "I was just looking at Splotch." I didn't say anything. After a moment he frowned. "What? Why are you looking at me like that?"

I shut the door behind me. "What do you think you're playing at, Darnay?"

Carefully he lowered himself again and tipped Splotch back into the box. But he didn't stand back up; he knelt there, looking up at me, while he held his finger out for her to chew on. "What are you talking about?"

I breathed in, slowly. "So Alta's going to meet a dark, handsome stranger, who's going to fall in love with her, is she?"

He shrugged. "Look, it wasn't — it was just a —"

243

"What? A joke? A game? It didn't occur to you when you made it up that she might —"

He raised an eyebrow. "What makes you think I made it up?"

"Because . . ." I hesitated. In a lower voice I said, "I suppose it was a coincidence, then. That you told her exactly what she wants to hear."

A flicker of something came and went in his face. "I thought all little girls wanted to meet a tall dark stranger."

"Damn it, Darnay!" I dropped to a crouch opposite him so I could look full into his face. "Don't be so disingenuous. How *dare* you tell her you love her?"

His face went blank. He pulled his hand away from Splotch. "I never said anything of the kind."

"Oh, of course, you had no idea what she was thinking!"

"Don't be absurd." He stood up. "I don't know what you're suggesting, exactly — but if you imagine I have designs on Alta's virtue . . ."

"You must think I'm stupid."

"Well . . ." He looked me up and down. "I'm not sure how to answer that."

I squared up to him. My heart was hammering. It was driving me mad, this constant desire — no, *need* — to hit him, when I knew I didn't dare. "Why can't you just leave her alone?"

A pause. He folded his arms and stared at me. At last he said, "All right. I admit it."

"What?"

"You're right. I'm going to seduce Alta — I mean, I know she's only a child, but that just adds spice — and then abandon her. If she's expecting my child, so much the better. Ruin her life. And yours, and your parents', as well. Just because I want to. I enjoy that sort of thing."

I stared at him. His eyes were like jet: inert, inhuman. My throat was so tight I could hardly breathe. "You — really . . ."

"No!" He spun round and took a few steps away from me. "No, not really! For goodness' sake, who do you think I am? I save your sister's life, I bring her home, I visit her when she's ill, I bring presents to cheer her up, I adopt a puppy to stop it getting killed. And you look at me like I'm planning a murder. Why?"

"Because you make my skin crawl!"

Silence.

"At least you're honest." He sounded tired. He unhooked his cloak from the peg on the wall and put it on. "Don't worry about Alta. She'll be fine."

I bent my head and turned away. I heard the door creak and swing shut, and his footsteps in the hall. A gust of wind rattled the tiles on the roof. It would be freezing out there; but then, he'd ridden here in snow and ice, he could ride home.

I went over to the dogs' box and looked in, but the pups were asleep. Only Springle turned her head and thumped her tail. If it hadn't been for Darnay, Splotch might have been dead by now.

But there *was* something wrong about him. I wasn't making it up.

I reached out and held my hand over the hottest part of the range, daring myself to touch it.

For the next few days I avoided them both. A while ago I'd promised to help Alfred repair the chimney of his cottage; it was freezing, and the wrong weather to do it, because we had to make sure the frost didn't get to the mortar, but I insisted. Ma and Pa swapped glances when I told them I'd be working in Fields Row for a while, but I'd finished the stackyard fence the day before and Pa only gave me a look over his slice of pie. Ma said, "Very well, dear, I'll do Alta's chores," and went back to her breakfast. I bent my head to hide my face, slicing my bread into smaller and smaller pieces.

But in a couple of days the job was finished, and it was back to work around the farm. It was nearly the Turning, and the pig had to be slaughtered, and the log and greenery brought in; normally I liked all the preparations, but it felt like every time I turned round I caught sight of Darnay coming or going. When Ma and I brought the pig back from the singeing fire he was riding into the yard. As he passed I felt Ma's eyes on my face. Suddenly the stench of burnt pig hair and blood on my clothes could have choked me. I wiped away the sweat on my forehead and trundled the wheelbarrow through the open gate. I didn't glance at Darnay, although I heard his boots click on the cobbles as he dismounted; I went straight to the pump and splashed my face with icy water. It took a couple of hours to butcher the carcass, and then I set up the smoker in the yard; it wasn't until late that afternoon, when it was dark, that I washed away the grime and strode upstairs. My heart drummed as I went into Alta's room, but Darnay nodded at me coolly, as if he'd forgotten what I'd said to him. "Hello, Farmer," he said.

"Darnay," I said.

He tilted his head a little, acknowledging me. Then he went back to the game he was playing with Alta. There was a silence, punctuated by the roll of dice, Darnay swearing softly and Alta giggling. I bent my head and fumbled with the harness I'd brought up to repair, but it was a long time before my fingers were steady enough.

After that it was as if we'd declared a truce. We didn't look at each other more than we could help; when we had to speak, it was in a bloodless, neutral way, as if we'd never met before. I was afraid Alta would notice that we were behaving differently — that I no longer glared at him when he tugged her plait, that he no longer treated me with mocking courtesy — but when Darnay was there she didn't notice anything or anyone else. She was happier than I'd ever seen her, and it made me ache all over. It couldn't last, like this; sooner or later, she'd see that Darnay didn't love her.

But the days passed. Somehow one afternoon I realised there were only two days to go before the Turning; everywhere I looked there were wreaths of evergreens, glittering gold-paper stars and red baubles, and the kitchen smelt of cinnamon and melted butter. Alta had spent the last week making ivy garlands — incessantly and carelessly, as if she couldn't bear to look away from Darnay for an instant — and he and I hung them up while Alta directed us from a settee, wrapped in a huddle of blankets. She was bright-eyed with excitement, and Darnay kept glancing at her and smiling. "No, that's lopsided, you've got to pin it up in the middle," she said.

"Very well, my lady." He swept her a bow — still holding one end of the garland — and then leant sideways so far that the chair he was standing on wobbled. "Here?"

I looked down at the heap of dark green leaves, which were already starting to lose their gloss. "I'm going to fetch more pins," I said.

"Good idea. Oh come on, Alta, does it have to be absolutely *perfect*?"

I went into the kitchen and started to root through the dresser drawer, looking for pins. Ma was rolling out pastry on the table, lightly dusted in flour and as flushed as Alta. "Oh — Emmett — get down that jar for me, will you? And while you're here, will you stoke up the range? And measure out a pound of sugar, will you, and put it on for caramel? Where did your father go? He promised to pluck the goose."

When I finally got back to the parlour, they were kissing.

I froze in the doorway. No. They were dancing. She was in Darnay's arms, but he was twirling her round, navigating smoothly past the furniture, their heads close together. Darnay was humming, a sort of melody that dropped into a breathless "One — two — three —" and then "Side — together — good — blast, my fault —" before he tried to pick up the tune in the same place. "La la la — yes, that's right — *la*," he sang, and Alta giggled. "Stop it, I can't — that was definitely *your* fault." They ground to a halt, laughing.

"Let's go again."

"You mustn't get tired."

"I won't." She smiled up at him, her breath coming quickly. She looked . . . beautiful. And his hand on her waist was elegant, aristocratic, a hand that had never done a day's work and would never need to.

"Well, *I'm* getting tired," Darnay said. He pushed a wisp of damp hair off her forehead and let go of her as if it was all one gesture. "What about the rest of these garlands? Didn't your brother go to find some pins?" He looked at the doorway, and saw me.

"Emmett!" Alta said. She skipped towards me, light-footed, as if she was still dancing. "Lucian's teaching me to waltz."

"I saw." I put the box of pins down and concentrated on prying off the lid.

"Did we look good?"

"I can see Darnay knows what he's doing."

"I've never done it before, Em, you can't expect me to do it properly straight away. I just need to practise."

She reached for Darnay, but he laughed and shook his head. "Sorry. I don't have your stamina."

"All right then, show Emmett what to do. Then by the time you come back I'll be perfect."

I said, "Alta, you've only just been allowed out of bed."

"I think I should be going," Darnay said at the same time.

"Oh no! *Please*, Lucian. Just a few minutes. It's Turning Eve tomorrow, you're meant to be kind."

He bit his lip, half-smiling, and caught my eye. "Why don't you teach him, Alta? Now you know what to do."

"All right, I will. But you have to stay and correct me when I teach him wrong." She manhandled me sideways, so that we were facing in the same direction. "Copy me. You step forward, side, together, like this — see? One, two, three . . ."

I tried to follow what she was doing. Darnay looked as if he was trying to bite back a grin.

"No, like this — oh, you're so slow!"

Darnay said, "Give him a chance, Alta." I paused and glanced at him, but he was watching my feet. "Don't rush him. You weren't much faster yourself."

Alta sighed and tugged at my elbow. "Got it? Now, if you stand there and I stand here — you put your arms like this." She tried to fold me into shape, like a puppet. "And then you lead, one — two — three — oh, for goodness' sake!"

"What did I do? I thought I got it right."

"You're meant to *lead*. It's not meant to be *me* pushing *you* around. It's different when Lucian does it."

"I'll bet," I said, under my breath.

"Lucian, show him." She grabbed Darnay's arm and pulled him towards me. "Show him what it's like."

I started to say, "I don't —"

250

Darnay said, at the same time, "I'm not —" We fell silent, staring at each other. Darnay's expression was guarded, and his cheeks were pink. "I don't think your brother wants my help," he said. "Especially not with waltzing."

"Don't be silly," Alta said. "Just show him."

Darnay didn't move. He was waiting for something. Belatedly, stupidly, I realised what it was. "It's all right," I said, in a tight, unfamiliar voice. "Show me."

"You want me to dance with you?"

I took a deep breath. "If you want. If that's what Alta wants."

He looked at me for a long time, his face unreadable. "Won't it . . . make your skin crawl?"

"No," I said, as steadily as I could. "I don't think so."

He narrowed his eyes as if I were an animal he was thinking of buying. I felt the blood building in my own cheeks, hotter and hotter. I looked away.

He laughed. It was a strange, wary, pleased sort of sound; the sound of winning without knowing why. "I think you were doing pretty well, actually," he said. "Your feet are fine. You need to get used to it, that's all." He reached out, and hesitated. "Are you sure?"

"*Show* him! Such a fuss about nothing," Alta said. "Honestly, *boys.*"

Darnay took a step closer to me. I flinched and felt him draw back; before I had time to think about it, I made myself reach out and take his hand, the way Alta had taken mine. It was warmer than I'd expected, and sticky with sweat: it felt ordinary, friendly, like Ma's or

251

Perannon Cooper's. "Go on, then," I said. "If we must."

"Ready? One, two, three — *one* two three, *one* two three . . ."

He was stronger than I expected. We waltzed round the room, and suddenly I understood what Alta meant: I hardly had to do anything, just let myself go. But it was like an embrace, sickeningly close, so close I couldn't catch my breath. One two three . . .

I stumbled. He let go of me instantly. "There. Now, you can show Alta."

"Yes." I blinked, trying to stop the room from spinning. The momentum wouldn't release me. I took a step sideways and reeled. Darnay caught my elbow to hold me steady. The heat of his hand seeped through the fabric of my shirt like water. I pulled away — foolishly, instinctively — and he sprang back, his face suddenly frozen. "Thanks, Darnay," I said, but it sounded thin.

"Alta!" Ma was standing in the doorway. "What are you doing? I said you could come down here if you stayed on the settee!"

"Oh — I was —"

"Back to bed. Excuse me, Mr Darnay. Happy Turning." Ma bundled the blankets into her arms and flapped at Alta. Alta sighed, gave Darnay an intimate flash of a smile, and followed her.

Darnay and I were left alone. He looked at me as if he was about to speak, but abruptly he picked up his cloak and went out into the hall. I hesitated, staring at

252

the forlorn pile of forgotten ivy garlands; then, in spite of myself, I went after him.

He was out in the yard. Fine snow had started to fall. He saw me, but he pulled on his gloves without pausing, as if I was part of the scenery.

"Are you going back to Castleford for the Turning?"

"No." He adjusted his gloves, and then glanced at me as if he wasn't sure why I was still standing there. "My uncle celebrates the Turning, in his own way. Or so the cook says. We'll get a haunch of venison, champagne, claret, port . . . Seven courses, the gold-plated china, the best silver. Just the two of us in a dining room the size of a barn."

"Right."

"Oh, it'll be fun, I expect. He'll be dead drunk by the second course, and then I can sit and watch him decay into his plate." He pulled his coat-collar closer round his chin. "I won't be back here for a few days, if that's why you're asking."

"Come to dinner here."

"What?"

He stared at me through the gathering dusk, flakes of snow clinging to his eyebrows. I swallowed. "Ma and Pa would like you to. And Alta, of course. There's enough food. We always invite the labourers and their families, one more won't make any difference."

"You're inviting me to Turning dinner?"

I raised one shoulder, but he went on staring at me until I muttered, "Yes."

His face changed. "No," he said. "Thank you."

"But —"

"You don't really want me to, do you?" He gave me a wry smile, as if I'd made a bad joke.

"I wasn't —"

"May your darkness be quiet and the light come sooner than you need," he said. It was the old, formal salutation at the Turning. Then he swung himself into the saddle and left me standing in the snow, shivering.

CHAPTER
FIFTEEN

Spring seemed to come earlier than usual. There were a few more snowstorms after the year had turned, but not many; and by the second full moon the snow was pockmarked and lacy, dissolving into piles of brown-edged slush. Until it was gone altogether, and every step plunged you ankle-deep in mud — and then overnight the trees woke up and sucked the water out of the ground, and the air smelt of greenness and growing. I'd always loved the first days of spring, when suddenly the prison of winter broke wide open; but this year it was like discovering an unknown country, as if seeing it through Darnay's town-bred eyes made everything new. Now that Alta was well again, and had chores to do, he wasn't there every day, or for hours at once; but he kept coming, and somehow he fitted in around the life of the farm so smoothly that he began to be a part of it all. He hovered at the edge of everything, not in the way exactly, but difficult to ignore: walking up to the High Field with Alta when she brought lunch to the sowers, sniffing the wind obediently when Alfred predicted rain, recoiling, his eyes watering, from the stench of chamber ley when we walked past the barn where Pa and I had been pickling wheat. The weeks when I stayed in the shepherd's hut for the lambing, Alta would come up in the evening with dinner; more than once he came with her and we sat for a long time drinking tea, not saying much, while the stars grew brighter and brighter. Once he was there when a lamb was born. Afterwards he knelt in the muck, his face lit by moonlight on one side and lamplight on the other, as he wiped the lamb's muzzle clean with straw. He had blood and mucus down his shirt, but he didn't seem to see it; he just leant over the lamb, staring, and finally looked up at me with an incredulous grin. I said to him, "You see? It wasn't hard," and he shook his head and laughed.

And there was Splotch, of course. We all joked about her excitement the first time she sensed a rabbit, revelled in her speed as she found her feet and ran, imagined the richness of the woody, earthy scents in her nose. As we walked home one evening from the field where we'd been turning the dunghill — directed by Darnay, who'd got tired after ten minutes of working beside us — Alta said, "I *wish* I could smell like her." I smirked and said, "Actually you do, stinker," but I knew exactly what she meant.

It was then, while the rest of us were too busy to watch him, that Darnay should have tried to insinuate himself into Alta's bed, if that was what he was after; but he didn't. He was never alone with her for long; often it seemed that he'd deliberately arrived when Pa or I would be in the farmyard, and he'd ask if he could help with whatever I was working on. At times, when he was throwing a stick for Splotch or trying to coax her away from a rabbit hole, I'd watch him and tell myself that we'd all been mistaken, that all he wanted was Splotch and some company. It must have been lonely, up at his uncle's house, and he never mentioned anyone else; maybe even his friendliness was skin-deep, and he was dallying with us out of sheer boredom. Then I'd look at Alta, and my insides would twist, because if he didn't care for her then she'd eat her heart out wishing. But when I heard him whistling as he rode into the yard, or caught his eye as he kissed Alta's hand in greeting, I couldn't kid myself any longer. He was as happy as she was; as if just being with her was enough. At least for now.

By then, Splotch was old enough to leave Springle. I thought about telling Darnay to take her home and not to come back; but somehow every time the words rose to the tip of my tongue I found myself swallowing them again, putting them off for another hour, or another day. I couldn't bear to think what it would be like once Splotch had left for good. Darnay gave us money for her food, but apart from that she wasn't exactly his but more or less *ours*. It had been so long since Springle was a pup that I'd forgotten what it was like, and how we could spend every spare moment playing tug-of-war or throwing sticks, or knotting bits of rope for her to chew. The dark brown blot on Splotch's back had gone black and her tail had been docked to a stub, but she was still small. When she wore herself out I'd put her into the canvas sack I sometimes used for poaching, with her head poking out of the top. Then Alta would walk along beside me, whispering, "Rabbits!" and giggling when Splotch pricked up her ears; and once Darnay announced, to no one in particular, "And here is Mademoiselle Emmie, modelling the latest fashion from the capital — note how the reticule worn stylishly over the shoulder displays an unusually excitable fur tippet . . ."

A few days later, though, I'd been pruning the thorn hedge on the slope of the High Field, and I hadn't brought the bag with me; so Darnay ended up carrying her back in his arms. Before we were halfway home he was muttering to her, "You spoilt lump, I can't believe I'm doing this, soon you'll be demanding a sedan chair," but when I offered to take her he shook his head. "No, it's all right, she's not heavy."

"So why are you complaining?"

"I'm enjoying it." He grinned.

I rolled my eyes, but his good humour was infectious. We went down the lane abreast of each other in companionable silence, while Alta wandered behind, singing under her breath. I stepped in front of Darnay to open the gate of the Upper Field — it was fallow, and there was a shortcut that took us home — but as soon as we were through it Splotch started wriggling and whining. Darnay swore under his breath, and tried to hold on to her. "She's got the scent of something. Stop it, Splotch. *Stop.*" But she didn't, until we got to the far edge of the field, where the wall of our courtyard met the hedge; then she gave a final spasmodic struggle. "Splotch, you half-witted cur, calm *down!*" Darnay said, elbowing his way awkwardly through the door in the wall. Then he added, in a different tone, "Damn. She's pissed on my shirt."

Alta snorted with laughter, and tried to convert the sound into something polite and ladylike.

Darnay put Splotch on the ground. She streaked away into one of the corners beside the barn where the rats liked to hang about. "Oh, hell," he said, looking down at his chest. "I'm soaked, and I stink."

"You'd better change," Alta said.

"It's all right, I can ride home like this. It's not too cold today, that's something."

"Don't be stupid," I said. "Alta, go and get one of my shirts, will you?" I didn't wait for her to answer. "Come into the kitchen, Darnay."

He followed me. I put a bowl of water on the range to take the chill off it. Behind me, I felt him hover in the doorway. "Farmer . . ."

"Yes?"

"You don't have to lend me anything."

I turned round. "What?"

For once he seemed to struggle for words. "If you'd rather not — I mean, I know you don't like it."

"What on earth are you blathering about?"

He hesitated; then he said, in a joking tone that wasn't joking, "Well, last time I borrowed one of your shirts you nearly throttled me."

I felt the blood rise in my face. "If I remember rightly," I said, "*you* offered to take your clothes off."

"Technically they were *your* clothes."

"How about I promise not to throttle you, and you promise not to take off *anyone's* clothes?"

"What about my pissy shirt? Can I take that off?"

"Shut the door. If Alta catches sight of your naked flesh she might fall into a swoon."

"In that case maybe you should avert your eyes, too."

I grinned. I couldn't help it.

"Just clean yourself up, Darnay."

He nodded to me in mock obedience and shut the kitchen door. I ducked into the pantry for a new slice of soap. When I came out he was already stripped to the waist. He wasn't as thin as he had been; he wasn't well-built either, but the long hours of walking and fresh air had put a layer of muscle on his ribs and chest, and his stomach was flat, not concave. "Thanks," he said, and reached for the soap.

I turned away. In spite of the jokes it made me uncomfortable to see him like that, like a labourer splashing off a day's dirt; especially when I was fully dressed, although I didn't know why that should make a difference.

There was a knock at the door. I opened it a fraction, plucked my spare shirt out of Alta's hand and shut the door on her as she said, "I brought the one without darned bi —"

"Ah," Darnay said, drawing it over his head, "thank you." It fitted him pretty well, although he had narrower shoulders than me. "Wait — is this the *very* shirt that drove you to fury?"

"No," I said, before I could stop myself. "Shut up, Darnay."

He laughed, with an easy, triumphant note, and adjusted the cuffs. I didn't care any more that it was getting threadbare; he never seemed to notice how old or dirty my clothes were.

"Can I come in yet?" Alta said. "What are you two doing in there?"

"Just a second," I said, and heard her sigh and tap the door with her fingernails.

Darnay was fully dressed now. He rolled the wet shirt into a ball and put it on the kitchen table. I hadn't lit a lamp, and in the dimness the pale bundle looked like a rose. Darnay stood still, watching me. At last he said, very quietly, "What is it?"

"I'm sorry," I said, so quickly the syllables ran into one another. "I was an idiot. Sorry."

"That's all right."

"No, I mean — all the time . . ."

"It's all right, Farmer."

"Stay for dinner. It's nothing fancy, probably just pie or something but I know Ma wouldn't mind —"

"I'd like to. Thanks."

"And this time I'm not just asking out of — oh. Good."

We looked at each other. It was too dark to see his expression; there was only the white shape of his face. Suddenly the room behind him — the dark bulk of the range and the gleaming rows of copper pans, the scrubbed stone floor and the faded prints on the walls — was unfamiliar. The pantry door was open, and the jars gleamed dimly like rows of polished stones.

"I'm just . . ." I gestured wildly. "Upstairs. Won't be a moment." I turned and pushed out into the hall.

"Darnay's staying to dinner," I said to Alta on my way past.

"What? You invited him? Why?" She grabbed my elbow and I nearly stumbled.

"Why not?"

She peered up at me. The passage was full of the blue half-light of a spring evening, so that the speckled pink of her dress was deepened to mauve, and the wall behind her smudged with shadows. The window was open, and a west wind blew in over the fields, driving the sour yard smells away; it had the sweetness of new grass — the scent, not of warmth, but the promise of warmth. Suddenly, standing there, I *felt* the spring, like the hairs rising on the backs of my arms. I shook her away, and laughed.

"What's going on? Emmett? Wait, are you two *friends*?"

Her voice was a mixture of relief and suspicion and — something else, something not quite as comfortable. I swung myself round the newel post and up the stairs, taking them two at a time. She called my name again, with a plaintive note; but I was on the landing by then, and didn't turn back.

I suppose, after that, we were friends. There was always a current under the surface, treacherous as a weir-stream, threatening to drag me under; but whenever I felt it start to tug I could move away, and after a while it was easy to pretend it wasn't real. That sense of danger, the fierce electricity that had made my hackles rise the day Darnay came into our lives — it had been nothing, just irrational dislike, and now I knew him better I could relax.

And it was as if Alta had seen the last barrier go down. I never said that now, if he asked, she had my permission to marry him — not that *my* permission would have mattered, anyway — but she seemed to feel that somehow, tacitly, I had. She launched herself into love as though she was hurling herself from a cliff: she seemed alight with happiness — incandescent with it — as if the new, golden world of being Darnay's wife was ripening within easy reach. Of course, she was a child, and like a child she cared about the trappings, the dress she'd wear, the house they'd live in, the ring he'd give her; once I walked past her sitting on a gate with Cissy Cooper, and before they saw me and burst into stifled giggles I heard Alta say, ". . . and a long veil! Edged with lace, you know the flowery patterns with pearls sewn in —" That didn't worry me; what made me lie awake at night were the other times, when the woman she'd be in ten years shone through her face, and I caught a glimpse of how much she wanted him. She moved differently now, light and languid at once; she let her fingers trail across the surfaces of things as if she'd only just discovered the sense of touch. She'd lost her appetite, and even the shape of her face had changed: her mouth was wider, her cheekbones more prominent.

But Darnay went on treating her as he always had: joking, teasing, as easy with her as if they were brother and sister. Maybe it was because he was so sure of her. Or maybe, I thought once, horrified, it was contempt

. . . But no. Darnay was unvaryingly kind to her; the only person he treated with an odd, goading affability that might have been disguised scorn was me.

I could have gone mad, thinking about it. So I didn't. There was more than enough to think about, anyway: spring was gathering speed, and the first crops were starting to sprout, in the garden as well as in the fields. The sap was rising, and when the other jobs were done Ma would send us out to gather wild garlic or gallons of dandelion flowers for wine. When we stood at the edge of the bluebells in Lord Archimbolt's wood, I laughed aloud at the spectacle: no wonder Alta was head-over-heels, it was the season for it. I almost felt like I was in love too.

That week everyone's spirits were high, because that Sunday was Wakening Fair. I'd never enjoyed it since I bought that book from the man with the stall, and Pa had been so angry; but this year I looked forward to it, and not just because it was a holiday. As I walked there with Darnay, Splotch and Alta — with my parents straggling behind, arm in arm as though they were as young as we were — I saw it all with new eyes. There were the tents, the strings of flags and the smoke of cooking fires, and everywhere people in their best clothes, flashes of colour and flushed faces, laughter and the clink of money changing hands, and the watery sun sparkling off overflowing tankards. At my side Darnay paused and whistled to himself — half amused, half daunted — and I laughed. "Come on," I said. "Aren't you hungry?"

"Yes, actually. I'll buy you a pie," he said.

"I can buy us pies, Darnay, we're not paupers."

"All right, I only — never mind." Splotch was going mad, tugging and choking at the end of her rope. We made a beeline for the nearest stall. Once we'd got our pies — after two gulps Splotch licked her chops and looked up hopefully for more — we turned down one of the narrower paths and wandered aimlessly between the rows of tents and trestles. Alta stopped, naked greed on her face, in front of a table of jewellery. Darnay followed her look and said, already reaching into his pocket, "How much are the blue beads?"

"Oh — thank you — Lucian, you shouldn't have."

Darnay turned away, dismissing her thanks with an easy gesture. For a second I disliked him intensely — the young lord, dispensing largesse — but he caught my eye and winked. At the next stall he bought three painted wooden eggs and flipped one towards me so quickly I almost fumbled it. "Darnay," I said, as he passed the other to Alta, "these are meant to be symbolic, you buy them for your sweetheart."

"And I have," he said, showing me the one he'd kept for himself. "For goodness' sake, Farmer, it's an egg. Don't look at me like I'm trying to buy your soul."

I laughed, with an effort, and shoved the egg into my pocket. Somewhere a bell rang, and Alta tugged me forward. "Come on, or I'll be late."

"You won't be late. It's the little girls first, not you. The ribbon dancing," I added to Darnay, who was looking quizzical. "You know, there's a big erect pole with ribbons tied to it, and the girls dance round it and sort of knot it to death."

"It's pretty," Alta said. "And Perannon Cooper's the Queen of the Wakening, Emmett — you'll want to see *that*." She waved at a clump of girls who were waiting in the centre of the green, gave Darnay a quick smile and ran to join them. They were all in their best dresses, pale as primroses, and a crown of straggling flowers was wilting on every head. Most of them had left their hair loose; only Alta had pulled two slim plaits back from her forehead, as if she wanted to look different. As she joined them there was muffled laughter and they all turned to stare at us. Cissy Cooper pointed at Darnay, tried to turn it into a ladylike wave, and then convulsed with giggles.

"I feel like a cake in a bakery window," Darnay said.

I snorted with laughter. That was precisely the way they were looking at him: hungry, envious, wistful . . . All except Alta, who knew the cake was already hers.

Darnay swivelled nonchalantly sideways, one hand raised to shield his face. He was blushing. "Do you desperately want to see the ribbon dancing? Or could we just . . . slip inconspicuously away?"

"Let's go," I said.

"Thank you." I didn't say that he couldn't ever be inconspicuous, especially not here, where every girl had her eye on him; instead I let him lead us back into the thick of the crowd, and tried to ignore Alta calling his name behind us. Once we had room we broke into a run, until at last we were at the far boundary of the fair, where the shabbiest stalls were dotted about like abandoned lean-tos. "Thank goodness," he said, leaning over to catch his breath. "Girls that age are frightening in groups, aren't they?"

"Packs," I said.

"Covens."

I grinned. "You don't have sisters, then?"

"Two, actually. Cecily and Lisette. Both older than me."

"Really? I didn't know that." It was funny how little I did know about Darnay; he'd never even mentioned his parents. I was about to say so when his face changed and I turned to see what had caught his attention.

The book stall. It was set apart from the other trestles, knee-deep in the taller grass; there was a half-empty barrow next to it that had left bruised tracks in the ground. It could have been the same man I had bought a book from, years ago — a greyer, leaner, shiftier version — or someone else. It didn't matter. The books were the same. Piles of coloured leather spines, gold-patterned; a few plainer ones; one or two with great metal clasps, the pages edged with spots of mildew . . . I took a step towards the stall. My heart sped up, for no reason.

Darnay gripped my arm so hard I almost yelped. "What the devil are you doing, Farmer?"

"Nothing. I just —" I blinked.

"Don't you know what they are?"

"I just want to look."

His eyes narrowed. Without another word he spun round and walked away so fast that Splotch choked and scrabbled after him on the end of her lead. I stood still, hesitating. The ribbon-dancers' pipe melody sang in my ears, high and shrill, coming and going on gusts of wind. The man at the stall was looking in another direction, his hair greasy under his hat; the stall itself was crooked and precarious, as if it might collapse at any moment. But the books shone in the quick spring sunlight, deep blues and reds and dusty gold-tooled green . . .

It was like snapping a thread: a second of effort, and then I ran after Darnay. "Hey! Wait! For goodness' sake —" But I was too out of breath to carry on. I knew he'd heard me, but he sped up, jogging through the deep grass and down into the hollow. I dodged the trees and caught up with him just as a low branch swiped him across the forehead. "What's going on?"

He turned to spit words at me as if we'd been fighting for a long time. "You like them, do you? Books? Do you have a secret stash somewhere? Something to keep you warm on a winter's night? Someone else's humiliation spread-eagled on a page, so you can read it over and over while you —"

"What?"

"You ought to be ashamed."

"What are you talking about?"

"You think it's all right, do you? For people's lives to be sold at a fair, to keep the peasants amused in the long winter evenings?" He hissed out a long breath through his teeth, and sagged against a tree. The swinging branch had left a thin streak of red above his eyebrow. After a moment he raised his eyes to mine and stared at me; I didn't know what he was looking for, but at last he looked away. When he spoke again, his voice was quieter, as if I'd passed a test. "You really don't know?"

"No."

He ran his fingers back and forth along the scratch on his forehead. Finally he said. "They're people's lives, Farmer. Stolen. Sucked out. Memories of the worst things that have ever happened to them."

"What?" I stared at him. "You mean, people write down —"

"Write down? No! They get bound into a book, and that makes them forget." He scowled. "It's — a kind of magic, I suppose. A dirty, sordid sort of magic. People pretend it's something glamorous — something *kind* — but it isn't. 'Poor Abigail, she's been through so much, wouldn't it be easier if we took her memories away?' And then men like that one get hold of the books and sell them for other people to . . ." He ground to a halt. "You knew that. You must have known that."

I shook my head. "I knew that there was something . . . wrong. But it can't be like that — I don't believe it." But I did. That was why my parents went pale at the mention of books, why they'd never told us about them. In my head, uninvited, I saw the shadows of a camp the night before a battle; and I saw Pa, furious, about to hit me. Perhaps I was lucky not to have read the rest.

"But you must have seen books," he said. "Even school bindings are memories. Didn't your teachers tell you?"

"At school we learnt from slates. And samplers, and letters." I shrugged, although my shoulders felt tight

269

and painful. "Never books. People round here don't read books."

His face had the thin, strained look it had used to have. It seemed hours before he nodded. "You're right," he said. "There's no reason why you should have known. The nearest binder is an old witch who lives miles away on the marsh, and why should you know about her? My uncle told me. Not that *he* bothers much with anything that isn't in a bottle."

There was a silence. Splotch was sniffing at something, straining at her lead. Darnay didn't move. His eyes were lowered, but there was nothing at his feet but trodden-down grass and leaf-mould, and gnarled tree-roots just breaking the surface. A burst of birdsong clattered out over our heads, and a cold wind blew the scent of earth into my face. I put my hand into my pocket and curled my palm around the painted egg that Darnay had given me.

"Darnay . . ."

"What?"

I didn't know what I'd wanted to say. After a moment he pushed himself upright and walked past me, along the path that led up over the ridge. The trees grew too close for us to walk abreast, so I followed him, glad that he couldn't see my face. I didn't want him to glimpse the obscure wash of shame that I felt when I remembered that book, and Pa's fury. Splotch gave a whine of excitement and darted sideways, and Darnay almost stumbled over her; but instead of laughing he tugged her sharply back to him, so that she had to abandon whatever she'd found.

He stopped at the top of the little rise, where the trees ended. From here you could see the New House on the horizon, almost veiled by the freshly green trees, and the ruins of the castle and the glint of the moat in the valley below. There was a thick grey storm coming towards us, in pleats and hanks of dark cloud. The sun came out in a final extravagant blaze of light, turning everything gold; then the clouds closed in on it again.

"Would you like to be my secretary?" Darnay said.

It took a second for the words to make sense. "What?"

"I need a secretary. It would be well paid, of course. It wouldn't be hard, just writing letters and advising me and things like that. *Don't*," he added, with a sudden sharp turn of the head. "Please, just once, listen to what I'm saying. I want y — I need someone who can think clearly, who isn't taken in by all the nonsense. Yes, you'd be paid. But I'm not asking you to be my servant. And if you didn't like it, you could leave."

I turned my head and stared at the approaching storm. Its edges were like the lip of an oyster, a frill of pearl-grey against dark cloud. He *was* asking for a servant. For a moment I imagined myself running his estate: managing the woods and the farmland, an office in the New House, what Ma and Pa could do with my wages . . .

"I have a job already," I said. "You may have noticed."

"I know that. But you don't want to stay on your father's farm forever. Do you?"

I clenched my toes in my boots, feeling the give and suck of the mud beneath my feet. "It'll be *my* farm when he's old."

"All right, but —"

"All right *what*? It's not good enough?" I turned to face him and drew myself up, to make the most of the tiny gap in our heights. "You mean, obviously, if someone had a choice, they'd choose to be you rather than me?"

"Stop it!" He shook his head. "I'm not saying that. I'm offering you something else. That's all."

"I don't need something else."

There was a silence. I kicked a clump of grass until it lay flat, smeared with clots of mud. I knew exactly how I'd use Darnay's estate. Pa wouldn't be able to argue with me, or tell me I was too young to know what I was talking about; I could make it yield twice what it did now *and* leave enough for the poachers . . . When I glanced at Darnay, he was watching me; there was a tightness around his eyes and mouth as if he was trying not to show what he was thinking.

He said, "Would you be prepared to try?"

I clenched my jaw. I wasn't sure I could bear to take orders from him. And when he and Alta were married . . .

"If I don't," I said, "how will you find someone else?"

"It's you I want. If you don't, then I'd rather have no one at all." His expression changed. "What did I say?"

"No," I said.

"Emmett —"

272

"No."

He shut his eyes. It was a gesture of defeat. Then he sighed and started to make his way down the hill into the field, towards home. "Your damnable pride," he said, without energy.

"Pride? *Me*?"

He didn't answer. I wasn't sure if he'd heard. I walked behind him. The mud gathered again on my boots and weighed me down.

I said, to break the silence, "Doesn't your uncle want to choose someone, anyway?"

"It's none of my uncle's business. When I go back to Castleford I'll be working for my father, running factories."

"Wait." I stopped. "I thought you were — you're going back to Castleford?"

"When my father judges me to be suitably chastened." He glanced over his shoulder and stopped walking too. "Why, what did you think? I was sent away as a punishment. It was my uncle's house or the insane asylum. I won't be here for ever. That's why I wanted y — Forget it. I'll be fine."

I dug my heel into the mud, grinding until I felt the grass break and the clay push up over my instep. "What about Alta?"

"What about her? I'm asking *you*." He started walking again so suddenly I nearly slid over trying to catch up with him. The clouds had clotted into a shadowy mass, and everything was tinged with grey. On the other side of the valley a pale curtain of rain had blown across the New House and the ruins.

We reached the stile at the bottom of the hill. Darnay climbed it without a word, and then stood waiting for me, his back still turned. The bluebells here had gone over, and the last muddy slope was covered with flattened, faded leaves. A raven cawed and fell silent.

I could hear him breathing. There was an inch of bark in his hair, almost the same colour, and a streak of greenish mould on the back of his neck.

I said, "What did you do?"

"What?"

"What are you being punished for?"

He turned his head, and hesitated. His eyes were wide and preoccupied. He wanted to tell me, but he couldn't — or he could tell me, but he didn't want to . . . "It doesn't matter," he said. "I'm never going to do it again."

It started to hail. Both of us hunched instinctively against the nearest tree, but it was still too early in the year for it to give much shelter. Splotch crouched against Darnay's knee, shivering. The hailstones hammered on my scalp and shoulders, melting into freezing trickles. "We'd better go back," I said, through the patter of ice. "We can get something hot to drink —"

"You go. I'm going home."

"Darnay —"

"Leave me alone. I'm fine."

He didn't give me time to answer. Before I had time not to believe him he'd leapt the stream and was halfway across the next field, his feet slipping in the mud, his clothes already soaked and dripping. Maybe I

274

should have followed him; but somehow it went from too soon to too late, without the right moment in between.

CHAPTER
SIXTEEN

Darnay didn't mention going back to Castleford again. Sometimes I wondered whether I'd misunderstood. Maybe he'd meant *occasionally* or *for a few days at a time*; surely this had been too long a stay to be a punishment? I tried to imagine Darnay's father, but it was like one of those fairground boards with a hole for the face: I could picture the clothes, the gold watch and stovepipe hat, but his features were a blank. Then I tried to imagine what Darnay could have done, to be threatened with the insane asylum. It was like picking a scab, at once painful and irresistible: it occupied me while we planted turnips and cleared the stones and rolled the grass fields, niggling at me, itching in the corner of my dreams while I was asleep. Sometimes I wondered whether I should tell Alta — but tell her what? Tell her that something was wrong with him, but that I didn't know exactly what? It was easier to keep it hidden, and to stare at her with a glazed, idiotic expression when she frowned and asked me what I was looking so thoughtful about.

The only cure was when I was actually with Darnay. When we were together, none of it seemed important. All that mattered was Splotch's newest trick, or the fence I was showing him how to repair, or whether we could bag a couple of pigeons on the way home. Darnay, to my surprise, had never fired a gun. He was bad at it, laughing at himself when the shots went wide, and in the end he'd shoved the gun at me, saying, "Go on, Farmer, you know you're dying to show me how it's done." Alta mourned the pigeons when they thudded into the undergrowth, but she ate pigeon pie with gusto, whether or not Darnay happened to have dinner with us.

Spring widened into summer, like a river turning from a clear spate to a slow green ribbon. Alta was busier, now that the calves were weaned and she had butter and cheese to make; and then there was the sheep shearing, first ours and then at Home Farm and Greats Farm, so that for a few days we only saw Darnay briefly, when he came to see Splotch. But the day after the sheep were sheared, Pa unexpectedly leant on the pigsty wall next to me as I was feeding the pigs, and said, "You've done a good job, these last few days, lad. You can take the rest of the day off if you want it. I'll get Alfred to do your chores." He reached over to scratch the sow's back with a piece of twig. "You'd better wait for young Mr Darnay, so he doesn't get under our feet here."

It was unheard of, a holiday for no reason in the middle of summer; but I didn't argue, and when Pa added, without looking at me, "Oh, and take that sister of yours with you," I realised that it was for Alta's sake, because they were afraid Darnay would lose interest. It didn't matter, or not really. I've never felt as free as I did that afternoon, as we wandered further and further, up through Lord Archimbolt's woods (that should have been ours) and past the New House. Splotch always came back when she was called, so we let her wander; but we forgot to call her for a long time, and when Alta asked, "Where's Splotch? Splo-otch!" she was too far away to hear. At first we didn't worry. Splotch was clever — *much* cleverer than other dogs, Darnay said — and always knew where she was. But after nearly an hour I could feel the anxiety building in my chest. Those man-traps were centuries old and rusted open, but she might somehow have caught a paw in one, or cut herself. Or she might be trapped somewhere, down a foxhole or face to face with a grumpy badger . . .

"Let's split up," Alta said. "We'll go that way, to the stream. Meet you in half an hour, Emmett." She had a dainty little pocket watch that Darnay had given her for the Turning. She brought it out now with an actressy flourish, as if the whole point of the exercise was to show Darnay how grateful she was for it.

"Good idea. You go that way, Alta," I said, grabbing Darnay's arm and swinging him round before he had time to respond. "We'll go uphill. We're faster. The two of us can cover more ground."

As we walked away Darnay gave me a sideways look, with a glint in his eye, but he didn't say anything except, "Splotch'll be all right, Farmer. Don't worry."

"I'm not."

We struggled up the wooded bank and found ourselves at the edge of the drive to the New House, just in front of the lodge. It was even more overgrown than it had been before, with a thick curtain of ivy half burying it, but the door was ajar. It was the perfect place to root out a rat — and the perfect place to get stuck, and sit marooned under the floorboards, whining for help. "Come on," I said, pushing the door open.

The floor was so dusty it crunched under our feet. There was a table in the middle of the room, two chairs — one with its seat collapsed — a heap of rotting unidentifiable canvas, piles of ancient rain-warped ledgers and wooden boxes. It smelt of damp, even now it was summer, but the sunlight streamed down from a hole in the ceiling and a warm breeze blew through one of the smashed windows. I took a look round, listening hard, but everything was still. And the floor was stone, without floorboards to get stuck under.

"What about upstairs?" Darnay said.

The staircase was rickety but more or less complete. At the top, the floor gaped like a toothless mouth, and sunshine blazed down through a matching hole in the roof. It looked as if something huge had fallen all the way through. I edged forward and called, "Splotch!" There was no answer. "I don't think she's here."

Darnay moved round me and took a few steps across the dusty floorboards. He grimaced. "This is exactly the sort of place she'd like. And I'm sure I heard something."

"Rats, probably."

"Splotch! Come on!" Nothing moved, except a slow plume of dust that rose and spun in a shaft of sunlight.

He edged past the hole to the far corner of the room, where a tall clock lurked in the shadows. "Splotch!"

I followed him, treading carefully. "Alta's probably found her by now," I said.

"What if she's got stuck here?"

"There's nowhere to get stuck," I said, looking round. All that was left here was the clock, and a few mouldy pictures; one last cupboard squatted in a corner, but the door and drawer above it had gone. If Splotch had been here we would have seen her.

Darnay tugged his lower lip. "All right," he said, at last. For a moment I thought he was going to add something else; then he sneezed three times in a row. "Let's go."

We went back the way we'd come, along the edge of the hole. I felt the planks start to sag under my feet, and grabbed the window sill to steady myself. Darnay reached out without touching me, letting his hand hover where I could grab it if I needed to. "Careful."

"I *am* being careful."

"It was just a piece of friendly advi —" He stopped. I glanced back at him; he was staring out of the window.

I started to say, "Is she out there?" But before I could finish my question he grabbed me, pulling me back and sideways into the corner. "What's —"

"Be quiet!" He slammed me against the wall. My head hit the side of the clock, and it rang gently with the noise of wood and rusty chimes. Darnay pressed himself into the space next to me. "My uncle," he said. "Coming in. Don't move."

280

I frowned. He pointed to my gun and drew his finger across his throat. I leant back, my heart hammering. As long as we didn't move . . . As long as he didn't come upstairs . . .

The door opened and closed. I concentrated on breathing silently, pushing down the panic. There were footsteps in the room below. For a chilling second I thought he was coming up the staircase; but no, he was pacing back and forth. What was he doing? A breath of pipe-smoke rose up, sickly sweet. I swallowed, trying not to cough. I felt Darnay's eyes on my face, and gave him a tiny nod: *I'm fine.*

The door opened again. Someone else. I clenched my jaw, resisting the urge to lean forward and see who it was. Light feet, a feminine rhythm.

"There you are. And you've been poaching, haven't you?"

My heart stopped.

"Oh, sir, I'm afraid I have," a voice said.

I collapsed back against the wall, drenched in sweat, soggy with relief. It wasn't Alta. It was . . . I blinked, suddenly recognising the lilt of her voice. Perannon Cooper. But — *Perannon?* What was she doing, poaching? Her brothers, yes — but Perannon never came into the woods at all, she was only interested in boys and fashion plates, she was planning to move to Castleford as soon as she could. It didn't make sense.

"I saw you," Lord Archimbolt said. "You've got a big — plump — juicy — *pheasant* in your bag."

Perannon, shoot a pheasant? I slid a sideways look at Darnay, but he was frowning at the floor.

281

"Oh sir," she said again. Her accent was broader than it should have been; she sounded like her grandmother. "You caught me. You're too clever for me."

"That's right. You've been a very naughty girl."

"I'm very sorry, sir." There was a little quaver in her voice.

"Say it!"

"Oh, sir. I've been a very naughty girl."

"And you know what happens to naughty little girls like you, don't you?"

"Oh . . ." She breathed out, with a hiccup. "Oh please don't, Lord Archimbolt, I'm only a naughty little poacher, I promise I won't —"

"Bend over. And take up your skirts."

Embarrassment flooded through me like boiling water; and then, an instant later, the insane desire to laugh. I screwed up my face, trying to repress it; beside me, Darnay put both hands over his mouth and took a long, shuddering breath. If he caught my eye . . . I curled my toes into the floor and clenched my fists. If we made a sound . . .

Thwack. A belt on bare skin. Then Perannon said, without emphasis, "Oooh."

I nearly burst out laughing, then. Who would have guessed that Perannon was such a bad actress? I willed myself not to look at Darnay. That was the most important thing. But I could feel him shaking with the effort to stay silent. One shared glance, and we'd both be on the floor.

"Six of the best, young lady!"

Thwack. "Ooh." *Thwack*. "Ooh." *Thwack* — an infinitesimal pause, as if she wasn't concentrating — "Ooh, please, sir!"

"Now, have you learnt your lesson?" A pause, and the rustle of fabric. Then he gave a long piggish grunt, and something started to creak rhythmically. Perannon moaned, slightly out of time.

Darnay shifted. "That was only four," he murmured, so low I only just caught the words.

I snorted. He slapped his palm over my mouth so quickly that I felt his skin against my teeth. "Sssh," he said. "They'll hear you." I bit him, not quite on purpose. He pulled away, and we stood shoulder to shoulder, both of us breathing in juddering gasps, fighting not to laugh out loud.

"Good girl," Lord Archimbolt said, "good girl. I mean, *bad* girl."

"Oh yes, oh sir, oh that's lovely, I am sorry, I won't do it again."

Now they were making wordless noises. That was better — less funny. Like animals. The table was creaking louder and louder, and there was another sound, too, the scrape of wood on bare flagstones . . . I was about to lean forward but Darnay moved before I could, bending and tilting his head to see through the hole in the floor. *Creak — squeak — scrape — creak —* "Uh!" *— squeak — scrape —*

He slammed me back against the wall, and stood with half his weight pressed against me, breathing hard. For a moment we were both frozen, horrified by the noise we'd made; but nothing changed in the pounding downstairs. Darnay muttered, "The table's moving. They're right underneath. If they look up they'll see us."

I gritted my teeth. The clock-case dug into my back, right between my shoulder blades. Darnay had his hand on my chest, holding me where I was, our faces close. It was difficult to breathe; his ribcage was crushed against mine, and the heat coming off his body made my head spin. I thought about pushing him away, but I didn't dare. *Creak — squeak — scrape*, came the sounds from downstairs. "Uh — ugh —"

Now Perannon was grunting too. I shut my eyes, trying to block out the sound: but suddenly I could see her in my mind's eye, all too clearly, working up to a passionate climax that might or might not be fake. My eyes snapped open again. I tried to think of something, anything else.

But there was no escape. And standing like this, with Darnay's breath on my neck, sweat crawling in my hair . . . I could feel the tension running through him. His hand was burning through my shirt, right over my heart. When I undressed tonight I'd find the print of it on my skin. No, that was idiotic. I tried to think of something cool — cold water, ice — but even with my eyes fixed on the ceiling all I saw was the fine sheen of moisture on Darnay's forehead, the dampness of his shirt-collar. And Perannon would be wet between her breasts, between her legs —

I dug my fingernails into my palms as hard as I could, and kept staring at the ceiling. I thought about the peeling plaster, the scrolls of paint that hung like

284

parchment. I counted the chipped roses that garlanded the cornice — one, two, three-fourfivesix —

But it was no good. I could feel the heat pooling in my groin, a familiar, delightful ache at the pit of my stomach. I bit the tip of my tongue until my mouth tasted of salt. But the blood pulsed, harder and harder, until I was tingling all over and weak at the knees. My body was betraying me, whatever I did. I swallowed, more loudly than I meant to, and Darnay shifted to look at me. I didn't meet his eyes. If only he'd step back. If only he wasn't so close to me.

Maybe he wouldn't notice.

I was blushing, my skin as hot as sunburn. If only he'd stop *looking* at me.

He leant sideways, so that his mouth brushed my earlobe. "Are you getting excited, Farmer?"

I wanted to die. Right here and now. I wanted the floor to collapse, killing all four of us. I kept my eyes on the ceiling and pretended I hadn't heard.

"If it's unbearable," he murmured, as intimate as a voice inside my head, "feel free to . . . er . . . deal with it. Quietly."

"Shut up."

"Would you like a hand?"

"Go to hell, Darnay."

In spite of myself I glanced at him. He was laughing silently, his forehead pressed against the wall. After a moment he caught my eye and winked. I took hold of his shoulder and squeezed slowly until I felt my fingers dig into the space between his bones. He twisted away, still grinning at me, mocking me, daring me — to do *what?* Hitting him would be too noisy.

"Oh — good girl — oh yes — uh, uh-huh, *urgghh* —"

After the crescendo came a pause. We stood frozen, listening. At last there was the rustle of fabric, the clink of a belt buckle, and the lighter chink of coins dropping into a purse. Perannon said, "Thank you, Lord Archimbolt." Her accent had magically disappeared; now she sounded like me or Alta. "Same time next week?"

"That's right, lass."

A few light footsteps, and then the door slammed. Darnay and I swapped glances, waiting: it would be stupid to relax too soon. But a few minutes later — after a yawn, and the crackle of a match, and a new blue cloud of pipe smoke drifting up through the floor — the door opened and shut again. Darnay eased sideways to stare out of the window.

He exhaled, in a large unguarded breath that seemed to go on forever. "Well," he said. "My uncle always *said* he came down hard on poachers."

We exploded with laughter at the same moment. It was a relief to be able to give in to it. We bent over, convulsing, and laughed so hard we choked. It took a long time before we were steady enough to clamber back across the hole on to the wider bit of floor, and then Darnay paused, shaking his head. "I can't believe that just happened," he said, through his giggles, and gave a sudden splutter that sent saliva flying through the sunlight. It set me off again to see him like that, and we staggered in a zigzag like drunks, clutching our ribs. "I was sure I was going to sneeze."

"Don't fall into the hole —" I reached out and grabbed Darnay's arm. Together we stumbled precariously down the stairs and out into the leafy sunlight.

"I bet you're glad I don't treat poachers like that."

I shook my head, trying to catch my breath. "Don't."

He sobered up before I did. When I finally managed to pull myself together, he was standing staring back at the lodge, a smile still playing around the corners of his mouth. "Who *was* that? I mean, the girl."

"Perannon Cooper." His glance at me was unreadable. I added, "I didn't know she was a whore."

"Perannon Cooper? You — like her, don't you?"

I remembered, with surprise, that I'd used to. "Not any more."

"No, well . . ." He gave me a crooked smile, as if he thought I was lying.

"No, I mean — not for ages, not since . . ." I stopped. "How did you know that, anyway?"

"Alta mentioned it once." He shrugged one shoulder, turning away. "I remembered the name, that's all."

"Right." The back of his neck was damp. His shirt had two long creases down his spine like knife-blades. I fiddled with the strap of my gun, wishing I knew what I wanted to say.

Suddenly he spun on his heel. "Splotch! We'd better go on looking. I completely — I can't believe we —"

"Of course. Let's go."

He set off, running through the trees until his shirt was just a flash of white in the green. I hesitated. I had to follow him, or I'd lose him. But there was something nagging at me, a dislocated feeling like the onset of an illness. Or like I'd left something behind.

A long way away I heard Splotch bark. I squashed the feeling down until it disappeared, and ran towards her voice.

After that, Darnay stopped coming to see us.

At first we thought — we told each other, anyway — that it was nothing, he hadn't had time that day, and that he'd be there tomorrow. But the days stretched to a week and there was no letter or message from him, and Alta begged me to go with her to the New House to see if he was there. That day I'd been relaying the stones around the cows' watering pool, and I was glad of the quiet walk and the breeze that dried the sweat on my shirt; but when we walked up the drive and rang the bell there was no answer at all, not even a curt dismissal from the housekeeper. Alta turned and looked at me. She looked shrivelled, like a flower that had been caught out by a frost. "What if he's *died*, Em?"

"Don't be stupid. We'd have heard by now."

"What if —"

"Shut *up*!"

We walked back in silence. It seemed obvious that he'd gone back to Castleford without a word, without even saying goodbye . . . But I couldn't bring myself to tell Alta. Surely he couldn't be so cruel. But he didn't come. The atmosphere at home was thick and crackling with tension; Ma and Pa shouted at each other, Alta threw a tantrum in the dairy and let two days' worth of unskimmed milk turn sour, and Splotch pricked up her ears and whined every time a horse went past the gate. I worked so hard and relentlessly in the heat that I came home every evening with a splitting headache, but even so I struggled to sleep; at night I sat by my window, my forehead pressed against the glass to cool it, wishes and curses so mixed up in my brain I hardly knew which were which.

Then it was Midsummer Eve. There was a row because Alta refused to show her face at the village bonfire, and a row because I called her a spoilt little madam who'd need to start looking for someone else, and a row because when I apologised she boxed my ears. We went to the bonfire, but it was no fun; every mouthful of beer tasted sour, and Pa drank too much and almost started a fight with Martin Cooper. I turned away and let Ma wrench them apart. But when I stared in the opposite direction, I found myself looking at Alta, standing a little way apart from the other girls. They were all in their best dresses, the way they'd been at Wakening Fair, and they had wreaths of summer flowers around their necks and wrists; but then Alta had been at the centre of the group, sleek with happiness, and the others had given her sidelong glances of envy. Now Cissy Cooper called, "Alta, come and listen, Gertie's engaged," and Gertie tossed her head and said, "Don't worry, Alta, you'll find someone soon," and I wanted to slap them both for the smug note in their voices. But I knew Alta was too proud to

289

let me catch her arm and take her home; and so was I, and so were Ma and Pa, and so we stayed and laughed and sang with the others. We walked home at dawn, like unwounded soldiers after a defeat, trying to pretend we hadn't lost.

I fell asleep late — well, early, just as the sun was slanting over the gate into the yard — with my face against the window. The image of Alta's face, withered with misery, haunted me. It was my fault. Somehow, it was my fault. If I had . . . I didn't know what I should have done differently, but it was my fault. The thought went round and round; it was maddening, but at least it kept the other thoughts at bay, the ones about Darnay.

Something rattled on the glass next to my cheek. I jerked upright, out of my doze; then it happened again, and I opened the window and peered out, blinking. It was already mid-morning, and already hot.

"Farmer," Darnay called up. "Where is everyone?"

"It's Midsummer Day," I said. "We're all asleep. Where have you *been*?"

"Come down, will you?" He bent to pat Splotch, who was turning excited circles at his feet.

I dragged my clothes on and wiped the dried spit from my chin. I paused at Alta's door, half wanting to pay her back for the slap, but made myself knock. "Alta! Darnay's come back," I said, and heard her bedsprings jingle as she sat upright.

"Tell him I don't want to see him," she said, and her feet padded across the room to the chest of drawers where she kept her best nightgown.

290

I pelted down the stairs and out into the yard, jamming my boots on as I went. Darnay looked round and laughed. "You look . . . improvised," he said.

"The bonfire ends at dawn," I said. "We come home and feed the animals, and then we can sleep till noon. Even Pa does. It's a holiday."

"Oh. Sorry, have I —"

"No," I said, too quickly. "No, it's good to see you."

There was a silence. Darnay bent to tug Splotch's ears.

"Alta won't talk to you," I said.

"That's a shame."

"I think she wants you to insist on seeing her. Beg her forgiveness. You know."

"Will *you* talk to me?"

"Yes. Obviously."

"That's all right, then. Come on." He clicked to Splotch and walked out of the gate before I had time to tie my bootlaces.

"Darnay," I said, catching up with him, "where have you been? We thought — Alta thought — I mean, we were worried."

"I was thinking," he said.

"Thinking? For a *week*?"

"I'm a very slow thinker."

It was meant to make me laugh, and it did; but I noticed when we went on walking that he'd dodged the question. I said, "Where are we going?"

"We're walking Splotch." I followed him without thinking, glad we were taking a path through the woods, dazzled by the green-gold play of sunlight through the trees; and it wasn't until he stopped at the edge of the wood that I realised where he'd brought us. At our feet there was a still expanse of water, a little darker blue than the sky; and on the other side was the ruined castle. We'd always avoided the ruins, as if neither of us wanted to be reminded of the day we'd met; but now, overhung with wisteria, with its reflection trembling gently in the moat, the old castle seemed so far from the haunted black-and-red of that winter afternoon that it could have been another place. I breathed in, and from across the water I caught a sweet, rich scent like cloves.

We circled the moat and sauntered across the bridge while Splotch ran ahead of us. I walked into the little courtyard and leant against the well-head, tilting my head back to feel the sun on my face. I could hardly open my eyes against the light; when I tried, the tower and the walls blurred into a shimmer of sand-coloured stone, dancing water-light, leaves and fierce blue sky. I was breathless and dizzy, as if my blood was too thin, and I wondered if I was still drunk. I wiped the last gritty flecks of sleep from my eyes and turned to shield my face from the sun. Dark shapes flickered over my vision.

Darnay had paused to look down at the water, staring as if he could read something in the mud at the bottom. At last he said, "I wanted to ask you something, Farmer."

"All right."

"It's about Alta."

"She's just sulking," I said. "You probably should have banged on her door and pleaded with her to see you, but if you play your cards right it won't take more than a couple of boxes of candied fruit."

"That's not what I was going to ask."

I took a deep breath. The sun was too hot, all of a sudden; if only I hadn't drunk so much last night. "She'll be fine," I said. "She's only fifteen. She'll get over it — only be gentle with her, Darnay, she's not as tough as she tries to b —"

"Will you *shut up!*" He dragged a hand over his face, and for a second it was as if he was the one who hadn't slept. He paused so long that it seemed deliberate. Then he said, "I thought I might ask her to marry me."

CHAPTER
SEVENTEEN

I stared at him. I couldn't remember when I had really looked at him, at his face: his eyes were dark, but one iris held tiny flecks of amber and ochre where the sun hit it; the skin across his cheekbones was flushed, freckled so faintly it was hardly visible. He bit his lip and I noticed the slight asymmetry of his teeth, and how white they were. I didn't feel anything. All this time, all these months, we'd waited for him to say that — or something like it; and now he'd said the words, and the rest of our lives could begin. I lowered my head and kicked at a stone on the base of the well-head. The brightness of the sun was stinging my eyes. The warm air smelt flat and flowery, like old rosewater.

"Right," I said.

He went on watching me with an open, direct gaze that made me feel like he was waiting for something more.

"Won't you . . ." I cleared my throat. "We're only farmers. Will your parents — your father —"

"He can't stop me. We could marry in secret, and then . . ." His eyes slid away and then back to my face. "I'll look after her. It'll be all right."

"Then . . . good," I said. "Alta'll be delighted."

He nodded. I turned away and went to look through the arch into the ruined hall. The sun slanted through the wisteria-hung windows and patterned the grass with squares of brighter green. My head ached.

"I thought you'd be pleased."

"I am." I forced myself to smile at him over my shoulder. "Of course I'm pleased. We were all hoping this would happen."

He didn't return the smile. "Were you?"

"Naturally. I mean — yes." *Naturally* made it sound as if we were after his money. But then, if he'd been poor, Ma and Pa would never have . . . I pressed my knuckle into a gap between the stones of the arch and leant my whole weight on it. "I hope you'll both be very happy together."

Silence. A stock dove called from the foliage above me, with a sound like a clanking bell.

"Is that it, then? No spontaneous outburst of joy? No fraternal handshake?"

"I *said* I was pleased. It's not about me, is it? I'm sure Alta will more than make up for my bad manners."

"I didn't mean that." He scuffed his shoe against the base of the wall. His face was lit from below by the sun dancing off the water. Shadows flickered across his eyes. "What's the matter, Farmer? Do you still think I'll break her heart?"

"No." It was true. Somehow, without knowing when, I'd learnt to trust him.

"You still hate me, then? It's fine, you can tell me the truth."

"Don't be daft."

295

"Then what? I really care about her. I won't let you down."

I pushed my knuckle harder into the sharp-edged stone. When I took it out again the skin was beaded with tiny specks of blood. He was right. I should be pleased. I should be relieved. Now Alta could have her long veil with pearls embroidered on the edge; and she could have a house in Castleford, and a lady's maid; and she could have Darnay. Everything she wanted — in that order. Distantly I knew that was unfair, but I didn't care.

"Why are you asking *me*?" I said. "Ask Ma and Pa. Ask Alta. Why does it matter what I think?"

"Because —" But I didn't wait to hear his answer. I went through the arch into the high roofless hall and stood at one end of it, breathing as slowly as I could, trying to focus on what was here and now: the roses that spilt down the walls, the wide mossy band of paving stones, the short grass . . . Someone looked after it, I realised, it was a garden, not just a ruin. Funny, when Lord Archimbolt let everything else fall apart.

"Emmett. Talk to me. What's wrong? If you don't want . . ."

"Please don't marry her," I said, and put my hands over my face.

"All right."

I heard the words, but they didn't make sense. "Sorry," I said, forcing the words past the fierce ache in my throat. "No, you should marry her, of course, I'm just — it's — I don't know why, it's stupid, I didn't

296

sleep much last night, that's all — forget it, I didn't mean —"

He took hold of my arm and pulled me round to face him.

Then he kissed me.

A bell chimed six o'clock. I knew it was the clock on the New House stables, nearly a mile away, but the warm air was so still it could have been just the other side of the moat. A few moments later it repeated the hour — another six notes — and it was as if time itself had paused. I'd never felt such quietness; nothing moved, except the faintest tremor in the water, the flick of a fish breaking the mirror. Birds sang suddenly and then lapsed back into silence. The sun had dipped behind the trees on the hill, but the sky was still bright; it was the longest day, it would be hours before it was dark.

"Emmett?"

I looked round. Darnay was standing in the half-ruined doorway. His shirt was buttoned wrong, and one corner hung lower than the other. I opened my mouth to speak, but all I could do was smile.

"Are you all right?"

"Yes."

"Good." He gestured to the grass next to me. "Do you mind?"

"No." He turned away, and my heart contracted. "I don't mind, I mean."

He hesitated before he sat down next to me. I glanced at him, and the peace was overlaid with

297

something else. It was like sitting next to a stranger. I didn't know this Darnay, this voice, this naked unmasked face; and yet I did, I knew him better than the other one, this was the Darnay I had always known, from the moment I set eyes on him. I pulled my knees up to my chest, trying to stop the shivers that had started running down my spine.

"Are you cold?"

"It's getting chilly."

"It's warmer in the sunshine."

"It's nice here." We looked at each other briefly and smiled, and looked away again.

After a long time he said, "Are you hungry?"

"No. You?"

"Not really."

Another pause. Splotch barked suddenly and then whined, and we both looked automatically towards the gap in the wall. "It's the frogs," Darnay said. "Good job she's tied up."

"Yes."

A wood-pigeon called sleepily to its mate. Just in front of us a fish arched its back and sank again, leaving arrow-trails of brightness in the green water. I tried to summon the serene emptiness I'd felt a moment before; but I couldn't, not with him next to me.

"Listen, Emmett."

"What?" It came out like an attack, from nowhere. We stared at each other, frozen.

"I want you to know," he said, so carefully it was as if he was giving dictation, "that if you want to pretend all this never happened . . ."

I had earth under my fingernails. I concentrated on getting it out. "Is that what you want?"

"It's up to you."

"I asked what *you* wanted." I didn't mean to look at him, but I couldn't stop myself. "Don't worry about my feelings, Darnay. The agricultural classes have earthy, primitive appetites that are easily sated."

"Stop it!" He flung up his arm as if he was warding off a blow. "What's the matter? All I said was —"

"That you want to run away. That — *all this* — didn't mean anything." I hated myself for saying it aloud.

"Don't be such an idiot." He caught my eye. I set my jaw and tried to stare him out. If I let him see how I felt, it would be the final humiliation.

I don't know what I did; but I failed. Abruptly his whole face lit up with a huge, relieved, joyous grin. "So you *don't* want that, then?" he said. "Good. Neither do I."

I felt my breath hiccup in my throat. Then, with a quiet jolt, something inside me fell apart: like a pot that had been broken years ago but somehow managed to cling to its shape until someone nudged it. I started to laugh too.

After a long time he reached out and brushed my cheek with the back of his knuckles; and something in the gesture made my heart turn over as much as anything else he'd done that afternoon.

Later. Was it when Midsummer Day dissolved into Midsummer Night that we stumbled home like drunkards, kissing in the dark at the crossroads before we separated? I remember that kiss, reckless and breathless, we were so desperate not to let go of each other that we left bruises. Or was that another *later*, the night after that when I crept out through the summer dark to meet him? The time blurred, thick as honey. The days after midsummer, while Alta was still sulking, ran into one another, shining. Nothing had changed, and everything had: life went on, overflowing with sweetness, ordinary and extraordinary at once. He helped me while I worked — we worked together — stripped to the waist in the heat, both of us running with sweat; when we stopped to drink the ginger beer that Ma had brought us he drank so quickly he almost choked, wiped his mouth on the back of his wrist and looked up at me, grinning. And later, later, later . . . There was one twilight — dusk or dawn, after or before, I don't know — when Darnay took my hand and laced his fingers through mine; a moment under the stars when I kissed his forehead, my heart hammering — stupid, after everything we'd done, but I was afraid he'd shy away. There was a rose he picked in the shadow of the wall and pushed into the buttonhole of my shirt, and when I winced he leant forward and licked away the tiny line of blood where a thorn had scratched me. And a hot, late afternoon — was it our last, before Alta forgave him? — when we had snatched an hour together, alone, in the ruins, and he turned to me and said, with a new gentleness that made me shiver, "Maybe now you could call me Lucian."

"I thought I did."

300

"No. It's always Darnay. It makes me feel ...
strange." He grinned. "When you say 'Darnay' and
'please' in the same sentence."

"Shut up, Dar — Lucian." I dug my elbow into his
ribs. He was laughing. "What about Alta? She'll notice.
She'll ask exactly when we got on to first-name terms."

"Does that matter?"

"Yes." I sat up. "We can't tell her —"

"Of course not, you fool. I didn't mean that." He
pushed himself upright, twisting so he could look into
my face. "We can't tell anyone, ever."

"I know that! That's why I said —"

"Fine. Call me Darnay, then." He got to his feet and
walked away.

I opened my mouth to say, "You're not the lord of
the manor, *Lucian*," but something stopped me just in
time. He was knocking his fist against the stone
doorway, over and over again. Slowly I stood up and
walked over to him. My heart was thumping. I put my
hands on his shoulders, waiting for him to push me
away, or say something else. He didn't.

"Lucian," I said. "No one will find out."

"I hate this. I fucking hate it."

"I know." There was nothing else to say. He leant
back. I bent my head and rested my forehead against
the back of his skull. His hair smelt of grass and
summer earth.

After a moment he laughed — a dry, painful sound,
like a gasp — and dug in his pocket. He held something
out to the side for me to take. It glittered.

"What's this?"

"An engagement ring. I bought it in Castleford."

I clenched my jaw. I wanted to push him away and send the ring flying into the moat. Instead I took hold of it and turned it over in my fingers. It was a plain band of silver set with a chunk of dark stone, striped with lustrous shadows that shone and melted as it caught the light. It was beautiful. "Alta wanted a gold garland with rubies and pearls," I said.

"I know." He turned to catch my eye and laughed again. This time it sounded real. "You know Alta, she's not shy to drop a hint."

"So why —"

"Keep it."

"What? Me? Why?"

"I'm not going to give it to Alta now, am I?"

"You could pawn it. Or take it back to the shop. It must've cost —"

"Wear it round your neck. Please." He closed my hand over it, squeezing until the ring dug into my palm. "I'll get you a chain or something."

"All right," I said, although I still didn't understand. "I'll use a bootlace."

He strolled to the edge of the moat and dipped his foot into the water. I looked at the ring, tilting it to make the colours come and go: kingfisher, purple, moss . . .

"Wait a minute," I said. "If you knew Alta wanted something different . . ."

"I listened to my heart," he said, without turning round.

302

"You mean ..." I stopped. I could just see the contour of his cheek: he was smiling. "You knew," I said, slowly. "You bought it for me, knowing."

"I hoped."

"You calculating, arrogant bastard. You planned it all."

"Hey," he said, "it's not arrogance if you're *right*."

I grabbed him. He tried to trip me up, but I pulled him off-balance and we wrestled with each other, teetering on the edge of the water. I could feel him laughing all the way down to my bones. "Don't take me for granted," I said. "I'm not your servant." I was laughing, too, as I said it; then I wasn't, and we were at arm's length, staring at each other.

"Never," he said. "I promise. Never."

Did Alta see something in my face when she announced that, next time Lucian came, she'd let him apologise? I hoped not; but it was hard, when the world had changed so much, not to let anyone suspect. And Alta knew me so well; sometimes I wondered how she could *not* notice, when every muscle and tendon in my body felt new and raw ... She said, "At least he hasn't tried to *force* himself on me," and I had to turn away. I would have laughed, except that I could have cried. Now we'd be back the way we were. I wouldn't be able to touch him or call him Lucian. I'd be too scared to *look* at him in case she read my expression. I couldn't bear it; but I'd have to.

The next day I hated him. He made it look so easy. Every smile was for Alta, every joke was aimed in her direction, every sideways glance made her blush and dip her head. I felt my heart winding tighter and tighter like a clock, until I thought a spring would snap. That day we drove to the stonemason's for a couple of misspelt tombstones to replace the shelves in the dairy, and the three of us sat side by side while he and Alta laughed and flirted as if they were already engaged. Part of me wished I'd come on my own, but I knew that it would have been worse to know that I'd passed up the chance to be within a few feet of him — even if he didn't meet my eyes once. As we lifted the last slab into the back of the cart, he glanced up and I thought he'd look at me; but a second later he was helping Alta onto the seat, teasing her about the lettering on the marble, asking her if all her butter would come out marked with "PREPARE FOR DEATH". Had I imagined it all? Or was this his way of showing me that I was just a plaything? Once, when we stopped for Alta to squat behind a bush, he put his hand on the back of my neck. I started to turn to him, but he dug his fingernails into my flesh, holding me still. Every nerve I had was knotted into the space where his skin met mine. Alta was still within earshot. We sat like that, silent, until she wandered back to us with a posy of flowers to maintain the pretence that she hadn't needed a piss.

I couldn't eat that night, or sleep. I crept out of my room at midnight. I had to see him; if he wasn't waiting for me at the crossroads then I'd go all the way to the New House. When my bedroom door closed behind me the passage was thick with darkness, and as I trailed my fingers along the wall to guide me I could hear the whisper and bump of every tiny irregularity in the plaster. I carried my boots, and under my bare feet the floorboards hardly creaked at all.

But as I passed Alta's room she called out softly, "Emmett? Is that you?"

I stumbled and took a second to catch my breath. "I'm just checking on Splotch."

Alta opened her door so quickly I knew she hadn't been in bed. She was silhouetted against the moonlight, her face in shadow. "Is she all right? Did you hear something?"

"No. Never mind. Go back to bed, squirt."

"Only if you come and sit with me. I can't sleep."

I clenched my teeth. If I didn't see Lucian I'd go mad. But with Alta awake, listening for me to come back, I couldn't risk it. I let her pull me into the moonlit room. The colour was bleached from everything; her quilt was a black-and-white pattern of hearts and thorns, and the ivy clinging to the edge of the window gleamed like charcoal. It felt unfamiliar, like a room seen in a mirror.

Alta got into bed and lay down. I sat beside her and waited, but I could hear from her breath that she wasn't falling asleep. She hadn't let go of me, and her palm was damp. I tried not to think of the last time I'd felt someone else's sweat against my skin.

"Em?"

"Go to sleep."

She thumped her pillow into shape and rolled over. For a moment there was silence. Then she sighed and

305

sat up, pushing herself back against the wall. "I can't. I don't want to. Emmett . . ."

"What?"

"Do you think Lucian's in love with me?"

I twitched like a plucked string; then I exhaled, silently, and concentrated on relaxing every muscle. My heart was thudding so loudly I thought Alta might hear it. "Don't be an idiot."

She shifted, her eyes dark in the dim moonlight, and I expected her to protest. But she only laced her fingers together and said, at last, "Why is it idiotic?"

"He's — you're . . ." I stopped and shrugged.

She laughed softly. "Never mind," she said, a smile in her voice. She brought her knees up and hugged them to her. "He's here every day, Emmett. He could have taken Splotch and gone, long ago. But he didn't."

I cleared my throat. "He's probably just bored."

"No. I know it's meant to be, Emmett. I *know*." She leant forward and grabbed my wrist; I'd moved in spite of myself. "You can't understand until it's happened to you. But it will, Em." She drew in her breath. "The first time I saw Lucian . . . everything changed. I'd been waiting my whole life. Nothing will ever be the same again."

I didn't answer. Something rustled and pounced in the yard outside.

Alta didn't say anything else. Her grip on my wrist stayed strong. I leant back in the chair and closed my eyes, trying not to think. The moonlight slid across the floor; every time I looked the shadows had crept lower and longer. I dozed, waiting for Alta to let go of me, but

306

in the end I must have fallen asleep before she did, because when I woke it was morning and we'd both overslept. I could hear the cows complaining. I slipped out of the room without waking Alta and went to milk them myself; I didn't know why, except that I wanted to be alone. As I poured the milk out and marked the pans in the dairy, and then saw to the other animals, I felt queasy with frustration and unease. We were breaking Alta's heart, now, both of us; she just didn't know it yet. Every day she spent with Lucian, thinking he was in love with her ... and every day I spent with them together, aching for a word or a look and getting nothing ... But it wasn't my fault, it wasn't *fair*. There had to be a neat, painless way to get rid of her. I racked my brain, trying to ignore the curl of shame in my stomach: I couldn't stand another day of agony.

When Lucian arrived — swinging himself easily off his horse as though he'd slept like a dormouse — Alta was running round in stockinged feet, one boot swinging from her hand. She called down, "I'm coming, Lucian!" and then shouted, "*Em!* Where's my other boot? It was here yesterday!"

"I expect one of the dogs got it." I watched her scamper from room to room. "Come in bare feet. I'm going up to look at the fallow land and see whether it's ready to be harrowed. Darnay won't care if you look like a beggar's brat."

"Wait for me! It must be somewhere."

"Catch us up when you find it, then." I went down the stairs, while she bent to peer under the bed. She wouldn't find it; it was in the attic, behind the furthest row of apple-boxes. I glanced casually at Lucian. "She's lost her boot. She'll be ages. Shall we go?"

"All right." He raised his voice. "See you later, Alta!" Then, in unison, we turned and half ran to the gate, knocking elbows as we jostled to be the first to get to the latch. When the gate shut behind us we sprinted away, giggling like kids. "That was mean," he said at last, breathless.

"I know. Do you want to go back?"

"No." We swapped a look, and ran faster. Splotch galloped beside us, barking with excitement as if it was a race.

And then we were diving through the archway, into the enclosed part of the ruins, out of sight; and finally we could touch each other, and for a long time nothing existed except his mouth and hands and skin against mine.

Afterwards, when we were quiet, he said, "Why did you hate me so much?"

"Because you were so . . . *lordly*."

He started to laugh. He was lying on his back with his forearm over his face to block the sun. In the end he rolled his head sideways, still grinning, so that he met my eyes. "Sorry. I've just never heard so much contempt in the word, before."

"You know what I mean. The way you stood there" — I couldn't be bothered to move, but I moved my shoulder in the direction of the courtyard — "like you owned the place."

"I *do* own the place. Well, almost."

I pushed myself up to sit with my back against the wall. There was a daisy next to my leg and I began to pull it apart, petal by petal, like Alta playing *a-little-a-lot-passionately-madly*. "Your grandfather cheated mine out of this place," I said. "Did you know that? The woods where you said I'd been 'poaching' . . . We owned all of this, until your grandfather hired a few lawyers and swore blind it had always belonged to the New House."

Outside, Splotch burst into a flurry of barks. We drew apart a little, and I fumbled with my shirt-buttons; but after a second she fell silent again. Lucian let his head drop back on to the ground. "Frogs," he said. "No, I didn't know that."

"And then you swept Alta off her feet like you had *droit du seigneur*. And when I got home my father was practically tugging his forelock."

"Because I'd just saved Alta's life!"

"I was there too. If you hadn't been there, *I'd* have rescued her."

"If I hadn't been there," Lucian said, "she wouldn't have gone through the ice."

"You know?"

"She told me."

I squashed the bare daisy head with the ball of my thumb. Oh, Alta. She thought she was so sophisticated, but then she told him something like that. "She shouldn't have."

"Emmett . . ." He reached out, but I didn't move. "You know I'm not going to hurt her, don't you?"

"What do you think this would do, if she knew?"

"I meant it, you know. Give me the word," he said, very softly, "and I'll marry her."

I rubbed my face, as if there was a stain there I could wipe away.

He rolled over and stared at the cushions of moss that clung to the base of the wall. There was an ant climbing the stone, and he put out his finger so that it crawled across his knuckle.

"Will you reconsider, about being my secretary? Forget the money. Save it for Alta's dowry."

I didn't answer. He propped himself up on his elbow to flick the ant into the grass.

"Please, Emmett. Think about it. You'd be good at it, I know you would. All that primitive peasant cunning — all right, all right!" He let me wrestle him half-heartedly to the ground. Then he raised one hand and ran it through my hair, without meeting my eyes. "Come and stay with me tonight, at the New House. When you go home you can tell your parents that I wanted to interview you for the post."

I let go of him. "What?"

"Just for a night. A few nights. Please. I'll send them a letter to explain."

"I can't. You know I can't. I have work to do. If I'm not there . . ."

"You can't be that important."

I sat up. The sun was high in the sky; it was later than I'd realised. "It's a farm, Lucian. The work doesn't wait for you."

"Alta was ill for weeks. They can do without you for a few days. Please, Emmett."

I struggled to my knees, fumbling with my shirt buttons. "I have to go."

He caught my wrist. "I can't stand being with you and Alta and having to pretend I only have eyes for *her*."

I looked at him, and then away. Something scuttled in the wisteria above us and a flurry of petals drifted past, ivory edged with brown. A wood-pigeon called across the water, lazy and contented; a long, long way away I heard the sound of sheep, and the chiming of a clock.

"All right," I said, and in spite of myself I let him draw me down to lie beside him.

He grinned. I thought that I'd never forget how he looked at that moment, his eyes narrowed against the light, a blade of grass clinging to his temple.

"I know why you hated me," he said. "Because you wanted me, and you were scared."

Lucian's room in the New House was high up, under the eaves; it was cramped, with a sloping ceiling and a tiny iron fireplace, but it had a casement window that looked out on to the terrace and the ruined castle below. "It used to be a maid's bedroom," he said, as I looked round. "I wanted to be as far from my uncle as possible." I glanced involuntarily towards the door, but he leant against the wall, his arms on either side of my head, trapping me. He smiled. "It's fine," he added, "he sleeps in the trophy room, he doesn't like the stairs because of his gout. Also, he's always drunk. So you can make as much noise as you want."

"Why would I want to make noise?" He leant forward and bit my ear, and I laughed; then the air caught in my throat, and I had to concentrate on breathing before I drowned.

Time expanded and shrank to instants and eternities: a spasm of pleasure, sunlight on the ceiling, his fingers digging into my shoulder, half-darkness and the rich smell of wine that was older than we were. The weight of his ring on a string round my neck. He bent over me, picked it up in his mouth, and kissed me. The feel of the metal grating against my teeth, the taste of salt and stone and his saliva. Being woken at midnight by the clock in the stable block, and seeing him sitting on the window sill, outlined by the moonlight. The moon itself beyond the latticed glass: a pearl caught in a net. I didn't even know who I was any more. I was new, I was a stranger, I was Lucian's.

I had never been so happy. I didn't know it was possible. When I woke in the morning I lay there, incredulous, nearly blinded by it, holding on to the edge of the bed as if I was shipwrecked. I should have been at home, working, but it felt as if I was thinking about someone else's life, not mine. One way or another, the jobs would get done; it was a luxurious pleasure to lie still, listening to the birds, knowing that I was playing truant, not caring. It was late, and the sun was creeping up the side of the bed over the rumpled sheets and Lucian's legs. He slept as though he'd been thrown away, one arm over his head, the veins on his wrist showing blue under the skin. In sleep his face seemed smoother, his mouth wider. I watched him for a long time, imagining him as a child and as an old man. Then, at last, I had to get up; partly because the pleasure of looking at him was too close to pain, and partly because I needed to piss.

I crept along the corridor in the thick summer silence, grimacing when the floorboards creaked. But I didn't dare open any doors, in case I stumbled on the housekeeper — or, worse, Lucian's uncle. In the end I opened a window at the top of a narrow flight of stairs and emptied my bladder into the flowerbed below. I thought I knew the way back to Lucian's room, but I'd wandered too far and lost my bearings; I found myself in a long dark passageway, with closed doors on every side. It was so featureless and symmetrical that it made me uneasy. Finally I opened one of the doors as slowly and silently as I could, hoping to catch a glimpse of the window and the world outside: then at least I'd know which side of the house I was on. But when I peered round the edge of the door I saw that I needn't have bothered to be careful. It was only a storeroom, with sloping ceilings and one stoury window at the far end, looking out over the drive and the woods beyond. The smell of baked dust wafted out, warm as a bath.

I yawned and stepped into the room. There were boxes and old bits of furniture, crammed in so tightly it was hard to pick a path between them. Leaning against the wall was a rectangle swathed in a grimy length of velvet. I pulled it away and found a portrait of a pale woman with dark eyes and ringlets, wilting languidly against a landscape of cascading flowers. At the bottom of the frame it said, *Elizabeth Sassoon Darnay.*

313

Lucian's mother? No, the picture was too old, it had to be his grandmother. I leant closer, trying to see his features in hers. She had a curiously blank, melancholic cast to her eyes — nothing like his sharp cleverness — but perhaps there was a similarity in the shape of the forehead . . . I stepped back to take it in and blundered into a tin trunk. Something tickled my nose and I sneezed. I sat down abruptly on the trunk and nearly smashed a glass-covered case of butterflies.

There was another box in front of me. Idly I dragged it forward and opened it.

Books.

I almost pushed it away; now that I knew what they were, I was afraid to touch them, as if they were something soiled. But nothing bad could happen to me — not now, in this warm quiet attic, with Lucian asleep under the same roof. And when I lifted the top volume out and opened it, there was none of the sick whirling sensation I remembered from the book I'd bought from Wakening Fair. The words were just . . . words. *I was in the very February of my years, being of so tender an age that the Frost of Childhood was stark and pale upon me, not yet having given way to the first Blossoms of Maidenhood, when the first touch of a Gentleman bruised my Virginal Innocence.* I flipped forward. Pages of the same flat text, scattered with references to Venus and Priapus. *His enormous Weapon, which he directed, not towards the open gate to my Garden of Delights but down to that Earthlier realm* . . . I laughed.

"What are you doing?"

I twisted round. Lucian was half-dressed, leaning against the doorway, his hair falling over his face. He was wearing my shirt, with only one button done up. He made his way towards me, smiling, his limbs loose. I thought he was going to kiss me, but he froze. "What's that?"

"A book. I found it. But it's not — it doesn't . . ."

"I can't believe you're actually *reading* that." He took it from me and swung away as if he was about to throw it into a corner. Then he stopped, flipping the pages. "Oh."

"What?"

"I think it's a fake, actually. A novel. That must be why it's up here, and not in my father's . . . Look." He held it open in front of me and pointed at the label inside the front cover, against the patterned paper. "There's no way this is a genuine Sourly. For one thing, they've left the 'e' off 'Madame'."

"I have no idea what you're talking about."

"Madame Sourly? The leading binder for pornography, a hundred years ago? Wait, you mean *novels*?" he added, with a flicker of mockery. "They're not real books. They're written, like magazines. They're not actual people, or actual memories. They're invented. Never mind." He closed the book and shook his head, half smiling. "I can't believe how innocent you are."

"How'm I supposed to know about things when no one ever tells me?"

"Of course, your pure-minded parents. Don't worry. It's delightful."

"Go to hell, Darnay."

"No, really. I love it." He leant forward, put his mouth to my cheek and murmured, "And I mean, innocent about *everything*. Never read a book, never fucked a girl — or a boy, apart from me." He ducked away, grinning, as I aimed a swipe at his head. Then he caught hold of me, and his smile faded. We stared at each other.

There was a distant thud downstairs. He turned his head to listen. "Was that someone knocking?"

"I don't know. Won't your housekeeper get it?" Suddenly the summer silence seemed fragile; I didn't want to let the rest of the world in, not for a split second.

"If you mean the cook, she's only here in the evenings."

"What about your uncle?"

"Hardly. I suppose I'd better go." He stood up and began to do up his shirt.

"Really?" I reached out and unbuttoned the shirt as fast as he tried to button it. "But what if something stops you getting dressed? Maybe you should go downstairs like this."

"Very funny, Emmett." But he was laughing. "It might be the baker's boy."

"We'll go hungry. I don't care." The pounding reached a crescendo, and then stopped. "You see? Problem solved."

"All right." He sat back, letting me pull the shirt over his head. There was sweat in the notch of his collarbone. But as I leant forward, he made a tiny movement, so that our lips didn't touch.

316

"What?"

"The book," he said. "How did you know it was a fake? You did know, didn't you?"

"I don't know. It just didn't — pull me in, somehow. Does it matter?"

"No. But it's impressive. My father would love you." There was a distant, ironic glint in his eye that made me uncomfortable. "You're a mystery, Emmett. So innocent and yet . . ."

"Will you shut up about my fucking *innocence*?"

"All right," he said, and grinned. "As long as you'll let me destroy it completely."

By the time the stable clock struck four we were ravenous. We climbed out of the space we'd made for ourselves between the boxes — "I can't believe we just did that in front of my *grandmother*," Lucian said — and crept down the stairs past the trophy room and into the huge, dingy kitchen. We gorged ourselves on cold pie and potted meat and tipsy cake. I hadn't realised how long it had been since we'd eaten. At the end, the kitchen table was like a battlefield, strewn with debris and crumbs and smears of chutney, but when I started to clear it up Lucian shook his head. "Leave it. That's what she's paid for."

"But —" Ma would kill me, if I left the kitchen like that at home.

Lucian picked up the last crust of pie. "Come on," he said, with his mouth full, "I don't want anyone to see us here." He walked out. I hesitated, piled the plates hastily into the sink, gave the table a quick wipe and hurried after him.

When I caught up with him he was standing in the bay window of the hall, reading something. He looked up. "Sorry," he said. "I'm really sorry, Emmett."

My heart jerked like a weight at the end of a rope. "What?"

"It's all right, don't look so horrified, it's just a message from my father." He waved a slip of blue paper in my direction. "I have to go to Castleford."

"Now? It can't be that urgent."

"I'm sorry."

"You could pretend you didn't get it. Messages get lost."

"You don't know him, Emmett." He stooped to pick up the torn blue envelope from the rug, taking longer than he needed to. "If I disobey him, he'll find a way to make me wish I hadn't."

"Come on, Lucian. You weren't worried about marrying Alta in secret, how can you be too afraid to disobey him over a *telegram*?" He didn't answer at once, and I took a deep breath. "Or were you lying when you said that?"

"No! Of course not." He rolled the slip of paper into a tight baton, without looking at me. "But I — maybe I wasn't thinking . . . I'm sorry. I'm a coward, all right?"

"He can't be that bad. And surely your mother . . . ?"

"You don't know him! He's — he does things." He folded and folded the paper until it was a tiny blue parcel. "My mother lets him do what he wants. She

318

pretends not to see. It's better that way than letting him wipe her memory every time."

There was a silence. I stared at him. His face was drawn and distant, his old mask. I understood now why he'd never talked about his family.

I said, "You'd better go, then."

"Emmett — honestly, I'm sorry."

"I'm going too, I'll just get my boots."

"You don't have to go this very moment."

"You want me to help you pack?" He winced, and I was pleased. I turned and ran upstairs, pounding up flight after flight until I reached the tiny hot room under the eaves. It smelt of sweat and the wine we'd drunk. Part of me wanted to stay there, gazing at the unmade bed and the little fireplace and the view beyond the window, until it was all burnt indelibly into my memory; but I grabbed my boots and shut the door behind me.

When I got into the hall again Lucian was standing by the window, staring out. He looked round, but he didn't smile. "I'll come and see you as soon as I get back."

"Yes."

"Look after Splotch."

"Yes."

There was a silence. I took a step towards him. At the same moment he moved towards me, so that we stumbled and almost collided. I took his face in my hands. We kissed as if we could stop the earth turning, as if we were enemies as well as lovers, as if we'd never see each other again.

I knew what I wanted to say; but I made myself leave him without another word.

When I got home the yard was empty, lying quietly in the sunshine like a painting of a farmyard. No one was in the barn, oiling the haymaker; no one had mucked the pigs out, either. As I opened the gate Springle and Soot rushed over and barked at me as if they wanted something. Their bowl was dry. I filled it again, gave Splotch a drink too, and crouched under the pump to splash my face and neck with icy water. My head ached and my eyes were itchy with tiredness, but if I worked quickly I could make up for the work I'd missed. Maybe then no one would mind. My stomach twisted uncomfortably when I remembered how Pa had been when Alfred took two days off without telling anyone; but that had been during the haymaking, and it turned out he'd been blind drunk in a gutter in Castleford. I'd only slept one night under someone else's roof, and now I was back, ready to work.

I went to the barn and took out the straw-fork. But the silence was so thick that I found myself leaning it against the wall of the pigsty and turning my head to listen. It was as if someone was ill; that muffled, stagnant feeling, like being underwater. I crossed the yard and went inside, and the house was the same. I tiptoed towards the stairs, my heart so loud it seemed to echo off the walls. Then someone spoke in a hushed voice, and I spun round. It had come from the parlour — which was strange, on a weekday, unless we had guests. The door was ajar, and I crept to it and looked in.

Ma was sitting on the settee, her head bowed. Pa was standing beside the fireplace.

I pushed the door open. Ma looked up and saw me. She'd been crying.

"Emmett," Pa said. And I saw that he'd been crying, too.

CHAPTER
EIGHTEEN

They stared at me without speaking. Motes danced in the air, drifting lazily in and out of the light, going from visible to invisible in a split second. Beyond the shaft of sunlight the darkness was tinged with sepia, and everything seemed faded; the wallpaper had a jaundiced tinge, and the prints on the walls were grimy and indistinct. The wax fruits in the bell jar on the dresser were touched with a faint bloom of grey; somehow dirt had got in under the glass. In the corner of the room a scrap of dead leaf clung to the ceiling, where an ivy garland had hung at the Turning.

Ma hadn't cried since the day when Joe Tanner had sneaked into the stallion's stall and been kicked to death; and before that, since tiny Freya Smith had gone under the mill-wheel. And I couldn't remember seeing Pa cry, ever. Now he had a flushed raw look where he had wiped away tears; his eyes were bloodshot, and his mouth was slack and damp. There was something indecent about it, like nakedness or uncooked meat.

Something had happened to Alta.

The knowledge sucked the air out of the room, until I thought I would lose my balance. I couldn't speak; I couldn't bear for the silence to go on, but whatever broke it would be worse.

Ma said, "Sit down."

A moment ago all my joints had been watery, threatening to pitch me forward; but suddenly I couldn't have bent them if I'd tried. "What's happened?"

"What do you think, lad?" Pa's voice was weary, almost soft.

"Where is she?" Ma took a deep breath, and my insides turned over. "It's Alta, isn't it? Is she all right? Tell me what's happened!"

"Alta?" Pa frowned. "She's upstairs."

"It's a bit late to think about your sister, isn't it, Emmett?"

Silence. Ma's face was like ice: steady, white, so unforgiving it took my breath away. I looked from her to Pa and back again; and then I understood.

"I," I said, and I hated the thinness of my voice, the way it trembled. "I — don't —"

"I don't know what to say to you," Pa said. I'd never thought of him as old, but he was holding on to the mantelpiece as if he'd fall otherwise. "My son. We thought you were a good lad. We were proud of you."

The silence stretched on and on, settling around me until I was afraid I'd choke on it. "I didn't," I said, "I only . . ." It was like learning to read again: the simplest words were out of reach.

"How *could* you?" For a moment Ma sounded like Alta — only an Alta who had grown up, got old, lost hope. "I don't understand, Emmett. Tell me why."

"Why — what?"

"Why you chose to destroy Alta's future. Why you lied to us all. Why you threw away everything we taught you."

"I didn't do any of that!" At last the breath hit the bottom of my lungs, and I could speak. "I never lied! I just — I never meant to hurt Alta."

"How dare you say that!" Ma leant forward, as if she had to concentrate to breathe. "You knew how Alta felt. You knew how we all felt, how we hoped . . ." She swallowed. "We let you spend time with them when you should have been working. We trusted you. And you wrecked it all. Deliberately. Why would you do that?"

"Because I —" I stopped. I felt my knees tremble as if I'd come upon an adder in the grass and checked just in time. I said, "It wasn't about Alta. It wasn't about you."

Pa took a few steps into the middle of the room. "Don't say that," he said. "You're not the kind of son who would forget his family like that. Whatever you did with — that boy . . . It wasn't because you wanted it. You're not like that."

I stared at him. He wanted me to be malicious, and jealous, and vindictive; he *wanted* me to have done it out of hatred. Because otherwise I would be — *like that* . . . The tremors in my legs spread upwards, shaking me like an earthquake. It was Lucian I wanted, no one else. What did that make me? "Please," I said. "It wasn't like you think. It wasn't — just mucking about, it was — we care about each other."

Ma drew in her breath. "Be quiet."

"Please," I said again, and heard my voice crack.

"Shut up!" Pa paced to one side of the room and back.

I fixed my eyes on the remnant of ivy clinging to the ceiling. I could remember Lucian balancing on the chair to pin it up, before the Turning; that was the day we'd waltzed, and his body against mine had left me breathless. The memory caught me off-guard; I bit the inside of my cheek as hard as I could, and focused on the pain.

"What's done is done," Pa said. "We won't mention this after today. If you ever do anything like this again, Emmett, you won't have a family. That's all. Do you understand?"

I said slowly, "Anything like this?"

"If you ever — *touch* — another boy — another man — again. If you let a man touch you. If we hear anything — any rumour, any nasty story, *anything*." A pause. "Is that clear?"

I couldn't bear the way Pa was staring at me, as if I was a stranger. If I said yes, they'd forgive me; everything would go back to how it was, and we could pretend . . .

"Please," I said, "just listen. Please — Ma." I turned to her, forcing myself not to see the expression on her face. "You want Alta and me to have better lives, don't you? He's offered me a job, in Castleford. I could work for him."

"What are you talking about?"

My voice was getting higher and faster, but I couldn't stop myself. "Why should it be Alta, who gets

325

to escape? You wanted him to rescue her. Why can't he rescue me? I can leave here and be his secretary . . ."

Pa said, "You mean, be his whore."

There was an abrupt quiet in the room, like the silence after you drop something fragile.

"Robert," Ma said.

"It's true, isn't it?"

Suddenly my voice was steady, although I didn't know how. "You wanted Alta to marry him," I said. "Well, she still can. He'll propose to her if I ask him to. Then that's your happy ending."

Ma got to her feet. "Tell me," she said, "do you mean that?"

I hesitated.

"You're thinking about it," Ma said, in the same quiet voice. "You honestly think that Alta could marry him, after you and he have — after all this . . . You imagine that we would allow a man like that to touch our daughter. And you think that it would be good enough for Alta to marry a man who asked her because *you* told him to."

"If she still wanted him —"

"How dare you? What makes you think that you can do whatever you want, while Alta has to take your leavings? How *dare* you say that she should be satisfied with so little?"

"I didn't say that!"

"That's enough!" Pa strode into the space between us. "Enough, Hilda. I don't want to hear any more. Emmett, go to your bedroom. Tomorrow we'll forget all this. Right now I can't look at you."

326

"Just let me explain —" I said, not knowing which of them I was talking to.

Ma stepped close to me, and raised her hand. Stupidly — horrifyingly — I flinched; but she ran her fingers down my cheek, very gently, as if I was a child. "Don't you understand, Emmett? We'll forgive you. We're giving you another chance. Take it. Please." Her voice wavered, and she cleared her throat. "You're getting one more chance to be our son."

I stumbled upstairs. I couldn't judge the right place to put my limbs. When I stubbed my toe on the top stair, or knocked my elbow against the newel post, I didn't feel anything except a vague impact, as though something had happened a long way away.

Alta's bedroom door was closed. I walked past it without pausing; but something made me stop and look back. The shadow under the door moved, and I knew she was there.

"Alta?"

Nothing. But she was there all right; the shadow slid imperceptibly sideways, as though she was creeping away from the door.

I wrenched it open. She gasped; but before I could speak she'd caught her breath, drawn herself up to her full height, and smacked my face.

The world fizzed and sparkled, dancing with red and black spots. My ear rang, like a glass about to shatter.

Alta was shouting at me. *Bloody*, I heard, *disgusting bastard. Dirty shit* . . . And more words, words I didn't know she knew, words that didn't hurt me now but would fester and throb like splinters.

I hit her back.

It shut her up. She stared at me, wide-eyed, the blood rising to the surface of her skin. I could see the mark of my fingers along her cheekbone. For the first time in my life I didn't care that I'd hurt her; and I didn't care that I didn't care.

I heard myself ask, "How did they know?"

"I followed you. Once you came back with a rose in your shirt, so I knew you went to the ruins. I knew where to go. And I saw you." She swallowed. I had never seen her look at anyone the way she was looking at me: her face trembling with hatred and misery, and a strange, adult indifference to whether I saw how she felt . . . "Do you want me to spell it out for you?" she said. "I saw you together. Fucking."

I shut my eyes.

"I know you hid my boot, Emmett. You left me behind on purpose. I looked for it for ages, and then I put on my good shoes and came after you. I wanted to see Lucian." She swallowed. "But when I found you both, I heard you talking. You talked about me. About how I didn't matter."

"I *never* said —"

"And about how he couldn't bear to pretend he loved me."

"Alta."

"It doesn't matter. You don't care, do you? You were *laughing* with him." Her voice rose and cracked, but after a moment she went on again. "So I came home. I tried not to tell Ma and Pa, but then you stayed away all night — and I couldn't *not*."

I squashed down the thought of how it must have felt. Alta had no right to feel like that. She'd known what damage it would do to tell them.

"They thought I was mistaken, at first. And then I told them that you'd kept the egg Lucian gave you at Wakening Fair —"

"You've been through my stuff?"

"And I told them that he has those freckles on his back. And what I saw you doing." Silence. Was I imagining a tiny tremble of triumph in her voice? She tilted her chin. "Then they believed me."

I put my hands up to my face. I wanted to stop existing.

"Pa wrote to Lucian's family in Castleford. He wanted to make sure you never saw him again."

"You shouldn't have told them," I said, and I sounded like a stranger. "It was none of your business, Alta."

"I *love* him." A pause. "I — *loved* him."

Of course. The trump card. The words that, if *I* said them . . . I didn't let myself finish the thought. I looked her straight in the eye, and put every ounce of disdain into my voice that I could. "It's a pity that you told on us, then," I said. "If you hadn't, he would have married you."

She stared at me. "That's a lie."

"It doesn't make any difference now, does it?" It was a sick, horrible satisfaction to see her face whiten and whiten, until at last she blinked and the tears spilt down her cheeks. Then the spark of gladness died, and all that was left was ash.

I turned to leave. Something in the corner of the room drew my eyes. Alta's dancing shoes — ivory silk slippers, her pride and joy — lay against the wall as if she'd kicked them across the floor without caring where they landed. I could remember her face lighting up when she unwrapped them from their tissue paper, two birthdays ago; she'd made such a fuss when she wore them to last year's Harvest Supper that I'd had to carry her over the muddiest part of the road to keep them spotless. Later someone had said, "You dance like a fairy in those." I'd nudged her and murmured, "More like a goblin," and we'd got the giggles so badly we had to go outside. Even then she'd demanded that I put my cloak on the ground for her to tread on. Now they were tide-marked with grass stains and flecked with mud.

"I'm sorry," I said. "I didn't mean to hurt you."

"Just go, Emmett."

I hesitated. Somehow I expected her to relent, like when she was small and throwing a tantrum; but she stared at me until I left.

I found myself in my own room without knowing how I'd got there. I curled up on my bed as if the smaller I made myself the less it would hurt. For a long time all I could do was keep breathing, trying not to think; then I heard Splotch bark at someone riding past, and I started to cry.

I missed Lucian so much it was like a wound. I could feel the outline of it, a desperate fiery ache that started

330

under my sternum and ended somewhere in my groin. If I moved, or spoke, or inhaled too deeply, it hurt more. I'd never thought I could want to die: but it was like drowning over and over again, except that the final blackness never came.

Lucian had gone away. I would have given anything to catch a glimpse of him or hear his voice, and he wasn't here. That was all I knew, all that mattered. But slowly the other things began to take shape, too: Ma and Pa would never forgive me, Alta hated me, I had ruined their lives as well as my own. Alta had seen us together, watched us.

And Lucian. His father would know about us, now. If Lucian was punished, that would be my fault too. The thought made me catch my breath and knot myself tighter: Lucian suffering because of me, Lucian despising me as much as Alta did . . . I clung to the memories I had — of us laughing together, touching each other, the words we'd said — but with every heartbeat they receded further. I needed to remember so badly that I couldn't be sure any more. Either he'd hate me now, or worse — what if he'd never really cared about me? What if he wasn't thinking of me at all? What if he was relieved to be rid of me?

I wasn't hungry. I'd never be hungry again. The only thing that made me move was Splotch whining outside in the yard; but the effort of getting up to feed her made me giddy, and as soon as I'd done it I came back to bed. A minute later I heard her scratching at my door. Dogs weren't allowed upstairs but I couldn't be in any more disgrace than I already was, so I let her in.

She nosed about, settled into the space next to me, and I put my arms around her; her warmth didn't fill the emptiness inside me, but her quiet breath and the weight of her chin on my shoulder calmed the ache. Finally I drowsed, exhausted.

When I jolted awake it was nearly dark. Splotch leapt to the floor and scampered away, her claws skittering on the wood. My heart was thumping as if I'd had a nightmare, but it was the real world that had woken me, sharp as a whiplash. I sat up, trembling, pushing the sweaty hair out of my face.

The parlour door shut. I heard the creak of footsteps and a muffled voice. It was a man, but it wasn't Pa; although a few seconds later Pa replied, with a low murmur that might be deferential.

I took Splotch downstairs and let her into the yard. The evening air was warm and sweet after the fustiness of my room, but I shut the front door again and walked along the hall to the parlour door. That voice . . . I paused, listening.

"I understand your disappointment, Mr Farmer."

For a juddering, overwhelming moment I thought it was Lucian. Then the buzzing in my ears faded, and I knew that it wasn't: the accent was the same, but the voice was deeper, hollow-sounding and bloodless.

"All right," Pa said. "I'll get him." I stumbled backwards, but not fast enough: when Pa opened the door and saw me there his eyes narrowed. But he didn't say anything except, "You'd better come in, lad."

I followed him into the parlour. There was a man sitting in the armchair, his legs crossed, his head resting indolently against the back of the chair. He was oldish, with thick sandy-grey whiskers but no moustache, so that his mouth sat in the middle of his face like an overripe fruit. He looked me up and down, and his lips broadened into a fleshy pink smile.

He knew. It was in the way he looked at me. "Emmett?"

"Yes," I said. My shirt was rumpled, and I stank of sweat and dog. "Who the hell are you?"

"My name is Acre. I am an employee of Mr Darnay. Mr Darnay *senior*," he added, as if anyone could have imagined he meant Lucian. "Please, sit down."

"This isn't your house."

"Sit down, Emmett," Pa said. He was standing close to the lamp, and his hairline was glinting with moisture.

I sat down. My ankle started to tremble, and I ground my heel into the floor, trying to get it to stop.

"Thank you, Mr Farmer," Acre said. He smiled up at Pa, and gestured towards the door. Pa swallowed, looked at me, then turned and left without a word.

"So, Emmett," Acre said. "This is all rather regrettable, isn't it? I feel for you. Lucian can sweep people off their feet and he tends to forget about the consequences, I'm afraid. I expect you feel very bruised at the moment. But I'm here to help."

I bit the tip of my tongue, and said nothing.

"I understand if you feel resentful at my interference. It must seem impertinent. But you must realise that we have long experience of dealing with these sorts of . . . problems. And we're on your side. Lucian is a good boy but he's young, and he leaves a trail of destruction for other people to clean up. So —"

"A trail of destruction?"

"He has inflicted great hurt on you and your sister. I can see that you're suffering. No" — he shook his head — "I'm not asking you to tell me. I know how . . . violated you must feel already. But I want you to know that I sympathise. And I'm here to offer you a solution."

A wild hope leapt inside me. "What?"

"I'm sorry, Emmett. What happened shouldn't have happened. Lucian was cruel — thoughtless, to let you think . . ." He cleared his throat. "What I can do is to make it all go away. You can go back to your old life — just as you were. You were content before you met him, I assume?"

I hesitated. "I suppose so."

"Good. Then let me make you an offer. We will cover all expenses — transport, and so on — to allow you to visit a binder. As a gesture of apology and goodwill, we will also give you and your family a small financial gift. These occasions can be very upsetting. You'd be surprised how important it is for close relatives to feel that something positive has come out of this sort of mistake."

"Wait." I tried to think. He had such a plausible, resonant voice, like a singer lulling me to sleep. "You want me to go to a binder? To put myself into a book? To forget it all?" I thought I heard the faint music of Wakening Fair, throbbing distantly in my ears.

"There is a lot of prejudice around binding, Emmett. Let me set your mind at rest. It's a safe, painless process, and at the end of it you would be exactly as you were before. No memory of Lucian, no memory of your family's disappointment, no memory of heartbreak. You would be, as it were" — he leant forward, one plump hand cupped as if he were begging — "*whole again.*"

"And you'd pay me to do it. Why?"

"Because Lucian is our responsibility. And when he takes advantage of someone impressionable, like you, we feel that it would simply be wrong to let it destroy lives. Your life, for example, or your family's."

"You said . . ." I swallowed. "You say, *when* he does this. Do you mean . . .?"

He shifted a little in the chair as if it had suddenly become too small for him. "You know, Emmett, we think we know someone very well, and often we don't. Lucian can be very charming. He made you think that you were the only person in the world, I expect. And he probably wasn't exactly . . . lying."

"Not *exactly* lying?" But I could hear his voice: *I'm sorry. I'm a coward.*

"He is rather prone to love affairs. Did you think you were the first?"

I turned my head, but whatever I was looking at was blurred.

"He was sent away from Castleford because he'd become involved with someone unsuitable. A scullery maid, who was rather — ah — *young*, as it happens; perhaps that's why he chose you over your sister. But please don't feel a fool. He is quite ruthless in some ways; he sees it all as a form of venery. Hunting, that is."

"That's not true."

"Well, never mind. It hardly matters now, does it? Let's think about the future. Suppose I come with a carriage tomorrow morning. We'll take you out to the bindery in the marshes. It's better to keep this sort of thing discreet. And when it's done I will give your father twenty guineas — gold or banker's note, whichever you would prefer. Does that sound acceptable?"

My heart was beating so hard that I could feel Lucian's ring bumping against my breastbone.

I said, "No."

His face changed. There was another silence.

"I see," he said at last. "How much?"

"What?"

"Twenty guineas isn't enough. So what would be?"

"It's not the money."

"It's always the money. Name your price. Thirty? Fifty?"

"No." I stood up. "You don't understand, do you? I don't care that Lucian's had other lovers." My voice wobbled on the word but I didn't care. "I want to remember. That's all I've got, now."

"Your fond memories of an arrogant, manipulative palone?"

I hadn't heard the word before, but I could guess what it meant. "Yes."

"Emmett." My name sounded heavy in his mouth, like a warning. "Be reasonable. Reconsider. Let's call it seventy-five, and that's generous."

"I'd rather *die*."

"Be careful what you wish for."

I glared at him, hating every inch of his pudgy, obscene face, and finally he shrugged and stood up. "Very well," he said. "A pity. We were only thinking of you." He dug in the recesses of his coat — a huge, sagging thing, much too warm for a summer evening — and brought out a parcel. "Apparently this is yours. A shirt you lent him. He didn't want you to have any excuse to contact him again."

I took it.

"If you need my help," he said, "your father will know where to find me. And if you lie awake tonight wishing the pain would go away . . . there's no shame in changing your mind."

"I won't change my mind."

He gave me a quick, unfriendly quirk of a smile. Then he bowed and left.

When I looked up, my mother was in the doorway. I held on to the shirt Acre had given me; but it was mine, she had no excuse to take it away. She didn't say anything.

"I'm not going," I said.

She gave a long, heavy blink, as if it was an effort to keep her eyes open. "We can put the money towards Alta's dowry."

"Ma . . ."

"We tried so hard to keep you away from books. That evil magic . . . But Mr Dar — your friend told you, didn't he? I should have known. We should have seen what sort of man he was."

"You mean —"

"We thought we'd protected you. We were so careful . . ." She leant against the doorway, twisting her apron into a slow knot. "My mother always said it was a disgusting, unnatural kind of magic. Sucking out memories, shame and pain and sorrow . . . She said that's why some binders live so long. Because they feed off every drop of life." She glanced down at the smudges of flour and soot she'd left on her skirt without seeming to see them. "But — if you could only come back as you were, before . . ."

Something caught in my throat. "Ma, listen. Lucian and I were —"

"Go," she said. "Please, just go. There's nothing more you can do, to shame us."

I pushed past her and up the stairs to my room. My heart was drumming in my ears, and I was shaking. I sat down on the bed, clutching my old shirt to me, fighting the ache in my throat. I bent my head and pressed my face into the linen. I would have given anything to feel Lucian's arms round me, smell his skin under the faint scent of lavender water.

Something crackled in the cloth.

A note, sewn into the collar. It took an eternity to pick the seam apart with the point of my knife; but then at last I could unfold it.

Meet me at sunrise at the crossroads between the marsh road and the Littlewater road.

I love you.

CHAPTER
NINETEEN

If I'd had to speak to anyone that night, they would have seen how I felt. I could feel it blazing on my skin as if I was drunk. I was lucky that I'd already missed dinner, and I could stay in my room on my own: not sleeping, cradling my happiness.

Once, when I came back from getting a drink of water, I crossed Alta on the stairs. As I pushed past her our eyes met. There was moonlight spilling in a wedge from the open door on the landing above, and the top steps were cut into triangles of black and white; but down here the light was dim, elusive, clinging like cobwebs to the planes of her cheek and temple. She might have been any age — maiden, mother, crone — but her eyes were her own, steady and dark.

"Emmett?" she said.

There was a softness in the way she'd spoken that made a wild hope leap inside me: she'd forgiven me, she'd never really loved him at all —

"Yes?"

"I'm sorry," she said.

An owl called, distant and then closer; something scuttled in the corner of the yard. I imagined the owl circling, silent now, waiting for the glint of tiny eyes, the twitch of a tail. A death like that, you wouldn't hear it coming.

"I'm sorry too."

I took a step down, towards her; but with a quick movement she turned away, muttered, "I've got to go to the privy. Women's things," and slid out into the yard. I turned to watch her pick her way across the cobbles, holding up her cloak to stop it dragging in the straw.

I might have called after her, I suppose; but I didn't. I went back to my room, to wait.

I was dressed and ready before the sky started to go blue; the moon had set, but the stars were still as thick as a harvest when I crept down the stairs and outside. I couldn't get the breath deep enough into my lungs. I went out on to the road, and ran all the way to the crossroads.

At first, in the dim pre-dawn light, all I saw was the glimmer of a lamp and a thick patch of darkness; as I got closer I could make out the shape of a horse and cart. I wanted to call out, but the silence lay everywhere like a spell, and I was afraid to break it. I could see Lucian — wrapped up against the chill, his hood over his face — stamping impatiently beside the horse's head. I felt a wide, idiotic grin spread over my face, and I broke into a sprint. "Lucian! *Lucian!*"

He turned as I reached out for him, my heart hammering.

It wasn't him.

I took it in all at once; as if, deep down, I'd already known. It was Acre standing beside the horse, his face half-covered by his hood. Another man was slumped in the back of the cart — yawning, now, with a casual weariness that made my backbone creep — and —

Alta.

She was asleep. No. There was a shadow across her forehead, cast by nothing; one of her eyes was swollen, and there was a dried trickle of blood between her nose and mouth. I opened my mouth, but when I tried to speak there was nothing but a dry gasp, like the wheeze of a bellows.

"Do as I tell you, and she'll be fine." Acre pushed his hood back. For a long time neither of us moved; then I realised he was pointing at the cart. He wanted me to get in. At last he said, "Don't make this harder than it has to be, boy."

"Where's Lucian?"

He snorted. "Lucian? Not very sharp, are you, boy?"

I should have known. I should have guessed.

I said, in a strangely steady voice, "And how did you get hold of Alta?"

"Same trick, of course. She was even more eager than you were."

The other man gave a high-pitched giggle that made me jump. "She's a madam, isn't she? She'll be a handful when she's a real woman."

"Don't talk about her like that."

Acre clicked his fingers. "Enough of this," he said. "Get in the cart, will you? It's a long way."

I stared at Alta, and then forced myself to look back at him. It was a bluff. They wouldn't hurt her more than they had already. A slap was one thing; anything more than that was a crime. "I'm not going anywhere with you."

"You're past the negotiation stage, boy."

"I'm *not going anywhere*."

"Get the bag, will you, Wright? Thank you." Acre reached into the cart and held up a sack. My gut flipped over. "Now. I believe in giving people second chances. I am going to show you how serious I am, but because I am a kind man I won't start with your sister. Do you understand?"

It was wriggling. Acre held it higher, so that I could see the bulges where paws and muzzle were scrabbling against the sackcloth. It whined: a desolate, lonely, terrier-whine.

"No," I said, "no — please!"

"I never thought I'd see a Darnay love anything, but apparently one overgrown rat-whelp can get fond of another," Acre said. "Wright picked up this little runt yesterday, when it tried to attack his ankles. What is it called again? Splat?"

"No."

"No? Not that it matters much. Wright, will you do the honours, please?"

"You can't — please don't — *please*."

He dropped the sack on to the bottom of the cart. It landed with a thud and a yelp. I flung myself forward, but before I could haul myself over the side Acre had grabbed my arm and wrenched it up behind my back. "Go on," he said, to the other man.

"No — Splotch, *no* —"

The man — Wright — stood up, unfolding like a giant. He had a cudgel next to him, and he hefted it and adjusted his grip. He was smiling. He nodded at Acre like a musician about to begin a tune; then he swung the cudgel into the sack. Once. Twice. Three times.

I was shouting. I fought so hard that Acre nearly lost his grip on my arm, but he hissed through his teeth and hauled me back. Then I was on my knees, retching, my mind empty of everything except the blazing pain in my shoulder. When it faded everything was quiet: no more thumps or whines, nothing but the faint whisper of a breeze. My face was wet. Threads of spit and stomach acid swung from my mouth.

"Get up." A foot smashed into my ribs. It knocked the air out of me, and for a second I clawed at the ground as if it could help me to breathe; then my lungs started working again, and I got to my feet. Acre nodded at the cart. "Get in."

I reached out and supported myself against a wheel, noticing with a numb interest how much my legs were shaking. My whole body was juddering, as though I was driving over a rough road. I took a few steps towards the back of the cart, where Wright had let down the end panel. I clambered up and collapsed on to the seat. If I looked sideways I could see the bloodied sack; it was so still I could almost imagine that they'd been bluffing. But I'd heard her bark, and the frantic heart-rending whine when she recognised my voice.

Every time I blinked, the world blurred. Water rolled off my chin and soaked my collar. It didn't feel like crying; it felt like I was dissolving from inside.

"Now," Acre said. He sighed as if the worst was over. "We're going to drive out to the binder's house, and when we get there you'll tell her that you want to forget all about Lucian Darnay. And then we'll drive back, and you and your sister will be fine, and no one will ever bother you again. How does that sound?"

Opposite me, Wright gave me an eerily childish smile and patted Alta's knee.

"All right," I said.

"And when she asks, it's because *you* want it, you understand? You say a word about us, or the Darnays, and — well, as I say, let's not go into that."

"I understand."

He seemed to be about to add something else, but he clicked to the horse and we set off.

The sun had risen. In the east the sky was too bright to look at. I bowed my head and stared into the jolting shadows. There was a ribbon of red unrolling along the boards, inching closer and closer to my feet. I stared at it and wondered whether, after all this, I'd remember Splotch — or would she be taken away, along with everything else?

Everything else gone. Every memory of Lucian — every time he'd looked at me, smiled, laughed at a joke — every touch, every detail of his body, his bony intelligent hands, his chest, the back of his neck, the base of his spine — everything he'd said . . . *Are you getting excited, Farmer? . . . I won't let you down . . . Trust me . . . Let me . . . Yes.*

I love you. But that wasn't real.

I clenched my eyes shut. If I went over and over it all, now, before I saw the binder . . . Maybe I could keep some of it, maybe some of it would stay — not all of it, but some — please, just the first time he kissed me, or the last time, the last thing he said to me — please, if I could only keep that memory, I'd give anything, because at least if I remembered I could live it again and again, even if I never saw him again that would still be something.

"Get a hold of yourself," Wright said, "you'll flood the cart."

"It's fine," Acre said from in front, "if he looks like he's upset she won't ask him too many questions."

I took a deep breath through my mouth, tasting the salt on my tongue. A wisp of grass had stuck to the line of blood on the bottom of the cart, between a shadow of a footprint and a badly-hammered nail. The blood ran into the slit between two planks, and I imagined red droplets falling on to the path like a trail of beads. The air had a different smell to it now, already tinged with the moist thick scent of the marsh; a bird called, high and plaintive. The only other sounds were the rumble of the cart and the quick step of the horse.

Perhaps I could lie. Or fake it. Perhaps there was a way I could keep my memories, as if my own heart was a secret book made of muscle and blood. No one would know.

If only I knew more about binding. When I thought about it, all I could think of was a kind of death: a door to walk through, and no way to imagine what was on the other side. Lucian was the only person who had ever spoken about it.

He had known they'd do this to me. Lucian had known.

I caught my breath. He'd hated the sight of books. Because, I thought, because . . . The thought was vast and sickening. Because this was what happened to everyone he'd seduced. The word sat and looked at me and wouldn't retreat. Yes, seduced. He'd seduced me. And he'd known that sooner or later this would happen; he hadn't wanted to think about it, but — yes — he'd *known*. It was a risk he'd been prepared to take.

I narrowed my eyes and looked into the brightest part of the sky. My vision blurred and stung, but nothing changed. When I turned my head away a black circle hovered in front of me, blotting out Alta's face.

I reached for the note in my pocket. There was no need to read it again, even if I could have blinked away that dark sun; it was burnt into my memory. *I love you.* It wasn't true — but maybe, after all, it *was* Lucian's handwriting. I held it out, over the side of the cart. The wind had dropped. When I let it go it fluttered straight down and stuck in a tuft of reeds by the side of the road.

When we came round the last curve and saw the house it looked as if it was burning. The sun was dipping behind us, and every window reflected a flat, coppery fire: too still to be real flames, but enough to send a prickle of unease down the back of my neck, as if I was about to walk into an inferno. I set my jaw and refused to look; instead I watched Alta, who was hunched into the corner of the cart, her eyes shut. She'd woken a few hours ago in a daze, and asked where we were and where we were going; but when they told her she didn't protest or try to run away. I didn't know if she was in pain, or if it was because she was afraid. Wright gave her water and she drank a few mouthfuls, avoiding my eyes. Once, after a long time, she murmured, "Em? Are you all right? Maybe it's for the best, anyway . . ." but I didn't answer. I hadn't told her what was in the bloodstained sack at our feet, and she didn't ask.

The cart turned off the main road and down a track. A breeze blew warmth into my face, tinged with a miasma of mud. I held on to the side of the cart and splinters dug into my palm. Under my shirt Lucian's ring knocked against my chest with every jolt. I could walk out of the other end of this, like a miner stumbling out into the sunshine. Start again. Fall in love with someone else. I'd be innocent again. It would be for the first time, again.

The cart rolled to a halt. A thick cud of bile pushed into the back of my mouth. I swallowed hard, fighting the urge to vomit.

"Go on."

I couldn't move. I couldn't think.

"Ring the bell," Acre said, with heavy patience. "Tell her you need her to bind you. She'll ask if you're sure, and what you need to forget. Then you tell her about Lucian. It's not hard." He dug in his pocket and passed me a card. "If she asks about money, give her that."

348

Somehow I took it. *Mr Piers Darnay, Factory Owner.* I stared at my other hand, clenched on the side of the cart, and wondered how to make it let go.

"Em . . .? Please."

I glanced at Alta. Wright was digging one finger into the side of her neck. He gave me another wide, infantile smile.

I got up. I had to think about it step by step: if I did it like that it was manageable. I promised myself that after the next step I could change my mind; just one more, and one more . . .

Then I was on the doorstep, tugging the bell-rope. The bell jangled, off-key.

After a long time the door opened. "Yes?" She was ancient, and she looked like a witch.

"I need to be bound," I said, as though I was reciting a lesson. I looked past her to the dark-panelled hall, the staircase, the doors that led off in every direction. Inside, it was dim; only a lattice of reddish sunlight lay on the floor, and shone. It was exactly the colours of a flame, a fire-varnish on the old wood, smooth and steady . . . I stared at it, because I didn't want to look into her face. "I need to forget."

"Are you sure? What's your name, boy?"

I answered; it must have been the truth, because I didn't have to think about it. The light on the floorboards shimmered. Outside there was sun and sky and sunset. I clung to that thought.

I don't know how much time passed. She took my arm and led me through a passage and into a workshop. I went with her, numb all the way to my feet.

There was a door that she unlocked. There was a quiet room where the last dregs of sunlight fell across a bare table. She gestured to a chair, and I sat. There was sympathy in her face, as if I could tell her everything and she would understand.

"Wait," she said. We waited for a long time, until the sunlight had crept all the way to the far wall, thinning and reddening on the grain of the floorboards — until, in spite of myself, I felt my heartbeat slow, and exhaustion start to unknot the threads that held me together. Then, at last, she reached out her hand and touched my sleeve, and I didn't move away. She said, "Tell me."

"Lucian," I said. "The ruins. We shouldn't have been there."

Darkness swooped out of nowhere and ripped me apart.

PART THREE

CHAPTER
TWENTY

Emmett Farmer's eyes bulge. He drops to his knees and gulps down his memories like a man being forced to drink water till his stomach splits.

The smell of burning leather is sickening. Smoke billows out of the fireplace and stings my eyes. My fingers slide off the bell-pull. I can't remember whether I rang or not. I can't move. I have never seen anything like this. His face is distorted. Swollen. His hands claw uselessly at the air. He chokes and bubbles like a sackful of drowning kittens.

I don't pity him. It's his own fault, isn't it? He put the book on the fire, not me. He must have known what would happen. And now if he's on all fours, scrabbling and retching, ruining my father's Persian rug, that's his problem. He asked for it. But all the same I can't look away.

"Lucian," he says. Or does he? A mumble, a vowel and a sibilant, deformed by the grimace on his face. Perhaps I hear my name the way we hear singing in the wind: because we want to find meaning in meaningless things.

Or else he's asking for help. But I can't help him. Even if I could bring myself to touch him, there's nothing I could do. And if he were asking for help he should call me Darnay. *Mr* Darnay, ideally. Who the hell does he think he is, to call me Lucian? Or to have said *I'm sorry*, with that look in his eyes? It's almost better to see him like this.

He says my name again, unmistakable now. And — how dare he — he reaches out, balancing precariously on his knees. It's revolting: like a beggar, only worse, because of the way he's dressed. A fop, like de Havilland. A weakling. No, he wasn't weak, when we struggled in the hallway earlier. Weak-minded, rather. A flicker in his eyes when he looked at me, as though he was afraid. Coward.

I take one deliberate step back. My heart is thudding like an engine. If he tries again to touch me I'll kick him like a dog. Smoke billows out from the hearth.

He coughs — no, he sobs. His face is wet. Strings of saliva swing from his open mouth. He bows his head and convulses until bile spatters across the pattern of my father's rug. I stumble sideways. Stay on your feet, you fool.

The book is almost gone. It's burning faster than you'd expect, as if the paper is only half real. But the smoke is thick and dark and gets into my throat. It aches. I swallow and swallow again. I wipe my face with my loose shirt-cuff. The linen comes away grimy and wet. Fury blazes through me. They have no right — Emmett Farmer has no right — to do this. To infect me with their dirty magic . . . He's a binder, he deserves what he gets, but I'm innocent. This is nothing to do with me. Whatever sick sadness is getting inside me, coating my lungs with sticky ash, it's not mine. I don't want the tiniest smear of Emmett Farmer's memories on my skin.

The book flares in a final crown of flame. Then it's over. There's a pile of ash — the pages powdery and grey like the gills of a mushroom — on the glowing coals. The leather has curled away into brittle rags. The smoke begins to clear.

"Lucian," Emmett Farmer says, one more time. He tries to get to his feet. He goes to grab the table for balance and misses. He blinks convulsively. "Please — Lucian —"

His eyes roll upwards. For an instant his stare is white and blank. Then he drops forward, his jaw thudding into the floor. Liquid gurgles out of his mouth. He's still breathing, so he isn't dead.

Silence.

What do I do? Now that Farmer isn't moving, the thought of touching him isn't quite so horrible. I could check his pulse, but I can see the rise and fall of his ribs. Or I could turn him so that he won't choke on his own vomit. But he's already face down and the spasms seem to have stopped. I drop to one knee next to him and reach tentatively for his shoulder. I don't know what I'm going to do. Find out whether he's really unconscious, perhaps. But as soon as my knuckles brush his clothes my body swarms with shivering heat. I recoil.

I have to get a grip on myself before someone comes.

I stagger to my feet and empty the last dregs of brandy into my glass. The decanter rattles against the rim like chattering teeth. I slop some brandy on my collar as I drink. It runs down my neck and mingles with the cold sweat on my chest. The red flowers on the walls gape like mouths, wider and wider, behind the lingering smoke. How my father would mock if he saw me trembling like this. I have to pull myself together.

There's a trick that I use more and more. In my mind I imagine a grey wall rising above me, vast and featureless, so smooth it cheats all sense of perspective. I close my eyes and stand in front of it. I imagine it rising up and over, curling round to meet itself, so that I'm enclosed in a grey bubble the size of infinity. I'm alone. There is nothing here to harm me. Nothing can get through.

When I open my eyes again the spasms of shivering have stopped. The room is back in focus: quiet, luxurious. Velvet and leather and ebony. Antique grand-father clock, china dogs on the mantelpiece, cabinet of curiosities. A gentleman's study, as seen in a picture paper. Apart from the body on the hearth.

I walk to the dark glass-covered painting of anonymous mountains and look into the glass. My reflection looks terrible, but at least I can meet my own eyes. I push my sweaty hair off my face. I straighten my tie, pulling the knot up so that it almost hides the damp stain on my collar. I stink of brandy, but that's not unusual.

At last I ring the bell. I sit down in the leather armchair in front of the hearth, crossing my ankle over my knee. I am relaxed. I am in charge. There will be no crack in my voice when Betty comes to ask me what I want. I will order some more brandy, and then I will ask her politely if she could remove the binder from the hearthrug and dispose of him in an appropriate manner. I have no idea what an appropriate manner is; if she asks me I'll shrug and suggest she ask someone else.

I'm determined not to stare at Farmer's body. I raise my eyes and focus on the oval table that my father uses for his desk. The books that Farmer delivered for him are spread out everywhere. It'll be obvious that I went through them, looking for something. I don't know if that will make him angry or not. That's the worst thing about my father, not knowing either way. If he's angry —

I breathe. I imagine the grey wall surrounding me. Featureless. Blank.

The door opens. I am so encased in grey that I manage not to jump. I clear my throat. "Clear up this mess, will you?"

No answer. A footstep. Not Betty's footstep.

The grey vanishes, leaving me in a world full of sharp edges and nausea. I swivel round and struggle to my feet. My head spins and I bite my tongue to try to focus. Pathetic.

My father gives me a faint smile, which to anyone who didn't know him would look absent-minded. I say, "I'm sorry, I thought you were one of the servants."

"One misplaced word," he says, with a little sigh, "can be the difference between victory and failure. Pay attention, fool."

My face goes hot. I clench my jaw.

My father steps around the dark splatters of vomit and nudges Emmett Farmer with his foot. "What a scene of carnage. I hope you are not to blame."

"No! I —" He raises one finger and I fall silent.

"Give me the salient facts as briefly as you can."

I swallow. I can't find words to tell him what just happened. My *salient facts* — the way Farmer looked as he collapsed, the way he said my name, the horror of seeing a man force-fed part of his own life — are not the ones that my father is asking for. He raises an eyebrow. "Take your time." He means the opposite.

"He collapsed." I glance at the fire. The book is gone now, or nearly, indistinguishable from the glowing bed of logs. Why don't I want to mention it to my father?

He twirls one finger in the air to tell me I haven't finished.

"I don't know what happened. He was about to leave. Then he threw up on your rug."

"Elegantly put. Is that all?"

He knows it isn't. I look away and shrug, because staring back will make him realise that in my inward, cowardly way I'm defying him. But I'm not sure how long I can bear the silence. If only someone would pick Farmer up off the floor.

A skitter of light feet. "Oh — I'm very sorry, sir, I didn't expect —" As I turn, Betty curtsys to my father and frantically pushes a stray lock of hair under her cap. She wouldn't do that for me. "Shall I . . .?" Her eyes go to the body on the floor, and she stifles a squeak. Clearly she thinks Farmer's dead.

My father doesn't bother to look at her. "Get him taken back to de Havilland's workshop. They can look after him there."

"Yes, sir." She doesn't understand what's going on, but she's too afraid of my father to do anything but bob again and duck out of the door. We hear her run along the passage, raising her voice as she goes out of earshot.

We stand in silence until the coachman and footman come in, smelling of tobacco and horses. They halt on the threshold when they see my father, but he beckons them in and together they manhandle Farmer until he's draped over the coachman's shoulder. Farmer moans and another gurgle of vomit splashes on to the floor. I don't react. It's unmanly to show disgust or pity. My father murmurs an instruction to the footman, who grabs the bag of papers from the table. Then, at last, they stagger out.

Unexpectedly my father chuckles. He sits down in the chair in front of the hearth. He stretches his legs out in front of him. "Oh dear, oh dear. And he looked so dapper when he came in. Handsome, even, in a rough-cut way. I saw you looking at him."

I don't answer. He's right. Farmer *was* good-looking. Before he turned into that obscenity.

"A feeble lot, these binders. De Havilland is no better. I had higher hopes of this one, but it seems he is cast from the same mould."

I don't say anything. I would like to be invisible.

"They mollycoddle themselves." He gestures for me to put another log on the fire. "Cultivate delicate constitutions as if weakness was a badge of honour. A spineless lot. De Havilland calls himself an artist, but ultimately a binder is merely the rectum through which waste is squeezed into another shape."

359

He leans forward to peer at the books spread out on the table, but they're too far away to reach and he doesn't get up.

I take a tiny step towards the sideboard where the decanters are. He doesn't even look at me. Sharp as a whip he says, "You've had enough. Sit down."

I swallow the dry edge in my throat that needs alcohol to soften it. Instead I imagine a grey fog that gets thicker and thicker as I drag a chair from the side of the table into the middle of the room. I sit down. Is it obedience? Or am I trying to goad him?

Silence. "At least he finished before he succumbed."

"Finished?"

"With Nell." My father watches me, smiling. "My dear Lucian, don't look so tense. Try to pretend you enjoy your old dad's company."

"If you despise them so much —" I stop.

"Yes? Relax, for goodness' sake, you look like you've just caught your hand in a fan-belt." He laughs. That happens, once every few months or so, to men in his factories: they lose their arms. And their jobs, obviously.

"The binders." Everything that's happened tonight has loosened my hatred, like a knot of phlegm I need to cough up. "If you think they're parasites, why do you pay them? If they're arseholes, why do you collect their shit?"

I want him to get angry. Even if I'm afraid of him. It would be a point to me, if he got angry. He doesn't.

"You're quite right, boy. It was unkind of me to use that metaphor." He leans back and puts his arms behind his head. His gaze rests on the display cabinet next to the window. If you didn't know, you'd think he was smiling gently at the ostrich egg and the bits of intricately carved ivory.

I turn my head sharply away and stare into the hearth. The fire has almost died. Grey ash lies thick on the embers. One curled length of charred leather has dropped into the bottom of the grate. The flames have eaten half of the words, but a few singed letters still stand out. *METT MER*. Two hours ago I had never heard of Emmett Farmer and now half of his name makes me shiver. I cross my arms over my chest.

My father shifts in his chair. I know without looking that he's turned his eyes to me.

I say, "What was it this time?"

His smile stays the same.

"Nell's memories. Tell me, do you change your *modus operandi*? Do you alternate seduction and blackmail and rape?" My voice breaks. How easily I can imagine it. Does that mean I'm like him, if I can see it all so clearly?

"Lucian, you know my library is at your disposal. Any time you feel curious . . ."

He enjoys it. He loves knowing that I know.

The gaslight flares and the raised ropes of plaster on the ceiling sway and tremble. When the jet subsides the room seems darker than before, and smaller.

The clock chimes. It's earlier than I thought. My father stretches and rolls his head back. I push myself to my feet. He watches me but he doesn't say anything.

"Goodnight."

"Goodnight." He yawns. "Oh — Lucian."

"Yes?"

"If you see Nell, tell her she's got a day to clean this rug or I'll take it out of her wages."

Someone has lit the lamps in my bedroom. There's a fire in the hearth, too. I stand as close to it as I can. At first I'm shivering. Then suddenly I'm too hot and I break out in a sweat. I turn to the window and pull open the curtains. A cold draught dries the moisture on my forehead. Raindrops patter against the window like something desperate to get in. Beyond my reflection the darkness is thick and blurred. The two lamps on either side of the gate glimmer through a veil of rain.

I turn back into the room. It's not like my father's study. It's almost empty: bed, chair, dressing table, chest. But in the lamplight the bare white walls are the colour of sandstone, soft with shadows. Everything else is tinged with flame-colours. Darkness clings to the edges of the furniture. The coverlet on my bed gleams like silk. If I felt safe anywhere, I'd feel safe here.

I'm chilly again. I wrap myself in a dressing gown and pull the chair towards the fireplace. I sit there for a few moments, staring at the fire. But I can't resist long. I get up again and go to the chest at the foot of my bed. Underneath the blankets I've improvised a secret compartment. The bottle of brandy is half full but that's not what I'm looking for. I take out the other bundle and sit down again to unwrap it.

The cloth falls to the floor. The lamp is too far away to read by, but I don't want to get up. I know the book almost by heart, anyway.

Childhood Memories of William Langland, Esquire.
My father gave it to me on my twelfth birthday. It was the first book I ever read all the way through. I'd seen books before, of course. We had them at school. The masters told us over and over again how precious they were. Priceless, they said. One of my friends was beaten for getting an ink-stain on one. But the subjects were doddering old scholars, desperate to earn a few pence before they died. Who cared about a life spent teaching geometry, or experimenting with prisms, or keeping bees? The library was where you went to hide, or cry, or (later) have quick, ungentle assignations. No one went there to *read*. When you went through the door you could hear the infinitesimal creak of books on the shelves, telling you to mind your own business. They were there to impress the parents, like the stained glass in the windows or the new cricket pavilion.

William Langland was different. That day ... My mother made an occasion of every birthday, making a fuss of us with a brittle enthusiasm that could turn to sharpness in a heartbeat. She was the one who gave us presents, not my father. That year I'd had my cricket bat, or my fencing foil, or whatever it was, and I'd thanked her for it as fervently as I could. I'd had a birthday tea, and a cake with decorations in Scheele's green that had to be taken off before we ate it. There were girls in frilled frocks, and other boys like me in Norfolk suits, and their nursemaids, who filled the room and made my mother's lips tighten with dislike. My head began to ache from too much sugar. As the other children started to leave I tried to slip outside onto the lawn, but my mother summoned me in again immediately. "Your father would like to see you in his study," she said, in the blank, disinterested voice she always used when she spoke about him. I thought I must have done something wrong. But when I went to him he ruffled my hair and put a parcel into my hands.

He watched as I unwrapped it. It was in a dark blue wrapping, stamped with gold. I undid the paper and didn't know what to say. I didn't know what I felt. At last I said, "Thank you," and opened it, anxious to look away from my father's eyes.

The frontispiece was a coloured plate. A forest on an autumn afternoon, the sun low over a moss-covered stone wall, bracken tinged with gold. I smelt the sweet applish scent of cooling earth and damp undergrowth. For a second I was there, not in my father's study at all.

I think I thanked him again. I think he showed me the title page, and the stamps that confirmed Langland had consented and that the bookseller had a licence. I think he told me how much it had cost. None of that mattered. I went upstairs and read it nearly all the way through. I was so absorbed I didn't hear the dinner gong; I didn't see Abigail when she came into the nursery to light the lamps. I was swept away on a gentle current of memory: wide fields and deep woods, a tree-house, a pet otter, an adventure in an old quarry . . . A plump, humorous mother, a father who could ride and poach, three older brothers, a trusty farmer's son who could always be relied on in a scrape . . . It was only at bedtime, when my nurse plucked it away from me, that I blinked and knew where I was, or who.

How many times have I read it, since then? I can shut my eyes and see Langland's village from the steep path that ran up to the top of the down. I can feel the hum of chalk under my back, under the sparse grass. I can smell wild thyme and sun-warmed soil.

At the end of the book he was married. I always liked that part least. *If I could express to the gentle reader one fraction of the joy that filled me as my dearest Agnes smiled at me under her crown of flowers, I would count my sacrifice well made* . . . But now I spread my hand to the fire and imagine the brush of orange-flower petals falling through my fingers.

I was such a fool. I got to know those memories so well they might have been my own; but I never thought about Langland himself, or how the book came to be bound. The memories were from years ago, and I guessed he was long dead; but I didn't understand, not really. Not until that night, only a year ago. Less than a year. Back when I was my father's favourite.

It was last autumn, a week or so before I was meant to take my entrance exam. It was early evening, starting to get dark. I was in my father's study after a lesson. Dr Ledbury had just left. I could still hear his voice in the hall, as Abigail gave him his hat. I suppose I must have been thinking about the text we had been translating. I stared idly across the room at my father's curiosity cabinet. The peacock feathers were pressed against the glass like ferns in a vivarium. One of the maids must have moved the Oriental dagger when she dusted it, and it was hanging crooked. I got up and tried the door, in case it was unlocked.

I felt the whole cabinet swing outward.

There was a tiny moment of resistance as the fireproof seal opened. Behind the cabinet was a bookshelf, set into the wall. I stared at rows of books — cheap cloth-bound books, most of them, not like the ones at school. The names niggled at me, as if they should have been familiar: *Marianne Smith. Mary Fletcher. Abigail Turner.* I suppose I should have known then, but I had never heard the servants' surnames. And I don't think I'd ever seen a book by a woman. Maybe that was why I slid one off the shelf. I sat down on the arm of the armchair and leant sideways to turn up the oil-lamp.

I can't remember how long it took me to realise what they were.

When my father came home I was in his chair, staring into the ashes of the fire. The wick of the lamp needed trimming, so the mantle was dim with soot.

I heard Abigail answer the door to him. I imagined him brushing her arm — the faintest touch, like a breath — as she took his coat. He murmured something, and she laughed.

He was whistling a tune when he came into the study. When he saw me he paused, just for a second. Then he lit the gas and turned to me in the sudden flare of light, still whistling.

"I see you've found my little library," he said.

It was the first time I thought I could fight with him and win. I was wrong. When I threatened to tell the *Castleford Herald*, he only shrugged; when I threatened to tell my mother, he raised an eyebrow and said, "My dear boy, your mother has a genius for not seeing what doesn't suit her. But if you think her book would look well next to the others . . ."

I never took my entrance exam. Three days later I was packed off to my uncle's house in the country.

Now I get to my feet. *William Langland* falls to the floor, but I don't pick it up. I don't want to think about those long months, when loneliness rotted me away from the inside. White fields under snow, the black woods, the way I could walk for hours and not see another soul — and if I did, it was only a glimpse of a poacher, muffled to the eyes, who slipped away so quickly I wasn't sure I hadn't imagined him. A Turning dinner with my uncle, who was drunk before the soup was taken away. A rainy spring, the world flaring green. High hot summer. Afternoons that crept past as slowly as the sunlight through my window. Half a year, as worthless as the bits of rubbish that I found in the bottom of my trunk when I came home: a torn jeweller's receipt, a few pheasant's feathers, a broken wooden egg painted with flowers.

Forget it. I bend and pick up the book. I smooth the cover. When I left, I told my father I'd burnt it. I wanted him to see that I wasn't like him. But I didn't do it. I've come close to putting it on the fire, but I can't bear to. William Langland is dead and it wouldn't do him any good — but that's not the reason. If he were here, I'd buy his memories from him at any price. I'd take his childhood like a shot. I wouldn't hesitate. And that makes me as bad as my father. Worse —

367

because Langland must have been desperate. How could he have chosen to give up those memories, otherwise?

I put it down on the window sill. Rain rattles against the glass. The sky is orange in the distance, through the bare trees. Another factory fire on the other side of Castleford. Not one of ours. The rain will put it out, probably. If not, we're the right side of the wind.

The same soot is clinging to the windows of de Havilland's bindery. Somewhere out there Emmett Farmer is breathing the same smell of fumes and wet stone.

How many people out there have been bound? How many memories are sitting in vaults, or locked in secret bookcases, or being read by other people at this very moment? How many people are walking around with half their lives missing, oblivious?

I undo the top button of my collar and tug at it until the stud bites into the nape of my neck. But the tightness in my throat isn't because of my shirt.

I turn away from the window. I should go to bed, but I don't.

I've come up three flights of stairs. Now I'm standing on the bare icy landing outside the bedrooms under the eaves. The rain drums on the roof, and I can smell mould. I don't know what I'm doing here; my hand holding the lamp is trembling so much the shadows jump like fleas. "Nell?"

No one replies. I knock on one door and then the other.

"Nell. *Nell!*"

The metal crunch of bedsprings. She opens the door. She is so white she's almost green. "Yes, sir? I'm sorry, sir."

"May I come in?"

She blinks. Her eyes are steady and liquid and pale blue, the same shade of blue that my sisters overuse in their water-colours. She's in her nightgown. The edge that touches her neck is frayed with age.

"Let me come in. I won't be long." She steps back and scurries to the far end of the room. The window doesn't have curtains and my reflection stares back at me, as solid as I am. I look around for somewhere to put the lamp, but the chair has her uniform hung over the back and there's nowhere else except the floor. It's a cramped, ugly little room. It reminds me of the room I stayed in at my uncle's, only smaller, without the view.

She sits on the edge of her bed and pleats the hem of her threadbare blanket. I clear my throat. "Nell."

"I'm all right, sir, truly. I'm sorry I was took bad." She looks up at me. She doesn't say that it's late, or that I woke her up.

My throat tightens. I hear myself say, "Can you trust me, Nell? I want to tell you something. It's going to be very hard to believe."

"Of course, sir."

"You have to trust me. I want you to pack, tonight. Pack your things ready to go. I'll give you some money. Tomorrow you can sneak out, early."

"With you, sir?"

"No!" I look away. The wind rattles the window. There's rainwater trickling in along the top of the sill. A thread like glass runs down the wall and spreads into a dark stain on the floorboards. "No, not with me. I'll find somewhere for you to stay for a few days. Then you can go home. Do you understand?"

"But, sir . . ." Her fingers burrow into the quilt. "I promise I won't be ill again."

"It's not a punishment. It's for your own safety. I want to protect you." I mean every word. But in the empty little room it sounds so pompous it makes my skin crawl. I keep my eyes on that spreading blot of water on the floorboards. Somewhere behind me another leak has started to drip. The wind ruffles the slates above our heads with a dull clatter. "Please, trust me, Nell. You're in danger here. Sooner or later bad things will happen to you, and I don't want that."

"Bad things?" She picks at the mattress, pulling strands of straw through the ticking.

I breathe in. I should have thought what to say when I was standing outside her door. Now I can't think of the right words. Any words.

The door opens.

For a moment I don't hear it. It's only when Nell leaps to her feet that I realise what it means. She dips into a curtsy and catches her foot on the bed.

I don't look round. The pause stretches for an eternity, from one heartbeat to the next. It's like the split second after a blow from a leather belt: the silence before the burn.

"Go on, then," my father says. "Tell her."

370

CHAPTER
TWENTY-ONE

A gust of wind hums in the chimney. Water pours on the floor in a sudden spate; then the wind falls silent and the drip slows to a stop. The room seems even darker than it was, mean and narrow and fragile against the winter night.

My father steps past me and I catch his smell of soap and silk. For a moment I think he's going to touch Nell, or even sit beside her on the crumpled bed. But he doesn't. He stands in front of me, where he can see both of us at once.

Nell looks from me to my father. Whatever happens, she knows she's in the wrong. I shut my eyes but I can still see her face.

"Tell her," my father says again. His voice is soft. When I was a boy he'd be so kind to me after a whipping that it was almost worth it. "It's all right, Lucian. Don't let me stop you. Tell her what I did."

"I —" My voice betrays me. I swallow hard. I can taste soot and alcohol on the back of my tongue.

"Please, Mr Darnay, I didn't . . . Mr Lucian asked to come in, he's only been here a moment, I *promise*, sir!"

"That's all right, Nell. Lucian, the sooner you speak the sooner this will be over."

I don't know what game he's playing. All I know is that — somehow — I'll lose.

"Nell." I make myself look at her. But she chews her bottom lip and doesn't meet my eyes. She knows better than to believe that she matters, any more. This is about my father and me. "Listen. This afternoon a binder made a book out of . . . You were bound. Do you understand what that means?"

"No, sir, that's not right. I washed the floor and then I came over all quivery —"

"You don't remember. Obviously. Because you had your memories taken away."

"But —" She stops. I want to think it's because she believes me. She gnaws at the chapped patch at the corner of her mouth and then starts to pick at it. She stares resolutely at the floor while her fingers pull at the flakes of skin. On the wall behind her the plaster is peeling too, as rough and scabbed as her lips.

"What you don't remember is that my father . . ." I'm very aware of how close he is to me.

"Go on, Lucian."

I clear my throat. "My father . . ." Nothing else comes. It's like wanting to vomit and only being able to gag.

Now he sits down next to Nell. She looks up at him as if he can rescue her from me. He smiles and brushes a lock of hair off her face. Her mouth is bleeding now. A drop of blood clings like a dark red petal to her lower lip. "I took you, Nell," he says, with infinite gentleness. "I came up here, night after night, and had my way with you. But not just here. The summer house, my

372

study, Lisette's room . . . And in all sorts of ways. You used to cry and beg me to stop." He doesn't move his head but his eyes meet mine. "Nelly, my poor darling . . . What *didn't* I do to you?"

Silence.

She doesn't move. Her eyes are still on his face.

"Ah, Nell . . . Are you angry with me? Do you remember, now?"

She frowns. "Remember what?"

Someone makes a noise. It's me. My father doesn't look at me but the corner of his mouth twitches. "Nelly, my little love," he says, "all those times I hurt you. All those times I made you bleed. How about the first time, surely you remember the *first* time? Shall I tell you how it was, how you lay there so still, as if you thought you deserved it, how I told you you'd asked for it and you nodded and wept and —"

"Stop — please!" My voice almost chokes me.

"You remember that, don't you? Now I've told you. Nell? Are you listening?"

She blinks. "I'm sorry, sir."

"What did I just say to you?"

Her mouth opens. The bead of blood trickles down and she wipes it away. It leaves a wide stripe of red on her chin. Her eyes slide from side to side. "I'm so very sorry, sir, I don't feel very well and things went all sort of blurry, if you know what I mean, I was trying to attend, honestly, I —"

"Repeat after me, Nell: 'Mr Darnay took —'"

"*Stop!*" Finally I have enough breath to shout. But it isn't the words, it's her face: set and afraid, desperate to understand. I drop to my knees in front of her. "It's all right, Nell. He's only teasing you. Don't worry. Please." She blinks rapidly. Tears slide down her cheeks. The sore patch on her lip starts to ooze blood again. Between us we're tearing her apart.

"Of course." My father stands up. "Only teasing. Now we'll leave you in peace. Get a good night's sleep and you'll be back to your old self tomorrow. Oh, that reminds me, try to get the stains out of the rug in my study, won't you? Otherwise I shall have to ask Cook to take it out of your wages."

She sniffs so hard it squelches. "Yes, sir. Thank you, sir."

"That's all, then. Lucian, come with me."

I reel as I get to my feet. A headache sucks and spins like a whirlpool inside my skull. Stay upright. Don't be sick. My father ushers me out. He follows me down the stairs so closely that I feel the warmth of his breath on the back of my neck. When I reach the door to my bedroom he gives my shoulder a gentle tap. "My study, Lucian."

I pause with one hand on the doorknob. My palm prickles with sweat. The house is very quiet. The carpets and curtains muffle the sound of rain. My father and I might be the only people in the world.

I don't look behind me as I walk down the passage and down the stairs. My father's footsteps are like an echo of mine as we cross the hall. I catch sight of my reflection in the mirror behind the ferns. In the pale gaslight you can see how like my father I'll be, when I'm his age.

His study door is ajar. The fire has died completely. He never meant to come back down here tonight; he was going to see Nell.

My father closes the door behind us and eases himself into the armchair. He looks at me through half-closed eyes. I walk to the other chair but he draws a line in the air with his finger, as if he's wiping dirt off a pane of glass. "I didn't say sit down."

I'm glad he said that. Being able to despise him is a gift. I stand there with my hands in my pockets and make myself smile. I cling to feigned insolence as if it can save me.

"My dear boy," he says, "perhaps you can tell me what you were trying to achieve up there." He points through the ceiling as if he's talking about the sky.

I can't keep the smile on my face. I don't know how he does it. Isn't it obvious what I was trying to do? "I wanted to warn her. Nell. I didn't want to let it all happen again."

He gives me a faint smirk. It's the expression he has when Cecily shows him one of her drawings: mildly indulgent, gently bored. "Ah, your finer feelings. Such compassion. Such delicacy. Such a *masculine* need to protect the feebler sex . . ."

"More compassion than you, at least."

"Oh, Lucian." He sighs. "When will you learn to see yourself as you are? Who would have thought my son would be so squeamish about the truth? Your little display of chivalry had nothing to do with Nell at all."

"I was trying to —"

"No." Again, the tiny flick of a finger to cut me off. "You were trying to make me angry. That's all. You are quite as bad as I am; worse, in fact, because at least I am honest. You didn't care how much pain you inflicted on the poor girl, as long as it made me notice you." He picks up the glass on the table beside him and tilts it to see the shine dance on the stem. A fragment of bee's-wing has stuck in the dark stain left by the dregs. "But you would rather not look at yourself clearly."

I try to summon the grey fog but nothing happens. I'm here in my father's study. The paintings and furniture and *objets d'art* have such bright edges they sting my eyes. I stare at the continents of vomit on the rug. A map of nowhere.

My father cracks his knuckles and gets up. "Let us say no more about it. You saw the utter uselessness of trying to undo a binding, so you won't try that again. And I'm sure you have no wish to humiliate yourself further."

He comes very close to me. I am slightly taller than him. I look down and nod.

He slaps me in the face. Hard.

I lose my balance. My mind is perfectly sharp, but my knees buckle and I stagger sideways. I should have expected it. I should have been ready. There is a long slow moment while the rug tilts like the deck of a ship. The side of the table smacks the side of my jaw. The crash seems to come later, like thunder after lightning, when I'm already on all fours. A glittering black snow falls round me. I can't breathe. I can't see properly. Stupid.

"Lucian? Dear boy, get up. No use grovelling on the floor like that. Foolish child." Something wet wipes my neck and ear. A red-stained handkerchief comes away. I look into my father's face. He drags me up until I'm sitting against the table-leg. "All this drinking, Lucian, you must try to master yourself. A tiny tap on the cheek and you collapse. Sit still. Let me see. Good boy."

"I'm sorry." In spite of everything I want him to love me.

"It's not as bad as it looks. Better? Good." He crumples his handkerchief and drops it on the floor. It lies on the rug, blotched dark and white, with his monogram crusted with blood. Then he gets up, grunting a little as his knees crack, and stretches a hand to me. I'm too tired not to take it. For an instant I can believe that my father is nothing more than a warm, firm grip, helping me to my feet. "Go to bed, boy."

I walk to the door. My head pounds. It takes concentration to open the door.

The armchair sighs as he sits down again. "When are you next seeing Miss Ormonde?"

"For tea, a week on Tuesday."

"Perhaps you'd better go to the kitchen before you go to bed. Get some steak on that bruise." He chuckles. "If she sees you looking like a ruffian she might call off the wedding."

Five days later I'm working in the Blue Room. Or meant to be working. In front of me there's an account ledger and piles of bills and letters. The whole desk is covered. But I can't concentrate on it. For once my father has asked me to look at something important, not just the lists of prices and importers. One of the under-clerks is accusing his superior of taking bribes. His superior says the clerk's been embezzling. I read the same accusations over and over again, as if the words might change the third time around. Then I raise my eyes and stare at the fern-patterned wallpaper. The shadows turn the blue-on-blue fronds to silver and mauve. Outside the sky is grey. The whole room is in shades of half-mourning. The clock whirs and tips into its elaborate tinkling chime. My head aches. At least the swelling on my eye has gone down.

A carriage draws up outside and footsteps crunch across the gravel. A moment later the bell rings. I hear Betty scamper down the stairs and past the Blue Room door. Someone squeaks and there's a clank and a splash. "Stupid sow, why are you kneeling *there* — well, mop it *up*," she hisses. I remember catching sight of Nell scrubbing the tiles in the hall earlier. I frown and knead my scalp. The paper in front of me crawls with ink, illegible.

I stand up and look out of the window. It's de Havilland's carriage. It has an elaborate coat of arms on the side panel: a gaudy purple and gold book with a lion brandishing its claws on either side. A stray brown leaf clings to the paint. The carriage wheels are gilded but apparently the suspension is so bad de Havilland uses the stagecoach — or the post cart — to go anywhere outside Castleford. I've heard my father compliment de Havilland on it; he called it "your fine appendage".

De Havilland. He must have come to present his bill. I tap the glass with my fingernail, staring out into the threadbare trees without seeing them. The sky is dark over the town, smoke-stained and threatening rain. There's the sound of the front door being opened, and Betty's voice. Then footsteps crossing the hall to my father's study. I hold my breath. But no one calls for Nell, and I hear the clank of the bucket and the sound of renewed scrubbing as she starts on a new patch of floor.

I lean against the wall. I force myself not to listen. There's a painting of water nymphs over the fireplace, decked with lotuses and lilies. They beckon me, all translucent skin and green eyes. I used to be fascinated by them, until I discovered that no real flesh lives up to that ivory perfection. It's the same with the chiaroscuro Bacchus on the landing: I used to shut my eyes at night and picture him — his mouth, his dark-shadowed torso, the sweaty gleam of grapes. Now I resent having been taken in. After my engagement was agreed my father offered to move the Bacchus into our bedroom, as a wedding gift. He had a glint in his eye. Somehow he knew — of course he did, my father is nothing if not efficient — about the other boys at school, as well as the whores in town. I refused. When my wedding night comes, there'll be no surprise or mystery: only the quick heat of desire and a few minutes of panting and friction. I think I can manage that, even for Honour Ormonde. But the last thing I want is those painted eyes looking at me, the lovely planes of chest and shoulder and stomach, the deceitful promise of something more than lust. The nymphs regard me placidly, as smooth-skinned as children. I turn away from them and go back to my desk.

I sit down. I manage to read a sentence of the clerk's letter. Outside, de Havilland's coachman climbs down from his seat and lights a cigarette. Smoke blows through the trees, unwinding like a bandage. I get up, go out into the hall, and cross to my father's study. Nell has retreated to the far door, leaving a vivid shine on the black-and-white floor. She glances up and hesitates, not knowing whether she should get to her feet to curtsy. I nod to her. She bends her head and goes on with the scrubbing.

A year ago I would have despised anyone who eavesdropped. Now I lean close to the door and hold my breath. My heart crashes in my ears like a tocsin. But the door is too thick and the voices are muffled. The only noise I hear clearly is the dip and splash of Nell's brush in the bucket.

"Excuse me, sir." I swing round. Betty is there with the pink-lustre tea set on a tray. She reaches past me and opens the door. I try to move away but it's too late. My father is standing next to the table, looking at something. As Betty comes in he looks up and sees me.

"Ah, Lucian." He says it as if he's been expecting me. "Come in. De Havilland, you've met my son, I believe."

"Yes, yes." De Havilland springs to his feet and shakes my hand. His skin is as smooth as soap. "Master Darnay."

My father gestures to a chair and I sit down. The blood stings my cheeks and throbs in the fading bruise over my eye. Betty arranges the tea things on the low table beside the fire. She's only brought two cups, but no one asks her to bring another. We wait in silence for her to finish. There are hothouse roses in a silver bowl on the mantelpiece, between the china spaniels. They're fat, blowsy bundles, dark-purplish red.

Betty leaves. My father strides over to the table, pours himself some tea and leaves the other cup empty. He saunters to where he was standing before and goes back to examining the book. A small, cloth-bound book, plain blue. "Helen," he says, looking at the spine, "of course, I had never thought ... *Miss* Helen, indeed. How quaint."

"I'm so sorry, Mr Darnay. My apprentice gave instructions without my knowledge. If you'd rather I asked the finisher to redo it . . .?"

"No, no. I rather like it. Look, Lucian." He holds it up. I see the shine of silver lettering. "'Miss Helen Taylor'. It makes her sound rather more important than she is, doesn't it?"

I lean forward and pour tea into the other cup. De Havilland shifts, as if he's expecting me to offer it to him. I catch his eye and sip. It's black and bitter.

"I must compliment you, de Havilland," my father continues. "The text of this is . . . elegant. Quite unlike your usual productions. Even the writing is less elaborate. Some day you must initiate me into the mysteries of what makes one binder's work so much more compelling than another's." De Havilland gives a bloodless smile but makes no riposte. "Your apprentice seems to show some promise. Such a pity he was ill."

"I must apologise again, Mr Darnay. He came to my bindery after his first master died, hardly two weeks ago. If I had had the slightest idea of his frailty . . ."

"No, no." My father waves the apology away like a fly. He comes over to me and holds out the book for me to take. "Don't you agree, Lucian? Lucian," he adds to de Havilland, "is something of a connoisseur himself. Or at least he will be, when he has more experience."

"Expertise is so often inherited," de Havilland says. "And what a privilege it must be to have access to your collection."

I swallow. I take the book. It's so light I nearly drop it. I open it at random and rub the paper between my finger and thumb. I look up at the clotted roses in their silver bowl. "Very nice," I say.

"Twenty guineas, I believe." My father writes out a cheque. He passes it to de Havilland, who puts it into his pocketbook with precise womanish fingers.

"Thank you, Mr Darnay. And once again my sincere apologies, my apprentice will certainly not be —"

I say, "How is he?"

They both look at me. My father raises an eyebrow. I put my cup of tea gently on the side table. The saucer chinks. I want to get up, but instead I cross my ankle over my knee and lean back. I tilt my head enquiringly at de Havilland. "Your apprentice. Is he recovered?"

"Please believe me, I am mortified." He clutches his pocketbook. "If it proves impossible to remove the stains from the rug . . ."

"Yes," I say. "But how is he?"

"Truly, if I'd had the slightest idea of his character —"

"I'm anxious to know about his health, de Havilland, not his morals."

There is a slight pause. My father sips his tea. When he lowers his cup there's a faint smile playing about his mouth.

De Havilland says, "Oh. I see. Ah . . . well, it was a bad attack of fever. Nothing contagious, I am sure of that, but he was delirious for a few days. The doctor's bill came to six shillings and twopence ha'penny, can you imagine? To tell you the truth, I don't know what I shall do with him. Perhaps he might be useful in the workshop. But it is kind of you to take an interest, Master Darnay."

"It is indeed," my father says. "Lucian bore the brunt of your deputy's indisposition. He was quite upset."

"That must have been most distressing."

De Havilland knows the exact amount of the doctor's bill, but he hasn't once mentioned Emmett Farmer's name. I put Nell's book to one side, go to the mantelpiece and brush one of the roses with my finger. It's like silk, so soft I can't feel where it begins.

"I hope — er — your face —" de Havilland glances at my father and stops suddenly. He fumbles for his handkerchief and coughs delicately into it.

"No," I say, "no, that was an accident a few days ago."

"That is a relief. I would be horrified if . . . Pardon me, I do hope I wasn't taking a liberty in mentioning it."

"Not at all," my father says. He joins me at the mantelpiece and bends his head to inhale the scent of the roses. "There's no denying that Lucian looks as if he's been in a bar-room brawl. But it was entirely his own fault." He rubs my temple with his thumb as if the bruise is an ink stain. "Never mind. Young men drink too much. It's a fact of life. Don't you agree, de Havilland? Especially when those young men are going to be married in ten days or so."

"Certainly, certainly. And may I offer my congratulations?" De Havilland inclines his head in a sort of half-bow. "And while I think of it . . ." He fumbles in his pocket and holds out his card to me. It has an embossed wreath on a dense cream background, a monogram of "d" and "H". I turn it over. *De Havilland, S.F.B., 12 Alderney Street, Castleford.* I know Alderney Street; one of the elegant houses with a discreet brass plaque is a brothel. "If you need my services . . ."

"Me?"

"You'd be surprised how many young couples find it useful to visit a binder before a wedding. Separately, of course." He tilts his head with a smile. "It's quite the thing, you know. Particularly for young men who want a clean slate before they marry. Those little white lies can become a burden. It's so much better to start a new life with nothing to regret or hide."

I glance at my father. He has plucked a rose from the bowl and is twirling it in his fingers. He meets my eye and smiles.

I say, "No, thank you."

384

"We have the securest vault in Castleford — at Lyon and Sons. And our storage rates are very reasonable." He glances from me to my father. "I have a very long and illustrious list of clients. Their books never see the light of day. I keep my true bindings entirely separate from trade."

"Assuredly," my father says. He plucks a petal from the rose he's holding. It flutters to the rug and lies there like a small wound. "Because selling a true binding while the subject is still alive is, as we all know, illegal. My dear de Havilland, I am quite confident that nobody" — he puts a subtle, dangerous weight on the word — "in this room would dream of breaking the law."

"Certainly not — but in a few cases there is a grey area."

"No," I say. "Thank you."

De Havilland falters and nods. "If you change your mind, you have my address. Or if Miss Ormonde feels differently. It would be an honour." He leans towards me and lowers his voice. "I dare say I could arrange for you to see her book. That is another advantage. Although naturally I wouldn't offer that to anyone else."

I turn away. The only sound is the murmur of the fire and the tiny rip of petals as my father dismembers the rose.

"Well, then," de Havilland says, "I must be going. I'm having lunch with Mrs von der Ahe. Thank you for your time, Mr Darnay. And if you change your mind," he adds, to me, "I am entirely at your disposal. Good morning."

"Good morning," my father says.

The door shuts behind him. My mouth is dry and my tongue tastes sour. I move towards the sideboard where the decanters are.

"Not now, Lucian."

I stop. I push my hands into my pockets. The corner of de Havilland's card digs into the base of my thumb. "If that's all," I say, "I need to get back to work."

"Must you?" He says it with faint amusement, as if I'm a child. He flicks the bare stem of his rose into the fire. "Dear de Havilland. He really has no idea, does he? A binder is only an asset as long as he can be trusted." He wanders over to the window. De Havilland's carriage is rolling awkwardly down the drive. "Trade bindings are one thing — no doubt de Havilland has a licence. And the occasional book without a stamp . . . well, who would bother? When he has Lord Latworthy as a collector . . ." My father taps the glass, idly. Outside a bird startles and flies away in a clap of wings. "But I've never heard him offer to show a true binding. If he's offering that to me . . ."

"Wasn't Nell's a true binding?"

"Don't be disingenuous, boy. A paying client. Someone like us."

"Someone who matters?"

"Exactly." He smiles at me. "What happens to a doctor, when he starts selling his clients' secrets?"

The question hangs in the air until I realise he isn't going to answer it. He watches until the carriage has

386

gone through the gate, and the wrought-iron "D" has clanged back into place. He yawns, picks up Nell's book and flips through. I want to leave, but some queasy impulse makes me stand there, watching him.

Then he turns a page, and something slips to the floor.

A thin, cheap envelope and ink that's already turning brown. *Mr Lucian Darnay*. It's careful, competent, day-school handwriting. My father sees it just as I do. A split second passes.

I fling myself forward. But he gets there first. He whisks the flimsy paper away from me. He examines it, raising his eyebrows. "I must say, mysterious *billets-doux* smuggled in by a bookbinder . . . Poor Miss Ormonde won't like that."

I struggle to my feet. My pulse drums in my ears. The writing is the same as Nell's book. But what has Emmett Farmer got to say to me? "I have no idea what it is."

"Then you won't mind my keeping it."

I say, "It's mine."

He taps the envelope against his thumbnail. The sound sets my teeth on edge. "Calm down, Lucian," he says. "I am merely curious."

"Give it to me. Please."

He smiles, twirling it at arm's length. "If you must continue to sow your wild oats, dear boy — and I suppose you must, you are my son, after all — please ensure they stay *manageable*, won't you? If you lose your head entirely . . . well, it is rather a bother to arrange a binding. Not to mention expensive."

I refuse to reach out. I take a deep breath. "I wouldn't let myself be bound. I'm not that cowardly. Or dishonest."

"I think we must be talking at cross-purposes," my father says. He tilts his head with a quizzical half-smile. "I would never encourage *you* to be bound . . . But I am intrigued by your point of view. I thought you despised me, not Nell."

"Nell didn't have a choice. Anyone who *chooses* . . ." I stop.

"Yes?"

I swallow. If I look down I'll see the stains on the rug where Emmett Farmer vomited, and the hearth where his memories went up in flames. I can see him retching and clutching at the air, his wet face. "I wouldn't do it, that's all," I say.

"Well," my father says, "may you live up to your high opinion of yourself." Now he's flicking the corner of the letter as if it were a playing card. Any moment now he'll make it disappear. Into his sleeve, into nowhere.

"Father," I say. "Please may I have —" In spite of myself I hold out my hand, like a beggar.

He slides one finger into the fold and starts to rip the envelope. He's going to read it here, in front of me.

My heart trips over itself. For a vivid instant I see Farmer as he was before he burnt his book: handsome, a little gauche, with his hair falling over his face. His shirt was too small and he hadn't done the top button up properly. When I called him a servant he looked at me as if he wanted to hit me.

I snatch the letter out of my father's grasp. Before he has time to react I cross to the hearth, pull the fireguard back and drop the envelope into the fire. It glows white and falls into swift golden holes. They meet in a flare of flames and the letter curls into a scrap of grey gauze. There's a tiny, dancing flicker of triumph in my belly. For once I've defeated him. Then the silence floods back into my ears and I feel sick. I'll be sorry. He'll make me pay for it.

His eyes narrow. But he only walks past me, picks up the poker and stirs the fire. Sparks swarm upwards. "How sensible," he says, at last. "I imagine you will find it hard enough to satisfy *one* . . . person."

I don't imagine I'm forgiven. My punishment will come later, when I've stopped expecting it. "I'd better get back to work."

"So you keep saying." He gestures to the door with a flourish, as though I don't know the way.

I go to the door. I glance over my shoulder at the hearth. Every trace of the letter is gone now. Whatever Emmett Farmer wanted to say. An apology for ruining the rug. An apology for looking at me as if he pitied me. What else could it be, but an apology? So there's no reason to feel the way I do now: as if I'm locked in a grey cell, and I've burnt the key.

CHAPTER
TWENTY-TWO

We're having tea in the drawing room. There are only five of us, but the room feels small. The yellow walls are giving me a headache, and the air is thick with my mother's toilet-water and the pomade Cecily and Lisette use on their hair. Even the smells of tea and lemon make my gorge rise. I take shallow breaths. There's a fire roaring in the hearth, but the air is chilly. One side of me is sticky with heat: the other is cold. Miss Ormonde is sitting opposite me, her ankles crossed demurely and her head bent. She's listening obediently to my mother, but every few seconds her eyes flick to me. Her gloved hands are fiddling with something. I see the lump on her third finger and realise it's her engagement ring. She catches herself, and stops. I don't meet her gaze. Outside, the garden is grizzled with a thin layer of snow. The white is like tissue paper that's been left out in the rain, ragged and forlorn. The deadish grass pokes through it. The gardener's footprints are dark with mud.

My mother strokes her skirts, patting the purplish watered silk and making her rings glitter in the pale daylight. Then she passes the plate of biscuits to Miss Ormonde with a smile. Miss Ormonde passes it to

Cecily. My mother coughs delicately. Cecily blushes and passes them to me without taking one. Her corset creaks as she lowers her arm, and she darts a look around, hoping no one noticed.

Lisette leans past me to take a biscuit, and then — with a glance at Cecily — another. She wanders to the piano and picks out a tune with her other hand.

"Lilies," my mother says, to Miss Ormonde. "Are you quite sure, my dear? One must be confident that one's bouquet is becoming."

"Yes, Miss Ormonde," Cecily says, "lilies are so sombre! And the scent is so overwhelming. Can't I put in a plea for freesias? You would look so perfectly *darling* with a fountain of freesias." She knocks the sugar bowl over. "Oh — silly me!"

Lisette strikes the same note twice, and pauses. "Perhaps she's right. Lilies are very stalky."

"I think it *would* be best to avoid anything too . . . straight," my mother says. For an instant they all stare at Miss Ormonde. "I adore lilies myself — our hothouse is full of them — but when one is, perhaps, a little lanky . . . No, I think roses are decidedly more forgiving."

Miss Ormonde dips her head. "Yes — whatever you think would be right — I expect I'll look a bit of a scarecrow, I always do."

There is a tiny silence. I am supposed to say something comforting. I watch a bird hop across the dark-prickled lawn.

"Nonsense," my mother says. "You will look like a beautiful blushing bride. But you can't possibly have lilies. Roses — no, Cecily, *roses*. But what concerns me most is the decoration of your sitting room. Now I know it will be yours and Lucian's, but after all you will be staying under this roof and I can't abide that awful grey-green. *Couldn't* we have something more cheerful?" She looks around at the sunshine-yellow walls, the colour my father calls "gambogian". "Lucian?"

"Whatever you want."

"Thank you, darling. You see, Miss Ormonde, how obliging he is. *You* don't mind a different colour, do you?"

"Well, I — no, after all this is your house, I wouldn't want to . . ."

"Good, that's settled. Lucian, sweetheart, you shouldn't really be listening to all of this! Not a man's business at all."

Lisette plays a high tinkling trill. "But that's Lucian for you, Mama. He's never been a *proper* man."

"Don't be unkind." My mother leans across and pats Miss Ormonde's knee. "She's being silly. Lucian won an awful lot of prizes at school. Riding, fencing . . ."

Lisette rolls her eyes. "Verse-speaking, dancing . . ."

"Those can be very manly accomplishments. A gentleman who can waltz is a credit to his sex."

I get to my feet. "We're already engaged, Mama. You don't need to advertise."

There's a split second before Mama laughs. She bends over the teapot and pours Miss Ormonde another cup of tea. "Do excuse him, my dear. He's always been modest. Now, tell me about your going-away clothes. I saw the loveliest chinchilla tippet in Gallant's. With your complexion . . ."

I stand at the window, looking out at the fraying snow. The drawing room is reflected palely in the glass; ghosts of my mother and Miss Ormonde sit under the trees. Miss Ormonde rubs her forehead with the inside of her wrist.

". . . charming," my mother says. "But in summer, they can be a little unfortunate, can't they? Our cook makes a wonderful lotion with lemon juice and soured cream that you might like to try. One doesn't want to look as if one has dropped a bucket of brown paint."

Miss Ormonde stands up. My mother falls silent. Lisette plays a long arpeggio, keeping the pedal down until all four notes hang in the air. Cecily hides a half-eaten biscuit under her saucer.

"Excuse me," Miss Ormonde says. "I feel rather faint."

"Sit down, my dear. Standing up certainly won't help."

"I'd like to go outside. It's very hot in here." She looks straight at me. "Could you show me the garden, please?"

"Certainly. Excuse us, Mama." I hold out my arm. She crosses the room to me. She's almost as tall as I am. I lead her out into the passage and through the back door into the garden. As we leave the drawing room the piano tinkles the beginning of the Wedding March.

It's freezing. The sky is white, criss-crossed by bare branches. She tilts back her head and blinks up at it.

393

Then, without looking at me, she sets off down one of the paths. I follow her. My shoes slide on the snow-slick stone. When I catch up with her she's standing in the circle of yew hedges, staring at the white-capped Cupid. She reaches out and touches his golden arrow with gloved fingers. "I'm sorry," she says.

"Don't be."

"Your mother —"

"I know."

She turns and meets my eyes. Her face changes, moving through a frown to something else. "You don't want to marry me, do you?"

It's so still I can almost see the shape of words in the clouds of her breath. "I don't want to marry anyone else," I say.

She laughs. It's a quick, bright sound, like a single note of birdsong. But then she's serious again. She pulls a leaf from the hedge and lets it fall. She walks away, down the narrow yew-lined avenue that leads to the end of the garden. She reaches the locked wooden gate and tries the handle. "Where does this go?"

"The river." Water murmurs and rattles on the other side of the wall.

The key is under an ornamental urn. When I pick it up the metal is stinging cold. I push it into the lock as quickly as I can. I throw the gate open and beckon Miss Ormonde through. We stand on the muddy, tufty riverbank, watching the current swirl round tree-roots and nibble the ice.

I blow out a plume of breath and watch it disperse. "Do you want to marry me?"

"More than I want to marry anyone else." She looks at me sideways.

"That's . . . satisfactory, then."

She takes a few steps through the deep grass. The snow clings to the hem of her skirt. A knobbly willow shudders as the river tugs at its branches. Then she swings round to face me. Her cheeks and nose are rosy with cold. "You don't love me. That's all right."

"I never —"

"It's all right, I said. But you have to promise to be . . . kind."

"Of course."

Her eyes narrow. She comes closer to me. I take an automatic step back and she clutches my arm, suddenly fierce. "My sister married three years ago. Before that, she was an artist, a painter, she was going to . . . But now she's no one. Her husband . . . My mother says he's very understanding, because he pays for her gin and her laudanum and her bindings." I pull away from her. "A book binder comes once a month. You must have heard of them. They make books of people's lives."

"I know what a binding is."

"I don't want to be like her. Please, Lucian. I've seen what you men do to people who don't fit in. Who make a nuisance of themselves. Promise me —"

"I said, *of course.*"

She blinks. Then she turns away. The wind whispers through the trees and sends stray snowflakes drifting past. She picks her way through the long grass back to the gate. "It's very cold, isn't it? I wonder if it will snow again."

I clear my throat. The icy air stings as it hits my lungs. "Miss Ormonde . . . Honour —" It's the first time I've called her by her first name.

"Perhaps we should go inside. I don't want your mother to think I'm rude."

She goes through the gate. She walks down the path ahead of me, holding up her skirts even though they're already wet round the bottom. Her hair is in a shiny elaborate knot, the colour of polished wood. Below it her neck is white and thin, flecked with moles. Her back is narrow and straight. She doesn't look back.

I hurry after her. As we get to the edge of the lawn, Betty steps out of the back door. She bobs a curtsy. "Mr Lucian?"

"Yes?" In front of me, Honour pauses, waiting for Betty to move out of her way.

"There's a gentleman to see you."

"Did he give you his card?"

"No." She hesitates. "He said you were expecting him."

"If it's the man from Esperand's, just tell him the grey is fine."

"It's the binder, sir. The one who came to see to Nell."

Honour looks over her shoulder. She gives me a long, weighing look. Then she slips past Betty, into the house.

"To see my father, you mean," I say.

396

"He particularly said, to see Mr Lucian Darnay, sir. Shall I tell him you're not at home?"

The door bangs. Through the drawing-room window I see Honour sit down, carefully arranging her damp-hemmed skirts. My mother gestures and smiles. No doubt she's talking about clothes again. Honour's face is set and blank. She doesn't glance at the window.

"No, thank you, Betty. I'll go and see what he wants."

"I put him in the Blue Room, sir." She steps aside.

It isn't until I'm halfway across the hall that I realise how fast my heart is beating. I stop in front of the mirror and stare at my reflection over the mass of ferns. I can see enough of myself to straighten my collar and smooth my hair. But there's a strained, hot look in my eyes that I can't get rid of, no matter how much I blink.

When I open the Blue Room door, Emmett Farmer is staring up at the water-nymph picture. He's wearing thick, baggy trousers and a brown collarless shirt. His hair is tousled, uncombed, and he hasn't shaved. When he swings round at the sound of the door he's as pale as the water nymphs. There are shadows under his eyes.

"Mr Farmer." He doesn't answer. I raise my eyebrows. "How can I be of service?"

"Lucian — Darnay," he says. Something catches in his throat. He swallows.

"Yes. What do you want?"

"To see you." He stammers, "I mean —"

The clock grinds a warning that it's about to strike. Farmer jumps and looks round. A cascade of chimes fills the room. As the notes die away I cross to the window and look out at another stretch of white-speckled lawn. The clouds are sagging over the town and the light is starting to fade. "Whatever it is, I'd be obliged if you'd be brief. I'm expecting my tailor to call."

"Your tailor?" I can't place his accent exactly but he's from somewhere even more provincial than Castleford. He sounds like my uncle's cook.

"Yes, my tailor. I'm getting married in just over a week and he hasn't finished my suit." I don't know why I bothered to tell him that. I cross my arms and wait, determined not to say anything else. He doesn't speak. He reaches out and takes hold of the mantelpiece as if the floor is about to give way. "If this is something to do with the letter you sent, I haven't read it."

He's staring at me. The skin under his eyes is so dark it looks bruised. Finally he says, "Why not?"

I shrug.

"You're getting married?" His voice cracks. He clears his throat. "I didn't know."

"Why should you?" I pick a loose silver thread from the curtain.

"I'm sorry."

"What?"

"Nothing." He shakes his head, twisting away from me so that I can't see his face. When he turns to me again his eyes are wet and I look away.

I pick another thread from the curtain. It puckers the embroidery. "What do you want, Farmer? I really don't have time for this." He doesn't answer. "It it something to do with Nell's book?"

"No. Not exactly. I wish you'd read my letter. I don't know." He grimaces.

"Did it say anything important? Your letter?"

"Yes." He gestures, as if he can see something I can't. I was moving towards the door. I stop. His outstretched hand is wide, muscular and blunt-fingered, the sort of hand that can sharpen a knife or build a wall. "I need to tell you something."

"Go on, then." I flip open my watch and glance at it.

"When I was an apprentice out on the marshes — I mean, before I came to de Havilland's bindery . . ." Suddenly his voice sounds strange, distant and unintelligible, like someone calling underwater. It only lasts a second. Then I can hear clearly again. There's a silence. He stares at me. "You've been bound. I've seen your book."

"That's absurd."

"No. It's all right. Listen —"

I try to put my watch back in my pocket but it won't obey me. I almost drop it. "You're lying. Why are you lying? What the devil are you playing at?"

He steps towards me. His mouth is still moving but the room glimmers and slides. The blue-grey drapery shimmers silver. My breathing is so loud it rings in my ears. The floor is dissolving under my feet, like sand sucked away by the sea. I steady myself on the back of the chair but the world keeps tilting. It's like being drunk. "Lucian?" He touches my wrist.

I jerk away. "Get off me!"

He takes a long breath. "No," he says, and it's like the answer to a question. "You didn't hear any of that, did you? And you wouldn't have been able to read the letter, even if you tried. Damn it, I should have known."

"Any of what?" But when he starts to speak I cut him off. "Get out."

"What?"

"Get out. Now. Or I'll ring for someone to throw you out."

"But — you understand, don't you? Somewhere there's a book of your memories. I can't tell you what you've forgotten but you have to believe me."

"Why should I believe you? This is outrageous. An outrageous lie."

"Why would I lie?" There's a pause. A draught hums in the chimney and rustles the papers on the desk. I catch the sharp, elusive scent of ash.

"I don't know," I say. "You still haven't said what you want. Blackmail, is it?"

He stares at me. Finally he says, "No." He puffs out a mouthful of air. "I thought . . . I don't know what I wanted."

"You'd better go."

He looks around, as if he's lost something. At last he says, "Goodbye, then."

"Good afternoon, Farmer."

He pauses at the door. He swings round. "Do you love her?"

"What?"

"The girl you're marrying."

I blink. The room is dim, lit only by the last bluish snow-light from the window. Farmer's clothes merge into the gloom. His face is all shadows and skull.

400

I reach for the bell-pull. It's so cold to the touch it feels damp. "Ask one more impertinent question," I say, "and I will make sure you regret it."

"What?"

"I don't know what you thought you were doing, coming here to threaten me —"

"I wasn't — I'm not."

"— but you are treading a very dangerous path. If my father hears about this . . ."

I don't finish the sentence. I don't have to. He stares at me, and even in the growing murk I can see how wide his eyes are. I ring the bell.

In the silence after the distant jangle, he bows his head. "I'll go," he says. "You don't have to call anyone to throw me out." He makes a strange, stiff kind of salute and goes through the door. "I'm sorry, Lucian," he says, without looking back at me.

"If you come near me or my family again . . ." I call after him. His footsteps pause, halfway across the hall, and I'm almost sure I hear him laugh. He stays still so long I think I've misheard, and he's already gone. Then he walks to the front door. "Oh, and . . ." he says, only just loud enough for me to hear, "congratulations."

The hall is full of lilies. They hang in swags from the walls and spill over the tops of benches. Everywhere I look there are banks of stiff green leaves and white waxy flowers. They open their star-shaped mouths. The pollen drifts down. A few grains land on my shirt. I try to wipe them away. They leave a wide ochreous smear across the perfect linen.

401

There's a whispering, rustling hush behind me. The noise of two hundred people trying to be quiet. A hundred starched shirts rasp, a hundred whaleboned bodices creak as they turn to look.

I can't move. I stare at the shimmering mass of lilies. The perfume is so sweet I can't quite breathe. I try to inhale and the scent is like a pillow over my face. I struggle but suddenly I'm smothering, panicking.

I open my eyes. The air rushes into my lungs with a gasp. I'm lying down and there's a dark grey window above me. Before-dawn grey, and I'm in bed. I'm not getting married. Not today, not now. It's not real. Pre-wedding nerves. Everyone jokes about it.

I breathe until my muscles loosen. I sit up, wipe the clammy moisture off my face and huddle in my blankets. But closing my eyes brings it back: the growing featureless fear, the flowers. A year ago I would have reached automatically for *William Langland*. I would have let the book lull me back to sleep, let it conjure up the high downs, the chalk land rippling in the summer heat, the smell of thyme. But it's no good. It's lost its old magic. Now it just makes me think of Langland, and what it must have cost him. And of Nell, and my father, and Emmett Farmer.

I don't believe him. Why would I? He came to our house, saw how rich we were, and thought he'd try his chances. It's an old trick. Like the fortune-teller who clawed at my mother's arm at Midsummer Fair one year, gasping, "You're cursed, madam, you must let me break it!" I'm not enough of a fool to fall for that. If Farmer seems guileless, and honest, and strange, it only means he's clever as well as a liar; and if he's beautiful — well. *That* only means that I should be even more careful not to trust him.

It isn't true. But if it were . . . I bring my knees up to my chest and shut my eyes. What would be so bad that I'd put it in a book? If I could wipe my life away now, I would. My father's secrets. The bruise on my face. The way Honour looked at me, open-eyed, illusionless. My mother, and her gaze deliberately sliding away when the maids enter the room. My own past, the sordid fumblings with other boys at school, the women in town. The dirty itch of desire, my cold determination never to be the one to show weakness. The whores that I leave as soon as it's over, without saying thank you; the moment I saw my old Head of House at the White Stag and stared at him blankly as if I didn't remember letting him kiss me on the last day of term. Since the night when I found my father's books — and those desolate, corrosive months with my uncle — I can't even summon a face to go with my fantasies. Only fragments of a body, orifices, obscenities. There's nothing about me I'd keep. There's only one thing to hold on to: that, no matter how perverted I am, I've never forced myself on anyone. I've never done what my father does.

As far as I remember, that is.

I scramble out of bed, pull on a robe and go downstairs. The house is silent. It's too early for my family to be awake. The only sound comes from behind the servants' door. I go into the Blue Room and light the fire that's already laid in the hearth. Then I ring for tea.

I draw the curtains and look out. The snow has melted and there's a fine drizzle falling. It sweeps across the drive like gauze. Grey, grey, grey. I want to drink it until it turns my blood into water and my brain to nothing.

"Good morning, sir."

I was expecting Betty, but it's Nell. She looks how I feel: red-eyed, shadowy, as if a nightmare is still loitering at her shoulder.

I order tea. She leaves. I go to the window. The silver pattern on the curtain is still puckered where I pulled at the loose thread. That means I was here, and Emmett Farmer was here, and it all happened. I clench my jaw. What was I hoping for? That I had dreamt that, too?

I go to the desk and look down at the piles of letters and ledgers. I flip the top of the inkwell back and forth on its hinges. When Emmett Farmer left yesterday I went back to the drawing room, sat beside Honour and went on chatting about the wedding and whether Esperand's would send my suit in time. I heard my own voice and marvelled at it. Once I glanced down and saw my hand pressed against my solar plexus, as if I was trying to staunch a wound. But if I'd been bound, I'd know. There'd be a hole in my brain somewhere. Trying to think about it is like rolling my eyes back to try to see inside my head. And there's nothing. Only the greyness. Grey as the day outside, soft-edged, almost kind.

"Shall I pour it, sir?"

Nell's voice makes me jump. Ink flicks off the lid of the inkwell and blots the front of my dressing gown. I

404

move away, wiping uselessly at the stains with the blotter. "Yes. Thank you."

She starts to say something, and stops. The china clinks as she sets out the tea things. I go on dabbing at the ink-stains for longer than I need to.

"Mr Lucian, sir." Nell has arranged everything in a neat cluster. Now she looks up at me. Her eyelids are red, and her mouth looks swollen. She hesitates.

"What is it, Nell? Is something wrong?"

She fumbles with the teacup. She almost knocks it off the table and then stands rigid, as if she's expecting me to box her ears. "I wanted to say thank you."

"What for?"

"You told me." She takes a breath. "You tried to help."

"Forget it." It's meant to sound kind, but it makes her shrink away from me. "I mean . . . Never mind. Just . . . Run along now."

She lowers her head and picks up the tray. Her dress gapes at the collar where it's too large for her. There's a shadow or a bruise on the side of her neck.

"Wait." I reach for my waistcoat pocket. But I'm wearing my dressing gown and I don't have one. I go to the desk and rummage in the box in the drawer. It takes me so long to find a coin that my scalp prickles with embarrassment. I shouldn't have bothered. I hold it out to her. I see, too late, that it's half a guinea. In the darkness of the drawer I thought it was half a crown.

She stares at it.

"You're a good girl, Nell." I push the coin at her and pour myself a cup of tea without looking up.

"Thank you, sir." Her voice is flat. Doesn't she realise that it's half a year's wages? She could take it and leave.

"You're welcome." I turn away.

"Will that be all, sir?"

"Yes, that's all."

She leaves. The door closes with a soft click. I sit down at the desk and start to reread yesterday's correspondence, but I can't concentrate. I don't want to see anyone and I don't want to be alone. Stupid.

I rub my temples until they burn with friction. The perfume of lilies lingers on my skin, sweet and heavy. In less than a week . . . I shut my eyes and think of a grey wall, curving up and over me. I'm alone, I'm safe.

I raise my head. There was a noise of something falling.

Silence. I take a mouthful of tea but it's nearly cold. I wait and listen but the house is completely still. The clock ticks, dropping seconds into the air like coins into a begging bowl. I pull the nearest letter towards me and rest my elbows on the desk. Betty's voice echoes in the hall; then there's the click of her feet as she crosses to my father's study. Then nothing.

Just as I lower my eyes again, she starts to scream.

My father's study door is open. I don't give myself time to think. "What's happening?"

Nell is hanging against the cabinet. Her head sags to one side. The sharp ammoniac smell of urine catches the back of my throat.

Betty is in the middle of the room, her hands pressed against her mouth. She's breathing in harsh sobs. I look round, surprised at how real everything is, at the rich sheen on the legs of the overturned chair and the minute reflections in the puddle of piss. There's a dried-up rose petal curled like a scab on the floor, the same colour as the wallpaper. The clock slows until there's more silence than tick. Then I realise that it isn't the clock at all, it's the sound of Nell's wet skirt dripping. With a rush the air fills my lungs and I take a step forward. "Get out."

Betty flinches as if I've hit her. "She's — I — she —"

"Tell the boot-boy to run for the doctor. Now."

I glance around for something to cut the rope — a letter-opener or a penknife. But it's all been tidied away. The ebony table is as bare as a dark mirror.

Panic floods through me. I can't think. I'm wasting time. If Nell is still alive . . .

I stumble towards the cabinet. My reflection slides into view in the glass behind her, behind the peacock feathers and gilded elephant's tusk. I look into my own eyes and smash my fist into the pane.

It breaks. Blades and triangles of glass fall into the cabinet and glint among the curios. I drag one of the shards away from the frame. It comes away with a sudden jolt that sends pain shooting up my arm. I set the chair upright and clamber on to it. I don't look at Nell's face. I saw at the rope — not a rope, a piece of fabric, a sash or a belt of some kind — with the edge of the glass until it parts and Nell collapses forward. I try to support her weight but she's too heavy. I sway and

407

nearly fall. The chair tips. I manage to put one foot flat on the floor. My knees buckle and I land awkwardly. Beside me Nell has fallen like a sack of cotton waste, slumped and shapeless.

I drop to my knees. I catch sight of her face and shut my eyes. I have to check her pulse but great icy shivers are running through me and I'm scared I'll vomit on her. I open my eyes and keep them focused on the wallpaper opposite me. I lean forward and push my fingers into the crease where the belt has bitten deep into her neck. Her skin feels tepid and doughy. Nothing. "Please, Nell," someone says, a friendly, reasonable voice. "Come on. Please. Stop this. Please."

She doesn't move. I pull at the knot. It doesn't give. I pick at it with shaking fingers. If I can undo the knot I can undo everything else. All the time I'm talking to her. "You don't want to do this, Nell. Please. Don't do this. Please." The knot comes apart. I drag the cloth out from under her jaw. Her head rolls to the side. Her eyes are . . .

I go to stand up but my head swims. I crouch on the floor and try not to be sick.

"Get up, boy."

I catch my breath so hard it sounds like a gulp of laughter.

"Get *up*." My father takes hold of my arm and pulls me to my feet. I stagger to the nearest chair and lean on it. "When did this happen?"

"She brought me tea. Maybe an hour ago."

He looks down at her. "She's pissed herself."

408

"I think she's dead." The word feels wrong, as if I've never said it before.

"Of course she's dead, look at her eyes. Stupid little bitch. Ah well, at least Sandown won't ask any questions."

There's a silence. He reaches for the bell-pull. "She hanged herself, did she? Where's all the blood come from?" He glances at me and his face changes. "Damn it, boy, what have you done?"

I look down. Blood is running down my wrist and soaking into the cuff of my dressing gown. There are smears everywhere. Nell looks as if someone slashed her throat. A cut gapes open on my palm. Surely it should hurt more than it does. "I'm fine. It's just a scratch."

"We'll ask Sandown to look at it. No harm in him knowing you hurt yourself trying to get her down. Ah. Betty." She's wet-faced and trembling but he clicks his fingers at Nell's body as if it's something he's spilt. "Call the coachman to get this moved. And then send the stable-boy for Dr Sandown."

"Yes, sir."

"Oh, and bring a bandage for Mr Lucian."

I watch my blood well up. He's right. It will be useful for him, if anyone asks why Nell would want to do . . . *that*. He can point to my scar. Look how much we loved her.

I tilt my hand and it drips on to the table. Tick, tick in the silence. Someone has let the clock run down, or it would be keeping time with me. I watch the puddle spread. Another housemaid will try to get the stain out

409

of the dark wood. Not Nell, with her bitten nails and chapped bony knuckles.

"You started again, didn't you?"

My father freezes. Slowly he turns to me. "What did you say?"

I can't repeat it. I don't need to. I can see his answer in his eyes.

"Don't you dare." He says it so softly it's almost a whisper. "Don't you ever, ever say that again."

I lift my chin. He can't laugh at me any more. Now, if I told, someone might believe me. Now it would matter.

He crosses the room and stands in front of me.

"You think you're clever, don't you, boy? I suppose you're pleased that she's killed herself. Finally someone might listen to you."

I shake my head.

"Hasn't it occurred to you that my secrets are your secrets too? That if I fail, if my business fails, if my reputation fails . . . It'll be your life, too. You think the Ormondes would still want you? You think anyone would want you?"

"It's a risk I'm prepared to take."

"Oh, Lucian. You think you're so different from me, don't you? You think you're the good one. I'm the old reprobate, and you're young and pure." He sighs. "You've forgotten a lot, haven't you?"

My heart judders as if something's hit it. I clench my fist and blood squeezes out between my fingers. "What do you mean?"

410

"Your own book, Lucian. Your own binding." He leans close to me. "Look at Nell. You think I killed her. You think you could never do something like that."

The world is very still. Obediently, stupidly, I look at Nell. Her eyes are half open and the whites are blotched and dark. It's not her. It's not human. Her tongue is protruding. My blood is caking on her livid cheek. My stomach heaves and I wrench myself away, swallowing hard. The wallpaper blurs in a mess of pink and dark red.

"My book," I hear myself say. "What do you mean?"

The door opens. "Thank you, Betty. Just leave it here." My father watches her leave before he dips the square of linen into the basin and wrings it out. "Show me where you've hurt yourself."

My pulse beats in my fingers and throbs all the way up my arm. "No." I keep my fist closed, holding on to the pain as if it's an object.

He sighs. "Don't be so childish."

The door again: the coachman and the ostler, treading warily in their muddy boots. The coachman startles back when he sees Nell on the floor, but he nods at my father's instructions and between them they pick her up and take her out. Another body on the hearth. Only this time it's dead, not just unconscious. I imagine them laying her on the kitchen table, her feet tilting away from each other, her damp skirt smearing urine into the grain of the wood. I can't stand up any more. I pull out a chair and sit.

My father takes my hand and uncurls my fingers. He wipes the wet linen across the mess of blood in my palm until I can see the clean line of the cut. He wrings it out into the white enamel bowl. A cloud of pink wafts into the water. "You poor boy," he says. "Does it hurt?"

I don't answer. I'm shaking. I let him hold on to me.

"Now. You're not going to do anything ill-advised. Are you, my dear?"

There's no sound but the splash of water. At last he reaches for a dry piece of cloth and folds it lengthwise to make a pledget. "You were bound a little over two months ago," he says. "You needn't look like that, it was nothing to do with me. I would never have let you, if I'd known."

"Then —" I stop. There's a distant whine in my ears, making it impossible to think.

"What was it you said? Anyone who chooses to forget is a coward. Although, considering . . ." He lays the pad of linen over the cut and ties it in place with a long strip.

I raise my eyes to his.

"Oh yes, I know what it was you wanted to forget," he says. "But I don't know which binder you went to. It could have been anyone." He finishes the knot and tucks the ends neatly under.

"I —" But I can't think. It wasn't me. I wouldn't have.

"Let me give you some advice, dear boy." He strokes my cheek. "Let it lie."

I pull away. "What?"

"This unfortunate episode — let it be a lesson to you." He gestures to the frayed end of fabric that still hangs from the curved top of the cabinet. "Don't do

412

anything stupid. You need my protection more than ever now. You're safe. Don't jeopardise that."

"You mean my book."

"You know I can't tell you what's in it." He rubs his eyes. "I'm not sure I'd want to. If you knew . . ."

I close my eyes. The scent of lilies rises from nowhere. "It's bad," I say. "Isn't it?"

He shifts in his seat. It seems a very long time before he replies. "I'm sorry, Lucian. I'm afraid it's very bad."

I get up. The shattered glass of the cabinet gapes at me. There are smears of blood and piss on the floor. I've left a red footprint on the rug. The other stains still show. It's ruined, that rug. My father might as well throw it away.

"Perhaps it's for the best. You can start a new life with Miss Ormonde."

I glance at him over my shoulder. That was where he sat when he threatened to send me to the insane asylum, the next time I defied him. Now he looks as weary as me.

"Yes," I say. There's nothing more to say. All I can do now is go upstairs and change my shirt. Wait until noon, when I can have a drink. Think of the grey wall in my head. Try to stay sane.

As I leave he adds, "I'm sure it won't fall into the wrong hands."

CHAPTER
TWENTY-THREE

Alderney Street is longer than I remember, all narrow white houses and railings and pavements deep with last night's snow. Every other door has a brass plaque beside it. By the time I find number twelve my feet are aching with cold and my eyes are stinging from the dazzle of the sun. I pause in front of the steps. A woman in mourning is coming out of the door. She snatches down her veil when she sees me looking at her.

I tip my hat to her and walk on. It's only when she's picked her way carefully down the street that I turn back and ring the bell.

A thin, plain woman answers the door. She's not a maid; she's wearing striped bombazine in heliotrope and yellow. She stares at me through a pair of pince-nez. "Good afternoon. May I help you?"

"I need to see Emmett Farmer."

"Who?"

"Emmett Farmer." The cold air catches in the back of my throat and I cough. She shifts, looking pointedly over my shoulder, tapping her fingers on the doorframe until I've stopped. "He's de Havilland's apprentice. Tall, light brown hair, clean-shaven."

She raises her eyebrows at me. "Oh. The new boy."

414

"A young man. Yes."

"I'm afraid he's not here."

"When will he be back?"

"He won't."

I stare at her. "What?"

She tilts her head so that the sun glares off her pince-nez and I can't see her eyes. "May I ask what this is about? If you would like an appointment with Mr de Havilland it must be made in advance."

"Excuse me." I step forward. She quivers and straightens her arm, barring my way in a rustle of bright purple and a waft of violet water and camphor. I keep my voice level. "Let me in, please."

"There's a two-week waiting list."

I push her out of the way. She squeaks in indignation but I'm already inside and I don't look back. "De Havilland?" On my left the door is ajar. I push it open. I get a vague impression of light blue-green walls, spindly chairs and orchids. There's another door at the far end of the room with a sign: *Consulting Room.* "De Havilland!"

De Havilland throws the far door open. "What on earth is going on? Miss Brettingham, I asked not to be disturbed." He sees me and adjusts his cravat. The diamond pin glitters. "My dear Mr Darnay, I wasn't expecting . . . What a pleasure. How can I be of service?"

"I came to see Emmett Farmer."

There's a silence. De Havilland shakes his head sharply, looking over my shoulder. When I glance round Miss Brettingham is just retiring into the room on the other side of the hall, the violent colours of her dress dimmed to mauve and cream by the shadows. De Havilland turns the corners of his mouth downwards. "I do apologise, Mr Darnay. Emmett Farmer has unfortunately left us. Perhaps I can help?"

"Where's he gone?"

He clears his throat. He gestures to a chair. When I don't sit his smile flickers and he smoothes his moustache. "My establishment has an excellent reputation and the highest standards. I can't employ anyone who shows the slightest sign of . . . vice." The stroking fingers pause on his top lip. Perhaps my face has changed. "I was obliged to send him away."

"Where is he now?"

"I really have no idea." He tilts his head at me. "May I ask why you wanted to see him, particularly? I would be honoured to assist you myself."

I rub my forehead. The snow-dazzle is still dancing in front of my eyes. "It's about a book," I say.

"Indeed?"

The room is too warm. It's making me queasy. I take a few steps, breathing deeply. My shirt is sticking to my ribs. "My book. It appears that I . . ." There's a vase on a pedestal in front of me and I reach out and touch the creamy bloom of an orchid. It's made of wax. I turn back to him. "I was bound. Emmett Farmer said — before he came to you, he worked at another bindery. Did you know? About my book?"

He tugs at his waistcoat, pulling it lower. "No, no, I'm afraid not," he says. "How could I possibly have known?"

416

"Emmett Farmer knew. I need to find it. I'm getting married." De Havilland knows that, of course. I fiddle with my gloves.

"I can't help you, Mr Darnay. I wish I could. If only you had come to me to be bound in the first place . . ." He tilts his head regretfully.

"I have to find him. Where would he have gone?"

"Oh." De Havilland inhales slowly. He bends and rearranges the illustrated papers on a low table. It seems to take a long time: as if it matters whether the aquamarine cover of *Parnassus* lies next to *The Illustrated Hunter* or *The Gentleman*. Finally he stands up again and meets my eyes. "Mr Darnay . . . You mustn't waste your time. Many young men have peccadilloes — no, please, listen to me. You cannot possibly find your book now. If, that is, it actually exists. Emmett Farmer was a liar and a thief. Please, take my advice. Forget about it. You have your whole life ahead of you. Let it go."

"It does exist. My father —" I break off. "De Havilland, I would be grateful. Very grateful. My book is worth a lot to me. Fifty guineas. A hundred."

He blinks twice, rapidly. A twitch of regret passes across his face, almost too brief to see. "I'm very sorry that I can't help you." He pulls his watch from his waistcoat pocket. "Now please excuse me. I have an important visit to make."

I catch him by the elbow. "When did he leave?"

"In the middle of the night, the day before yesterday."

"And you don't know where he was going?"

He dabs at his sleeve to check whether I've left a mark, and brushes a grain of invisible dust away. Then he looks up at me. "I really am terribly sorry, Mr Darnay," he says. "But to be quite frank, for all I care he has frozen to death."

When I go out into the street the shadows are pale blue, picking out the tiny cliffs and glaciers of footprints. The air is icy. A hansom creaks slowly past. Steam rises from the horse, thick as a momentary fog. A passer-by skids and throws his arms out to steady himself. Otherwise the street is empty.

I breathe in and it burns the back of my throat. I wrap my gloved hand around one of the spearheads that top the railing. The metal is cold. I bow my head and squeeze until fierce pain from my cut runs up my arm.

Without looking up I know that someone has drawn back the lace curtain across the waiting room window. De Havilland is watching me, waiting for me to go.

I walk down the steps and turn back the way I came. At the corner there's an alley, its walls high and crusted with soot. I step into the shadows and make my way to the end. In front of me is a narrow muddy lane with a scatter of leantos, gates and open yards. About halfway along there's a ramshackle wooden building, a little higher than the others. I stop in front of it and squint through a window. Behind a veil of grime, men bend over benches. One is hammering; one is hunched over something. Another glances up, and the book he's holding shines red and gold.

I knock on the pane and point sideways. I hold the man's gaze until he shrugs, puts the book down and disappears out of sight. A moment later he opens the street door and stares out at me. "Yes?"

"Is this de Havilland's bindery?"

"Front door's on Alderney Street."

"I'm looking for Emmett Farmer. The apprentice."

"He got sacked," he says, and starts to close the door.

I reach into my pocket. He hesitates. "I know," I say, and let the edge of a half-sovereign show between my thumb and forefinger. "Where did he go?"

The man clears his throat and spits on the ground, without emphasis. "I don't know."

"Did he go home? Where did he come from?"

"Somewhere out in the country, I think. Some other bindery." He eyes the coin. "Why don't you ask de Havilland?"

"Did he say anything about where he was going?"

"Look." He shakes his head. "He got thrown out in the middle of the night. I wasn't even awake. I don't know what he did, or where he went, or whether he's still alive. He's probably in a gutter somewhere, like everyone else who's out of work."

I lean forward, until I can smell tobacco on his breath. "Please. I need to find him."

"And it's more than my job's worth to talk about bindery business," he says, and shuts the door. I hear him walk away. I knock again. I keep knocking until he opens a workshop window and cranes sideways. "He left without taking anything with him," he says. "His coat and knapsack's still upstairs. No one here knows anything else. Now go away or I'll call the police."

He pulls the window shut and latches it. Through the grime I see him go back to his work. He's telling the truth.

I'm so cold it takes an effort to move. I pick my way across the frozen ruts to the end of the lane, turn one corner and then another. There's nowhere to go but I keep walking, as if my hopelessness is one step behind me, unable to catch up. I lose my bearings. I must be going in circles, because when I finally come to a halt I'm in Alderney Crescent, outside a gin palace. I look up at the Corinthian columns and the gold letters painted on black: *THE PRINCESS*. Or perhaps I came here on purpose, I don't know. It doesn't matter.

Inside, gaslight reflects off polished brass and dark wood and engraved glass. Warm air gusts into my face, smelling of stale flesh and spilt drink. As soon as I step over the threshold my cheeks begin to tingle where the wind has scraped them raw. I put a shilling on the counter, drink one glass of gin without pausing and order another. Then I sit down in a corner and shut my eyes.

Emmett Farmer has gone. I'll never find him, even if he's still in Castleford, and still breathing. I only have de Havilland's word for it that he was alive when he left the bindery.

I finish the second glass of gin. When I stand up to go back to the bar, my vision slides and I have to pause to focus. I reach out and take hold of a marbled pillar. The edges of things are starting to soften. The glare of the brass is a little dimmer, the world less tawdry. It's better. I dig in my pocket for more money. At the same time the door opens. A freezing draught kicks at my ankles. A crumpled piece of paper skims the tiles at my feet and presses itself against my shoe. I bend to pick it up and smooth it out on the bar.

It's a piece of headed notepaper. At the top, there's a gold crest, and a motto: *Liber Vos Liberabit*. Underneath it says, *Simms and Evelyn, Fine Binders*. The rest of the paper is full of instructions in a spidery, careless hand. *Go to Madam Halter's at 89 ALDERNEY ST and ask for MISS PEARL and her speciality. An engagement of at least TWO HOURS is required. Immediately afterwards you are required to attend for binding. Any memories lost through attrition, abuse of drink or any other cause will result in a proportional REDUCTION OF FEE, which has been agreed to be a sum NOT EXCEEDING 10s.*

The barman glances at me, takes my money and puts another glass down in front of me. "I wouldn't, if I were you, sir," he says. For a second I think he's talking about the gin. Then he nods at the sheet of paper. "I've known people go mad, after. They're full of promises, the binders, but if someone says something before you've had time to heal, you can end up knowing you've been bound. They say that's the worst, when you don't know what you've forgotten."

I roll it into a ball and throw it away. "That's all," I say. "Thank you."

He nods, registering my tone. He reaches for a cloth and begins to polish the row of gleaming taps.

But the page is still floating in front of my eyes. I know Madam Halter's place. It's classy, relatively speaking; but I've heard of Miss Pearl and her . . . preferences. In spite of myself I can imagine the girl who must have read those instructions. I don't know any girls younger than Lisette, but somehow I can picture her: gap-toothed, her hair in a plait. In my mind's eye she walks up the steps to the door and tugs the bell-pull. She's desperate, and brave. But she doesn't know what she's doing. She's so guileless it hurts. And it will hurt more, when the door opens, and the door behind that . . . I shake my head, trying to clear it. But I can't. I can see her so clearly. She's not like Nell — she's more like Farmer, somehow, with the same gallant tilt of the head, the same wide-set eyes. What if it was a girl like that?

"Hey." I catch at the barman's sleeve. "Did someone — did you see . . .?" I feel light-headed, weak with urgency. It doesn't make sense, but my stomach is churning. What they've done to her is my fault.

"Yes, sir?"

"The girl . . ." I swallow. She's not real. "I mean, whoever dropped that piece of paper. Did you see them?"

"Can't recall, sir." He detaches himself. "Lost someone, sir?"

"No. I mean — yes." I force myself to sit back. What am I doing? I'm going off my head. She doesn't even exist. "Never mind."

He gives me a long stare. Finally he says, "Your sweetheart made herself a page-turner, has she? Well, plenty more fish in the sea, if I may say so, sir."

422

"What? No. I don't mean that." But I feel so ill I can't think. As if this girl, and Nell, and my father, and my book are all part of the same thing. Fear crackles in my gut like broken glass. What have I done?

The barman wipes his rag over the bar. It leaves an oily, iridescent sheen. "Binders," he says, and hawks a lump of phlegm into the spittoon. "You seen the queues on Library Row? Turning people away, they are. It's the weather. Freezing cold and the workhouses full. Give me an honest whore any day."

"Yes." I bow my head. I can't bear it. In my mind's eye I see Madam Halter's door swinging open. I can see Miss Pearl, waiting at the end of the curtained gallery, all in black. The girl stands at the foot of the stairs, looking up. Panic quickens in her eyes. But the scene blurs into my father's study, and Nell's body. Emmett Farmer choking out my name. De Havilland's waiting room, and his secretary glaring at me over her pince-nez. De Havilland smoothly wishing Farmer dead. I push my fists into my face, until bloody colours blossom against my eyelids.

Perhaps Farmer *is* dead. Part of me wants to think he is. It's his fault I feel like this. I was fine before he came. Now I can't think about anything but what I might have done, and my book, and him. And the way he looked at me, and the way — in spite of everything — it made the blood rush to my heart. No, of course I don't want him dead. If I could only find him, I could find my book. I could lock it away for ever. I'd never have to wonder why the thought of a girl's face makes me sick with guilt.

Through the haze of nausea something is niggling at me. Something the barman said. *Turning people away, they are . . . and the workhouses full . . .*

I flounder to my feet before I know why. I sway, pushing my hands into my pockets as if the reason is mixed up with my latchkey and loose change. Then I get hold of it. Hope.

Bindings are for desperate people. People who can't go anywhere else. And if Emmett Farmer is alive, he must be desperate by now. I stagger to the door and out into the street. The barman calls something after me, but it's lost in the cacophony of voices. I slip on a patch of ice and nearly go flying. It's foolish. I'm drunk. I should go home. But if there's a chance — any chance at all . . . I turn my back to the blazing evening sun, hurry around the corner, cross the junction with Alderney Street, and come out on to Library Row.

But the street outside Simms and Evelyn is empty, and they've shut for the day. Next to the trade entrance there's a notice in the window: *No Soliciting.* A gaggle of women and children are waiting silently on the steps of Barratt and Lowe, huddled against the cold; but that door is closed too, and no one goes in or out. A little further down, an aproned man with a broom is jabbing at a beggar in the doorway of Marden's. He says, "We're shut, come back tomorrow," with weary resignation. The beggar gets up and shuffles away.

None of those people is Emmett Farmer.

I keep walking, past the fine binders and the Bibliophiles Club and the school binders, checking each one as I go. I get further and further away from

424

Alderney Street, and Library Row gets narrower and dirtier and shabbier. Now the shops are down-at-heel, the doorways deep with shadows, and the houses almost meet overhead. The booksellers' shop-fronts are peeling, black paint faded to grey. Their curved windows are cloudy with grime. Above me a rusty book-shaped sign rasps as the wind catches it. *Trade Binding*, it says across two stylised pages; and on the other side, *Pawn Broker*. I stop to peer into the shop and catch a glimpse of a cramped room full of cheap trinkets in cabinets, a cluster of people, muttering. A dishevelled woman in an archway looks up as I pass, but she doesn't call out or beckon to me. An indigo glass bottle glints at her feet, an octagonal label. Laudanum.

A chill wind kicks up rubbish and grit. I pull my coat closer round myself and keep walking.

O'Breen and Sons. Licenst Bookseller. All Stamps Genuine. I pause to look through the window at a dim landscape of shelves and spines. A plump shopkeeper is behind the counter, talking to a woman in tears. He reaches out, pats her cheek, and smirks at her. Behind me a man pulls up in a carriage. He ducks past me through the door in a tang of leather and expensive cologne. I don't see his face. At the same time a door slams. I look round to see a woman coming out of an alley that runs between two shops. She's holding two children by the hand. The little one is grizzling; the older one is blank-eyed and dazed. "All right, ducky," she says, "we can go home now."

I clench my jaw and turn away. I'm wasting my time. If Farmer did come here when de Havilland threw him out, he's earned his money and gone, long ago. Now he'll be sleeping it off in an inn somewhere, slack-mouthed, undone.

I come out into a square, hardly wide enough for a carriage to turn. A single unlit streetlamp stands like a gibbet in a meagre drift of ashy snow. A girl is huddled by a cart, shivering and stamping her feet. A couple of men crouch on the kerb, warming themselves at a fire in a bucket. A gust of wind blows the stench of factory smoke into my face. I pull into a doorway to wipe the dust out of my eyes. The strip of sky above the houses is starting to unravel into thick strands of grey. It'll snow again before nightfall.

On the corner is *A. Fogatini, Pawnbroker and Licens'd Bookseller*. It's the smallest and shabbiest of all. It's famous for it. Fogatini's, the rubbish heap of memory. One window is roughly bricked up. The other is covered with pages of newspaper that have faded to the colour of old skin. The door opens, setting a bell jangling, and bilious light spills out on to the cobblestones. A man comes out — two men — and they walk towards me, laughing. Instinctively I lower my head.

". . . pass a long winter evening," one of them says. "Classic Fogatini."

The other one laughs. "Quite right. He's the absolute best for that sort of thing."

They go past. Their voices are whirled away in a gust of wind.

426

I wait until their footsteps have faded. Then I walk towards the wedge of light that's still gleaming on the cobbles. Through the open door I see piles and shelves and boxes of books. A small boy is sweeping the floor, sending up a cloud of coal dust. In the flickering lamplight I can just make out the label on the box beside the door: *INCOMPLETE (TRADE), 1d*. The shelf beside it is marked *CURIOSITY'S 2s6d EACH*. A man turns his back to the draught without looking up from the book he's holding. There's no one else in the shop. My head is aching. I should go home. This is the last bindery, and I haven't found him. As I step back I tread in something soft and the stink of shit wafts through the frosty air.

Outside, set into the wall a little further along, is a smaller door. Next to it there's a rain-stained notice: *For Trade Bindings. Please Knock. We Pay Good Rates*. Two men are standing there, arguing; one of them is in shirtsleeves, hugging himself against the cold. He glances round, and for the first time he shows his face.

It's Emmett Farmer.

A ray of red sunlight blazes over my shoulder, swift as a curtain being drawn back. Shadows sharpen on the pavement. Frost sparkles scarlet on the edges of bricks and window sills. Then it's gone. My breath comes short. For a second I can't move. Then the other man says, in a high foreign voice, "I told you, half a crown is too much. Suppose we say sixpence."

I grab Farmer's arm. I shove him backwards so hard I feel the breath go out of him. "No thanks," I say over my shoulder, "he's changed his mind." Behind me someone clicks his tongue in disgust and shuts the door. Farmer's feet scrabble on the cobbles. Suddenly I'm taking his whole weight. He sags to the ground. "Get *up*." The last time someone's body was in my arms it was Nell.

"Lucian." He starts to laugh. He doesn't stop. I drag him to his feet again and steer him towards the nearest doorway.

I fight to keep us both upright. I'm weak at the knees with triumph and euphoria and fury. "What on earth do you think you're doing?"

"What are *you* doing?" His pupils slide upwards and he staggers.

"Don't you dare wipe your memory — don't you *dare* —"

He blinks. "I wasn't."

"I need you to remember. Tell me where my book is and then you can do whatever you want."

He stares at me. At last he says, "I was asking for a job. That was the only one where they even considered it."

A job. Of course. Not a binding, another apprenticeship. And I dragged him away from the door as though he was about to jump under a train. But it doesn't matter. I've found him, at last. I loosen my grip on his shoulders, but I can't bring myself to let go of him. "I've been looking for you for hours." At least I sound calmer. "I just want my book back. I want to know it's safe. Where is it?"

"I haven't got it."

"*Where is it?*" I dig my fingers into his shoulder. Another wave of shivering goes through him. I can feel his bones judder in my grip. "For goodness' sake," I hiss. I take off my coat and push it at him. But he's huddled into himself, his eyes half closed. I have to wrap him in it. His skin is freezing.

He says, through rattling teeth, "De Havilland threw me out. I didn't have time to pack."

"I know. I heard."

"All I want . . ." He stops and clears his throat. "I want to go home. I'd walk, but in this snow . . ."

"You'd freeze to death."

"Yes." He pushes his arms into the sleeves of the coat and rubs his cheek with one cuff.

"How much do you need for a bed somewhere?" I reach into my pocket. The chill is starting to creep through my jacket. "Half a crown?"

He stiffens. "I'm not asking you for money."

"It's fine. It's half a crown. Here." I hold it out to him. It gleams, a small cold weight in the palm of my glove.

"No." He tries to step back and bumps into the wall. "No, I don't want your money."

I stare at him. "You'd rather work for Fogatini than let me give you half a crown? Two shillings and sixpence? You can't possibly be serious."

He turns his head away. "I'm not taking money from you. I'm not a beggar."

"It's not charity. I need my book back. Think of it as payment for that."

"I told you before, I haven't got it."

"But you know where it is."

He exhales through his teeth. "I can't get it. If I could . . ." He bows his head, burrowing his chin into the collar of my coat. "It's a long way away. In a bindery on the marshes. Locked in a vault. It's strong, a big bronze lock, you couldn't break it open. De Havilland has the key."

"De Havilland? He said he didn't know anything about it."

"And you believed him?" Farmer's face is in shadow but I see the glitter of his eyes as he glances at me. "It doesn't matter, anyway. I know where your book is, I know where the key is. But I can't get it. And neither can you."

"I offered de Havilland money. A hundred guineas. Surely he would . . ."

"He knows. Trust me." The words hang in the air. There's no reason to trust him. He shrugs.

"If I get the key from him, will you take me there?" I ask.

He laughs, croakily. "He keeps it with him all the time. Even at night. I don't care who you are, he won't let you take it. Why do you think he chucked me out into the snow without time to grab my coat?"

There's a yell and a thud from the crossroads behind us, the clatter of an overturned bucket. The smell of burning paraffin catches the back of my throat. Farmer cranes over my shoulder, his eyes narrowed. A moment later I hear footsteps running the other way and he relaxes.

430

"You mean . . ." I pull my jacket tighter but I'm getting colder by the second. "You tried, and that's why he sacked you?"

He opens his mouth as if he's going to speak. But he only nods.

"Why? Why do you want it? The key? You burnt your own book, it's not that." He doesn't answer. He won't meet my eyes. I say slowly, "I see. You're going to blackmail me. That's why you came to see me."

"Blackmail you? When I won't take half a crown?" He laughs again, for longer this time. But when I stare at him his eyes slide away and his grin fades. "Lucian."

"Call me Darnay." I fold my arms against the cold. "I understand. Half a crown is nothing. You want more. I'll give you whatever you want. Just help me get my book."

He hesitates. "Why do you want it back?"

"Because it's driving me mad, knowing that anyone could . . ." I draw in my breath. The doorway, the street, everything is covered by a grainy dark mist. The walls on either side of me seem to be closing in. I catch his eye. He's watching me so intently my throat tightens. Something makes me say, "I'm getting married in three days. I just want it all to be over. To be safe."

He makes a small helpless sound. "Of course I'll help you, if I can. But de Havilland won't just let you have it."

"I'll get the key. Somehow."

"But, Lucian —"

"*Don't call me that.*"

Silence. There's the distant jangle of someone going into Fogatini's shop. The wind picks up again and blows gritty snow-dust into our faces. Farmer slumps against the wall and rubs his eyes. A rat scuttles somewhere around our feet.

"All right," he says, finally. "If you can get the key, I'll help you. But on condition you treat me as an equal. I'm not your servant." He holds up his hand, palm turned to me. There are callouses on his fingertips. "And I'm calling you Lucian. It's your name."

His eyes are level and blank. I stare at him. Abruptly I recognise his expression. It's the way I look at my father, fighting to conceal hatred.

He's read my book. He hates me the way I hate my father.

I shut my eyes. My skin crawls as if he can see all the way through me. I blunder forwards into the blank darkness behind my eyelids. The wind drives freezing air down the back of my neck. I feel fingers drag at my elbow but I shake them off.

"I'm sorry. Don't run away. Please." He stands in front of me. We're in the middle of the street. A tiny edge of the sun flames above grey shreds of cloud, tinting the sky with crimson. My eyes smart. "It doesn't matter. If you can somehow get the key . . ."

I turn sideways, putting more space between us. I fumble in my pocket. "Stay at the Eight Bells, that's not far from here." I pull out a handful of coins and thrust them towards him. Six shillings or so. "That should last a couple of days. Think of it as payment in advance. I'll send you a note as soon as I've got it. Then you can take me to the bindery."

"I don't want that."

"Take it."

He raises his eyes to me. The wind tosses his hair, and one corner of his mouth pulls tight. He lets me tip the money into his palm. He goes to drop it into the pocket of my coat, and then grimaces. "Oh. Wait." He shoves the coins into his trouser pocket instead. He starts to slide his arms out of the coat-sleeves.

"Give it back to me next time. I've got a jacket."

There's a silence. "Thank you."

"If you need more money, send me a note. You know my address."

He nods. We stare at each other. The sun flares behind him, spilling red through the gap between the tenements. It glitters in his hair. His temple and jaw and the tip of one ear glow scarlet. Unexpectedly, as sudden as the flood of sunlight, he smiles at me. It changes his face completely. I can't remember anyone looking at me like that, ever. It makes the sunset redder, the scent of soot and paraffin sharper, the cold ache in my fingers more intense. The wind sings in a chimney somewhere above us. A crumple of paper whispers and swoops across the cobbles. The horn of a distant factory blares. He reaches out and brushes my cheek.

My heart gives one heavy thump. Then I recoil. *A binding, or standing on a street corner.*

"What's wrong? Wait, Lu — Darnay, I'm sorry."

"It's not a payment for *that*." I don't know why I'm so angry. It's not as if I've never had a whore before. But — *him*?

"I wasn't . . . I'm not . . ." He stares at me. Suddenly his mouth twists and he sputters with laughter.

"Keep your bloody hands off me." I can still feel the trace of his caress on my cheek, like a cobweb. I want it there forever, and I want it gone.

He stops laughing. "I'm sorry. Truly. I shouldn't have —"

"I don't care how you earn your money. I don't care what de Havilland sacked you for. Just help me find my book and then *leave me alone.*"

He opens his mouth. But whatever he wants to say, he doesn't say it. He gives me a tight nod, and turns on his heel. It takes an effort not to watch him leave. His footsteps die away. Now he's gone I notice how cold I am. I'm a fool to trust him. I shouldn't have given him the money. I should have given him more.

The red light is so shallow now that every cobblestone is picked out in shadow. My shoes slide on the kerb. Crumbs of broken glass crunch under my soles. I cross the band of sunlight into the darkness on the other side of the road. Fogatini's window shines around the edge of the papered panes. It's not far to Alderney Street, and the world of carriages and street lamps. The wind lifts spindrift off the cobbles and sends it whipping around my ankles. I walk as quickly as I can, trying to warm up. My reflection slides past me in murky shop-windows, huddled against the cold. I see it out of the corner of my eye and for a second it's as if someone's hurrying along beside me.

I emerge on to Alderney Street, then hesitate. I stare down the line of lamps, the railings throwing their shadow-cage on the new dusting of snow. De Havilland's window has a light in it. There must be a way to get the key from him. But if money won't work . . . The answer will come to me. It has to.

Finally the cold makes me turn towards home. My cheek is still tingling, as if Farmer's touch went deeper than my skin. I find myself stumbling to a standstill on the pavement, staring at the last streak of the sunset. A shadow moves behind me. Foolishly I glance over my shoulder, as if I'll see Farmer there. But I'm alone.

CHAPTER
TWENTY-FOUR

The next morning everything is pale and grainy and flickering, as if I'm getting a migraine. When I open the study door the fire in the hearth snaps and dips in the draught. I'm sick of this room. The red clotted walls waver and close in on me. My father isn't expecting me, as far as I know, but he gestures to the chair opposite him without looking up. I sit. I haven't slept and a long ache runs down my temple and jaw. I massage the side of my face as subtly as I can, trying to ease the tension.

"Lucian, my dear boy," my father says at last, putting down his pen. He raises his eyebrows. "I do hope it isn't the prospect of your fast-approaching nuptials that's reduced you to this condition."

"No. Thank you."

There's a pause. It's still my turn to speak. My father glances at the clock.

I swallow. I've been rehearsing this in my head all night, but the words won't come. In the darkness, while all the clocks of Castleford counted off the hours, it seemed like the only thing I could do. Now it sticks in my throat. "Father."

"Perhaps it would —" he says at the same moment. We both fall silent, watching each other. Pain gnaws at

436

the edge of my jawbone and licks down into my shoulder.

He leans back in his chair. He runs one finger along his bottom lip. "My dear boy," he says. He puts his sheet of blotting paper to one side. "Whatever you have to say, I'm listening."

I nod. I stare past him at the wallpaper and then shut my eyes. The elaborate curlicues still hang in front of my eyelids, like the last thing a dead man sees. I try to summon the greyness, but since I saw Emmett Farmer it's refused to come. Everything stays in colour, pulsing blood-red.

"That said," my father adds, "I do have other demands on my time."

I force myself to look at him. "I need your help."

"Indeed?" He picks up his pen and rolls it between his finger and thumb. His face is neutral, attentive, kindly. If I didn't know him I'd think he loved me.

"De Havilland," I say. It comes out like a stutter. "I mean . . ."

"Yes?" He hasn't moved, but something sharpens in his expression.

"He knows — he has . . ."

"What is it, my boy?" He gets up, and squeezes my shoulder. There's a choking smell of sandalwood shaving soap. I look up at him. "You are in a state, Lucian. Tell me what's wrong. I'm sure we can sort it out."

I take a deep breath. A gust of wind bubbles in the chimney and drives smoke into the room. My eyes water. If anyone can get the key off de Havilland, it's my father. But it takes an effort to form the words. "His apprentice told me . . ."

"Yes?" My father's grip clenches, and relaxes. "Ah, I see. Your book, is it? So you did go to de Havilland, after all. My goodness, he is a duplicitous fellow. Well, well. There's no need to worry. Lyon and Sons is very secure, but if you'd rather I'll have your book transferred to Simpson's."

"It isn't that." I stop. His face is avid. The collector's instinct.

There's a silence. "What?"

I swallow. I turn my head away and wipe my running eyes with the inside of my cuff. When I lower my arm I catch sight of the curiosity cabinet. The glass has been replaced. In spite of myself I glance at the floor, where the stains were. Someone has cleaned it all. The rug has been replaced, too. There's nothing in this room to show that a girl died here.

I look back at my father. He's bending towards me. Perhaps I imagined the greed in his eyes. Now they have a familiar benevolent gleam. It makes you feel special, that expression. It promises you that everything will be all right. It's how he looks at me just after he's hit me. "I'm glad you came to me, Lucian. It was foolish of you not to tell me before you were bound, so that I could take the necessary steps. Now I can protect you from any . . . unpleasantness."

I stumble to my feet. I take a clumsy step away from him.

"What on earth is the matter?"

438

I don't answer. My reflection stares at me from the curiosity cabinet, suspended among the ivory and the fossils. No one would know that there were shelves of books behind it. But I can feel them, fierce as heat from a furnace, as if Abigail and Marianne and Nell are in the room with me. "No," I say. "No, it's not that. It's nothing. Forget it."

"No? What then?"

"Nothing. It doesn't matter." I go to the door. I'm shaking, as if I've just stepped back from an abyss.

"Lucian." It stops me dead.

"I'm sorry. It's not important."

"I will decide that, not you. Now, what were you going to tell me? If it isn't about your own book, what was it?" All the benevolence has gone. His voice is like the edge of a piece of paper: sharp and deceptively soft.

I turn. A drop of sweat crawls down the back of my neck. I take a breath to argue but he's watching me and my mouth is suddenly too dry. I clear my throat.

He waits.

"I just — I heard —" I'm glad when the fireplace billows an ashy cloud and I have an excuse to cough. "De Havilland . . ." I grope hurriedly for a lie. "His apprentice said he was producing fakes."

"Fakes? Novels?" My father frowns. "You mean, copies?"

"Yes. Copies. In the bindery. He said they copied Nell's book."

He is silent for a moment. At last he nods. "I see."

"It may not even be true."

"I've had my doubts about de Havilland for a while." He's not talking to me. "Thank you. You may go."

"Yes." I don't wait for him to change his mind. When I step into the cooler air of the hall my shirt is wet and sticking to my back and under the arms. I don't pause until I'm in the Blue Room and the door is shut behind me. I lean against it. My heart is thundering in my ears and my headache has come back with a vengeance.

I shouldn't have been such a coward. I'd made up my mind to ask my father for help. I don't even know what made me hesitate. If I'd told him the truth, it would be out of my control by now.

I stare up at the painting of the water nymphs. But instead of their wet bare flesh all I can see is Emmett Farmer, waiting for me at the Eight Bells.

I drink wine and sherry with lunch and a brandy afterwards, but it doesn't have any effect. Clouds build up over the sun and it starts to snow again. Even the softer light hurts my eyes.

Before my grandmother died she'd roam from room to room, searching for something. If you asked her what she was looking for, she'd pause and regard you for a moment. Then she'd turn away and go on wandering, until she was so tired she staggered. Cecily and Lisette used to giggle behind her back. So did I. But now I feel the same. I can't settle. It's as if someone is just ahead of me, leaving every room just before I open the door. No matter where I go I have the same sensation, as if the warmth of someone else's breath still hangs in the air. I go to my bedroom and take *William Langland* out of the chest where I keep it. But I can't read. I never want to read it again. I stare out at the snow. My mother's voice crosses the hall downstairs but outside there's deep, dead silence.

I don't know how long I stay there, watching the snow, before something snaps inside me. I hurry down the stairs. No one sees me.

The main streets are full of traffic, mired in the frozen mud. Cabbies shout at each other. Pedestrians curse as they pick their way along the pavements. Beggars glower from doorways. But as soon as I turn into a side street, everything is quiet. The snow swallows every sound.

Alderney Street is empty and silent. When I get to number twelve I go up the steps without giving myself time to think. The door is opened almost immediately. It's the same woman as before. This time she's wearing green with jet beading. I say, "I'm here to see de Havilland."

"Do you have an appointment?" She doesn't give me time to answer. "I'm afraid he's out."

"I'll wait."

She glares at me through her pince-nez. She remembers me. "May I ask what it's regarding?"

"No." I take a step forward. She holds her ground just long enough to make it clear that she doesn't *have* to let me pass. Then she sighs, draws aside and gestures me to the waiting room.

There's no one else there. I take off my coat and hat and sit down. I leaf through *Parnassus* and *The Gentleman*. I crush one of the false orchids into a stiff

441

pad of wax. I stand by the window and watch for de Havilland. The street is still empty. The snow goes on falling. The light is starting to fade.

I'm here to get the key. That's why I've come. At least, I thought it was. But now, standing here watching the snow, I'm not so sure. I don't have a plan. I don't have a hope. What I want, most of all, is to forget all this. To go home blank-headed. To sleep without thinking. I'd do almost anything not to have to be myself any more. I imagine a binding like a doorway, leading you into an empty room. You can clear your life away. Start again.

My chest is tight. There's a sour taste at the back of my mouth. It would almost be a relief, not to know that Emmett Farmer is waiting for me at the Eight Bells. Not to feel that sting of unease when I think of his face, Not to look at Honour, the day after tomorrow, knowing that part of me is locked away, out of sight. And there's a simple solution. When de Havilland comes . . .

I snatch up my coat and hat. A moment later I'm out in the street, clenching my teeth as the cold wind sends needles of snow into my face. I need to find the nearest public house.

It's not far to the Eight Bells, but I can't go there. I don't want Emmett Farmer to see me in this state. Something makes me avoid the Princess Palace, too. I turn down Library Row. There's one solitary lamp on the corner. Beyond that, the growing dusk is spotted with soot-blotched shop windows. Surely somewhere, in the maze of booksellers, there'll be a tavern. But I get

442

to the corner where Fogatini's is without finding one. I turn round. I'm not too far from the bar of the Theatre Royal, where the whores congregate. That would do.

I start back the way I came. The snow comes and goes in gusts. A man hurries through the chilly pool of light under the lantern, clutching his hat to stop it blowing away. The brim casts a shadow over his eyes but for a moment the lower part of his face is illuminated. Greasy ringlets brush his shoulders.

It's de Havilland. It shouldn't be surprising — we're only a few streets away from his bindery — but it makes my heart jump into my mouth.

I stop dead. But I don't want to accost him here; it'll be too easy for him to walk away from me. I pull back into the nearest doorway and wait.

There are two men sauntering down the street behind him. When they pass the lamp they move casually to the edge of the pavement, keeping to the shadows. With a jolt, I recognise one man by his size and the other by his gait: Acre, my father's advisor, and his right-hand man. As they move into the unlit part of the street, Acre and his man — Wright, I think — swap a single glance. With a few swift steps, Wright comes up behind de Havilland. He knocks de Havilland's hat off. In the same second he swings his arm so quickly there's no time to see if he has a weapon. De Havilland drops, clean as a shot.

I hold on to the edge of the doorway. The mortar crumbles under my fingers. Why didn't I call out?

Wright puts his cosh back in his jacket and manhandles de Havilland's limp body into the little

443

alley just in front of us. Acre bends for de Havilland's hat and follows Wright into the shadows. It's so slick it's like a music-hall turn. But there's no applause or laughter. Now the wind has died down I can't hear anything but my heartbeat.

I make my way to the mouth of the alleyway and stare in. Slowly my eyes adjust to the blackness.

The men are crouching beside de Havilland. Wright is holding something over his face. De Havilland's feet jerk about and his body convulses. As I watch, it slows and stops. His ankles roll outwards. Everything is still. Acre puts a handkerchief and a bottle of ether back in his pocket. Wright lets go of de Havilland and rolls his head from side to side, grunting.

I clear my throat.

Acre looks round. For an instant I see the weariness in his eyes. I was stupid enough to let him see me. Now I'm another problem to be solved. Then he recognises my face.

If he's surprised he doesn't show it. He gives me a half-smile. "Mr Lucian," he says. "Good evening."

"Good evening, Acre." The words come out easy and assured. I tilt my head to look at de Havilland's face. He's breathing. If there's a bruise, it's on the back of his head. He could be asleep. I keep my eyes on his face but I can hear my father's voice. *I've had my doubts about de Havilland for a while.* "Did — my father — order this?"

Acre smiles. "Perhaps you should be getting home, sir. These back ways can be dangerous after sunset."

444

I catch myself before I ask anything else. I don't want to hear the answer. I brush the soot from my sleeve until I'm sure I can control my tongue. "And the — the others?"

"Probably a fire at the bindery," Wright says. "Terrible thing, a bindery fire. A binder gets stuck in it, no one even hears him screaming. Lucky the workers decided to leave early."

"Shut up." It's so quick and low I barely hear it. Acre turns to me. The look in his eyes has changed. If my father decided he didn't need a male heir, after all . . . "This is nothing to do with you, sir. With all due respect."

"Certainly." I smile at him. "I'm sorry to stumble in like this. As it happens, though . . ." I drop into a crouch beside de Havilland's body. I've turned out his pockets before Acre has time to react. Coins and a watch and a pillbox clink on the cobbles. A handkerchief. A cigarette case. A bunch of keys. I pick it up and they rattle on the ring. Latchkeys; the key to a cupboard and a tantalus; a little shiny key with a label, *Lyon & Sons*. A bigger, bronze key, older and plainer than the others.

Acre holds out his hand. "We need those."

I meet his eyes. "Yes. Of course." If they're staging a fire in de Havilland's bindery, they'll need to get in without breaking the locks. I fumble. If I take too long, Acre will pluck the whole bunch away from me. His arm twitches. Just in time I slide the big key off the ring and slip it into my pocket. I look at him and smile, again. "That was all I needed. Thanks."

445

"Your father knows about that, does he?"

"Naturally." After a moment he shrugs and picks a tooth with his thumbnail. His mouth is floppy and raw. I get to my feet. "Good luck with — the rest."

"Thank you, sir." You wouldn't know from his voice that he's staring at me, taking my measure.

I nod and walk away. For the first ten yards the space between my shoulder blades is prickling. At every moment I'm expecting a foot in the back of my knee, or a flash of pain across my skull. But nothing touches me. At last I grind to a halt beside a shop window. When I glance down the street Acre and Wright are only just emerging from the alleyway. Wright has de Havilland over his shoulder. They cross the road and turn down a narrow passage that isn't wide enough to be an alley. At the corner a ragged man is loitering, trying to light a damp cigarette end. He looks up and quickly away again. It must be a sight that they're used to, in these dark lanes.

It's started to snow again. Shabby clumps of snowflakes drift past me like feathers.

I hurry towards the junction with Alderney Street, sliding on lumps of frozen slush half-hidden by the new snow. The cold is like lead in my bones, weighing me down. But I don't slow my pace until I'm halfway down Alderney Street, within reach of the corner of Station Road and Market Square. Here the lamps are all lit. Traffic is clogging the centre of the road. The ladies of pleasure are congregating under the portico of the Theatre Royal, wrapped in cloaks edged with dyed rabbit and moulting plumes. One of them waves at me,

446

but a shiver catches her halfway through the gesture and her smile turns to a grimace.

I need to send a note to Farmer, telling him to meet me. Midnight would be best, somewhere quiet, where there's no one around. He didn't tell me where we were going. I was counting on borrowing horses from our own stable, but I can't go home now. I can't risk my father seeing me. Acre will tell him about the key. I'll have to find a hotel where I can write a note and stay warm until it's time to leave. I'll hire the horses from a livery stable. I check the key in my pocket. Still there. I look round, wondering whether the Feathers or the Grosvenor would be safer. The movement makes me giddy. Suddenly, out of nowhere, a wave of nausea goes through me. Acid bubbles in my stomach, spreads upwards into my chest. I lean against the window of the nearest shop. I'm trembling so hard my forehead knocks against the icy glass.

If de Havilland isn't dead already, he soon will be. Because of what I told my father. Because I didn't call out to him, I didn't warn him. I shift from foot to foot, helpless, despising myself. If I went back now . . . But I'm afraid. If my father finds out I lied — if he decides to punish me . . . He threatened me once with the lunatic asylum. He wasn't bluffing. The thought sends ice down my spine. If only I were a hero. The sort of person who would risk that, to save de Havilland. But I'm not.

I huddle into myself, shaking. I must have known what I was doing. But it's only now that it's real. I've killed someone. That noise when Wright hit him — the choking, bubbling sound of ether going into his lungs — the spasms, the terrible juddering as he clenched all over . . . My fault. Me.

I wait for it to pass. My vision clears. In the shop window a fan of coloured gloves stretches empty fingers towards me. The horror subsides into a dull shame. This is what it feels like to be a murderer. And a coward. No wonder I got myself bound. If my book is anything like this . . . I have to find it.

And I have the key. I bought it with de Havilland's life.

I wipe my face dry with my sleeve. There's no way back, even if I were brave enough. I take a deep breath and turn to hail a cab.

CHAPTER
TWENTY-FIVE

Later that evening the snow stops. The wind is stronger than ever. It scours the clouds away, strips twigs from the trees and grit from mortar and stone. By the time I get to the fish market the sky is clear and milky with the light of the full moon. The market square is like an empty stage, glistening limelight-bright. The traffic on the High Street is muffled by the buildings between and the silence is only broken by the clipped sound of hooves. I don't like riding like this, leading another horse behind mine. I'm afraid I'll draw too much attention, and someone will tell my father. But no one looks at me, except the few last whores outside the Theatre Royal.

It's so like a dream that I don't quite expect Farmer to be there. But he is. He's standing under the clock. He's huddled in my coat, stamping his feet. When he hears me coming he withdraws into the shadows. Then he sees it's me. "Darnay," he says, "I'd started to think you —" He breaks off. He steps forward into the moonlight, pulls himself easily into the saddle and sets off a few paces in front of me, without another word. I click to my own horse and follow him. Behind us the clock strikes twelve.

For the first few miles all I care about is getting out of Castleford. At every turning — every shadow and alleyway — flashes of memory mix with premonitions of disaster in my head: the sound of metal on bone, Acre's voice warning me to stop, Farmer brought down, choking on his own blood, the final spasm as he loses consciousness . . . But as the road takes us past the last half-built houses I relax. The air is clearer here, out of the stench of coal fires and factories. There's more space, more light. I tilt my head back. On the horizon, furthest from the moon, the sky is rich with stars.

We're on the outskirts of the forest now. At first the snow is striped black and silver. Further in, the shadows deepen. There'll be enough light to ride by, on the road. But within a few yards on either side there's a glittering net of darkness. Here and there something scuttles. A fox flashes its eyes at us. My horse catches up with Farmer's and whinnies.

We ride side by side. Up till now Farmer has been silent. The horses trudge on. The rhythm of their steps is so regular it nearly lulls me to sleep.

He says, "What happened to de Havilland?"

In the absolute quiet it's as loud as a gunshot. Without thinking I almost bring my horse to a halt.

He raises his eyebrows. His eyes are sharper than they were. There's more colour in his cheeks.

My voice is clogged up, as if I haven't spoken for days. I say, "What makes you think I'll tell you that?"

"You might as well trust me. What have you got to lose?"

"Everything."

"Come on, Darnay. I already know more about you than you do." He gives me a half-smile.

It's true. And I don't care as much as I should. Not any more. I look away. The sharp black-and-white of the forest blurs and dazzles. I'm too tired to go on lying. "They drugged him. They're going to burn the bindery down. With him in it."

"What?" Farmer pulls up short.

I shouldn't have told him. He stares at me. In the silence I see his expression go from disbelief to belief. "I couldn't stop them."

"The whole bindery? What about the others?"

"It's only de Havilland," I say, as if that excuses everything. As if one sordid death doesn't count.

"Even so, we can't ..." He pulls on the reins, swinging his horse round. "Don't you understand? It's *murder*."

I've said the word to myself. But hearing it aloud makes me catch my breath. "Of course I understand. But we can't stop them. I wish we could."

"We have to try. Come on!"

I bite my lip. He'll go back. Any decent person would. I should have done. If only I had . . . But it's too late. "We can't help," I say. "It won't do any good."

"We could —"

"My father's made up his mind. You can't stop it. If you get in the way, you'll end up in the bindery with de Havilland."

"We have to!" He stares at me. "You're not going to let them *kill* him."

I can't speak. The pause answers him better than I could have done.

"Lucian —"

"Please. Please don't. You'll die too. If you died, because of me —" My voice cracks. It doesn't matter. Let him think I only care about myself. "And if my father finds out about this ... he'll put me in a madhouse." But why should Emmett believe me? Why should he care? I've condoned murder, by my own admission. And I'm a coward. He must despise me now, if he didn't already.

There's a silence. I bow my head and swallow the taste of metal on my tongue. Then I gesture at the road in front of me. "Just tell me where I need to go, will you?"

He starts to speak, and stops. A fine vapour of snow curls along the bank at the side of the road. At last he clicks to the horse and pulls it back round. He rides past me in the direction we were going before. I watch him get further and further away until at last he looks back over his shoulder. Incredulous warmth pulses through me. I don't know why he's changed his mind, but it feels like a kind of miracle.

I'm worth a lot of money to him. That's all. It must be.

I nudge my horse with my heels and it lurches into a reluctant trot. When I'm within a few metres of Farmer he starts to move again. Neither of us speaks. The path looks the same as it did a minute ago. I imagine us walking round a wheel, the snowy path unrolling and

452

the diorama of wintry trees repeating itself for ever. I wouldn't care.

After a long time he says, "Was I meant to be in the bindery, too? Burnt to death with de Havilland?"

I don't answer. But in spite of myself I glance at him. He makes a grim little noise.

"Why didn't Acre take de Havilland to another binder? Isn't that what he normally does?"

"I don't know." I push my hair out of my eyes. The frost has frozen it into clumps. Farmer looks away. "How do you know what he normally does?"

The corners of his mouth tighten. At last he shrugs. "Long story."

"Go on."

He snorts. "I can't. Believe me, I'd like to."

"Did you — tell me you didn't try to blackmail my father?"

"For pity's sake, shut up about blackmail!" He wheels his horse sideways. Mine stumbles to a halt. "I'm not blackmailing you. Can you get that into your head? I'll give you back every penny of your damned money. I'm only wearing this coat because I'd freeze to death without it."

I don't say anything. Slowly he pulls his horse round to face the road. He wipes his mouth. The vein on his forehead stands out like a thread.

I ride past him. I stare at the shadows under the horse's hooves, watching them fold and slide over the uneven snowdrifts.

The road curves. A clearing opens and disappears to our right. A charcoal-burner's stack smoulders in the middle of it. Then it's gone. An owl calls, and my horse spooks sideways. Blood thunders in my ears.

Farmer catches up with me. The path winds up a hill and down a rocky gully.

He says, "You could have told them where I was."

"Don't be a fool. Why would I do that?"

"Why didn't you?"

"Are you saying that's what I should have done?"

"I'm asking if you wish you had."

I rub my forehead, trying to bring some feeling back to the numb skin. "Because you can lead me to my book."

He nods. "Your book. Yes. Of course."

"Yes." Even my lips and tongue are stiff with cold. "What are you trying to say? Why else would I care what happened to you?"

"Why else, indeed." He coughs, clears his throat, and spits. The knot of phlegm sinks into the snow. It leaves a clean outline like a leaf. Then he flicks the reins and his horse speeds up. He doesn't look back. I ride after him in silence.

We ride on and on. Everything looks the same. I start to drift into a dream. Suddenly everything is lighter and I jolt awake. The end of the woods. In front of us the marshes stretch bare and shining under the moon. The road is only just visible, like a watermark. Where it curves I can make out a dark smudge that might be a house or an outcrop of rock.

Farmer calls over his shoulder, "Let's stop here. I need to piss."

I rein in my horse next to him as he dismounts. He lands with a thud and staggers. He points at the trees and disappears into the shadows. I get down too. The muscles in my legs have frozen solid. I'm chilled and aching all over. How long have we been riding? Hours. The moon is lower than it was. I get out my watch but I've forgotten to wind it. The case is sticky with frost.

When Farmer steps back into the moonlight I pick my way through the deep snow into another patch of trees. At first I think it's too cold to undo my trousers. I have to take off my gloves. When I'm finished I fumble with my flies for a long time, wrestling with my buttons.

"Come on, I'm freezing," Farmer calls over his shoulder. Then he catches sight of what I'm doing. "Need a hand with that?"

A flush prickles on my skin like pins-and-needles. "Don't be stupid."

"I was joking."

"Oh." I manage to do the last button. When I look up he's still watching me. He smiles. It's a crooked, reluctant smile, but there's no mockery in it. For a split second colour dances on the edge of my vision, a sense of light and space as if someone has lifted the lid of a box.

"Here." He stands beside my horse and laces his fingers together into a step. "Need a bunk-up?"

I want to refuse. In Market Square he mounted easily, graceful and thoughtless, as if he's been doing it all his life. I can only just clamber onto a horse when there's a mounting-block and a following wind. But without his help I'm not sure I'll be able to get into the saddle at all. "Thank you." The words stick in my teeth. He grins, as if he knows exactly how I feel.

"Come on, then." He hoists me up easily. My muscles are clumsy from the cold but I find myself in the saddle without any effort. He hauls himself up on to the other horse. He's still smiling, but not at me.

"What do you want, Farmer?"

The smile fades. He looks around, as if he's woken up and doesn't know where he is. "What?"

"I don't understand you. You say you don't want money. You're not blackmailing me. You help me — but you despise me. Why?"

"Despise you? Lucian . . ."

"Don't call me Lucian!"

He blinks. His face is expressionless. After a long time he shrugs.

"All right. Never mind." I flick the reins. "Let's go."

"I know you don't remember. I know that. But I wish . . ."

I straighten up, digging my heels into the horse's sides. His voice dips into a murmur, suddenly distorted as if I'm hearing it underwater. Then everything slides away. I'm alone, nowhere. The air shimmers, full of light. Like a blizzard of stars. I blink and it's gone. I'm back. I shake my head, scattering the last shimmering flakes.

We haven't moved. He stares at me.

"What?" Stars drop across my vision and burn out.

"Never mind. It's stupid, I can't stop myself trying."

"What? What happened?"

"Don't worry. You're right. It's getting late. Early. Let's go."

"Wait — you tried to tell me something, didn't you?" This is what it was like for Nell. The world sliding between your fingers like water. Nothing to hold on to. If I reached out for the nearest branch my hand would go straight through it, like a shadow in smoke.

"Forget it." After a second he laughs, shortly.

"You did that before. Didn't you? When you came to see me. You made the world go . . . strange. Don't do it again."

But he doesn't look at me. "Come on. I'm freezing."

"Did you hear me?"

"We'll find your book. It'll be all right." He clicks to his horse and it sets off.

I stare at his back. It won't be all right, ever. I've killed a man. But it will be . . . better. From nowhere a picture flashes into my head: the secret compartment of my blanket chest. A bottle of brandy, *William Langland, Lucian Darnay*. Perhaps it would be better to rent a bank vault — like my family's vault at Simpson's, where my father's share certificates and my grandmother's diamonds moulder in the dark. But would I rest easy, knowing it was out of my reach?

Farmer has left me behind. I kick my horse, urging it to catch up. It accelerates into a weary trot. But Farmer stays ahead of me, quickening his pace so I can't catch up. He doesn't look round.

By the time we reach the house the moon has set. A wide cloudbank is sweeping in from the west, but with

457

the stars and the snow there's still enough light to see by. The horses trudge on. I'm almost asleep when at last Farmer stops and dismounts in front of me. "We're here."

My eyes are gritty with fatigue and cold. I wipe them on my sleeve. The house is bigger than I expected, thatched and half-timbered, with lattice-paned windows and a carved pattern on the front door. A mountain of snow has drifted up against the front wall, waist-height. An icicle clings to the tip of the bell-rope.

Farmer leads us round the side of the house into a yard. The house forms one side of the square. Opposite it there are storehouses and a stable. I take in the stone paving and the newish thatch. Whoever lives here, they're not poor, but they're lazy. A tuft of straw has blown free of the gable and hangs down, garlanded with beads of ice. The snow is deep here, too, marked by seams of bird-feet and rats' paws. But the walls have kept out the north wind and the drifts are shallow. It's easy enough for Farmer to get the stable door open and the horses inside. I help him haul the door through the last part of its arc. The place stinks of damp and rot. He grimaces. "It'll be all right for a few hours. We'll leave as soon as the sun comes up."

I'm too cold to care. I huddle in a corner while he leads the horses into the stalls. He cracks the ice in a bucket. My brain has frozen. I can't even think.

He glances at me, but doesn't pause until the horses are comfortable and he's given them a wipe-down with a handful of straw. Then he beckons to me. A path leads out of the yard and round the back of the house to

458

another door. The marshes gape on the other side, so empty and white I can't look at them. It feels like vertigo. I stumble inside, glad to be surrounded by walls.

But in here it's just as cold. Colder, even. The air scrapes my throat as it goes down. It's only now that I realise the house is empty. There's a dead, stale smell in the air, and dry flecks of grass have blown in under the door. I follow Farmer numbly into a long room. There are tables and shelves and strange pieces of equipment. Needles and knives.

"Give me the key, and we'll go downstairs." He glances at me. "Are you all right?"

"Just cold."

"Get the fire going. There're matches on the shelf. Never mind, I'll do it. Sit down." He starts to load logs into the stove.

"Do you have any brandy?"

"Drunkard." He straightens up to look at me and the grin dies off his face. "I'll look."

I nod. Every thought I have is limp and mushy, like a frost-bitten plant. I draw out a stool and sit. At last a faint tendril of warmth reaches my legs. I lean forward and pull off my gloves.

"Here." I didn't notice him go but now he's back. He pushes a glass at me. The perfume of honey and lavender makes me cough. "Mead," he adds. "There's no brandy. De Havilland drank all of it." He raises his own glass in a wordless toast.

It's good. Medicinal. It feels virtuous and nourishing. Not like my father's expensive stuff, which I drink to get drunk on. Heat and sweetness pool on my tongue. This is like drinking sunlight.

"Better?"

"Thank you."

He takes his coat off and drops it on the bench. He leans against the wall next to the stove. He's watching me. I watch him watching me. He smiles. He lowers his head to hide it, but he's definitely smiling.

"What?"

"Nothing."

"*What?*"

He raises one shoulder. "I can't help it."

"You're laughing at me."

He inclines his head. He takes a mouthful of mead. "Not you." He stares at the stove. He's left the door open and the fire casts red light on the floor. The flames are like ragged satin. He laughs under his breath.

I push my stool back and rest my elbows on the bench behind me. Now that I'm warm, the room reminds me of Esperand's workshop, with its dummies and boxes and rolls of cloth. Or of our kitchen, the walls hung with pans and shape-moulds and the table scrubbed almost to silver . . . Nothing here is luxurious; and because of that, it's beautiful. Even the painted tiles around the stove have a reason to be there. I try to make out the patterns of leaves and animals. Lamplight plays on Farmer's face. It glints gold off his eyelashes. There's a tiny scar on his top lip.

He spreads his hands over the hottest part of the stove. Then he lowers them, slowly, until he's nearly touching the metal. My own palms tingle. He pulls back, catches my eye, and laughs. "Right." He drinks the last mouthful of mead. "Are you ready?"

"What for?"

"For your book, of course. You've got the key?"

"Yes." I dig it out of my pocket. It falls to the floor.

Farmer scrabbles for it. His movements are clumsy, but he's eager, not afraid. When he picks it up he looks up at me as if he's expecting something else. "All right. Let's go." He straightens and moves towards me as if he thinks I need his help to get to my feet. When I catch his eye, he shrugs and steps away.

He picks up the lamp, unlocks the door at the end of the room, and goes through. It smells like a tomb but the air beyond the doorway is mild, almost warm. I can imagine mould and spongy growths on the walls. I follow him quickly because otherwise I'll be walking down the steps in the dark.

We're in a storeroom. It's a mess. Boxes are stacked against the walls. Tools I don't recognise are scattered everywhere.

Farmer puts down the lamp, glances at me and sets his jaw. "Ready?"

"I've already said so."

His cheeks are flushed. Sweat glints in his hairline. He fits the key into the lock. I reach out and take hold of the edge of the table. My pulse twangs like a bow-string.

The lock clicks and the whole wall swings on hidden hinges. Behind it there's a dark room lined with empty shelves. Farmer catches his breath. Slowly he reaches out and puts the key down. He misses the table and it falls to the floor. The clunk is answered by a tiny echo from the darkness beyond, as if the safe has its own voice.

There's nothing there.

I turn on my heel and go up the stairs. Farmer says my name but I don't look back. The darkness sucks at my heels like mud.

Footsteps come up the stairs behind me. He stops at the top, in the doorway. The silence goes on and on.

"Damn, damn, *damn*." He's breathless. He thumps the wall with his fist.

I pick up my gloves. The chill makes them feel damp, as if the leather has only just been peeled off the carcass. Beside them on the bench there's some kind of knife. It's half the length of my forearm, the blade cut at an angle. Streaks of stove-light dance on the bevelled edge.

I put my gloves on, lacing my fingers together so that the seams fit well between my knuckles. I pick up my hat. Then, finally, I turn and look at him.

"Naturally," I say, "there's no question of payment."

He stares at me. "What?"

I smooth my hair off my forehead. I check my hatband isn't creased and put my hat on. "Shall we go?"

"Lucian . . ." He takes a step towards me. "Wait. I didn't know. I thought it would be there."

I shrug, with tight shoulders.

462

"De Havilland must have changed his mind. Come back later — while I was ill, maybe — and taken them all. Sold them."

"To whom?"

"It could be anyone. Any collector." He rocks back and forth. Then he kicks the bench so hard it jumps a few inches sideways. "There's only one person who would know." He raises his eyes to mine. "And he's probably dead by now."

He doesn't say that it's my fault. He doesn't need to. A glimpse of the alley, de Havilland's body.

I adjust the brim of my hat. I don't want him to see my face. "I'm going home." I'm dreading the cold ride back to Castleford so much my bones feel like lead. "No point in staying here."

He turns away. A gust of wind rattles the windows.

"Are you coming?"

He doesn't answer. Outside a curtain of snow blows across the marshes. We have to leave now, before it gets worse. I'm getting married the day after tomorrow. If I get trapped here . . .

"Come on. Let's go." I wait for him to move. When he doesn't, I pick up his coat from the side and thrust it at him. "I need to get the horses back to the livery stable."

There's a silence. He doesn't take his coat. My coat. I drop it on the floor.

He glances down, but he doesn't bend to pick it up. "What if we don't go back?"

"What?"

He turns and meets my eyes. "You don't have to go back." There's something in his expression that I don't understand. "You don't have to."

"What on earth are you talking about?"

"We could . . ." He gives a small, helpless shrug. "If we stayed here . . ."

"Of course I have to go back."

"Lucian." He reaches out for me.

"Stop calling me that, damn you!" I knock his arm out of the way and try to push past. But I'm clumsy and drunk and my hand hits the side of the bench, hard. Pain blazes down my wrist and my fingers. I reel sideways and collapse on to the workbench, trying to breathe.

"What's the matter?"

"Nothing." I cradle it against my chest. Automatic tears sting my eyes.

"Lucian, you're bleeding — your glove —"

"I know." I exhale, inhale slowly, exhale again. "It wasn't you."

"I'm sorry, I didn't know."

"It's nothing." He reaches out and takes hold of my wrist. I tense.

"Let me see. Please." He stays still, watching me, until I nod. Then he pulls me gently toward him. He peels off my glove. He drags up a stool and sits down. All the while he's holding on to me.

"That looks painful. What happened?"

"I —" I clear my throat and wipe my eyes on my cuff. "I broke some glass. I was trying to . . ." I stop. He

464

waits. "Nell hanged herself. I was trying to cut her down."

"Hanged herself? Nell? The one who — the one I bound?"

"Yes."

There's a silence. He stands up. For a moment I think he's walking out. But he only goes to the end of the room and picks up an empty jar. He opens the window and scrapes snow into it. He puts it on the stove to melt. We watch the white feathers collapse into water. Then he brings it back to me, picks up the bottle of mead with his other hand and nudges the window shut with his elbow. Without a word he dips a bobble of sponge into the water and cleans the blood off my palm. Then he wets the sponge with the mead. "This will hurt."

It does. But after a second the burn softens to warmth, and the pain eases. Farmer rinses the sponge. I don't look up.

"Are you all right?"

I nod.

"Are you sure?" He puts the sponge down on the bench. He leans forward. I tense, waiting for him to touch me, but he doesn't. "I'm sorry."

I shake my head. Snow crackles against the window.

I say, "I could have saved Nell, if I'd tried harder."

He shifts his weight, but he doesn't answer.

I draw in my breath. "They killed de Havilland because of me. Because I lied to my father. That's my fault, too."

He's very still. "You didn't kill him."

465

"I knew what would happen. I knew, when I said it." In spite of myself I meet his eyes. He doesn't waver. I'm the one who glances away.

After a while he says, "I'll get a bandage."

Suddenly I think of my father, knotting the ends of white linen neatly around my thumb. "No." I curl my fingers over the cut. "It's fine."

"But —"

"No!" I get up. "Thanks. I have to go home."

"It'll bleed more, if you don't let me —"

"Please, will you just *stop* —" My voice breaks. I shut my eyes. Now he's on his feet, closer than arm's length. I can feel the heat of his body.

He takes hold of my wrist. He unfolds my fingers, very gently, one by one. It sets off a fierce dangerous ache in my heart and throat, nothing to do with the cut. He tilts my palm to look at it. "Fine," he says, at last. "But keep it clean."

I'm so tired. I have to pull away. If he looks at me, he'll see . . . But my head is spinning. If I fell now, he'd catch me. A gust of wind whines in the chimney and blows cold air down the back of my neck. Slowly, as if something inside me is dissolving, I lean forward. My forehead touches his shoulder. I feel him freeze. We stand still, hardly breathing. Every part of me is concentrated on the place where my skin is against his shirt.

"It's all right." His voice is very low.

It isn't all right. But he grips my shoulders and holds me steady. I let him take my whole weight. I can hear his heartbeat. When I raise my head he stares at me, eyes intent and hesitant. It sends a sting of exposure through me.

That's the moment when I should move away. But I don't.

CHAPTER
TWENTY-SIX

Sometime in the night, the blizzard stops. When I wake, the bedroom is quieter than anywhere I've ever slept. There's only the wind humming in the roof, and my own breathing, and Emmett's.

The bed is next to the window. The light kindles from dull to bright and back again as clouds blow across the sun. There's a blue patch in the corner of the sky. It moves sideways, shredded by the wind. Sunlight glints off an icicle and throws rings of light on to the bare floorboards.

I untangle myself, trying not to wake Emmett. He sighs and draws his knees up to his chest, nestling into the blankets. His face is buried in the pillow. All I can see is his ear and the curve of his cheek. My lips tingle with the memory of his skin: hot and slightly rough, tasting of sweat. A faint warmth runs through me, an echo of last night. I want to do it all again, over and over. I want to forget everything else: my life, my father, my wedding, my book.

For a moment I let myself imagine staying here. If I missed the wedding, my father would probably disown me. But that might not be so bad. My mother would miss me, but she'd have my sisters. She's good at turning away from unpleasantness, at pretending. I look sideways at Emmett's body curled under the covers. If I nudged him now, rolled him over to me and told him I couldn't bear to leave . . . He stretches, and his eyes flutter open. He sees me, smiles, and goes back to sleep. I almost kiss him. I shut my eyes. My heart is beating too fast. I've never known anything like this before. Last night it was exhilarating, the way desire swept me away. I wanted him so much I didn't know who I was. I didn't care any more. I gave in to it. And he went with me, like a dance — he let me, he made me . . . As if he knew me already, knew my body right down to my bones. I cried out at the end as if I was lost. But now, in this cold light, a spasm of shivers passes through me. He's a stranger.

I wish I could believe that last night mattered. But what he showed me wasn't tenderness; it was experience. When he first kissed me I thought — in spite of everything — he was innocent. As if he'd never touched anyone else. But that's absurd. No one fucks like that unless they've done it a lot. Even if he hasn't asked me for money, yet . . . He's more like me than I thought. If I told him I wanted to stay here with him, he'd laugh in my face.

And even if he didn't . . . there's de Havilland. Nell. My book. I don't deserve any better. None of this, nothing, no matter what happened last night, can change that.

The floor is like ice. Most of my clothes are in a pile under the window sill. When I drag them on they're clammy. My teeth chatter and my hands fumble with the buttons. In the end I leave my collar open. I shove my cravat into my pocket. I pick up my boots and tiptoe out of the room. I go down the stairs. A loose piece of thatch rattles against the front door. It makes me stop dead. No one there.

The stove in the workshop has gone out. In the soft white light the room looks like a still life, one of those bare Northern interiors, all drab brown and ivory. My cloak is hanging over a tall press.

I unhook it with numb fingers. As I turn to leave I nearly trip over Emmett's shirt. It lies where I dropped it before he led me upstairs. I pick it up, remembering the way he shivered when I unbuttoned it. I was shivering too, but not from cold. Now the linen is soft and chilly against my face. It smells of him, the cedarwood and pepper of his sweat. I want to put it on.

No. Suddenly it's as if I'm outside the window, looking in. I can see myself: red-eyed, unshaven, languishing over another man's dirty shirt. A man I can't trust. How my father would laugh. One fuck has turned me soft inside, like an infection. I drop the shirt and kick it out of the way. It slides under one of the wooden chests. If Emmett looks for it he'll see the trail in the dust. He can fish it out with a ruler or something. It's cheap, anyway. Old. Hardly worth him kneeling for.

I have to shove the back door open. A drift has built up on the doorstep and for a few seconds I'm not sure I'll be able to get out. I wade out into it and the wind bites me almost in half. Tiny particles of ice hiss against my face. My cheeks sting. I trudge, knee-deep, round the side of the house. The hinges on the stable door are coated with ice. I have to kick the door-frame to break it. I pause and look at the horses contentedly chewing their straw. If I leave one here, I'll have to tell the livery stable to send the bill to my father. If I take them both, Emmett will be stuck.

I tell myself that the reason I only take one of them is the prospect of sorting out both bridles in this withering cold. I lead my mount into the yard and hoist myself awkwardly into the saddle.

All the way to the road I keep glancing over my shoulder. He'll wake up. He'll hear. He'll wonder where I've gone. But nothing moves. The house stares back at me with blank windows.

It's a long ride back to Castleford.

It's dark when I get home. There's light in all the windows. When Betty answers the door her hair is falling out of her cap and there are smears of pollen on her pinafore. Behind her a new scullery maid picks her way across the freshly polished floor with a fish on a silver platter. She gives me a sidelong, excited glance as Betty says, "Oh, Mr Lucian. The man from Esperand's is here. In the drawing room."

There are great bouquets of flowers on pedestals at the foot of the stairs and by the entrance to the dining room. Red roses, ferns, dark waxy leaves like saw-blades. Lilies the colour of raw skin. Betty hovers, anxious to get back to her work. "Sir? Are you all right?"

"Yes. Of course." The sudden warmth is making me nauseous. Betty darts forward to take my hat and coat but I wave her away. The scullery maid elbows open the door to the dining room and I catch a glimpse of the dinner *à la française* laid out on the sideboard. I can smell poached fish and something meatier, like game. I hang up my own hat and coat and push past Betty into the drawing room.

My mother gets to her feet. "Darling," she says. "At last." She waves Esperand's deputy forward. "Mr — what was it? — Mr Alcock has been waiting very patiently."

"Good afternoon." I nod to him. The movement makes me giddy, as if the world is rippling outwards. "Mama, would you ring for tea? I haven't eaten since . . ." I stop. There's a pause. Lisette raises her head from her circle of embroidery. She watches me, her eyes narrowed, like a cat.

"I'm afraid you're too late," my mother says. "The servants are all very busy. That's why we had tea early." She smiles at me. But there's something in the silence afterwards — while Cecily furtively crunches a sugar-lump and Lisette lets her eyes linger on my unshaven chin — that tells me that my father has ordered her not to ask where I've been.

I let Alcock adjust my waistcoat. He pins it without meeting my eyes. Every so often he suggests I raise and lower my arms, in a tactful undertone. My shirt is drenched in sweat. I stink of horses and wet wool. Lisette wrinkles her nose. But no one mentions it. And maybe I'm the only one who can smell, underneath that, the musky brackenish scent of Emmett Farmer's body.

At last Alcock goes. He tips me a little salute, man-to-man. When he's gone Mama smiles at me. She says, as she moves the sugar-bowl out of Cecily's reach,

472

"I'm so glad you're not *nervous*, darling. So many grooms would be anxious the day before their wedding. It's good that you haven't let it interfere with . . . whatever you've been doing."

I walk to the window and pull the curtain aside. I look past my reflection to the garden, luminous with snow. Coloured lanterns border every path. "Why should I be nervous, Mama?" Her reflection plucks at a tasselled cushion. "Now my suit finally fits, there's nothing to worry about."

"Quite right. And you look splendid in it." I turn so that we can smile at each other. She adds, "Don't forget, full evening dress tonight. Sherry in an hour."

"I'd better go and have my bath."

"I think that's a good idea, my precious."

I shut the door on her tinkling laugh and cross the hall to the foot of the stairs. There are even more flowers than before, dark and lush as a jungle. A tray of empty champagne glasses sits on the console table. The swing door to the servants' quarters clunks. The new scullery maid giggles. She stops when she sees me. She dips in a curtsy — carefully, because she's holding a silver epergne loaded with fruit.

"Ask Betty to run me a bath, will you?"

"Yes, sir." I feel her eyes on me as I go up the curve of the staircase.

All I want is to lie down and sleep. But my clothes have been laid out for me on my bed. A red rose in a little vase waits to be my buttonhole.

Tomorrow Honour and I will sleep in the room at the back of the house that's been set aside for us. It's a nice room. It overlooks the garden. It has pomegranates on the wallpaper, like mouths stuffed with seeds. The bed is a four-poster, draped with burgundy velvet. When I was small I sometimes drew the curtains and crawled inside. I remember the red darkness, the hot muffled silence. I used to pretend I was dead.

A knock on my door. "Your bath is ready, sir."

"Thank you." A second later I turn to tell her to bring me a drink, but she's already gone.

There's so much steam in the bathroom it's like a hammam. Someone has tipped oil of roses into the bathtub, too much of it. I lower myself into the hot water as quickly as I can. I scrub myself for longer than I need to. Then I let my head tilt back against the rim of the tub and shut my eyes. When I hear the clock strike downstairs I haul myself out of the bath and go to my own room to dress. I've taken too long. If I don't hurry I'm going to be late. The carriages are arriving outside. Feet crunch on the drive. High-pitched voices giggle. A bray: "Oh, indeed, *painfully* plain, but the Ormondes' money covers a multitude . . ."

I knot my tie. My flushed cheeks have faded. The face in the mirror is a study in black-and-white. When I slide the rose into my buttonhole it's like a blot of red ink on a charcoal drawing.

"Mr Lucian? Your mother wondered if you needed any help."

I shake my head. Betty stares at me a little too long and closes the door.

A last look at my reflection. I can do this. I straighten my tie. I smile.

474

The dining room glitters with silverware and candelabra and jewels on naked flesh. Everywhere I look there are women wearing low-cut gowns in bright colours — vermilion, royal blue, jade — and men in black-and-white evening dress. More flowers fill the corners of the room. An enormous centrepiece trails dark green leaves over the white tablecloth. The noise of voices blurs into a high chattering as if we're in an aviary.

I pause in the doorway. My mother swoops towards me. "Darling! You look lovely. Now, you know Sir Lionel and Lady Jerwood." I shake hands. I kiss a woman's satin glove. I hardly have time to look into their faces before my mother steers me towards the next knot of guests. I nod and smile and joke. I can't hear my own voice. It's hot. The colours are so bright I feel like I've got a fever. Tiny details catch my eye: the lustre on a string of pearls, the starry bubbles in a glass of champagne, a beauty spot on a bare shoulder. It takes an effort to wrench my attention back to the man I'm talking to. On the sideboard behind him the biggest shape is starting to collapse. Milky juices have nearly submerged the crown of pansies and candied ginger that runs round the bottom of the mould. The buttery parsley sauce for the fish has congealed into green-flecked golden grease.

People are eating now. The smells of strawberry mousse and poached salmon mingle with the scents of hot skin and candle-wax. I put a few things on my plate and sit down. On my right a lady fiddles with her collapsing hairpiece and says, "Well, it may be more

475

fashionable, but this isn't quite what *I* would call dinner *à la française*." Her husband rolls his eyes discreetly. "The Darnays have always been so modish. *Nouveau riche* —" She catches sight of me and breaks off, a flush rising to her cheeks.

I bend my head and jab my fork into the crust of my pigeon pie. On the other side of me another woman is leaning over her plate. Her string of turquoises chinks against the china. She's talking in a breathless stuttering voice. "I heard he was invited tonight — doesn't Florence Darnay know Lady Runsham? But he's absolutely prostrated, my dears."

The grey-haired lady opposite her raises an eyebrow. "I can imagine." She turns to the man next to her. "Did you hear about Sir Percival Runsham, James?"

"Who?" He balances a pink morsel of mousse on his spoon. "Oh, *Runsham*. The liability. Haven't seen him since he stood on Rosa Marsden's dress. I enjoyed that."

"He used to see de Havilland."

"Or whatever his real name was," someone interrupts, "I heard it was a *nom de plume*."

"Smith or Jones, I expect."

The grey-haired woman cuts through them as if they haven't spoken. "And last night the bindery burnt down, and Runsham's most recent binding . . ." She lets the words hang. They all swap a glance.

"Bloody hell," the man says, licking the bowl of his spoon. "Imagine remembering you were Percival Runsham."

"Language, James," the grey-haired woman says. But they're all laughing. "Well, I'm glad to say that none of

476

our family has ever been bound. Even if it didn't show a lack of moral backbone, this sort of thing is an excellent reason not to indulge."

"Come on, Harriet, that's a bit . . ." The man makes a conciliatory gesture with his spoon and grins at the others. "She may sound like a Crusader, but I assure you all that sixty years ago she was far too young to lynch anyone."

"Just think, though," the first woman says. "The secrets de Havilland must have known . . ."

I get to my feet. A few people glance up and go straight back to their conversations. They don't seem to care about being overheard. Gossip is public property. I go to the side-board and pour myself another glass of champagne. It's tepid. A young lady hovers, batting her eyelashes, until I realise she wants me to serve her. As she points at the dishes, she says. "It's very romantic, isn't it? You and Miss Ormonde. You're like a prince in a fairy tale, choosing her even though she's . . . She's not here, is she? Are the Ormondes having their own party tonight? I don't expect they can afford anything like this, can they? Yes, some grapes, please. Oh, and a spoonful of blancmange. Thank you."

I smile at her. She tosses her blonde curls and turns away.

My mother bears down on me. She leans close and murmurs, "I'm glad you're enjoying yourself, my darling. You are quite the handsomest man in the room. And you have made a great conquest of Lady Jerwood. Your father will be so pleased." Her breath smells of parsley. My father catches my eye across the room and raises his glass to me. I acknowledge him, then push my way through a group of moist-faced men into the hall. I skirt the sharp-edged flowers to go upstairs, but there are two giggling girls leaning over the banister. I turn away before they see me. My shirt is clammy and my eyes are stinging. All I want is to find a shadow somewhere and dissolve into it.

I go down the passageway and open the door to the Blue Room. The lamps are lit and there's a fire in the grate, but the room is empty. The painted nymphs look at me from over the mantelpiece, their wet limbs glistening like mother-of-pearl, their eyes vacant. Water lilies cluster round them like funeral wreaths. I shut the door behind me and breathe.

Someone has stubbed a cigarette out in the inkwell. It's still smouldering. I cross to the desk and extinguish the thread of smoke. The ledger is open on the last month's receipts, and the clerk's letters are no longer in the right order.

"Forgive me. I'm afraid I am endlessly curious. And they *were* lying around."

There's a man by the window. He gives me a little bow. I rock back on my heels, but at least I haven't flinched; I'm cushioned by the champagne I've drunk.

"You must be Piers' son," he says. "Lucian, isn't it? I'm Lord Latworthy, one of your father's . . . Well, we share some interests. How do you do?"

"How do you do?" I say, and tap the letters back into a neat pile. I can see that he's not going to look embarrassed, however long I wait.

"Did I startle you? Forgive me." He sounds magnanimous, as if I'm the one trespassing. He steps forward and looks at me, not quite smiling. He has a dark beard and very straight eyebrows. He's middle-aged, younger than my father. "Lucian Darnay. A pleasure to meet you. Face to face, I mean."

"Thank you."

"No doubt, all this . . ." He waves at the door, in a way that includes the rest of the house, the guests, the wedding, the world. "It must be . . . overwhelming." His face is intent and curious. It's the first time tonight anyone has really paid attention to me. The last person who looked at me like that . . .

"Please, sit down," he says, and in spite of myself I obey him. He sinks on to the chaise longue opposite me, tips his head back and heaves a sigh. "It's rather a circus, isn't it? So difficult for a sensitive young man like yourself."

"What makes you think I'm sensitive?"

"A young man who may not be . . . *entirely* enamoured of his bride-to-be."

"I have nothing but respect for Miss Ormonde."

He laughs under his breath. "There's no need to pretend, Lucian." He leans forward, crossing his ankle on his knee. The expression in his eyes isn't exactly sympathy. "Surely I'm not the only one to have noticed, tonight? You must feel very alone."

"I don't know what you mean."

"Don't you?" But his look doesn't waver. "I'm simply . . . well. Shall we say, I can imagine myself in your place?"

I stare at him. A sudden ache throbs between my temples, quick and gone in a heartbeat. "Excuse me," I say. I get to my feet, propping myself up on the arm of the settee. "I must get back to my father's guests."

As I try to move past he stands up in one smooth movement. Before I can react we're eye to eye. He's too close. Under the bitterness of tobacco there's the perfume of something sharp and resinous. Amber, wood. "Lucian," he says, and his voice is soft. "Wait."

"What do you want?"

He seems about to speak. Instead he reaches for my collar and loosens my tie. I can't move. It's like being back at school, in a sixth-former's study, too confused to be afraid. Surely he isn't . . . But he tugs my tie slowly out of its knot, while the silk whispers. His skin radiates heat through my waistcoat and shirt.

I freeze. A wave of sick warmth goes through me. For a second, wavering in front of my eyes, his face is Emmett's: clear-eyed, intent, almost afraid. "I have to go."

"Why?"

I look into his eyes. They're brown. Emmett's are brown, too.

I take a breath. All I want is to stop existing. Or to return to that moment yesterday, when the rest of the world was blotted out.

Then Latworthy clears his throat, and the dry sound breaks the spell. I pull away. He laughs. I hear him still chuckling as I stumble out into the passageway. In the hall people are saying goodbye to my mother. She looks round, sees my unbuttoned shirt and loose tie, and

480

wipes her expression clean, the same way she would look at my father coming out of the servants' door. She goes back to her farewells, the gleaming, chattering crowd of top hats and furs, while laughter washes out in waves from the dining room. I cross to the staircase and pull myself up, step by step.

I shut my bedroom door and sit on the bed. The world melts into ribbons. My head is spinning; not only from the drink.

I thought for an instant, last night, that I wasn't so bad. But now I disgust myself. There are easy words for the sort of man I am: depraved, pathetic. I don't understand. How did Lord Latworthy know? But somehow he did. I must stink of it, like sweat. Like blood. And whatever I've forgotten is worse. Whatever I did, it was so bad even my father despises me for it.

It's gone. Forgotten. As long as it stays locked away. I can go on.

And this time tomorrow it'll be over.

"I feel sick. Honestly. I can't believe how calm you look. I'm a quivering wreck and all I have to do is not drop the rings."

I glance sideways. Henry Ormonde's face is greenish where it isn't freckled. His hair is stiff with pomade. He ducks his head and it wobbles. "Sorry. It's a family thing. Honour was practically vomiting last night with nerves."

I don't answer.

"How many people are here? Must be hundreds. Poor old Honour, she hates being stared at."

"Two hundred."

"Goodness. I don't even *know* two hundred people."

"Neither do I." I turn away. The hall has a ceiling like the hull of a ship, higher than I remembered. Somehow the beams have been strung with white ribbon and orange blossom. More garlands hang along the walls. The wood panelling has a silver sheen that makes the windows seem bigger than they are. But as the seats fill, the walls seem to creep inwards. The noise rises like water. Voices, laughter, apologies as men tread on expensive skirts. Thumps and scuffles as they find their seats. Everything echoes.

"What's the time?"

I nod at the golden clock above the entrance. I wish I didn't have to stand here, waiting. Ten more minutes. My skin is itching. I want to pull off my gloves and scratch till I bleed. I'd kill for a drink. There's a hip flask in my pocket but everyone's watching me.

"Nice roses."

"Thanks." Today the flowers are pale and delicate, roses and freesias and loose ruffled blooms like petticoats. No lilies.

"Your sisters look pretty."

"Good." I glance over at them. They're sitting at the front with my parents. Cecily is swelling out of a mauve taffeta dress. She has a lace handkerchief poised for action. Lisette is in dark peacock-blue, a sprig of monkshood wilting in her hair. She's cleaning under her nails with the point of a jewelled hatpin. I let my eyes slide sideways. My father gives me a nod. I look away so sharply Henry jumps.

"You all right?"

"Fine."

"Sorry, sorry. You want me to stop talking, don't you?"

"Yes. Please."

But the silence doesn't help. I wish he'd start talking again. I turn and count the parchment-coloured roses in the biggest display. In front of it is the table where we'll sign our certificate. It's draped in lace and satin bows, but it's just a table.

My shoulders prickle. I want to throw up. Behind me the noise grows louder and louder. Surely they're all here. Surely I don't have to wait any longer . . . But when I glance at the clock there's still five minutes. I check my watch but it says the same thing.

I can't think. When I was small my father once broke a thermometer just to show me the quicksilver. You couldn't pick it up. It split and darted everywhere. This is like that: gleaming, uncatchable.

I turn back to face the front again. Everyone's in place now. The Hambledons. Charity and Eleanor Stock-Browne. Renée Devereux is wearing a sable that still has teeth. Simon and Stephen Simmonds are there with their mother. Simon is wearing our old school tie. I catch his eye by mistake. He gives me a sympathetic grimace. I force myself to smile back. I turn my head to look at the other side of the room. The Ormondes' half.

I only recognise a few of these people. Rosa Belle Marsden. Alec Finglass looks like an undertaker. Two of the Norwoods sit side-by-side. Identical noses, identical over-jewelled wives. Lord and Lady Latworthy.

He's reading the order of service and she says something to him and laughs. He looks up. Our eyes meet. He smiles and nods, as if what happened last night was nothing out of the ordinary. He turns aside. He replies to his wife.

A second later he looks back at me. He's not expecting me still to be watching him. His expression is interested. Intimate. Knowing.

He's read my book.

My breath checks in my throat. I don't know how I know. Suddenly my heart is sucking blood in the wrong direction, swollen, hammering. Heat and cold run over me in waves.

"Lucian? You all right?"

I turn aside. I must be imagining this. The stress of the occasion. The overscented air. The rows of eyes on me. The creep of the clock's ornate minute hand towards the hour. I try not to look at him again. But I do.

"Lucian? *Lucian!* Where are you going? You can't just . . ."

I knock Henry out of the way with my shoulder. There's a door at this end of the room, an antechamber. I don't care if I have to scramble out of the window. He bleats something. I don't look at him. "I'll be back in a moment."

"But she'll be here in two minutes."

I shut the door on him.

I'm in a sunken alley at the side of the building. I walk blindly to the end of it. Suddenly I'm at the front, where a wide staircase leads down from the main entrance. A carriage is drawing up. A pale lacy figure clambers out on to the pavement and nearly trips. The wind whips her dress into a white flag. Mr Ormonde steadies her and leads her up the stairs. A gust lifts her veil. I catch sight of flushed cheeks. Bright eyes. A thin lace-mittened hand holding a bunch of roses. The flash of the diamond I gave her.

If I hurried I could get back before anyone noticed.

I swing sideways and cross the road. There's a queue for the omnibus. A few men stare into the window of a butcher's. A woman with a basket over her arm tuts at me. I turn round, borne on the current of passers-by. A spatter of sleet strikes my face.

"Daily news," a man shouts. "Taxes to go down! Bookbinder killed in fire!"

A man pauses and buys a paper. I approach the stall, fumbling in my pocket. I don't have any money. I go on fumbling and lean over to scan the dense columns of print. *A tragic accident last night led to . . . secretary, Miss Elizabeth Brettingham, said there were no survivors . . . called upon to accelerate the inquiry into the storage of inflammable materials . . .* My gorge rises.

The newspaper-seller steps between me and the page. "You going to buy one, or not?"

"No. Excuse me."

I wrench myself away. Any moment now Henry will emerge into the forecourt of the Town Hall. But there's nowhere to run to. I can't go home. I'm stuck on the pavement as if it's quicksand. Make a decision. Move.

I duck into the archway that leads to the arcade. At least here I'll be under a roof. I push past a man standing in a doorway. He reaches out and grabs my wrist. I try to shake him off. But his grip is stronger than I expected. I start to say, "I haven't got any —"

"Playing truant?" he says.

It's Emmett Farmer.

I stare at him. Surely if I were hallucinating he'd look exactly the way he did the last time I saw him. Or at the very least, he'd be flushed and laughing, reeling with fatigue, with his shirt open at the neck. But now he's dressed differently, in rougher, warmer clothes. His eyes are clearer. Steadier. He has a knapsack over his shoulder, and a woollen cap.

Behind him the omnibus arrives. The newspaper man goes on calling his headlines. The sleet makes a silver fan on the floor at the entrance to the arcade.

"What on earth . . .?"

He said it. Or did I? Doesn't matter. He's still holding my wrist like a handcuff.

I clear my throat to make sure I know my own voice. "What are you doing here?"

"It's a free country," he says, but the bravado doesn't reach his face. "I wanted to see you. And her." He hesitates. "Your wife."

"Well." I try to bite back a foolish, painful laugh. "I'm afraid you might be waiting longer than you thought, for that."

It's no good. I giggle once, violently, as if I'm being sick.

486

"What's going on? You should still be in there." He nods at the Town Hall.

"I ran away."

"You *ran away*? Just like that?" There's a split-second pause. Maybe we're both thinking the same thing: that I ran away from him, too. But he doesn't give me time to explain, or apologise, even if I could. "What about Miss Ormonde?"

"I don't know."

His eyes narrow. "What?"

I shake my head. I can still see her, at the centre of that whirling veil, her face flushed. She asked me to be kind.

"Lucian, what are you doing?"

"I can't marry her. She's a good — a good person. She deserves better."

He lets go of me and turns away. A couple of young women hurry into the arcade. One of them skids on the damp marble and the other catches her. They laugh like machines clanking. He watches them go past. "So she should be grateful that you're jilting her at the altar."

"I didn't say . . ." I look down. Of everyone in the world, I thought Farmer would understand. I can feel wetness inside my glove, but it hasn't soaked through. I stretch my fingers to feel the kid pull away from the stickiness on my skin. "It's just . . . wrong. For her. For me. Does it matter?"

"And me? Should *I* have been grateful that you . . .? Never mind." He turns away as I open my mouth. "No, I said *never mind*."

There's a silence, full of the newspaper man and hurrying footsteps and the crunch of wheels on half-frozen mud. Inside the hall she'll be waiting for me. Or someone will have taken her to one side. Henry will be searching, frantically trying not to seem frantic.

Farmer sighs. He takes off his cap, wipes his forehead with the inside of his wrist, and puts it back on. At last he says, "You're serious, aren't you?"

"I saw one of them look at me." My mouth tastes sour. Metallic. "He'd read my book. I saw it in his face. He was watching me." I don't want to tell Farmer about Lord Latworthy, and what happened last night. Silence. In the street a wheel-axle smashes. Someone shouts. Someone else shouts back, louder. I shrug. "That's it."

"Someone looked at you, and you walked out of your wedding."

I tug uselessly at my glove. "Yes."

"I didn't know you were so brave."

"To abandon Honour at the altar?"

He tilts his head to concede the point. A gust of wind whirls down the arcade, scattering bits of rubbish around our feet. I shiver. Somehow I thought that leaving the hall would make things different. I lean against the wall and take a sip from my hip flask. I offer it to him. He shakes his head.

I look at my shoes. The sleet and mud have tarnished their perfect shine. "What will you do now?"

"I pawned some of my old master's things," he says. "I've got enough money for the train to Newton. I thought I might try to find a bindery there."

"A bindery? Why?"

He takes a deep breath and adjusts the strap of his knapsack. "Because I'm a binder, Lucian."

I nod. He's right. He has a trade. A living. He can have a life like de Havilland's. Why not?

"I wish . . ." Emmett shifts from side to side. "I'm sorry."

"Don't be." I drain the last fiery dregs of brandy.

"I can't stay here, Lucian."

Can I hear Henry's voice, coming and going on a gust of wind, or am I imagining it? I lean my head back and stare at the intricate panes of smut-stained glass. Directly above us there's a shatter-mark. A star. "Well then," I say. "Good luck."

"Yes."

I hold out my hand. "Thanks for trying to help."

"Yes." He swallows, and takes it. Neither of us has taken off our gloves. He's wearing a ring and it digs into my fingers. My cut stings. It goes on aching as he steps backwards. The pain runs up my arm like a rope. It catches round my heart and pulls tight.

"Goodbye, Emmett."

He nods. He goes on nodding. I put my hip flask in my pocket. I'm so cold. A child runs past us, bowling a hoop, screeching with laughter. A gaunt governess in half-mourning follows a few paces behind.

He doesn't say goodbye. He holds my gaze for one more breath. Then he turns and walks down the arcade, away from me.

I put my forearm over my face. It must look as if I'm crying. It doesn't matter now.

489

I should have stayed in the hall. By now it would be done.

My shirt itches. My shoes have chafed my ankles. My breath smells of brandy. I didn't have breakfast and the alcohol has already gone to my head. I could pawn my watch. Go to a public house and get drunk. Walk into the river. No, of course not. Go home. When I left this morning the garlands over the staircase were starting to wilt. Red petals fell as I walked past. Empty rooms, dead flowers.

"Wait. *Wait.*" Someone is running down the arcade, shouting. I open my eyes. My vision breaks into a kaleidoscope of colours. I blink. It's Emmett.

He drops his bag at his feet and takes hold of my shoulders. "*What* did you say?"

"What? When?"

"You said someone had read your book."

I try to shake him off but he's stronger than me. "Yes. Lord Latworthy. It made me —"

"Lord Latworthy. *Lord Latworthy* has read your book. Are you sure?"

"Yes."

He stares at me. He's not seeing me at all. The blood thuds through my veins.

"And he was there. At your wedding. He's" — he points backwards — "there. Right now?"

"Yes. Why?"

He smacks his forehead. "I'm such an *idiot*. Come on, I know where he lives."

It takes me a second to understand what he means. "Just because he's read it, doesn't mean he has it now."

"I took a delivery there myself. I should have realised." He breathes out, half laughing, and catches my wrist. "Stop arguing, Lucian." He starts to run. I nearly trip as he drags me after him. "We don't have long. Come *on*."

CHAPTER
TWENTY-SEVEN

The hansom takes us to the gates. It's a mile or so out of town. A dark stone wall runs alongside the road, topped with ranks of iron arrow-heads. Beyond it the parkland slopes up towards the house. Bare oaks are scattered on snow-blotched grass. The gate is massive and wrought iron, hung with fruit and leaves. In the monochrome landscape it's a parody of summer.

We roll to a stop. A sudden panic grabs me. I have nothing in my pockets except my hip flask and my watch. But Farmer jumps out ahead of me and pays. As the cab drives away he catches my eye. Without a word he digs in his pocket again. He holds out a coin to me.

"I don't want that."

He lets the money fall into the gutter. It sticks in a grainy ripple of slush, edge upwards, almost invisible. Something has changed in the way he moves. There's light behind his eyes even when he's not smiling. But all he says is, "Come on. We have to hurry."

"What's the plan, exactly?"

"We go in. We find your book. We get out. Before Lord Latworthy gets back from your wedding."

Latworthy might be on his way already. How long will it take? I can see the Town Hall in my mind's eye.

A growing unease. No, a growing enjoyment. Men swapping sidelong looks. Hidden smiles. Flowers and feathers nodding as women put their heads together to whisper. When Henry comes back in, wilting with defeat, there'll be some kind of council-of-war. My father and the Ormondes. Twenty minutes? Then to explain to the guests . . . With any luck there'll be more delay as people take in the news. Gossip. Speculate. Have breakfast anyway. Some people have travelled from miles away. I kick at a ridge of muddy ice until my shoe is caked in it.

Farmer touches my shoulder. "Don't think about it."

"I can't not."

"Let's go." He sets off up the drive. The meadows on either side are wide open. Foothills of unmelted snow are being eaten away by the brown sea of grass. Anyone looking down from the turrets of the house would see us immediately. The clouds hang above like a ceiling. Every time I glance up they seem to have dropped lower.

Get in. Find book. Get out. Simple.

The drive curves. It takes us through a grove of trees and round the crest of the hill. The house is the same dark stone as the wall. It looks like a fortress. The fountain in front is a dry basin of alabaster. The mermaids are streaked with green. I hurry to catch up with Emmett. "Wait!"

"Come on." He turns left, towards the back of the house. There's a huge stable yard, double the size of the one at my uncle's house. Windows look down on us from every side. The cobbles are gleaming wet. At the far corner a man in working clothes looks up. I stop dead. He stares for a second and goes back to sluicing the ground clean with a bucket of water. Emmett beckons me. "What's the matter?"

"That man saw us."

He shrugs. He crosses the yard to a door set into the wall. I follow him. He rings the bell.

"Emmett." I glance around. Any moment now someone will ask what we're doing here. The man at the corner of the yard catches my eye again. He picks up his empty bucket and takes it into a lean-to. He's whistling. It sounds too loud.

Emmett frowns at me. "What?"

"We can't just ring the bell and ask if we can ransack the library."

"It's all right. Trust me."

Footsteps come down the passage. I can hear them patter on stone.

I drag him away from the door. He stumbles sideways. "What are you doing? Lucian?"

"Let's go round to the front. I can try to convince the butler. We won't get anywhere with the tradesman's entrance."

"What, they'll trust you because you're wearing a flashy waistcoat?"

"Better than *you* trying to —"

The door swings open. A scullery-maid in a drab dress and grey pinafore peers out. She's wearing grimy cotton cuffs around her wrists and holding a smeared rag. "Sally," Emmett says. "You remember me. From de Havilland's. I brought those boxes, last week."

She stares at him. Her mouth makes a silent O.

He steps forward. She squeaks, and nearly trips over the mat. Then, as if the noise has released something, she whispers, "Mr Emmett?"

"Yes. Listen —"

"You're dead. They said you were dead. Mr Enningtree said it was in the paper —"

He blinks. "I'm definitely not dead." He spreads his arms wide and his knapsack slides down to his elbow. "Look."

"But . . ." She screws up her mouth. For the first time her eyes go to me. She frowns. She bounces slightly as if she isn't sure whether to curtsy. "All right then . . . I suppose . . . But what're you doing here? Mr Enningtree didn't say anything about a delivery."

"Listen, Sally. I need to talk to Lord Latworthy. It's important."

"He's not here. He's gone to a wedding." Her eyes slide back to me. Surreptitiously I take the rose out of my buttonhole and push it into my pocket.

"I'll wait. Show us into the library. We won't be any trouble."

"I ought to ask Mr Enningtree — I can't just let you in, you're only an apprentice — I mean, even Mr de Havilland has to make an appointment."

"Don't. It has to be secret. Please, Sally."

"A secret? It's more than my position's worth."

"It's binder's business. Come on. You know who I am. Please."

She looks at him, furrowing her brow, and then at me. "No."

There's a silence. Sally twists the rag into a scrawny knot. I can smell silver polish. Pink paste has got into the cracks around her knuckles. She dips her head briefly, regretfully, at the space between Emmett and me. Then she starts to swing the door shut.

Emmett pushes his foot into the gap. "Wait."

"I'm sorry, Mr Emmett. But I can't."

"Look at me." He steps close to her. She stands still in the doorway. She's staring at her feet. "*Look* at me, Sally."

"Slowly she raises her head."

He leans forward. His mouth is almost touching her ear. In a low voice, he says, "Do what I say, right now. Or I'll take your whole life away."

She catches her breath. Her eyes flicker. "Mr Farmer, sir . . ."

"You know what I mean, don't you? I'll put your memories in a book. You won't even remember your own name." There's a pause. My own breath is coming short. Emmett pushes gently against the door and she steps backwards, giving up ground. "I don't want to do that. I like you. But I need to get into the library *now*."

She raises her face. She's gone white. "Please — don't . . ."

"Good girl." He steps past her into a dingy little passage. He beckons to me without turning his head. "Now. We're going to be in the library. If you make sure we're not disturbed, everything will be all right. Do you understand?"

She nods. She clears her throat. "When milord comes back . . .?"

"Then you can come and tell us he's here."

She nods again. She keeps nodding. Her eyes are fixed on Emmett's face. She gestures to the end of the corridor. "Shall I show you to the library?"

"I remember the way. Go back to work. And don't tell anyone we're here. Promise?"

"I promise." She waits for Emmett to dismiss her with a gesture. Then she scurries away. When she gets to the door she fumbles with the handle for a long time before it finally turns. Then the door closes behind her.

Emmett breathes out. He bends over, bracing himself against the wall. He's shaking as much as she was. After a moment he stands up straight. "Come on. It's this way, I think. Maybe I should have let her show us. I wasn't thinking." He pushes open a different door. An identical passage disappears into darkness like a tunnel. It's painted green-and-cream like the servants' quarters at home. He hurries along, counting doors. At last he stops and pushes one open. He swears under his breath. He tries the next. Then he grabs my arm and pulls me through.

We're in the main hall. On our left there's a great marble-balustraded staircase. A drawing room opens on the other side. We go down a long wide gallery paved with lozenges of daylight. Huge paintings hang on the walls. Battles. Hunting scenes. Bared teeth and blood.

We walk to the last door at the end. My head pounds with the effort it takes not to run. Emmett opens the door. He exhales slowly. He steps to one side like a footman to let me pass. Then he follows me through the doorway.

The library is a tall, light room. High mullioned windows on two sides look out on an avenue of limes. The other walls are bookcases. More books than we had at school. A gleaming spiral staircase leads to a walkway above our heads. The fireplace is carved white marble. Plump cherubs balance heavy tomes on their dimpled knees. Nymphs peep between vine leaves, their eyes wide. Satyrs write. There's the end of a fire in the grate, still flickering. Fire-buckets filled with sand stand ready on either side. The armchair on the hearthrug holds the shape of someone's body. I imagine Latworthy taking coffee in here before he left for my wedding: relaxed, amused, flicking idly through my book. A mixture of hope and shame pulses, deep in my gut. But if he was reading my book, he's put it back on the shelf. Everything is in its place.

A desk stands in front of the windows. I pull out the narrow wooden chair and sit down. My palms are slick with sweat.

Emmett shuts the door and shoots the bolt across. He laughs under his breath. Finally he pulls off his gloves and pushes his hair off his face. I was right before, when I thought he was wearing a ring. It's a thick silver band, set with a blue-green stone. The sort of thing de Havilland might wear, or my father. Not ugly, but surprising. He wasn't wearing it yesterday; he must have stolen it from somewhere. He turns to me. "Lucian? What's the matter?"

I pull one drawer of the desk open. It's full of creamy paper. The other drawer is locked.

498

"What is it? Are you all right?"

I tilt the inkwell. It's nearly empty. I hold it still, wondering if what I can see is ink or shadow. I clear my throat. "Would you have done it?"

"Done what?"

"Bound her. The maid. If she'd refused . . ."

"What are you talking about?"

I put the inkwell down. I swing round to face him. I keep my voice level. "You threatened to take all her memories. Even her name."

He blinks. A smile comes and goes at the corner of his mouth. "Of course not. I couldn't."

"You threatened to."

"No, I mean I *couldn't*. It's not possible. You need someone to let you bind them, you can't just . . . I'm a binder, not a wizard."

"But . . ."

"You need someone's consent. Always. Even with Nell."

"I thought . . ." My voice breaks. I find myself adjusting my cravat. I check my cuffs. They're dirty. My stomach is churning. "Good. That's good."

"You didn't think — seriously, Lucian?"

"No, I thought I'd ask, that's all."

"Yes, I see. Better to be quite clear about these things." He scratches his head and looks away.

"Don't laugh. How could I have known?"

"I'm not laughing," he says. His eyes are bright hazel, like rain on growing wood. "I wouldn't have hurt her."

A clock strikes somewhere. I jump to my feet. He straightens and looks round. Suddenly his face is different: alert, concentrated. We don't have much time.

"Right." He turns on his heel in a circle.

I look round too. I open my mouth. But there's no need to say it. We can both see how many books there are. I start to scan the nearest bookcase. Names. Names and names and names. Any of them could be mine. "There's no kind of order to these."

"Those are too old, anyway. Your book is silk, not book-cloth or leather. It's a kind of grey-green." He runs his finger along the shelf nearest to him, so quickly he can't be reading the spines. He glances over his shoulder. "It's all right. We'll find it."

I look round. Hundreds of books. Thousands.

"No . . . no . . . no . . ." He steps sideways. His fingernail flicks over the backs of the books. In the quiet it sounds as loud as a child dragging a stick along railings. He gets to the corner of the room. The clock strikes again. Fifteen minutes gone. We look at each other. "There has to be an order to them. They're not alphabetical. There *has* to be . . ."

I shrug. I can't think.

He steps back and surveys the bookcases. "Look for the colour. Unless he's had library covers put on . . ." He stops, as if the thought is too heavy to hold. "I promise we'll find it. We just have to look. We can't give up."

I nod. At the Town Hall the first carriages must be rolling away. What is Honour doing right now? What is my father doing? Lord Latworthy will be on his way back here. I raise my head and look out of the window. But you can't see the drive. There's only the avenue of bare limes, pointing upwards like black feathers.

500

Brownish grass. A mound of snow that's sooty at the edges. A raven flashes out of nowhere. Its call is like cloth ripping, a little at a time.

Emmett says, "What are you waiting for?"

I turn back into the room. He's staring at me. He looks white and strained. As if he cares about this as much as I do. If he gets caught here it'll be transportation. At least my father will make sure I stay out of gaol. "Sorry."

"Just look, will you?"

"Yes." I head towards the spiral stair. The iron treads ring dully as I climb.

Emmett mutters, "No . . . no . . . no . . ."

Up here the covers are more varied. It's harder to be sure I'd spot a grey-green spine. I go back to reading the names. I can feel time being used up like oxygen.

"Damn it. I can't see the names properly. This lowest shelf . . ."

I glance over the railing. He's tugging at the lock, trying to break open the bookcase. "Don't be stupid! Break the glass."

"Yes. Right." He shoots a look at the door to the rest of the house. He pulls his elbow back and jabs it into the glass. It shatters with a deafening, world-wrenching smash.

Silence. For an instant I hear footsteps running towards us. I realise it's my heart.

Emmett puffs out his breath. He reaches gingerly through the jagged hole in the pane and picks out the books one by one. He checks the spines, throws them into a pile, reaches for more. He sags. "No."

"Keep looking." But he's a statue, staring down at the book which has fallen open in his grasp. "Are you *reading* that?"

He snaps it shut. He sways. "Sorry — I can't — I didn't mean to . . ." He reels to the desk and puts the book down. "It gets hold of me and I see it. Sorry."

"Damn it, Farmer!"

"I *said* I can't help it! I'm a binder, it sucks me in." He's gone even paler than before. "At least we know they're not fakes."

I turn back to the shelves. Names and names and names. Not mine. Once I see *Darnay* and it's like an electric shock. But it's *Elizabeth Sassoon Darnay*.

Sassoon was my grandmother's maiden name. She was cold to us all, distant, haughty, hardly pausing as she searched every room for something she never found. But the book isn't like that. It's pretty. There are gold-and-blue irises curling over the brown leather. I press my finger against the glass. I want to know what happened to her. But I don't have time.

Emmett climbs the stairs behind me. I move aside to let him go past. But he doesn't. He bends over the banister at the top. His eyes are closed. His face is white.

"What's the matter? Farmer?"

"I'm all right."

"You look ill."

"It was the memories. Bluebell woods — his daughter's wedding . . ." He catches my eye and tries to smile. "It's horrible, that's all. They stole his *life*."

502

"Yes." In the back of my mind I can see William Langland, lying in the thin downland grass. Butterflies dancing in the hot air. A cloudless sky above him. Or raising his bride's veil, bending to kiss the freckle at the side of her mouth. I turn away, crossing my arms across my chest. My mouth is sour and dry.

Emmett shifts. I don't look round. I don't want him to see my face. I can still feel his arms round me, the night we spent together, the slow warmth seeping into my bones. But that's gone. Over. I look up at the plaster on the ceiling. Frozen white fruit hangs above us, hard enough to break your teeth.

Abruptly, he moves towards me. I turn automatically, ready to reach out for him. I'm about to say something. I don't know what.

He pushes past. I stumble backwards into the bookcase. "It's there. I think — yes!"

For a blank instant I don't know what he's talking about.

"Your book. It's there!" He wrenches the handle of the bookcase. "These must be the illegal ones. The ones where people are still alive, or their families . . . Look."

He's right. Grey-green, with my name on the spine in silver. *Lucian Darnay*. I should be glad, but waves of cold run through me. Maybe I never really believed it was real.

I look away. I let my eyes rest on the nymphs carved on the fireplace. Their smooth thighs and parted lips. The satyrs lounging with their pens erect in their hands. I clear my throat. "Good. Take it and we'll go."

"Of course, what do you think I . . .?" He breaks off. He wrenches the handle. He puts his whole body weight into it and hisses with the strain.

I push him out of the way. "Why are you wasting time? Just break it!"

There's a grille. An iron grille, behind the glass.

I stare at it. The metal is dark and decorative. It's knotted with tendrils and spirals and buds. It looks like something growing. Or something dead. The bars are too close together to let anything pass through.

The clock strikes again. Emmett looks at me and then back at the bookcase. "We can get it out somehow."

"Somehow?"

"Yes. Break the glass, and . . . Maybe we could . . ." He tails off. The silence answers my question better than the words.

I take a deep breath. For a moment everything looks like it's *trompe l'oeil*: the plasterwork, the books, the furniture. Like Lisette's old dolls' house. Even the trees and sky outside are like a drawing on paper, pressed against the glass. I could be made of wood and wax.

I turn my back on him. "Let's get out of here." I go down the spiral staircase. He doesn't follow me. "Leave it, Farmer."

"What? You're not — you can't give up. Lucian!" He glances down over the banister, at the fire in the hearth. "Wait, what am I thinking? We don't have to get it out. If we break the glass we can burn it here. Get the tongs — and one of those sand-buckets, I don't want to set the whole house alight."

504

"No."

"Come on! If Lord Latworthy gets back . . ."

"I said no!" There's a silence. Over the fireplace a smug little cherub chortles over someone's secrets.

"I don't understand," he says, at last. "Why did we come here, if not for your book?"

I draw in a long breath. "I want my book," I say. "I want it — safe. I want to keep it somewhere out of sight. I want to know that no one can read it. That's all."

"But don't you want to know?"

"No."

More silence. I look up. He's leaning on the banister, hair falling over his eyes, cheeks flushed. With his brown coat and leather knapsack he looks out-of-place. A thief. A binder. I don't even know what he wants. He says quietly, "Why not?"

"Let's go." I glance at the door, but the thought of running into someone makes me shiver. I turn to the window. A magpie hops along the paving just outside. It pauses and slirts its head at me. There's something sparkling in its beak. I step closer. No. I'm imagining it. There's a headache starting in my temples. I unlatch the nearest casement. It's narrow but there's room to squeeze through.

"What's the matter?" A pause. "There's nothing to be afraid of —"

"Oh, really?" I swing round. "I saw you when your book was burned. I thought you were dying."

"I meant the memories."

"Don't you dare . . ." I catch myself. We both glance at the door. I lower my voice. "Whatever I did, I chose to get rid of it. I *chose*. All the things my father does — it must be worse than that, worse than anything I can imagine . . . So don't you dare tell me that I should *want* it back."

"All I'm saying . . ." He hesitates. For a moment a shrill hum swells in my ears, as if he's on the brink of saying something I won't be able to hear. "You don't have to be afraid. I promise. Burn it."

"Stop telling me what to do!" He winces, and I'm glad. "It's my life, Farmer. *I* choose."

"Please, Lucian. Trust me."

"Trust you?" I spit the words at him. I can remember how he wept and vomited the first time I saw him. Now he's looking at me the same way I looked at him then. Pity, and contempt, and disbelief. It hurts so much it takes my breath away. "Why should I trust you? Because we fucked, once?" He bends over the banister, his face lowered. I take a step towards him. "You think you know better than me? Well, Nell's dead. De Havilland's dead. Because of you. So tell me, why should I trust you?"

Somehow, in spite of everything, I expect him to have an answer. He raises his head and meets my eyes. But he doesn't reply. For a moment it's as if he's not there any more. He's gone somewhere I can't follow.

I turn back to the unlatched window. I push it as wide as it will go. The magpie flies away. I catch the blue-green sheen of its feathers, like black pearl. The raw air makes my eyes sting. I clamber on to the

506

window sill, swing one leg over and duck through the casement. I land with a painful, undignified grunt in the flowerbed. The side of my ribcage smarts where I've knocked it against the window frame. I glance from side to side, but there's no one in sight. I set off down the path between the skeletal limes.

Behind me there's the rattle of the window as Emmett scrambles through, and the crunch of wintry plants underfoot. He's running after me. I keep walking.

"Where are you going to go, Lucian? Back to the Town Hall?"

I shrug. I can't look at him. Looking at him would be like deliberately putting my hand in a flame.

He's beside me now. He's breathing hard. "And what happens to your book? You'd rather leave it here?"

"I know where it is now. I'll get my father to buy it."

He snorts. "And naturally after today your father will pander to your every whim."

I still don't look at him. A few miles away, the Town Hall will be emptying. My father will be saying goodbye to the guests, making jokes, complimenting the women, smiling as if this was exactly what he had in mind. In a little while I will have to go home.

"Or you could ask Lord Latworthy," Emmett says. He catches my arm and spins me round so that I have to meet his eyes. He gives me a sharp derisive smile. "If he was at your wedding. I'm sure he'd give it up without a second thought, if you just explained that you wanted it back."

Lord Latworthy's face flashes into my mind's eye: avid, predatory, curious. *That* was why he wanted me, last night. I was a specimen. I swallow, refusing to let Emmett see how queasy I feel. "Maybe he would," I say. "Maybe we could come to some arrangement."

There's something in my tone that makes him blink and falter. "All right," he says slowly. "And then what? Even if you get your hands on it . . . What will you do with it? Keep it in a bank vault, out of sight?"

"Yes, exactly!"

"And lie awake worrying about who else has the key? Get up in the middle of the night and walk halfway across Castleford to check it's still there? Get bound again, so you can sleep at night?"

"Bank vaults don't work like that, you can't go and open them yourself whenever you want —"

He doesn't seem to hear me. "You'll be afraid. You'll be constantly afraid. For ever. Is that what you want?"

I force myself to face him. "I'll be fine," I say.

He lets go of me. He steps back. My arm aches where he was touching me.

"What are you going to do?" he asks, and I know he's not talking about my book any more.

"Don't worry about me. I dare say I can numb my fear and self-loathing with alcohol and meaningless liaisons."

"Leave off, Lucian."

"Why do you care? You're off to Newton to find a job. You never have to see me again."

He opens his mouth as if he's about to say something else, but in the end he only nods. He fumbles with the

508

strap of his knapsack. A gust of cold wind flicks fragments of twig and leaf into our faces.

I walk away. My eyes are stinging worse than ever. I break into a stumbling trot; I want to get as far away from him as possible. But a few steps later I realise he's not following me. I glance round.

He's running back towards the house.

It takes me a second to understand what he's doing. Then I'm pelting after him, sliding on the mud-slick grass. I shout after him, "Hey!"

He doesn't even pause. He launches himself through the window, swears, and stumbles into the room clutching his elbow. By the time I've climbed through he's crouching by the hearth, digging in the fire with the tongs.

"You can't," I say.

"You can't stop me." He stands up, holding a flaming chunk of coal in the tongs. I reach out and he takes an instinctive step backwards, swinging the ember away from me.

"I forbid it," I say. He raises his eyebrows and walks past me, holding the tongs out to the side. The flame clings to the coal, shrinking in the draught. "Hey — you said — what happened to consent?" But he's not listening. "What about the other books? If you set light to mine — *Farmer!*" He starts to go up the stairs. I grab his arm. He twists away, grimacing as the coal nearly slips. I try to get hold of him again and he stumbles up two stairs at once.

"I said I *forbid* you!"

"Let go!" But I drag him down. He totters on the edge of a step, tries to grab at the banister, and misses. He staggers backwards, almost into my arms. I lean over him, trying to get to the tongs. He fights to keep them at arm's length. I grind my thumb into his shoulder, until he gasps; but when he wrenches himself free he's laughing. We wrestle, teetering on the same narrow step. It's almost a dance. "Come on, just let me — oh, this is so stupid . . ." He's *laughing*.

I smack the side of his face. He drops to his knees. The tongs fall through a gap in the banisters and the ember skitters along the floor, spraying sparks. He blows air through his teeth. I take a helpless step down, and another, until I'm on solid ground. At least he's not bleeding. I watch him get to his feet. His eyes flick past me to the tongs on the floor, and then to me.

We both move at once. As he dives for them I throw myself into his path. We grapple, pushing and pulling at each other like kids. He wrests one hand out of my grasp, but he doesn't hit me. Instead he pulls ineffectually at my fingers, trying to prise them off his upper arm. He's not laughing any more. "We don't have time . . ."

I haven't got the breath to reply. My throat is burning. I force him backwards. He gives way suddenly and we reel together towards the window. I feel the impact in my arms as his leg catches the desk and he sags, yelping with pain. I let my grip slacken. Instantly he grabs my wrists and slides away. "No!" I launch myself at him, clawing at his shoulders, his collar, his throat, anything. He spins and ducks, trying to dodge.

510

For a split second he pauses, staring over my shoulder, and a frown flickers over his face. I turn to see what he's looking at and lose my footing. My elbow catches his jaw. His head snaps sideways and slams against the desk. He falls to his knees, his breath hoarse. There's a silence.

Not quite silence. Something crackles, murmurs . . . Fire.

It must have been the ember, skidding across the floor — or a stray spark — catching the pile of books that Farmer threw aside . . . It doesn't matter how it happened. There are flames licking up the bookshelves, ragged ribbons of heat snapping against the glass. The varnished wood blisters and turns black. The books are burning like camphor: furious, exuberant. Light flares inside the bookcase, leaping up and up until the very top shelf is blazing. New sparks burst like seed-pods, take root, grow. Smoke pours upwards. Already it's catching in my throat.

I glance stupidly at the buckets of sand beside the hearth. But it's too late for that. A shelf collapses. Glass shatters. The fire pounces on a new mound of books. Talons of flame rake the pages apart. Volumes sigh and gasp their memories at the ceiling in a skirl of glittering ash.

I try to get my breath back. "It can't be — it's so fast . . ."

"Books want to burn," he says. "They go up like that because — they're unstable, memories don't *want* to stay . . ." He tails off into a fit of coughing. There's a knock at the door, and Sally's voice, pleading to be let in. "Stop this. We have to go," he says, forcing the words out. "Now."

I bend and grab the poker from beside the hearth.

Then I run up the staircase, into the heart of the fire.

CHAPTER
TWENTY-EIGHT

The smoke is so thick I could get lost in it. It chokes me. It scratches my throat and burns my lungs. I fumble along the walkway, blinded by tears. The fire roars underneath. The heat is like a wall. I keep my grip on the poker. The warmth of the metal seeps through the calfskin of my glove. I hear glass break close by. Dark stars swarm and pulse.

I don't have time to think. I stumble into the bookcase. I try to right myself. Pain grows suddenly from nothing. It shoots down my arm. The iron grille. The glass has gone and the bars are hot. They're burning through my glove. But it means I'm in the right place. My book is here, somewhere. The shelf at eye-level. I swing the poker back and smash it against the grille. It judders.

Shouting. Confused voices. Farmer calls my name. He's pounding up the stairs.

I hit the grille again. I can't get my breath. I cough and cough. Inside I'm scalded raw. The stars boil up over my vision. I try to blink them away.

One more time. But it's no good.

I slide the poker through the bars and twist. I lean my whole weight on it. I won't give up. If the bars don't give way I'll go on trying till the smoke gets me. At least I'll be unconscious before the walkway collapses. I won't feel the flames.

"Lucian! *Lucian!*"

My heart is labouring. A flabby beat like a broken drum. Every cough rips deeper into my lungs. My mouth is clogged with phlegm that tastes of soot.

The grille gives way. I nearly fall.

I press myself against the case. Colours swim in a fog of grey that burns my eyes. I pull the corner of the grille out enough to get my hand past it. I scrabble at the spines. My gloves are scorched through at the fingertips. Somewhere there's my book. Will I know when I touch it? Books tumble to the floor. I'm disorientated in the smoke. Someone whispers words of love. Scent of bluebells. There's the high sickening creak of wood on fire. Shouting, too, somewhere. The floor lurches. Clouds of blackness threaten to engulf me. I'm breathing acid. My head is spinning. The books are warm. They feel alive. Any moment now they'll twist out of my fingers, throwing themselves towards the flames. They burn so fast. They *want* to burn.

I fall.

I fall forever. I crash. Time flips: I land, I fall again. Pain lifts me up like a tide. I gasp for breath. I push myself up. I realise I'm not dead. My head spins. I'm on the floor. Down here there's more space between the veils of smoke. More glimpses of bookcases and carved plaster. More colours that aren't fiery amber-red or blank grey. There's a sudden crash of wood. Books slither and thud. Then a new column of smoke gushes

514

upwards. It spills and billows on the ceiling. Grey fumes dance in front of my eyes.

"Lucian." A croak through the roar and frush of the fire. A sobbing laugh. Someone in pain. Emmett. "Damn it," he says, "are you trying to kill yourself?" I blink away the tears and squint up through narrowed eyelids. The staircase is still there — it's only a section of the gallery floor that's given way —

"Stop!" He grabs hold of me. "This is dangerous — we have to go — *please!*"

I laugh. It hurts. The heat pulses in my veins.

"They're trying to break down the door now." There are shouts in the passage outside. Men's voices. The door judders in its frame. "That bolt won't last for ever."

"I'm not leaving without my book." I wrench away from him. He staggers. He's still holding on to me; but this time his grip is weak, as if he's at the end of his strength. He's hurt. We're wasting time. If I hit him, hard, he'll let go.

"Listen." He raises his voice. "Let it burn. If you ask me to rebind you afterwards I will, I promise I will."

My eyes are watering. I glance up. The flames dance through the hole in the walkway, glowing crimson and gold through the haze. The bookcase with the broken glass will be the next to catch light.

"What is it you think you did, Lucian? What's worth dying for?"

I open my mouth, and the smoke rushes in. Stinging tears pour down my face. I thought I knew what I was afraid of — murder, perhaps. But how could I have thought that was the worst thing? Now, in the blinding heat and the fumes, as the fire roars and fists pound on the door, it's as if something inside me — some last protective barrier — collapses. My mind floods with fragments of nightmare, vivid and plausible and sickening. The real memories are bad enough: Nell's stained eyes as she hung from her make-shift noose, the blank-faced maids, de Havilland as he was attacked, my father . . . But behind them are shadowy pictures of worse things. Things my father might have done, things he might have made me do. Things that are so depraved and vicious I can only just imagine them. Only just . . . but if I'm capable of imagining them, I'm capable of doing them.

I fight for breath. My face is wet. "You don't understand. I'm — if you knew . . ."

He puts his mouth to mine. It's so rough it's hardly a kiss: our teeth knock together, my skull jolts, a bolt of pain goes through my lower lip. I'm still speaking and for an instant I feel my voice in his mouth. He pulls back, just far enough to look into my eyes.

"I love you," he says.

For a moment it's as if I'm somewhere else. The furious heat and noise is only the foreground: I can hear the silence beyond, the emptiness at the furthest edge of the world. There's such stillness inside me that I could be dying.

Then he glances up. Reflected fire glints in his eyes. There's anxiety on his face, followed by a flash of something like triumph. The fire. The bookcase.

516

I push him aside. But it's too late. I gulp a breath as heat washes over me. The flames leap, catch at my mind, throw sparks across my vision.

The truth flares in my head, dazzling, so bright I can't see it. Then it burns through me.

When I open my eyes the world has changed.

I don't know where I am. I don't know who I am. I'm cold. My lungs hurt. When I try to clear my throat it feels as if I've swallowed a live coal. Vicious pain. My face is scraped raw by smoke.

Under everything is happiness so deep and rich it's like dark wet earth. I don't know what it means. I don't know why it's there. But I could reach out and grab a fistful of it.

"All right?"

Emmett. His name comes to me before I remember my own.

"I — think so . . ." My voice creaks. It hurts to speak. I sit up. I'm dizzy.

"Stay still. Don't worry. You're safe."

I blink until my vision steadies. I don't know where we are. Some kind of stone structure, the sides open to the air. Flaking pillars frame a field bordered by trees. The grass is the tired green-brown of winter. A greying mat of snow clings to a slope. No time has passed. It feels as if I've been away for years. A whole life.

"Better?"

"I nod."

"It'll get easier. The first few days will be . . . strange."

"Yes."

"After that, it'll settle."

"Right."

I breathe in the smell of mud and dead leaves. Old smoke. Scorched calfskin. Vomit. There's a puddle on the stone floor. I must have thrown up. Like Emmett, when he burnt his book . . . I grimace. I'm glad I was unconscious. I look down and peel off my gloves. I was lucky to be wearing them. Underneath my fingers are pink and tender. Pain prickles on the skin. Why am I so happy?

Because of the colours. Because the drab wintry world is so bright I can hardly bear it. Because the pain is closer and the taste of soot in my mouth is as solid as any food I've ever eaten. Because I can smell roots and things asleep and seeds waiting to grow. Because . . .

I look sideways. Emmett meets my eyes. He looks afraid.

I laugh. *Now* he looks afraid.

"It's all right."

He nods, unsure. There's a smudge of black on his forehead. His eyes are red at the edges. A wine-coloured bruise covers his jaw.

On the roof there's a bird singing. A raven answers from the other side of the field. High watery chirrups and truculent cawing. Both of the sounds are lovely. Beyond that there's a bell ringing and distant shouts. A tall column of smoke rises over the trees to our right.

"I think we're safe. Sally won't tell anyone she let us in."

"I wasn't worried." It hadn't occurred to me to worry.

"Probably best not to stay here, though. I don't know where we go now."

I glance at him. It sends a shiver to my heart. Soon I'll want to stare at him and go on staring. I'll want to relearn every freckle, every trick of his mouth, every eyelash. But not yet. It's as much as I can do to catch his eye and go on breathing.

When you're starving, it's dangerous to eat too much, too soon. But it takes an effort to turn away. I blink at the green field and see a ruined castle, a farm yard, a jagged hole in a frozen moat. Too many memories to get hold of. They spin round me like a merry-go-round. Gradually they slow down. Now I can glimpse shapes, details. The light glinting on a blue-purple stone in a jeweller's hand. A line of playing cards on a dingy quilt. A terrier pup wriggling in my arms. A garden, an unbuttoned shirt, a bleeding scratch on sun-warm skin. If I slide my mind's eye sideways there will be worse things: a locked door, food congealing on a tray, my father with his belt in his hand . . . Weeks later, a farmyard baked to dust. Alta spitting at me. The open window above, and screams that died to sobs. Her face as she shrugged and stepped aside. *Go on, then. If you really want to see what you've done to him* . . . Emmett at the bindery, looking at me with a stranger's eyes.

But even those memories are bearable, now. I breathe. It still hurts but it's getting easier.

Remembering and not remembering overlap with each other. After I'd been bound . . . Those months of numbness. Contempt from my father, snide looks from Lisette. Distant misery, like it happened to someone else. And — I wince — the first time I saw Emmett . . . When he came to bind Nell. Something inside me shrivels at the way I spoke to him. Then, and later. And the night we spent together, when he knew, and I didn't.

I push that thought away. It wasn't his fault. If it had been the other way round I'd have done the same.

I turn to him. He looks back at me, wary.

"I'm sorry," I say. "For leaving you. And for — everything else . . ."

He shrugs. "It doesn't matter."

"I never even asked about *your* book. Your memories. I saw you burn it and I never even . . ."

"It does funny things to you, being bound," he says. A hint of a grin tugs at his mouth. "Especially if you were pretty self-absorbed to start with."

"Hey." We catch each other's eye and look away at the same time. I lean back against a pillar of the summer house and push my hands into my pockets. My fingertips touch something soft and damp. I pull it out. It's the rose I was wearing in my buttonhole this morning. It seems like an eternity ago. I throw it on to the grass, as far away as possible. Emmett's eyes follow the movement but he doesn't say anything. I take a deep breath. I don't know what I mean to say, but it isn't what comes out. "Did you mean it?"

"What?"

"What you said. Just before . . ."

"Oh." He shifts. "I was trying to distract you. Stop you throwing yourself into the fire."

"That's not what I asked."

"No, well . . ." He gets up. He stands with his back to me. At last he says, "Ask me again tomorrow morning."

I nod. I go on nodding. A huge grin is building inside me but for the moment I can keep it at bay. "You burnt my book. I forbade it, and you did it anyway."

"Yes."

"Right." A pause. The smoke mushrooms over the trees. "And you burnt all those other people's books. You burnt the whole library."

"Yes." He turns to look at the smoke.

"Isn't that dangerous? I mean, all those people, remembering?"

"I don't know," he says. "I didn't mean to." He glances at me. "It's just a guess, but I think most of them were trade. They won't mind getting the memories back, if they sold them in the first place. I hope so."

Where are they now? Dropping to their knees in the streets. In fields. In kitchens. Stopping halfway through a kiss or a fight. Imagine getting it all back. Your daughter's wedding. The first time you held your son. Bluebells. An ache builds in my throat that has nothing to do with the smoke.

I get up. My head spins. I walk past Emmett, out of the summer house on to the grass. The wind buffets me. Even though it's icy it's laden with the scent of soil and moisture, the end of winter. I lean against the pillar, drinking it in. Out of the whirl of memories, one surfaces: a damp, blue evening last spring, when I walked back to the New House from the farm. I'd stayed to dinner, because Emmett had asked me to. When I said goodnight he'd grinned at me, that awkward quick-quenched grin that made me feel like we were the only people in the world. I walked home whistling, dancing on the path like a music-hall turn, laughing softly to myself. I was wearing Emmett's shirt. My heart was so light I could have flown. The memory of it takes my breath away. I didn't know happiness was that simple.

It won't ever be again. Things have been broken that can't be made whole. But now . . . I tilt my head back, taking in the blank sky, the criss-cross paths of birds. I'm not a rapist. I'm not a murderer. I start to laugh; and then I start to cry, and Emmett keeps his gaze turned away from me, and finally I wipe my face on my sleeve.

"Emmett," I say, and then I can't think of anything else.

He offers his hand, with a crease between his eyebrows as if he isn't sure of me. I take it in mine. Our fingers knot together. His ring digs into my knuckle.

He swallows. "You remember, then?"

"Yes, I remember."

"Everything?"

"As far as I know." Another laugh catches in my throat. It's so true it shouldn't be funny.

522

He closes his eyes. His eyelids flutter as if he's asleep and dreaming. His eyelashes are clogged with soot. His bruise is already darkening. Soon I'm going to kiss him. But right now I stay where I am, watching.

There's the sound of a carriage rumbling along the drive, towards the house. Abruptly he leans forward and squints through the trees.

"Well then," he says. "Let's go."

CAVAN COUNTY LIBRARY

Acknowledgements

The generosity, wisdom, enthusiasm and expertise I've encountered while writing and editing *The Binding* has been overwhelming, and the list of people I want to thank is still growing as I type — which means I've almost certainly missed someone out! My apologies to you, whoever you are. Remind me to buy you a drink in person.

I'm hugely grateful to Sarah Ballard, my brilliant agent, whose intelligent, incisive and tactful feedback transformed the first draft into . . . well, the second. And third. Thank you so much for your support, warmth and humour — I can't believe how lucky I am to have you in my corner! Thanks too to Eli Keren, and the rest of the team at United Agents.

I also have to pinch myself that I get to work with Suzie Dooré, my editor at The Borough Press (who is not only a fantastic editor but an excellent person to have cocktails with), and the same goes for everyone else at The Borough Press and HarperCollins — from the moment I first met you all, I was swept away by your energy and passion. Thank you all so much for everything! It's also been wonderful to work with the

HarperCollins cousins in the US, especially Jessica Williams at William Morrow.

Thank you to Abby Fenton, who gave me not only space and time to write in her house in Galicia, but also a lovely photo of myself trying to write that I can now stare at while I'm trying to write. Also, thanks to Paul Jarvis, who has put up with me asking silly questions in his bookbinding class for several years. (Any mistakes about bookbinding are definitely my own.)

And finally, thank you to Nick Green, the most generous person I've ever met, without whom *The Binding* would never have been written.

Other titles published by Ulverscroft:

WASHINGTON BLACK

Esi Edugyan

Washington Black is an eleven-year-old field slave who knows no other life than the Barbados sugar plantation where he was born. When his master's eccentric brother chooses him to be his manservant, Wash is terrified of the cruelties he is certain await him. But Christopher Wilde, or "Titch", is a naturalist, explorer, scientist, inventor, and abolitionist. He initiates Wash into a world where a flying machine can carry a man across the sky; where two people, separated by an impossible divide, might begin to see each other as human; and where a boy born in chains can embrace a life of dignity and meaning. But when a man is killed and a bounty is placed on Wash's head, Titch abandons everything to save him . . .

WRECKER

Noel O'Reilly

Shipwrecks are part of life in the remote village of Porthmorvoren, Cornwall. When, after a fierce storm, Mary Blight rescues a man half-dead from the sea, she ignores the whispers of her neighbours and carries him home to nurse better. Gideon Stone is a Methodist minister from Newlyn, a married man. Touched by Mary's sacrifice and horrified by the superstitions and pagan beliefs the villagers cling to, he sets out to bring light and salvation to Porthmorvoren by building a chapel on the hill. But the village has many secrets, and not everyone wants to be saved. As Mary and Gideon find themselves increasingly drawn together, jealousy, rumour and suspicion are rife. Gideon has demons of his own to face, and soon Mary's enemies are plotting against her . . .